SEASON OF MAGIC

THE WITCHES OF MINGUS MOUNTAIN - BOOK 7

CHRISTINE POPE

This is a work of fiction. Names, characters, places, and incidents are either the product of the author's imagination or are used fictitiously. Any resemblance to actual events, places, organizations, or persons, whether living or dead, is entirely coincidental.

SEASON OF MAGIC

ISBN: 978-1-946435-92-7

Published by Dark Valentine Press

Cover design by Indie Author Services

Ebook formatting by Indie Author Services

1

ROSA SANDOVAL GLANCED OVER AT THE CLOCK on her bedside table. 1:11. Her cousin Maria would have called that an angel number, a sure sign that the universe was supporting her decisions. Rosa had the uncharitable thought that Maria was into all the woo-woo stuff because her witchy magic wasn't very strong, and so her cousin was trying to compensate, but right now, she figured she'd take any support she could get.

The important thing, however, was that Rosa's mother Zoe had gone to her beloved Los Altos ranch market down on Roosevelt in the heart of Phoenix…the stores were a chain in the greater Phoenix area, but Zoe swore that the one on Roosevelt was the best…and that meant Rosa had almost a whole precious afternoon to herself.

An afternoon during which she'd decided to disappear.

She hadn't come to the decision lightly, had done her best to accept her situation with a sort of Zen equanimity. After all, she was a Libra, right? That meant she was supposed to look at both sides of an issue and weigh them equally before coming to any sort of a conclusion.

However, most Libras weren't the de la Paz clan's *prima*-in-waiting. After she'd turned twenty-one back in early October, Rosa had tried to bear the burden as best she could, had attempted to make herself understand that this was how it had always been done and that she'd just have to put up with kissing random guy after random guy until she found the one who would send the *prima* energy within her flaring and let her know that he was the one, the man who would be her partner in life and magic.

In the abstract, she understood completely how all this was supposed to work. In practice, though....

And okay, it wasn't as if the parade of guys who'd come to the *prima's* house in Scottsdale, Rosa's family home, were random at all. No, they were chosen carefully from among the extended de la Paz clan, her mother and the collection of de la Paz cousins who acted as the clan elders deciding who was a distant enough relation for him to be safe as a possible match. They hadn't stopped there, either, and had also reached out to the McAllister clan in Jerome —Rosa's father's clan—as well as the Wilcoxes in Flagstaff and even the Castillos in New Mexico.

She couldn't lie—a lot of them had been pretty damn cute. The problem, though, was that none of them was her soul mate.

After eight months of dealing with a parade of eligible guys coming to the big, hacienda-style house that had been her only home, she was beyond fed up. Even when she tried to remind herself that her mother's search had gone on even longer and had even driven Zoe to try to create her perfect match—a plan that hadn't worked out so well, although at least the mishap had allowed her to meet Evan McAllister, Rosa's father—Rosa had found herself increasingly impatient.

Which was why she was now sitting on the edge of the bed in her room, staring at the oversized leather tote that sat on the floor. She'd bought it only a week earlier, telling her mother she liked how big it was because it allowed her to stash all her purchases in there when she went shopping instead of having to lug multiple bags around, and it seemed as if Zoe had bought the story.

In reality, Rosa had purchased the tote because she could stuff a couple of changes of clothes in there, along with her toiletries and the little sketchbook and box of pencils she took with her most everywhere.

It was packed now, ready to go.

The question was…was Rosa?

She knew if she didn't take this opportunity, she'd be stuck with another month of kissing guys she didn't know but whom she would be expected to spend the rest of her life with if one of them turned out to have the consort spark.

Stupid custom.

No one could even tell her where it had come from, except that it had been going on among the various witch clans for generations…centuries, really. The only exception seemed to be the Wilcoxes, who had a man as their leader rather than a woman. But since the Wilcoxes were relative upstarts, having split off from the Winfield clan in Connecticut in the 1870s while the de la Paz family had been in Arizona for almost four hundred years, Rosa knew that a lot of people in her clan didn't have much use for the Wilcoxes' so-called traditions.

Hesitation could cost her a month, maybe more.

She pulled in a breath and made herself get up from the bed. It wasn't as if she planned to run away forever—she knew her family would never allow her to get away with something like that, not when she was expected to be the head of the clan after her mother was gone—but she needed some space to think. In her mind, she'd thought that maybe the best thing to do would be to go to Jerome so she could talk to Levi, the man her mother had conjured all those years ago, and see if he could give her any advice. What had it felt like for him to be summoned to this world, only to be rejected once Zoe realized Ethan was actually her consort? It sounded as if Levi had made a life for himself in Jerome and was happy, but surely he must have had some rough ground to cover before he reached that sort of equilibrium?

Besides, Rosa was half McAllister. What was wrong about going to spend some time with her relatives? Her family—her parents and her older brother Zack and her younger sister Lira—had visited Jerome a few times over the years, but with Zoe being the *prima* of the de la Paz clan, it wasn't as if she could drop everything and head up there whenever she liked.

But both of Rosa's paternal grandparents were still living there, in the small, two-bedroom cottage where Evan had grown up. The place wasn't really big enough for her to crash there, because it had been decades since that second bedroom was used as anything except an office, but still, there were hotels in town where she could stay.

What would be so bad about going to visit some of the family she didn't get to see very often?

That seemed to be the final rationalization she needed, because Rosa got up from the bed and grasped the tote, then slung it over her shoulder. A pause to let her power assert itself, rendering her not just invisible and inaudible, but also masking her witchy abilities. She knew that hers was a very rare gift; although the de la Paz clan had a few mentions in its records of other witches and warlocks with the power to turn themselves invisible, it didn't sound as if any of them also could hide their witch natures.

And the strength of her gift, of course, was what had made her the *prima*-in-waiting. Sure, her mother was the *prima,* but if Rosa hadn't been powerful enough to ensure she'd be able to protect the clan when her time came to lead, she would have been passed over for someone more suitable.

After the thirty-second kiss or whatever it had been, Rosa had found herself wishing she had the wimpiest power imaginable, just so she wouldn't be stuck in this predicament.

But wishing didn't get you very far. No, sometimes you had to take direct action.

The house was quiet as she moved down the long, cool corridors, Saltillo tile glimmering beneath her feet. Her mother was off shopping, of course, but her father had gone with her as well, and Rosa's little sister was visiting some friends for the day, now that school was out for the summer and Lira could do as she liked with her time, while Zack had already graduated from the University of Arizona and had gotten a job at a winery in Gilbert. Rosa knew he wasn't all that into wine…but he was definitely into one of the women who worked there.

Anyway, maybe the invisibility was overkill, considering how no one was even around. Still, she figured it was a good idea to stay undetectable. The last thing she needed was to have any of the neighbors notice her walking down the street.

Because obviously, she couldn't take her car. It could easily be tracked, and although she knew her parents would figure out where she'd gone eventually, she figured she might as well give herself as much time as possible before that day arrived.

Instead, she made her way out of the neighborhood where she'd grown up, doing her best to ignore the oppressive heat. Even though it wasn't even noon yet, temperatures had passed ninety a good hour or so ago and were now hovering in the low 100s. About a month from now, the monsoon storms should arrive to provide some relief, but early June in the greater Phoenix area was always brutal.

She'd arranged everything through her friend

Natalie, who had a cousin with a friend named Aaron who ran a sort of informal shuttle between Phoenix and points north, whether people wanted to go to the Verde Valley for wine tasting or Sedona for shopping and hiking. Rosa had gotten Natalie to set things up with the strict admonition that she couldn't breathe a word of the plan. Although Rosa and Natalie had been friends since their freshman year of high school, Rosa had never said anything about being a witch, and had done her best to pass off her inability to casually date as a family tradition that really sucked but which she couldn't do anything about.

She dropped her invisibility behind a stand of palm trees, made her way to the rendezvous point in the parking lot of a local shopping center, and was infinitely relieved to see the dark gray SUV Natalie had described waiting near the T.J. Maxx, as planned.

The driver's window rolled down, and a guy with sandy brown hair who looked as if he was around twenty-five or so stuck his head out. "Rosa?"

"Yes," she said.

He grinned. "Right on time. Get in."

She climbed into the passenger seat, pausing for a second to wedge her oversized tote into the footwell before she fastened her seatbelt.

"Jerome, right?" Aaron asked.

"Yes," she said. "The Haunted Hamburger."

"Got it," he replied, and pulled out of the lot.

Rosa settled against the seatback. Aaron didn't seem too inclined toward conversation, which was just fine by her. She could take the hour and a half or so of the drive to settle into her resolve, to get herself centered before she showed up at her grandparents' house out of the blue.

Because that was her real destination, of course. She'd told Aaron to take her to the Haunted Hamburger because it was well known and not too far from the little Victorian cottage where her grandparents lived. It was by far the smallest house on Paradise Lane, the street at the top of Jerome that was also home base for Levi McAllister, and although Rosa had heard that some civilians lived there, it just seemed safer to go someplace more public first and then make her way to the quiet neighborhood where so many of the McAllister clan lived.

Aaron's car climbed out of the Phoenix valley and wound through New River, gained almost two thousand feet where the saguaros disappeared and miles of dry grass stretched to mountains on every horizon. Another half hour, and then they dropped down into Camp Verde and took Highway 260 into the heart of the Verde Valley. Rosa did her best to sit calmly in the passenger seat and pretend as if all this was utterly commonplace for her, although it was harder than she'd thought. Sure, this wasn't her first visit to this part of the world, but she hadn't been here since she'd graduated from high school, and everything felt fresh and new.

Or maybe it was simply because this time, she was all on her own. She'd always had her parents with her before, and now....

Well, she was twenty-one. Her family might have wanted to treat her like a baby, might have tried to shelter and coddle her, but she was still an adult.

And all right, she knew that view of the situation wasn't entirely fair. Her parents had done what they could to give her a normal life, hadn't tried to restrict her—well, except for not allowing any boyfriends, thanks to all the *prima*-in-waiting b.s.—and she knew she'd fared better than a lot of young women in the past who'd shared her unfortunate destiny.

But it still felt weirder than weird to have Aaron drop her off in front of the Haunted Hamburger, to shoulder her tote bag and wave goodbye to him as if she did this sort of thing every day. Obviously, she wasn't invisible right now, but she could still turn off the witchy signature that would let others of witch-kind know what she was. People only got that tingle or ringing in their ears or itch at the back of their necks or whatever when they met another witch or warlock for the first time, but there were plenty of McAllister cousins she'd never met, and she figured it was better to play it safe.

The aromas drifting out from the restaurant were divine, and her stomach growled. Should she grab something to eat before she headed up to her grandparents' house? It was an odd hour of the afternoon, nearly two-thirty and kind of late for lunch, but she thought it might be rude to expect them to feed her when she showed up out of the blue.

And she had plenty of cash on hand. She'd started squirreling it away as soon as she thought of running away like this, twenty bucks here and fifty bucks there, and currently had about a grand shoved in her wallet and zipped up in an inner pocket of her tote. Sooner or later, she knew her parents would find out she was here, but it couldn't hurt to keep things on the down-low for a while longer.

She went inside. More people filled the tables than she'd expected at this hour, but she was still seated soon enough. A Coke and a burger and some fries definitely made her feel a bit better about life, and after her impromptu meal, she headed out for Paradise Lane and her true destination.

When she was younger, the little street had

positively enchanted her, with its carefully preserved Victorian homes and lush gardens. She'd never seen anything like it in Scottsdale or Phoenix; even though there were some older neighborhoods in the city where she'd grown up, they weren't old enough to have any true Victorian architecture.

Her grandparents' house was one of the first on the street, set well back from the road and shaded by big oak and sycamore trees. The cobblestone path that led to the front door was bordered by old-fashioned flowers like hollyhocks and snapdragons and foxgloves, and the porch was cool and shady as well, welcome on a hot afternoon. True, it wasn't nearly as warm here as it had been down in Phoenix, but Rosa guessed the temperature must still be in the upper eighties, or maybe even ninety.

She pressed the doorbell and heard a *ding-dong* from within the house. All the windows were shut tight, and an A/C compressor hummed from the side yard, which made sense.

But no one answered the door.

Frowning, she glanced over her shoulder. Paradise Lane appeared almost abandoned on that Saturday afternoon, with no cars coming and going and no one outside, either. True, it was pretty warm, but she'd been here in the summer before and had still seen people outside watering their yards or going to fetch the mail or whatever.

Well, maybe her grandparents hadn't heard the doorbell. The house wasn't very big, but if they were both in the kitchen, which overlooked the backyard, or in the service porch, which was set right off the kitchen, she supposed it was possible the sound hadn't traveled all the way back there.

Okay, she'd just ring again.

The doorbell had almost a forlorn sound to it this time, as if it knew no one was going to answer.

Right then, Rosa was beginning to question whether her decision to come up here without calling first had been all that smart. True, she'd wanted to surprise her grandparents, hadn't wanted to give away her plan, and yet she hadn't really expected to find no one home. Her grandfather still worked in his studio at least a few hours a day, creating the metal sculptures that he'd sold all over the Verde Valley and points beyond, but she'd thought her grandmother would be home at least.

Still frowning, she turned away from the door and surveyed Paradise Lane. Across the street and halfway down the block was the big yellow house where Levi McAllister lived with his wife, Hayley, although Rosa thought she'd heard that their son and daughter, both older than she, had already moved out.

Of course they had. They were in their mid-twenties and could do what they liked, since they weren't stuck being the *prima*-in-waiting.

Rosa shoved that self-pitying thought out of her head. It wouldn't do her any good to think that way, and besides, she obviously needed to come up with a Plan B.

And that meant maybe going over and talking to Levi first instead of her grandparents. She'd always intended to speak with him anyway, and maybe this would be better. Although she'd never met him, it sounded to her as if he generally gave good advice.

Well, that seemed to settle things.

She adjusted her sunglasses and headed across Paradise Lane, her overstuffed tote banging against her hip as she went. It wasn't the best match for her outfit, since she was wearing a white sundress and sandals, and it was dark brown leather, but maybe no one would notice.

Of course, when she got to Levi's house and rang the doorbell, it didn't seem as if her tote bag's mismatch was too big a deal, since no one was answering the door there, either.

Now she planted her hands on her hips and scowled. Where the hell was everybody? Had they all gotten raptured or something?

That would be ironic, considering most of the McAllisters were pagans and practiced the old religion.

Not that the staunchly Catholic de la Paz clan had much use for the Rapture, either.

So…no one was home. Just a few doors down was the large white house with the green shutters that Rosa knew belonged to Angela McAllister and her consort, Connor Wilcox. No reason to believe anyone was there, considering how deserted the neighborhood seemed to be. Also, she would prefer to avoid Angela for as long as possible, since she had a feeling the *prima* would call Rosa's mother just as soon as she discovered that the de la Paz *prima*-in-waiting had gone wandering a little too far afield.

Was she supposed to just turn around and go home after all the trouble she'd taken to get here?

Fat chance.

Down the street, a darling little pink house caught her eye. It wasn't much bigger than her grandparents' cottage, but the pink made it about a thousand times cuter. Rosa didn't like to play favorites with colors because, as an aspiring artist, she loved them all, but she knew pink probably played a larger role in her wardrobe than most colors.

Without even thinking about what she was doing, she started moving in that direction. She had no idea who lived in the house and had no reason to believe they were home when everyone else seemed to be busy elsewhere, but if nothing else, she could get a closer look at the place and then shelter on its shady porch while she decided what to do next.

A breeze picked up while she walked, helping to lessen the heat somewhat. It pulled at her loose hair, and she had to reach up with her free hand to brush it out of her eyes. Still, something about the little wind seemed almost welcoming, as if it was coaxing her along. Silly, she knew, especially since weather magic wasn't her gift.

And yet....

As she'd hoped, it was even cooler under the shade of the front porch. Up close, she saw that the pink house had accents of dark teal and warm cream, unusual but striking. The front door was painted that same teal, and....

Was it slightly ajar?

She stepped a little closer. Sure enough, the door was almost closed, but not all the way, as if whoever had left had been in such a hurry that they hadn't checked to make sure it had shut and locked behind them.

Through the crack in the door, she caught the smallest glimpse of a big couch covered in teal fabric almost the same shade as the exterior accents. It looked nice and comfy, too.

Inviting.

No, you can't, she told herself. *You absolutely cannot go in there and make yourself at home. You have no idea who even lives here.*

But she was hot and tired and thirsty, and even though she knew a few civilians lived on this street, the odds were much higher that this house belonged to a McAllister. And since her father was a McAllister, that meant the owner was a cousin of some sort, if probably a very distant one.

Her hand reached out almost of its own volition, pushing the door farther open so she could step inside. At the same time, though, she summoned her magic to cloak herself. If someone was home, they'd just think the wind had pushed at the door.

Almost as soon as she stepped inside and carefully closed the door behind her, however, she realized no one was here. The only sound was the hum of the air conditioning in the background and another, lower hum that she guessed was probably the refrigerator.

Whoever lived in the house, they hadn't spent much time on decorating. Yes, that big couch looked comfy and cozy, but the only other piece of furniture was a metal and stone coffee table that faced it, and then a matching console table directly opposite that had a big TV perched on it. The fireplace had a beautiful tile surround in a deep turquoise shade, but no pictures sat on the wide mantel, and the only painting was a landscape on the far wall, one that showed a river under a warmly dusky sky.

Rosa recognized the work at once, though. That was one of Connor's paintings. She supposed if you weren't going to have many decorations in your house, you might as well have something that counted.

The lure of that sofa was too enticing, though. She went over to it and sat down, telling herself she was only going to rest for a few minutes to gather herself and then head back out, even if it was only to go down the hill to get a room at the Connor Hotel or at the Clinkscale. Maybe it would have made more sense to go up to the Grand Hotel at the top of Jerome, since that would be closer, but the place was rumored to be pretty haunted, and she wasn't sure if she really wanted to sleep there by herself.

Of course, the Connor and the Clinkscale were also supposed to be haunted, and yet they still didn't seem quite as intimidating.

Glad she had a backup plan, she found herself sinking farther down onto the couch, her head sliding onto the pillows. She hadn't slept at all well the past few days, keyed up as the moment of her escape came ever closer.

Maybe if she shut her eyes for just a minute….

Her lids slipped closed, and she was gone.

2

No more weddings, Shane McAllister told himself as he pulled the van into his driveway and shut off the engine. By that point, it was past ten o'clock, and although he certainly worked later than that most of the time, he'd been running since five that morning, and right then, he just wanted to go inside, maybe pour himself some brandy, and go to sleep.

It wasn't that he hadn't been glad to be there for his sister Bree on her big day, to be the one to make sure the food at the reception was everything she wanted and more, but her wedding had come barely a month after his cousin Bellamy's wedding, and having two of them clustered so closely together—and both held down in Page Springs, which meant he had to schlep everything a half hour away from Jerome— had been a bigger pain in the ass than he'd thought.

But Bree had been thrilled, and Shane was glad to see her so happy. Her new husband, Bill Garrett—well, that was what the extradimensional being Belshegar called himself, although everyone in the McAllister clan knew he wasn't any more human than Shane's own father—was a good guy, and after Bree being so aimless and uncertain of herself for so many years, Shane could only be grateful that she seemed to have found the right man for her.

All the same, he hoped no one else in the McAllister clan planned to get married any time soon…or if they did, that they'd look elsewhere for someone to do the catering. Normally, he would never have offered to provide all the food for both receptions, since he had his hands full as it was with his position as head chef at the Asylum, the restaurant in the Grand Hotel, but family was family.

Although maybe he should reexamine his definition of "family" when it came to putting himself out like this.

He got out from behind the wheel and closed the door, then clicked the key fob to lock things up. The back of the van was full of empty trays and other detritus from the wedding, but he figured he could take care of all that in the morning. True, he had to work—his days off were Tuesday and Wednesday—but he didn't come on shift until eleven, so he had time.

And although he supposed he could have just barely squeezed the van into a garage constructed in an era when cars were much smaller…the house itself had been built in the 1890s, but the garage was a 1920s add-on…he knew the place was too full of crap for him to fit anything bigger than a bicycle in there.

He headed up the front steps and put his hand on the door handle. No need for a key, not when all witches and warlocks could unlock a door just by thinking about it.

Except…the door wasn't locked.

At once, he frowned. Had he forgotten to lock up when he left? It wouldn't have been the first time. He'd been pretty distracted this morning, focused on making sure he didn't leave anything important behind, and he supposed it might have slipped his mind. This was a safe neighborhood, and it wasn't too big a deal if a door was left unlocked.

Still, he chided himself for being so careless. He'd have to pay more attention next time.

As soon as he stepped inside the living room and closed the door behind him, though, he paused, head lifting as he looked around.

Something felt wrong.

Exactly what, he wasn't sure, since at first glance, everything seemed just as it should be. The torchiere lamp in the corner was on, and he remembered turning it on in the morning right before he left so he wouldn't come home to a dark house. The air conditioning chose that moment to turn itself on, and he jumped a little at the sound of the condenser coming to life.

It was more than that, though.

For some reason, he sniffed at the air. He never used air fresheners or even scented candles since he didn't want anything interfering with the aromas of the food he cooked, but something smelled different now. A slight fragrance seemed to hang in the room, not completely sweet, almost warm, like amber and vanilla mixed together.

Had he brushed up against someone at the reception who'd been wearing a perfume that smelled like vanilla and amber, and it had rubbed off on his clothing? But he didn't remember making contact with anyone like that, and besides, he'd taken off the chef's smock he'd worn while he was preparing the food and now just had on a plain gray T-shirt.

"Is someone here?" he said aloud, feeling like a complete idiot.

Or maybe it wasn't so idiotic. Jerome was one of the most haunted places in the country, and although he'd never heard of any ghosts residing in the little pink house that had been his home for almost two years now, he supposed it wasn't impossible that a spirit had suddenly decided to make its presence known.

And then....

The cushions on the couch seemed to move and shift, almost as if someone had just sat upright on them, even though no one was there.

He resisted the urge to rub his eyes. Maybe he was more tired than he'd thought....

"If you're a ghost, you've picked the wrong house to haunt," he said. "I keep terrible hours, and I use a lot of garlic."

A sound that sounded almost like a muffled snicker reached his ears.

Maybe he was just going crazy.

"And the only thing here that's really valuable is the stove, and I guarantee you won't be able to carry that thing out of here by yourself."

Another of those chuckles, and then a woman appeared out of thin air, sitting on the sofa, her eyes—an unusual hazel green—dancing with amusement.

"I didn't come here to steal your stove," she said, her tone almost severe despite the glint in her eyes. "And it's vampires that are scared of garlic, not ghosts."

A small tingle at the back of his neck told him the strange young woman had to be a witch. With those unusual eyes and her long dark hair and warm-toned complexion, she definitely wasn't a McAllister, though. Probably a de la Paz, Shane thought, or maybe even a Castillo.

However, none of that explained why she was sitting on his couch…or how she'd suddenly become visible.

"It's my gift," she said then, almost as if she'd guessed what was going through his mind. "I can turn myself invisible and inaudible…and turn off my witchiness, or whatever you want to call it. No one can detect me when I do that."

A pretty fancy gift, that was for sure. Shane knew that Devynn Rowe was able to hide her witch nature, same as her father could, but he'd never heard of anyone being able to turn themselves invisible and inaudible as well.

"And you broke into my house because…?" he said, although he stopped there, since her eyes now sparkled with indignation.

"I did *not* break in," she replied as she rose from the couch. Standing, she still wasn't very tall, maybe five feet four at best, much shorter than his own six foot one. "The door was unlocked."

All right, he'd already admitted to himself that he'd probably forgotten to lock the door when he left this morning, but….

"That still doesn't give you the right to come waltzing in here and make yourself at home," he said.

Now she glanced away, her full lips pressed together. Shane found himself noticing with some reluctance how pretty she actually was, with those striking eyes and heavily arched brows and the rosy curve of her mouth. And that didn't even take into account the slender lushness of a body accentuated by the almost demure white sundress she wore.

"I didn't 'waltz in,'" she returned. "The door was ajar. So I stuck my head inside to see if anyone was at home."

"And then you fell asleep on my couch?"

Those striking hazel eyes met his. "It was kind of a long day."

Well, he could relate to that. At the same time, he couldn't help thinking that this was why he preferred to focus on work. Having random invisible women falling asleep on his couch was exactly the kind of complication he didn't need.

"All right," he said next. Although he wasn't about to concede the point on breaking and entering, he figured it was better if they got down to brass tacks. "Who are you, anyway?"

"Rosa Sandoval," she replied with a lift of her chin.

Seriously? The de la Paz *prima*-in-waiting?

Shane didn't pretend to pay much attention to the goings-on of the other witch clans—the McAllisters were a big enough handful as it was—but even he'd heard of Rosa.

She was a long way from home, that was for sure.

"Okay," he said, and crossed his arms. "And I'm Shane McAllister. Now that we've been properly introduced, you can tell me just what the hell you're doing in Jerome."

Rosa's pulse sped up at the edge in his voice, although she did her best not to let her nervousness show. She'd come all this way, had worked so hard to get here without anyone tracking her movements, and now she was standing in some stranger's living room while he glared at her as if she'd just run over his dog.

Not that it seemed as if he had a dog, but whatever.

And okay, maybe breaking into his house—or not breaking in, to be more exact, since the door had been unlocked—hadn't been her brightest move. But she'd been tired and overwhelmed, and the pink house had looked so welcoming, and it wasn't as if she'd meant to fall asleep on his couch, like some witchy version of Goldilocks.

Shane's eyes…an impossibly deep blue, so unlike anyone's eyes in her own clan…narrowed slightly. "Your father's Evan McAllister, right?"

"Yes," she replied, a little relieved that she wouldn't have to explain every single detail to him. "So I'm here visiting family. Technically."

"Technically," Shane repeated, his tone bone-dry. He crossed his arms over his chest, and Rosa found herself noticing the way the movement pulled his gray T-shirt taut across his shoulders… his very broad shoulders.

Oh, stop it, she scolded herself. So he was cute. At the moment, he was also extremely annoyed, and she knew she needed to focus on that.

"Let me guess," he went on. "Your family doesn't actually know you're here."

A flush touched her cheeks. "They will…eventually."

"So, you're a runaway *prima*-in-waiting." It wasn't a question, and Rosa found herself bristling.

"I'm not running away," she said, even though that was basically what she'd done. Or at least, it must have looked that way on the surface, even though she knew she'd never be able to completely escape her fate. "I just needed some space," she continued. "I wanted some time to think without everyone hovering over me and scheduling my entire life."

As she spoke, she heard the note of petulance in her voice and gave an internal wince. She was twenty-one, not twelve, and she knew she needed to sound like it.

And act like it.

Shane McAllister was quiet then as he studied her. He had the kind of strong, even features that made her itch to break out her sketchbook, although she kind of doubted he would appreciate her stopping everything so she could draw him.

"And you decided to take a nap in a stranger's house while you were 'thinking'?" he said.

"I was looking for my grandparents," Rosa said, grateful she could steer the conversation back to a topic that she hoped would make her sound slightly less foolish. "They weren't home. And I tried Levi's house, but no one was there, either. The whole street seemed deserted."

"That's because almost everyone was at my sister's wedding," Shane said. "It was down in Page Springs. I just got home, and I assume everyone else will come trickling back at some point."

Oh. That explained the empty neighborhood, as well as Shane's general air of a man who'd been working for sixteen hours straight. Guilt pricked at her.

"Your sister got married today?" Rosa said. "Congratulations. That's wonderful."

"Yes," he agreed. His expression softened just slightly, enough that Rosa could see the genuine affection beneath his prickly exterior. "It was a good day."

For a moment, they just stood there. Rosa became acutely aware of how she must look—rumpled sundress, hair probably a mess from sleeping on the sofa, makeup long since worn off. She'd left Scottsdale looking put-together, and now she must look like… well, like someone who'd fallen asleep uninvited on a stranger's couch.

"I'm sorry," she said at last. She knew she owed him that much. "For barging in like this, I mean. I wasn't thinking clearly. It's been a long day, and I just…." The words trailed off there, since she wasn't sure how she could ever adequately explain the mounting pressure of the past eight months, the desperation that had driven her to flee to Jerome in the first place.

Shane's expression didn't change, but something in his posture seemed to ease slightly. "You said you were looking for Levi?"

Rosa nodded. "I wanted to talk to him. About…about consort stuff." Her cheeks burned as she said those words out loud, but there was no point in pretending. If Shane was a McAllister, then he must know all about how witch consorts worked. "My mother conjured him years ago, before she found my father. I thought maybe he could give me some advice about how to deal with all of it."

"And by 'all of it,' you mean the *prima*-in-waiting tradition of finding your magical partner before your twenty-second birthday," Shane said. It wasn't a question this time, either. He seemed to do that a lot, she noticed—make statements instead of asking questions, as if he already knew the answers.

It should have been annoying. Instead, she found it oddly comforting not to have to explain herself.

"Exactly," Rosa said. "I've been trying for eight months. Thirty-four guys. Thirty-four failed kisses." She heard bitterness creeping into her voice but couldn't quite stop it. "And everyone keeps telling me I have plenty of time, that I shouldn't worry, but I'm tired of kissing strangers and hoping for magic that never comes."

Shane's gaze sharpened on her face, and Rosa had the uncomfortable feeling that he was seeing more than she wanted him to…much more than she'd intended to reveal to a man she'd met a scant fifteen minutes ago.

"That's rough," he said after a pause, and she noticed how his voice had lost some of its edge.

"But Levi's going to be exhausted tonight. Everyone is. The wedding was great, and everyone had a good time, but it was also a long day. I can pretty much guarantee that my dad won't be up for deep philosophical conversations about consort bonds until at least noon tomorrow."

"Your dad?" Rosa blinked, wondering if she'd heard him right, or if she was just that tired. "Levi's your father?"

"Yes." Shane's mouth quirked in something that wasn't quite a smile. "I suppose that makes us cousins, technically. Very distant cousins, since your father and I are only related by clan, not by blood. But still."

Well, she'd already tried to reassure herself that coming into a stranger's house wasn't so bad if they happened to be a member of your clan. In theory, it had sounded all right, but when faced with the reality of an obviously exhausted man who'd only wanted to come home and crash and instead had been confronted by an intruder, Rosa thought she was on pretty shaky footing.

"So you're Levi's son," she said as she tried to put her worries aside. Done was done, after all. "Which means your mother is Hayley. And your sister is…." She tried to remember what she'd heard about Levi's children, but her mother hadn't talked about them much, for obvious reasons. Still, she knew there was a daughter a few years older than she was, and a son who was a couple of years older than that, and that they'd both been living on their own.

"Brianna," Shane supplied. "Bree. She's the one who got married today. To a guy named Bill Garrett, although that's not his real name. It's complicated."

She felt her eyebrows lift. "Complicated" in a witch clan could mean a whole lot of things. However, she got the feeling it was probably better not to pry.

Shane rubbed a hand over his chin, and Rosa noticed the faint shadows under his eyes, the exhaustion that pulled at the corners of his mouth. "Look," he went on, "here's the situation. It's late, and everyone's tired. You don't have anywhere to go, and even if you did, I'm guessing you don't want to go back to Scottsdale tonight."

"I can get a hotel room," Rosa said quickly. "I have cash. I don't need to impose—"

"At this hour?" Shane glanced at the clock on the mantel, its only ornament. "It's past ten-thirty on a Saturday night. The Connor and the Clinkscale are probably fully booked, and the Grand Hotel…." He paused. "Let's just say that you probably don't want to stay there by yourself if you're not used to Jerome's particular brand of supernatural activity."

His words only confirmed what she'd thought

earlier, and Rosa suppressed a shiver. She'd heard plenty of stories about Jerome's ghosts, about the spirits that supposedly wandered the old mining town. Her family's house in Scottsdale was old, but it wasn't haunted. Not like this.

"So, what are you suggesting?" she asked.

Shane was quiet for a moment, his jaw working as if he was chewing over something he didn't particularly like the taste of. At last, he sighed.

"You can stay here tonight," he said. "I have a guest room. But I want to be very clear about the terms here. This is one night. Tomorrow, you talk to Levi, you figure out your next move, and you don't make this my problem. I have a kitchen to run and a restaurant that needs my full attention. I don't have time to babysit a runaway *prima*-in-waiting, no matter how distant a cousin she is."

The words should have stung. Instead, a complicated mix of relief and irritation washed over her—relief because she had a place to sleep that wasn't a haunted hotel room, and irritation because of the way he'd said "babysit," as if she was some kind of child who couldn't take care of herself.

"I'm not running a bed and breakfast for wayward witches," he added, and now there was a definite note of amusement in his voice, as if he was enjoying needling her just a little.

She straightened her spine and gave him her best *prima*-in-waiting look, the one she'd been working on since she was sixteen. All that practice told her she should look cool, composed, utterly unruffled.

Whether she'd come anywhere close to that impression, she had no idea.

"I wouldn't dream of imposing on your clearly overwhelming hospitality," she said sweetly.

For a second, his eyes widened, and then—impossibly—he almost smiled. Not quite, but close enough that Rosa felt what she thought was an answering flutter in her chest. Damn it. She didn't want to find him attractive. She didn't want to notice the way humor transformed his face, softening his chiseled features and making him look younger, more approachable.

"Come on," Shane said, and tilted his head toward the hallway. "Let me show you where you'll be sleeping."

Rosa picked up her leather tote and followed him through the living room. The house was small, much smaller than the home where she'd grown up, but there was something appealing about it. The rooms were cozy rather than cramped, and even with the minimal furniture, the space had a warmth to it that her family's much larger home sometimes lacked.

The hallway was short and narrow, with four

doors that opened off it. Shane gestured to the first one on the left.

"Bathroom," he said briefly. "The shower's a little temperamental, but it works if you're patient with it. Towels are in the cabinet under the sink." He moved to the next door on the right. "This is the guest room. It's not fancy, but it's clean, and the bed's comfortable enough. I think there are sheets already on it, but if not, there's a stack in the closet."

Rosa peered inside. The room was indeed not fancy—a double bed with a plain wooden frame, a nightstand, and a dresser that looked like it had seen better days. But it was neat, and when she stepped inside and flipped the light switch, warm golden light flooded the space, making it feel almost welcoming.

"It's perfect," she said, and meant it. "Thank you."

Shane shrugged, as if her gratitude made him uncomfortable. "Don't mention it. Seriously… don't mention it. If anyone in the clan finds out that I let you crash here, I'll never hear the end of it." He moved to the doorway, then paused, one hand on the frame. "Have you eaten?"

Rosa's stomach chose that moment to growl, loud enough that she was sure he must have heard it. She'd had the burger and fries at the Haunted Hamburger, true, but that had been hours and hours ago, and she'd been running on adrenaline and anxiety for most of the day.

"I'm fine," she said, even though she wasn't. Pride wouldn't let her admit that she was hungry. She didn't want to impose on him even more than she already had.

Shane gave her a look that suggested he knew exactly what she was doing. "When's the last time you ate?"

"Around two-thirty," she admitted. "But really, I don't need—"

"Wait here," he said, and disappeared down the hallway before she could protest further.

Rosa set her tote down on the bed and looked around the guest room again. Everything about this situation was surreal. This morning, she'd been in Scottsdale, playing the perfect *prima*-in-waiting, pretending everything was fine. And now she was in Jerome, in a stranger's house—no, her extremely distant cousin's house—about to accept food from a man who clearly would rather be doing anything else.

Her mother was going to kill her when she found out. *If* she found out. Rosa hadn't exactly left a note, and she'd been careful to pay for everything with cash rather than her credit card. With any luck, she'd have at least a day or two before Zoe realized she wasn't just spending time with friends or holed up in her room, painting. It wouldn't be the first time that she'd gone full hermit mode while she worked, but she knew at some point, her mother would figure out that her *prima*-in-waiting daughter wasn't working on her latest creation but had in fact flown the coop.

The scent of butter and bread reached her nose, and Rosa's stomach growled again. She should probably stay in the guest room, should give Shane space after intruding on his evening. But curiosity pulled at her, and besides, it would be rude not to at least say thank you for whatever he was making.

She found him in the kitchen, which opened off the back of the living room. Unlike the sparsely decorated main spaces, the kitchen looked lived-in and well-loved. Professional-grade appliances gleamed against butcher-block countertops, and a pot rack hung from the ceiling, displaying an impressive array of copper cookware. Herbs grew in small pots on the windowsill above the sink, and the air smelled of warm butter and fresh rosemary and something else, a scent she couldn't quite identify but thought was probably a combination of the ghosts of dozens of different spices.

Shane stood at the stove, his back to her. He'd tied a dish towel around his waist instead of an apron, and Rosa watched as he flipped something in the pan with a practiced flick of his wrist.

"You didn't have to do this," she said from the doorway.

He glanced over his shoulder. "You're hungry. I'm making you a grilled cheese. It's not a big deal."

But it felt like a big deal, the simple fact that he was feeding her even though she'd broken into his house and disrupted his evening and generally made a nuisance of herself.

"Can I help?" she asked.

The answer was immediate and unequivocal. "No. This is my kitchen. Guests don't work in my kitchen."

Rosa bit back a smile. "I'm not a guest. I'm an intruder, remember?"

"Semantics." He flipped the sandwich again, and Rosa caught a glimpse of perfectly golden-brown bread, the kind that only came from someone who knew exactly how much butter to use and exactly how hot the pan should be. "Sit down. This'll be ready in a minute."

She pulled out one of the two stools tucked under a small breakfast bar and settled onto it, watching him work. Something was mesmerizing about the way he moved—economical, elegant, never wasting a motion. His hands were large and capable, the hands of someone who created things, and she found herself studying them perhaps more closely than was strictly appropriate.

No, she told herself firmly. *This is exactly the kind of distraction you don't need right now.*

She'd come to Jerome to escape the endless parade of potential consorts, to breathe for a minute without everyone watching to see if this kiss would be the one that sparked the magic. The last thing she needed was to start noticing things about Shane McAllister—the way his hair was slightly too long and fell forward when he bent over the stove, or the careful attention he paid to every detail of what he was doing.

He was an artist, she realized. Just like her, in his own way. He took something simple—bread, cheese, butter—and transformed it into something that was so much more. That was art, even if it wasn't the kind that hung in galleries.

Shane slid the sandwich onto a plate, cut it diagonally with a single deft movement, and set it in front of her, along with a paper napkin. "There. One grilled cheese."

Rosa looked down at the sandwich. The bread was gorgeously browned, crispy at the edges, and when she picked up one half, she could see the cheese stretching between the two pieces in perfect, melted strings. It looked like something out of a magazine spread, far too beautiful to be a simple midnight—well, ten-thirty—snack.

"Thank you," she said, and took a bite.

Wow. That wasn't just a grilled cheese sandwich. No, it was the Platonic ideal of a grilled cheese sandwich, the sandwich that all other grilled cheese sandwiches aspired to be. The bread was crispy outside and soft inside, buttery and rich without being greasy. The cheese—and there was more than one kind, she could taste that now, something sharp and something nutty and something with just a hint of sweetness—had melted perfectly, coating her tongue with warmth and comfort and home.

She made a sound that was embarrassingly close to a moan.

Shane raised an eyebrow, a glint of amusement in his dark blue eyes. "That good?"

"That's good," Rosa confirmed once she'd swallowed. "Holy—" She took another bite and closed her eyes so she could savor it properly. "What did you *do* to this?"

"Nothing special," he replied, still looking amused. But she heard satisfaction in his voice, the pleasure of someone who knew exactly how good they were at what they did. "Just good bread, good cheese, good butter, and proper technique."

"This isn't 'nothing special,'" Rosa said. She opened her eyes and sent him a very direct look. "This is magic. *Your* magic."

He gave a casual shrug, but she could see she'd

hit close to the truth. "Cooking magic is what I've got. It makes me good at what I do."

"Good?" Rosa gestured at the sandwich with her free hand. "This isn't good. This is...." She struggled to find the right words and realized they probably didn't exist. "This is the best thing I've ever tasted, and it's a grilled cheese sandwich you threw together in five minutes. What's your actual cooking like?"

Was that a flicker of pride in his expression? For just a second, Rosa caught a glimpse of the passion underneath his offhand exterior, the dedication to his craft that had clearly driven him to hone his natural magical talent with years of training and practice.

"I'm the head chef at the Asylum," he said. "It's the restaurant at the Grand Hotel. If you stick around Jerome long enough, maybe you can come by and find out."

It was an olive branch, she realized. A small one, grudgingly extended, but an olive branch nonetheless.

"I'd like that," she said, and took another bite of the sandwich. She wasn't just being polite. She genuinely wanted to taste more of what he could create, wanted to see what his magic could do when he really let it loose.

They fell into silence while she ate, but it was a comfortable silence, the kind that didn't need to be filled with chatter. Shane busied himself cleaning up the pan and putting things away, moving through his kitchen with the ease of long familiarity. Rosa finished the sandwich slowly, making sure she savored every bite as she tried to commit the taste to memory.

When she was done, she folded the napkin and set it on the plate. "Thank you. That was amazing."

"You're welcome." Shane took the plate and rinsed it in the sink. "You should probably get some sleep. It's late, and you've had a long day."

He was right, of course. Rosa could feel the exhaustion pulling at her now that she'd eaten, the adrenaline that had carried her through the day finally ebbing away. But she found herself reluctant to leave the kitchen, to break this strange, fragile peace they'd found.

"What you said earlier," she began, then hesitated. "About not having time to babysit me. I just want you to know—I'm not here to be anyone's burden. I can take care of myself. I just needed to get away for a little while."

Shane turned from the sink and studied her with those dark blue eyes. They reminded her of the ocean at dusk, even though of course she'd never been to the beach. "Running away from something…or running toward something?"

Both, Rosa thought. *Neither.* She was running

from the suffocating pressure of being the *prima*-in-waiting, from the endless parade of potential consorts, from the fear that she'd never find what she was supposed to find. And she was running toward…what? Answers? Freedom? A moment to breathe?

"I don't know yet," she said honestly. "Maybe I'll figure it out while I'm here."

Shane gave a brief nod, as if that answer satisfied him. "Fair enough. But Rosa?"

"Yes?"

"Whatever you're running from—it's going to catch up with you eventually. It always does."

The words settled on her, heavy with truth. He was right. Her mother would find her, or her mother would call Angela McAllister, or someone would spot her in Jerome and word would get back. You couldn't hide forever, not when you were the *prima*-in-waiting of a major witch clan.

But maybe she could hide for a little while, and maybe that would be enough.

"I know," Rosa said quietly. "But I'll deal with that when it happens."

Shane studied her for another long moment, then glanced toward the hallway. "Get some sleep. We'll figure out the rest in the morning."

Rosa slid off the stool and headed for the guest room. At the doorway, she paused and looked back. Shane had returned to his cleanup, wiping down the counters with an economy of effort that told her he done the same thing countless times before.

"Shane?"

He glanced up. "Yes?"

"Thank you for letting me stay, and for the sandwich," she replied, then went on, "And for… well, for not calling my mother the second you figured out who I was."

"Don't thank me yet," he said dryly. "I might still change my mind."

But there was a hint of amusement in his voice, and Rosa found herself smiling as she headed down the hallway to the guest room.

She closed the door behind her and leaned against it, then let out a long breath. Her gaze fell on her tote bag, which still sat on the bed where she'd left it. Inside was her sketchbook and the little box of pencils she always carried with her, along with the clothes and toiletries she'd packed in such a hurry this morning.

Everything she needed to hide out for a few days while she figured out what came next.

Rosa moved away from the door and started getting ready for bed. As she brushed her teeth in the cramped bathroom and changed into the oversized T-shirt she slept in, she found her thoughts returning to Shane.

She'd noticed everything about him, she realized as she climbed into the guest bed and pulled the covers up to her chin—the way he moved through his kitchen like he was born there, and the care he took with his space, with his craft. The strong, elegant lines of his face, the capable hands, the blue eyes that seemed to see too much.

Damn it.

Rosa stared up at the ceiling and willed her racing thoughts to slow down and focus somewhere else. She'd come here to escape the consort search, not to start developing a completely inappropriate attraction to her—what was he, even? Her cousin by clan affiliation? The son of the man her mother had accidentally conjured almost thirty years ago?

Whatever he was, he'd made it clear that she was a temporary inconvenience. One night, he'd said. Tomorrow she'd talk to Levi, and then she'd figure out her next move.

She wouldn't complicate things by letting herself notice how the corners of Shane's eyes crinkled when he almost smiled, or the way his voice softened when he talked about his sister's wedding, or the fact that he'd fed her even though she'd broken into his house.

She definitely wouldn't think about the way his hands had moved over the bread and cheese, deft and sure.

Rosa closed her eyes and willed herself to

sleep. Tomorrow would be complicated enough without adding tonight's inconvenient awareness into the mix.

But even as she drifted off, she could still taste that perfect grilled cheese sandwich on her tongue, and she knew—with a sinking certainty—that she was already in much more trouble than she'd bargained for.

3

SHANE OPENED HIS EYES AND SQUINTED AT the bars of bright sunlight that had managed to poke their way past the blinds that covered his bedroom window. For one glorious minute, he felt completely relaxed, allowing himself to bask in the realization that Bree's wedding was now over and done with, and all he had to do now was get on with his regular day-to-day life.

Then he remembered that he had a *prima*-in-waiting sleeping in his guest room.

Crap.

He lay there for a while, staring at the ceiling and trying to figure out how his life had gone from mostly normal to beyond weird in the space of twelve hours. Last night, he'd been laser-focused on getting through his sister's wedding without any major disasters, and to his relief, everything had gone off without a hitch, and now Bree and Bill were on their way to New Mexico, granted permission by the Castillo *prima*...who also happened to be Angela's youngest daughter, Miranda...to spend their honeymoon in Santa Fe and Taos.

But then Shane had come home to find an invisible woman napping on his couch, and somehow—against all his better instincts—he'd agreed to let her stay the night. Temporary insanity brought on by exhaustion?

Probably.

He picked up his phone from the place where it had been resting on the nightstand and glanced at the screen. Seven minutes after seven. Early for a Sunday morning, he supposed, especially after yesterday's marathon, but his body was used to chef's hours, and he'd never really understood the concept of sleeping in.

Why lie in bed when there was so much to do?

He got up, pulled on a pair of jeans and a T-shirt, and padded barefoot down the hallway. The guest room door was still closed, and he couldn't hear any sounds coming from within. Good. Rosa could sleep as long as she needed, giving him some necessary mental space to prepare for the talk they needed to have. He'd make breakfast, and then they could have a conversation about what came next.

The conversation where he politely but firmly sent her on her way to talk to his father.

In the kitchen, he got to work making coffee. Good beans, freshly ground, the water at exactly the right temperature. His magic hummed beneath his skin as he worked, a familiar warmth that guided his hands and sharpened his senses. He could feel the potential in every ingredient he touched, could sense how flavors would combine and transform.

While the coffee brewed, he pulled eggs from the refrigerator, along with cream and butter and a wedge of good Gruyère, and gathered some fresh chives from the pots on his windowsill. The sourdough he'd baked two days ago was still good and would make excellent toast.

Just like always, he didn't really have to think about what he was doing. His hands moved through the familiar motions while his mind wandered, replaying the previous night's unexpected encounter. Rosa Sandoval, with her unusual hazel eyes and her desperate search for a consort she couldn't seem to find. Thirty-four failed attempts. That had to be rough, especially for someone just twenty-one, still trying to figure out who she was while the weight of an entire clan's future rested on her shoulders.

He cracked eggs into a bowl and whisked them with cream and a pinch of salt. He understood pressure. It was something he'd dealt with his whole life—the pressure to make something of himself beyond his magical gift, to prove he was more than merely a warlock who could cook. That was why he'd gone to culinary school in Phoenix, why he'd worked his ass off to get the head chef position at the Asylum by the time he was twenty-seven.

But at least he'd gotten to choose his own path. Rosa Sandoval didn't have that luxury.

He heated butter in a pan, let it foam and subside, and then poured in the eggs. Low and slow, that was the key to perfect scrambled eggs. They required patience and attention, and he let the curds form gently, folding them over themselves until they were creamy and soft and just barely set.

The smell of brewing coffee filled the kitchen, rich and dark and promising. Shane poured himself a cup and took a sip, then closed his eyes for a moment to savor it.

Behind him, he heard a soft sound from the doorway.

"That smells amazing," Rosa said, her voice still slightly husky with sleep.

Shane turned. She'd changed out of yesterday's sundress and now wore faded jeans and a soft pink

T-shirt that made her skin look warm and golden. Her long dark hair was pulled back in a careless braid, and without makeup, she seemed younger and somehow more vulnerable.

Also, annoyingly, even prettier than she'd looked last night.

"Coffee?" he asked, because that seemed like a safe neutral ground.

"Please." She moved into the kitchen and accepted the mug he poured for her, and wrapped both hands around it like she needed the warmth, even though it was already heating up outside, promising another day in the low nineties. "Thank you." She took a sip, and her eyes widened. "Wow."

Shane felt the corner of his mouth twitch. "Good?"

"Good doesn't even begin to cover it." She sipped again, slower this time, clearly savoring the flavor. "This is the best coffee I've ever had. What did you do to it?"

"Nothing special," he said, which was true. It was just good beans and proper technique. His magic helped, of course—it made everything a little more intense, a little more perfect—but the fundamentals were still the same. "Have a seat. Breakfast will be ready in a few minutes."

Rosa settled onto one of the stools and watched him work. Shane returned his attention to the eggs, folding them gently, checking their consistency. Almost there. He grabbed the chives and chopped them quickly, then grated some cheese.

While he worked, he could feel Rosa's gaze on him, tracking his movements, and something about being observed while he cooked made him hyperaware of everything he was doing. The way he held the knife, the rhythm of his chopping… the careful attention he paid to the eggs as they grew firmer and ever so slightly browned.

Stop showing off, he told himself. *She's not staying. She's leaving today.*

He folded the chives and cheese into the eggs, killed the heat, and let the residual warmth of the pan finish cooking them. Once they were done, he plated the eggs alongside thick slices of sourdough toast, buttered and lightly grilled, and set one plate in front of Rosa before he took the other for himself.

"This looks incredible," she said, staring down at her plate like he'd just presented her with something from a Michelin-starred restaurant instead of a simple Sunday breakfast.

"It's just scrambled eggs," he replied, but he couldn't quite keep a pleased note out of his voice. He liked feeding people, liked watching them experience his food. It was one of the reasons he'd become a chef in the first place.

Well, that and the magic that had set him on that course in the first place.

Rosa took a bite and closed her eyes, and Shane found himself watching her face as she tasted what he'd created. Her expression shifted through surprise and delight to something close to wonder, and a warm satisfaction settled somewhere deep inside him.

"Shane," she said after she'd swallowed and taken another sip of coffee to wash things down. "I need you to know something."

He tilted his head at her. "What's that?"

"I'm never leaving." She opened her eyes and gave him a mock-serious look. "I'm going to live in your guest room forever, and you're going to feed me like this every day, and I will never be hungry or sad again."

He couldn't help laughing at her comment. And he was a little surprised to realize it was actual laughter, not just the dry amusement he usually allowed himself. "I'm not sure your mother would approve of that plan."

"What my mother doesn't know won't hurt her." Rosa took another bite and made a soft sound of appreciation that did absolutely nothing to help with his resolve to keep her at a distance. "Seriously, though. How are you not, like, a celebrity chef or something? This is ridiculous.

You could charge a hundred dollars for these eggs, and people would pay it."

"The Asylum charges forty-five for my breakfast special," Shane said. "So you're not too far off."

"I would pay twice that." Rosa pointed at him with her fork. "And I'm not just saying that because you're letting me crash here. This is objectively spectacular food."

Something about her genuine enthusiasm warmed him in a way that had nothing to do with his magic. He'd gotten plenty of compliments over the years from both professional reviewers and his customers, but there was something different about Rosa's unfiltered delight. She wasn't trying to impress him or curry favor. No, she was only responding honestly to something he'd made, and that honesty felt like a gift.

Dangerous territory, he reminded himself. *She's not staying.*

They ate in friendly silence for a few minutes. The whole time, he found himself far too aware of her presence, from the happy gleam in her greenish eyes as she ate to the way the morning light coming through the kitchen window caught in her dark hair.

Somehow, he managed to force his attention back to his own plate.

"So," Rosa said eventually as she set down her fork. "I was thinking."

Here it comes, Shane thought. *The part where she asks for something else.*

"I know you said I should talk to your father today," Rosa went on, "but I was wondering if maybe I could stay in Jerome for a little while longer. Like, a few days? A week, maybe?"

Shane kept his expression neutral, even as his brain immediately started calculating all the nightmarish ramifications of having Rosa Sandoval hang around Jerome any longer than a day. "Where would you stay?" he asked, and was glad that he sounded casual enough.

"I could get a hotel room. The Connor, or—"

"They're booked solid through next weekend," Shane said. "There's a gem and mineral show down in Clarkdale, and it draws collectors from all over. Every room in Jerome—and Clarkdale and Cottonwood—is probably taken."

Rosa's expression immediately fell. "Oh. I didn't know about that."

Shane knew he should have left it there, should have said something sympathetic and helped her maybe find accommodations in Sedona or even Prescott if she insisted on staying in the area.

Instead, he found himself saying, "You could stay here."

The words were out of his mouth before he'd fully thought them through, and her expression immediately brightened. "Really?" she said, hope tremulous in her voice. "Are you sure?"

Of course he wasn't sure. Having a beautiful *prima*-in-waiting staying in his guest room was a complication he definitely didn't need. But the alternative was sending her away, and something about that felt wrong in a way he couldn't quite articulate.

"I mean—" she began, and he could see her trying to find the right words, trying to figure out the best way to assure him her presence wouldn't be a problem. "I wouldn't be in your way, I promise. I'll stay out of your hair, and—"

Shane's phone rang.

He pulled it from his jeans pocket and glanced down at the screen. Jared. His sous chef calling him at seven-thirty on a Sunday morning was never a good sign.

"I need to take this," Shane told Rosa, then held the phone to his ear. "Jared. What's up?"

"Hey, chef." Jared's voice sounded strained, and Shane already found himself tensing. "I'm really sorry to do this, but I can't come in today. Or, actually, I can't come in at all anymore. I'm quitting."

For a second, the words didn't quite register. Then he said, "You're *what?*"

"My girlfriend got a job in Seattle," Jared told him, the words spoken quickly, as though he was afraid Shane would interrupt before he had a chance to get it all off his chest. "She leaves next week, and I'm going with her. I know this is terrible timing, but I need to give notice. Like, effective immediately."

Shane got up from the stool, his hand tightening on the phone as Rosa stared at him with worried eyes. "Jared, the review is this week. The *Arizona Republic*. This could make or break the restaurant. You know that."

"I know, and I'm sorry, Shane. I really am. But I have to go. This is my relationship we're talking about."

Shane wanted to point out that being a professional meant you didn't just abandon your job in the middle of the most important week of the season, but he forced himself to take a breath. Getting angry wouldn't help. Jared was gone, and he'd just have to deal with the consequences.

"Fine," he said, knowing how brusque he sounded. "Just let me know where to mail your final check."

He ended the call before Jared could say anything else and set the phone down on the counter with something close to a slam. Luckily, its protective rubber case protected it from any real damage.

"Problem?" Rosa asked. Her voice was quiet, as if she understood that being too strident would only rile him up further.

Shane ran a hand through his hair and tried to push aside the anger flaring within so he could concentrate on logistics. Jared had been his sous chef for three months. That wasn't long enough to be fully trained to Shane's exacting standards, but certainly long enough to be competent and to handle the less critical stations, freeing him up to focus on the complex dishes that made the Asylum's reputation.

And now he was gone.

"My sous chef just quit," Shane said. "Right before Sunday brunch."

Rosa's eyes widened. "That's terrible timing."

"You don't know the half of it." He got the pan from the stove and took it over to the sink, unable to stand still while he tried to work through the disaster unfolding in front of him. "The *Arizona Republic* is sending a food critic this week. It could be any day between tomorrow and Saturday. This review could establish the Asylum as one of the premier restaurants in northern Arizona...or it could turn us into not much more than a gimmick in a tourist destination."

He heard the edge of panic in his own voice and hated it. He didn't do panic. He always had a plan, always knew exactly what needed to happen next.

Except right now, he didn't.

"And you can't run the kitchen alone during a review," Rosa said simply.

"No." The admission felt like pulling teeth, but he forced himself to continue, confronted by the obvious sympathy in her eyes. "I can't. I mean, I could if it was just a normal weekend. It would be brutal, but I could do it. But during a review?" He shook his head. "Every dish has to be perfect. The timing has to be flawless. The presentation has to be publication-quality. I can't do all of that, and also handle prep and line work and all the other things a sous chef does."

"Can you hire someone else?" she asked.

"Not in three days." He set the pan in the sink and then leaned against the counter, the weight of the situation pressing down on him even as the granite counter pressed against his back. "Maybe not even in three weeks. Good sous chefs don't grow on trees, and the ones who are available are usually available for a reason."

Rosa was quiet for a moment, her brow furrowed. Shane could practically see her thinking, working through something.

"What if I helped?" she asked at length.

Shane blinked. "What?"

"What if I worked in your kitchen?" She

leaned forward slightly, luminous eyes intent on his face. "Just through the review. However long you need. I could do prep work, basic tasks, whatever you need an extra pair of hands for."

"You don't have any commercial kitchen experience," Shane said. At least, he assumed she didn't. Somehow, he doubted the de la Paz *prima*-in-waiting had been earning spare cash while working at Chipotle or something.

"No," Rosa replied at once, "but I can follow directions. And I'm good with my hands—I'm an artist, so I understand attention to detail." She was getting more animated as she spoke, clearly warming to the idea. "You could teach me what I need to know. I'm a fast learner."

Shane opened his mouth to say no, to explain all the reasons why having an untrained *prima*-in-waiting working in his kitchen during the most important week of his career was a spectacularly bad idea.

But then he stopped.

Because the alternative was running the kitchen alone, and that was impossible.

"You'll have to do exactly what I tell you," he heard himself say. "No arguments, no complaints. In the kitchen, I'm the boss."

"Of course," she responded at once. "I understand."

"And you'd need to learn fast. I don't have time to hand-hold or repeat myself."

Maybe he was being too brutal, but better to have her get a taste of what she'd be getting herself into.

Not a single second of hesitation. "I can do that."

Shane studied her for a moment, trying to gauge whether she really understood what she was offering. Kitchen work was hard, especially in a high-end restaurant. It involved long hours, intense heat, and constant pressure. And Rosa came from privilege—she was the *prima's* daughter, probably used to people catering to her needs rather than the other way around.

But she was also desperate enough to run away from home, desperate enough to hide in a stranger's house. Maybe she had more grit than he was giving her credit for.

"Why?" he asked. "Why would you want to do this?"

Rosa's gaze didn't waver for a second. "Because you need help, and I need a place to hide. And because...." She paused there for a moment, then continued. "Because if I can't handle a few days working in a kitchen, how am I supposed to lead an entire clan? I need to know I can do hard things. That I'm not just a *prima*-in-waiting who failed to find her consort."

The raw honesty in her voice caught Shane off guard. He recognized that need to prove yourself, to demonstrate competence beyond what people expected.

He'd felt it his whole life.

"Okay," he said slowly, his mind already shifting gears, moving from problem to solution. "Here's the deal. You can stay here and work in my kitchen through next weekend. That'll get us past the review and give me time to find a replacement sous chef."

Those amazing eyes were still fixed on him. "That works for me."

"But there are conditions," he went on, holding up a hand so she wouldn't interrupt him. "First, you do what I say, when I say it, no questions asked. Second, you show up on time, and you work the full shift, even when you're tired. Third, if you can't handle it—if it's too much or you realize you're in over your head—you tell me immediately. I can't afford to have someone in my kitchen who isn't pulling their weight."

"I understand," Rosa said, chin up and her expression confident. "I won't let you down."

"And fourth," Shane added, "you still have to talk to my father and get his advice about your consort situation. That's why you came here, remember?"

"I will." Rosa rose from her stool and moved closer, extending her hand. "So we have a deal?"

Shane looked down at her outstretched hand. In his gut, he knew this was a terrible idea. The last thing he should be doing was bringing an untrained worker into his kitchen during the most important week of the season, let alone letting her stay in his house and tying himself to someone who was clearly running from problems that would eventually catch up with her.

But he needed help, and she was offering it. And something about the resolute set of her jaw, the steady way she met his eyes, made him think that maybe she could actually do this.

If she couldn't, he'd find out soon enough.

He reached out and took her hand. "Deal."

The moment their palms touched, something strange happened.

It wasn't dramatic—no flash of light, no surge of obvious magic, just an odd warmth that spread from the point of contact, traveling up Shane's arm and settling somewhere in the center of his chest.

And from the way Rosa's eyes widened, he knew she felt it, too.

They held the handshake for a beat longer than necessary, both of them frozen, before Rosa pulled her hand back. She flexed her fingers, staring at them like she couldn't understand what had just happened.

"That was…." she began, then stopped there, as if she couldn't quite think of the right word.

"Weird," Shane supplied.

"I was going to say 'unexpected.'"

"Same thing." He glanced down at his own hand, but there was nothing visible to show what might have caused the odd sensation, only a lingering warmth that was already fading. "Probably just static electricity."

"Right." Rosa nodded, but she didn't sound entirely convinced. "Static electricity."

That seemed logical enough. They might have both been of witch-kind, but physics affected them the same way it did ordinary people.

Well, most of the time, anyway.

No point in worrying about it. He didn't have time to analyze weird magical sensations. No, he had a kitchen to run, a review to prepare for…and now a *prima*-in-waiting to train.

"We'll start tomorrow," he said, forcing his voice back to business. "I still have to be at work at eleven today, but I figure you need a little time to get settled in. Tomorrow at 9 a.m., though, you're in my kitchen at the Asylum, and we'll start going over basics."

"Nine o'clock," Rosa said. "I'll be there."

"Don't make me regret this," Shane said, but his tone was lighter than his words suggested.

Rosa smiled, and Shane noticed the way the expression illuminated her face, erasing the shadows of worry that had settled there. "Don't make me regret hiding in your house," she returned.

Despite everything, Shane felt himself smile in return. "Fair enough," he said.

Rosa moved back to her stool and picked up her coffee mug, cradling it in both hands. "So... what should I know before tomorrow? Any tips for a complete kitchen novice?"

Shane leaned against the counter, considering. "Comfortable shoes," he said. "You'll be on your feet for hours. And you'll want to pull your hair back—nothing loose that can fall into the food. No jewelry except small earrings, nothing that can catch on equipment or end up in a dish."

"Got it." Rosa looked like she was committing every word to memory, brows drawn together in concentration. "What else?"

"Bring a good attitude and be ready to work harder than you've probably ever worked in your life," he said bluntly. "Kitchen work isn't glamorous. It's hot and loud and stressful. And when service starts, it's controlled chaos. You'll get burned, you'll get cut, you'll want to quit. But if you can push through all of that, if you can keep going even when everything in you wants to stop...." He paused there for a moment before adding, "Then maybe you'll understand what it takes to lead people through hard times."

Her head tilted as she considered his comment. "Is that what cooking teaches you?"

"It's what it taught me," Shane said. "How to stay focused under pressure, I mean...how to trust your training even when everything's falling apart, and how to lead a team through the worst service of their lives and come out the other side."

Was that a faint shadow of concern he saw in her eyes?

"And you think I can learn that in a week?"

"I think you can start learning it," he replied. He met her gaze, noting how she hadn't seemed to waver at all as he spoke. "The question is whether you're really willing to try."

Rosa set down her mug and squared her shoulders. "I am."

Shane studied her for a moment longer, trying to gauge her sincerity. He saw determination in her eyes, but also something else. Fear, possibly, or simple uncertainty, not so strange for a *prima*-in-waiting who'd run away from home because she couldn't face another failed consort kiss.

But she was here. She was trying. And Shane had to respect that, even if he wasn't entirely sure she knew what she was getting into.

"Okay," he said finally. "Then let's do this."

Rosa smiled again, even wider this time. "Thank you, Shane."

"Thank me after you've survived your first dinner service," he said dryly. "You might feel differently about it then."

But despite those words, despite all his reservations about this plan, he felt almost light now. Relief, he supposed, knowing that he wouldn't have to face the anonymous food critic while short-staffed. Or maybe it was something else entirely, something he wasn't quite ready to examine too closely.

He'd made a deal with Rosa Sandoval. For better or worse, they were in this together now.

"I should probably go talk to Levi this morning," she said then, breaking into his thoughts. "Get that conversation out of the way before I start working for you tomorrow."

"Good idea." Shane straightened and started clearing their breakfast plates. "He'll be at the big yellow house with the green shutters. You can't miss it."

"The one I tried yesterday?"

"That's the one." Shane ran water in the sink. "Just knock on the door. Sunday mornings, he's usually home."

Rosa slid off the stool. "Should I tell him

about our arrangement? That I'm working for you, I mean?"

Shane paused for a moment, considering her question. His father would probably have opinions about this plan...lots of opinions. But this was Shane's decision to make, not Levi's.

"Tell him whatever you want," he said carelessly. "But Rosa?"

"Yes?"

"Don't let him talk you out of it." Shane sent her a very direct look. "I need the help, and you need the hiding place. That's the deal we made, and I'm holding you to it."

Rosa's mouth curved in a small smile. "I wouldn't dream of backing out."

"Good."

She headed toward the hallway, then paused at the doorway. "Shane? Those eggs really were incredible."

Then she was gone, leaving Shane alone in his kitchen with dirty dishes and a plan that was either brilliant or completely insane.

Probably insane, he decided as he started washing the plates. No, *definitely* insane.

But he was committed now. And Shane McAllister always saw his commitments through, no matter how complicated they got.

Even when they involved a beautiful *prima*-in-waiting whose hand sparked something unexpected when it touched his.

Maybe especially then.

Shane dried the last dish and put it away, then pulled out his phone. He had a lot to do before he went into work—meal prep to reorganize now that he was down a sous chef, schedules to rework, a training plan to devise for someone with zero kitchen experience.

But first, he needed to text his sister.

> You're never going to believe what just happened.

He stared down at the words on his phone's screen, then deleted them. Bree was on her honeymoon, or at least the beginning of it. She didn't need to be bothered with his problems.

Instead, he opened his notes app and started making a list of everything Rosa would need to learn and everything he'd need to teach her…all the ways this could go spectacularly wrong.

It was going to be a long week.

But as Shane worked through his mental checklist, organizing and planning and preparing the way he always did, he couldn't quite suppress the small spark of anticipation that went through him.

Rosa Sandoval was a complication, that was for sure.

But maybe she was also exactly what he needed.

4

Rosa spent Sunday alone in Shane's house, trying not to think about the way she was hiding again.

She'd really meant to walk over to Levi's place, but somehow the morning had slipped away while she scrolled through social media on her phone, wondering if anyone had noticed the way she'd gone missing, even though she knew that there was no way in the world her mother would have let that kind of information become public. Then it was afternoon, and she told herself it would be rude to show up at Levi's during lunch, so instead she watched TV and tried not to think about much of anything at all. By evening, she'd convinced herself that a Monday visit with Levi would be better anyway. That would give her a kind of fresh start to the week.

Besides, Shane wouldn't be home from the restaurant until late, and Rosa didn't particularly want to sit alone with her thoughts after a possibly emotional conversation with Levi McAllister about her consort failures.

So instead, she ordered Thai food from a place in Cottonwood that delivered, ate pad see ew straight from the container while sitting cross-legged on Shane's couch, and tried to ignore the guilt that settled in her stomach alongside the noodles.

After the weekend rush, she promised herself. *After the whole food critic thing…and after I've proven I can do this one thing without failing.*

The rationalization felt thin even as it passed through her mind, but Rosa knew she'd gotten pretty good at building walls between herself and uncomfortable truths.

She went to bed early in the guest room, staring at the ceiling and listening to the unfamiliar sounds of Shane's house settling around her. Somewhere around eleven, she heard the front door open and close, and then heard Shane's footsteps in the hallway outside her door. A few minutes later, the shower in the bathroom across from the guest room turned on.

No way was she going to let herself imagine what Shane might look like in that shower. Instead, she pulled the blanket up to her chin and tried not to think about what she'd gotten herself into.

~

The next morning, the alarm on her phone went off at seven-thirty, which she hoped would give her plenty of time to shower, dress, and mentally prepare herself for her first day in a professional kitchen. She'd followed Shane's instructions from the day before and had put on her favorite slip-on sneakers, pulled her hair back into a tight French braid, and left all her jewelry in its bag except for a pair of turquoise studs her sister Lira had given her for her eighteenth birthday.

Afterward, she inspected herself in the bathroom mirror and barely recognized the woman staring back. No makeup, hair scraped away from her face, wearing jeans and a plain black scoop-neck T-shirt that she'd bought at Target because she'd thought it might come in handy one day, even if it wasn't exactly her style. The woman in the mirror looked almost normal, almost like someone who could hold down a job in a restaurant kitchen instead of a *prima*-in-waiting who'd spent eight months failing to find the one thing her entire future depended on.

She squared her shoulders and headed down the hall.

Shane was already in the kitchen, dressed in chef's whites—and looking way too damn gorgeous—while he drank coffee and gazed down at something on his phone. He glanced up when she entered, and she caught the brief moment of assessment in his eyes before he gave an approving nod.

"Good," he said. "You followed directions. That's a start."

"I told you I'm a quick learner," she replied, and went over to pour herself a cup of coffee from the pot he'd already brewed.

"You'll need to be." He set down his phone and crossed his arms, then leaned back against the counter in a way that was probably meant to look casual but came across more smoldering than anything else. "The Asylum isn't like other restaurants. We do elevated Southwest cuisine with French technique. Every plate has to be perfect, and every element has to be balanced. One bad dish, one sloppy presentation, and we could lose the trust we've spent years building. We get a lot of repeat tourist business, and it's important that people think they'll be able to have the same fine dining experience now that they did five years ago."

"I understand," Rosa said, then lifted her cup of coffee to her lips. Just like the day before, it was perfect…not that she'd expected anything less.

"Do you?" The question wasn't unkind, but it was direct in that way Shane seemed to favor—cutting straight to the heart of things without wasting time on pleasantries. "Because you're the *prima*-in-waiting of the de la Paz clan, I'm guessing you've never had to answer to anyone except maybe your parents. In my kitchen, you answer to me. You do exactly what I tell you, when I tell you, without argument. If you can't handle that, you need to let me know now."

She met his gaze steadily. Part of her was wondering just what she'd gotten herself into, but she wasn't about to back out. "I can handle it."

Something shifted in Shane's expression. It wasn't quite approval, but she thought it might be the beginning of respect. "Good. Finish your coffee. We leave in ten minutes."

The Asylum was walkable from Shane's house, but they took his van anyway, probably because they'd be coming back late and he didn't want to have her stumbling through unfamiliar streets after dark. He drove in silence, his attention fixed on the narrow, twisting road, and Rosa found herself studying him in brief glances she hoped he wouldn't notice.

His hands on the steering wheel were strong

and capable, the kind of hands that knew exactly what they were doing at all times. He'd rolled up the sleeves of his chef's coat, revealing forearms marked with the faint scars that seemed to be the badge of anyone who worked with knives and hot pans. His profile was sharp in the morning light, the bright sun making a halo of his dark blond hair.

As best she could, she pulled her gaze away and stared out the window instead, watching Jerome's colorful buildings slide past. This town was so different from Scottsdale—rough where her home was polished, eccentric where the de la Paz compound was traditional. She wasn't sure yet if she liked it, but she had to admit there was something appealing about the lack of pretense.

The Asylum occupied the main floor of the Grand Hotel. Her reading on the subject had told her the place was a sanatorium back in the 1920s—which probably explained all the ghosts—but now it just looked like a big, historic building. Shane parked in the small lot behind the hotel, and Rosa followed him up the back stairs and through a service entrance that led directly into the kitchen.

The space was smaller than Rosa had expected but immaculately organized. Stainless steel surfaces gleamed under bright lights, and pots and pans hung from overhead racks in neat arrangements. The air smelled like coffee and something sweet—cinnamon or vanilla, or maybe a mixture of the two.

Three people were already there, moving through morning prep with the kind of ease that seemed to indicate they'd been doing this for a while. They all looked up when Shane entered, their expressions shifting from casual to alert.

"Morning, chef," said a young woman with dark hair tucked under a bright bandana. She had warm brown eyes and a scattering of freckles across her nose.

"Morning, Kelli." Shane gestured toward Rosa. "Everyone, this is Rosa. She's going to be helping out for the next week or so while I find a replacement for Jared."

The kitchen staff exchanged glances. Rosa didn't think they were hostile, but they were definitely curious.

"Rosa, this is Kelli, my line cook," Shane continued. "That's Mike on prep"—he indicated a tall man in his thirties with a neat beard—"and Carlos on pastry."

Carlos, who looked barely twenty and had the kind of baby face that probably got him carded everywhere, gave Rosa a shy smile. "Nice to meet you."

"You, too," Rosa said, acutely aware that she was being evaluated by people who knew what they were doing, while she most definitely did not.

Shane moved deeper into the kitchen, and Rosa followed him, trying to absorb everything at once—the layout, the equipment, the casual but brisk rhythm of movement as the other staff members went about their tasks.

"You'll start on prep," Shane said as he led her to a station near Mike. "Basic knife work. Today you're going to learn how to dice an onion properly. By the end of the week, you'll be doing it in your sleep."

He pulled out a cutting board and set it in front of her, then retrieved several onions from a storage bin and lined them up with the careful economy of movement that Rosa was beginning to realize was characteristic of everything Shane did.

"Watch," he said.

Then he proceeded to demonstrate the technique—how to cut the onion in half through the root, how to make horizontal cuts without severing the root end, how to make vertical cuts and then slice across to create perfect dice. His movements were fluid and sure, the knife an extension of his hand rather than a separate tool.

"Your turn," he said, then handed her the knife.

Rosa took it, feeling the weight of the blade

and the texture of the handle against her palm. She positioned the first onion the way Shane had shown her and made the initial cut.

So far, so good.

But then she tried to mimic the horizontal cuts, and the onion started sliding across the board. She pressed down harder to stabilize it, and the knife skipped sideways.

"Stop." Shane's hand closed over hers, stilling the blade before she could do any damage. His palm was warm against her knuckles, and Rosa was suddenly all too aware of how close he stood, of a faint, clean scent that she guessed must be his soap. "You're gripping too hard. Let the knife do the work."

He guided her hand through the motion, his fingers wrapped around hers, and Rosa felt that strange warmth again—the same sensation from yesterday's handshake, only stronger now, like heat radiating up her arm and settling somewhere in the center of her body.

Shane must have felt it, too, because he stepped back abruptly and cleared his throat.

"Like that," he said. "Try again."

Rosa tried again. And again. And again.

By her tenth onion, her eyes were streaming from all the onion juice, her fingers ached from maintaining the proper grip, and her dice were still embarrassingly uneven.

"Better," Shane said, which Rosa suspected was chef-speak for "still terrible but marginally less terrible than before."

"They look like dice a drunk person would make," she muttered as she stared down at the cutting board.

To her surprise, Shane laughed—an actual laugh, one that sounded amused rather than sarcastic. "They kind of do. But you're getting the hang of the technique. That's what matters right now. Precision comes with practice."

He moved away to check on something Kelli was doing, and Rosa blew out a breath and reached for another onion.

This was going to be a long week.

By the time lunch service started, Rosa's hands were cramping, her back ached from standing in one position, and she'd gained a newfound respect for anyone who worked in a professional kitchen.

Shane had kept her on prep throughout the morning—onions, then garlic, then shallots, and finally moving on to carrots that needed to be cut into perfect batons. Every time Rosa thought she'd gotten the hang of something, Shane would inspect her work with those sharp blue eyes and find a flaw.

Too big. They won't cook evenly.

You're not paying attention to the angle of your cuts.

Faster. In a real service rush, we don't have time for you to contemplate each carrot like it's a philosophical question.

But he never raised his voice, and he never made her feel stupid. He simply corrected and moved on, showing her the right way and then expecting her to execute it according to his instructions.

And in between the corrections, Rosa watched him work.

She'd thought she understood Shane's gift after tasting his cooking, but seeing him in his element was something else entirely. He moved through the kitchen like a conductor leading an orchestra, coordinating multiple elements with the timing and intensity of someone directing Beethoven's *Ninth*. He'd check on something Kelli was grilling, taste and adjust a sauce Mike had prepared, and then offer a quiet word of encouragement to Carlos about the dessert he was plating.

Shane's magic hummed beneath everything he did. Rosa could somehow feel it even though she couldn't see it, a warm undercurrent that made the food better than it had any right to be. But the magic was only part of it. The rest was skill and knowledge, along with an artist's eye for balance and beauty.

When Shane plated a dish, it wasn't like he just dumped the food there and moved on. No, he created a composition—colors and textures and heights that pleased the eye before the first bite even happened. He'd adjust an element by millimeters, tilt his head to assess the visual impact, add a microgreen or a drizzle of sauce to complete the picture.

It was art. Maybe not the kind she created with pencils or oils or acrylics, but art nonetheless.

Rosa found herself mesmerized despite her exhaustion.

"Stop staring and start moving," Shane said without looking up from the scallops he was searing. "I need you to run these dishes out to table seven."

Rosa grabbed the plates—carefully, because they were hot—and pushed her way past the swinging door into the dining room.

The Asylum's dining room was elegant, with wood-paneled walls and brass and glass fixtures meant to harmonize with the early twentieth-century architecture. The lunch crowd was smaller than she'd expected, maybe a dozen tables occupied, but everyone seemed absorbed in their food.

She delivered the plates to table seven—a

couple in their fifties who barely acknowledged her—and hurried back to the kitchen.

For the rest of the afternoon, Shane kept her moving—running plates, fetching ingredients from the walk-in cooler, washing dishes when they started piling up, learning how to properly clean and organize the prep station.

By the time the last lunch customer left and the kitchen settled into the lull before dinner prep, she was ready to collapse in a heap where she stood.

"You did okay," Shane said, appearing at her side while she scrubbed down her cutting board for what felt like the hundredth time. "Better than I expected for your first day."

Rosa looked up at him, startled by the compliment. "Really?"

"Really." His mouth curved in something that wasn't quite a smile but suggested he was capable of the expression if sufficiently motivated. "You followed directions, you didn't complain, and you didn't cut yourself. That puts you ahead of the last three kitchen assistants I tried to train."

She couldn't help cracking a grin. "The bar is apparently very low."

"In this industry? Sometimes." Shane picked up a towel and started drying the pans she'd just washed. "But you also paid attention. I saw you watching how I plated the special. You've got an eye for composition."

"I'm an artist," Rosa said, then immediately thought that sounded way too pretentious. "Or I'm trying to be one, anyway. I study studio art at Scottsdale Community College. Mostly painting."

Shane's hands paused on the pan he was drying. "You paint?"

"When I have time," she replied. "Which isn't often lately." She rinsed another pan and set it in the drying rack. "I've been a little busy failing to find my consort."

She'd meant it as a joke—a dark one, but still a joke—but Shane didn't chuckle or even smile. Instead, he set down the pan he was holding and turned to face her.

"Is that how you see yourself?" he asked. He spoke quietly, probably because he didn't want anyone to overhear what he was saying, but there was a quiet intensity to his words nonetheless. "As a failure?"

Rosa opened her mouth to deflect, to make light of her comment, but something in Shane's expression stopped her. He was looking at her the way he looked at his food before he plated it—carefully attentive, assessing and considering.

"Sometimes," she admitted. "Thirty-four attempts, Shane. Thirty-four men who could have been my consort, and I felt nothing with any of them. At some point, you have to wonder if the problem is you."

"Or maybe the problem is that you're looking for something that can't be found by following a formula," he said. "Magic doesn't work like that… especially the consort bond, from what I've heard. It's not like it's a recipe you can execute perfectly and get the expected result."

Rosa studied him for a moment, this warlock who poured magic into food but still had gone to culinary school so he could back his gift up with credentials. "You sound like you have experience with that."

"I have experience with people who expect magic to solve everything." Shane picked up another pan, his attention clearly returning to the task at hand. "But we should get back to prep. Dinner service starts in two hours, and you still have a lot to learn."

He moved away before Rosa could ask what he meant, leaving her standing at the sink with her hands in soapy water and her mind sorting through what he'd just said.

Shane McAllister was more complicated than she'd initially thought. Brusque and demanding on the surface, yes, but underneath that exterior was someone who understood pressure and expectation and the gap between what people assumed and what was real.

Someone who might actually understand her.

Rosa dried her hands and returned to her station, where a new pile of vegetables waited to be prepped.

She had a lot to learn about working in a kitchen.

But she was beginning to suspect she might learn even more about herself—and about the chef who'd agreed to let her hide in plain sight.

Shane had trained enough kitchen staff over the years to recognize when someone had natural aptitude, and by the end of Rosa's first dinner service, he had to admit she had something.

Not knife skills—those were still objectively terrible. And not speed, because she moved through the kitchen with the cautious deliberation of someone afraid she'd break something or set herself on fire. But she had an eye. When he plated the evening special—seared duck breast with cherry *gastrique* and roasted fingerling potatoes—she'd studied his hands with the kind of focused attention most people reserved for watching a brain surgeon at work.

"The potatoes go at seven o'clock," she'd murmured, more to herself than to him. "And the microgreens balance the height of the duck. It's a triangle composition."

Shane had glanced at her, startled that she'd noticed. Most kitchen assistants watched him plate and saw only food going onto dishes. But Rosa saw the architecture of those creations and the way each element related to the others in space and color.

"Exactly right," he'd said, and she'd looked pleased in a way that made that same warm sensation flare within him, if only for a moment before he pushed it away and moved on to the next thing.

Now, two hours later, the last table had been served, and the kitchen was winding down for the night. Kelli and Mike had already left, and Carlos was finishing up the dessert station. Shane should have been focused on inventory or prep lists for tomorrow, but instead, he found his attention drifting to the place where Rosa stood at the dish station, strands of dark hair coming loose from her braid and her black T-shirt damp with steam.

She looked exhausted but also determined as she scrubbed away at a particularly stubborn pan with the same intensity she'd brought to dicing onions earlier in the day.

"You can leave that," Shane said as he came over to her. "I'll finish up."

"I'm almost done." Rosa didn't look up from

the pan as she added, "Besides, you said in the kitchen that I'm supposed to do what you tell me. You didn't tell me to stop."

He didn't quite sigh. "Well, I'm telling you now."

She looked up at him then, and Shane caught the faint smile tugging at the corner of her mouth. "Yes, chef."

He took the pan from her hands and set it in the drying rack. "You did good work today. Better than good, to be honest. You kept up during service, and you didn't fall apart when things got hectic."

"I mostly just tried not to get in anyone's way," Rosa replied, but he could see the pleased light in her eyes despite the self-deprecating words.

"That's harder than it sounds." He dried his hands on a towel and glanced toward the spot at the other end of the kitchen where Carlos was boxing up leftover pastries. "You hungry?"

Rosa blinked at him, obviously surprised by the question. "Starving, actually."

"Good," he said. "I'll make something for us. You should eat before we head home."

He headed over to the walk-in and retrieved the necessary ingredients while Rosa watched from the doorway. This had always been one of his favorite parts of the day, something that gave him the chance to cook simple and satisfying food without the pressure of perfection that came with plating for customers. Sometimes it was for the whole kitchen staff if they decided to linger, and sometimes it was just for himself. Since he was going to cook for Rosa tonight, he was thinking he'd make pasta carbonara, the classic Roman version with guanciale and pecorino and nothing else.

By the time he returned to his station, Carlos had finished cleaning and was hovering near the back door.

"You heading out?" Shane asked.

"Yeah, if that's okay." Carlos glanced at Rosa, then back over at Shane. "My girlfriend's picking me up."

Right. Carlos had mentioned something earlier about his car being in the shop. "Go ahead," Shane told him. "We'll see you tomorrow."

After Carlos left, the kitchen fell into a comfortable quiet broken only by the sound of Shane's knife against the cutting board as he diced the guanciale. Rosa had settled onto a stool near his station, watching him work with the same focused attention she'd shown all day.

He set a pot of water to boil and started rendering the guanciale in a pan, filling the kitchen with the rich scent of pork fat and smoke.

In the meantime, he separated eggs, whisked the yolks with grated pecorino, and tried not to think about the way her presence in his kitchen seemed increasingly natural.

"Can I help?" she asked. Clearly, she didn't think it fair for her to sit on the sidelines and do nothing.

"You can grate more cheese." He pushed the pecorino and grater toward her. "We'll need about another cup."

She took the cheese and started grating, her movements careful and deliberate, as though she wanted to make sure all the shreds were of uniform size. Shane added pasta to the boiling water and tended to the guanciale, adjusting the heat to get the fat crispy without burning it.

"I've never seen anyone cook like you do," Rosa said after a moment. "It's like watching someone paint, except with food."

Shane glanced at her, surprised by the observation. "That's basically what it is. Cooking at this level is as much about aesthetics as flavor. Maybe more, sometimes."

Her brows drew together, and she looked very thoughtful. "Do you ever paint? Or draw, or anything like that?"

"Not really." He stirred the pasta, checking the texture. "I'm good with food. That's where my magic lives. But I think I understand what visual artists do, at least a little. The way you're thinking about composition and color and balance—that's exactly what I'm doing when I plate a dish."

Rosa gave a slow nod, even as she continued to grate the cheese. "That makes sense. It's just different media."

"Exactly." Shane drained the pasta and reserved some of the starchy cooking water, then killed the heat under the guanciale. This was the tricky part—combining everything while the pan was still hot enough to cook the eggs, but not so hot that they scrambled. He worked quickly, adding pasta to the guanciale pan, then the egg mixture, and then pasta water to create a silky sauce that clung to every strand.

He plated two portions and set one in front of Rosa before he grabbed a couple of forks and the pepper grinder.

"This looks amazing," Rosa said, staring down at her plate as if to memorize every element it contained.

"It's simple food," he said, his tone casual. "Peasant food, really." He ground black pepper over both plates and took the stool next to hers. "But sometimes, simple is best."

They ate in silence for a few minutes. He watched her take her first bite and saw the moment the flavors registered—the salt of the guanciale and cheese, the richness of the egg, the sharp bite of black pepper.

"Oh, my God," she said after she'd swallowed. "Shane, this is incredible."

"It's carbonara," he said, knowing he sounded way too amused. "It's supposed to be good."

"No, it's better than good. It's—" She paused, obviously searching for the right words. "It's perfect. Like, this is exactly what this dish is supposed to taste like, and I didn't even know that before I ate it."

That warm sensation filled him again, the one that seemed to keep popping up whenever Rosa praised his cooking. He told himself it was just professional pride, the satisfaction any chef felt when their food was received the way they intended. But he knew that wasn't entirely true.

"You actually listened today," he told her. "When I told you how to prep the garlic, you paid attention to the size I wanted. Most people don't listen. They think they know better, or they don't care enough to get it right."

Rosa gazed at him, her hazel eyes serious. "Of course I listened. You're the expert. Why would I come into your kitchen and then ignore what you're teaching me?"

Now he couldn't help smiling. "You'd be surprised how many people do exactly that." He twirled more pasta onto his fork, then paused to add, "Especially people who're used to being in charge. They don't like taking direction."

"I'm not used to being in charge," she said quietly. "I'm used to being prepared to be in charge someday, which is completely different. Right now I'm just...."

The words seemed to disappear into the ether as she continued to stare down at her plate.

"Just what?" he prompted.

"I guess I'm just trying to figure out who I am when I'm not performing the role I'm supposed to play." She looked up at him at last, hazel eyes now intense, almost smoky. "Does that make any sense?"

He thought about the years he'd spent in culinary school, working twice as hard as everyone else because he needed to prove his success came from skill as well and not merely magic. And then his thoughts moved to the long hours he'd put in at the Asylum, the constant pressure to be perfect, the way he'd built his entire identity around being the best.

"Yes," he said. "It makes sense."

They fell into a companionable silence after that, the kind of quiet that didn't need to be filled with conversation. Shane found himself relaxing in a way he rarely did, the constant tension in his shoulders somehow easing.

"Can I ask you something?" Rosa said after a few minutes.

Well, there was a loaded question. But he only replied, "Sure."

She was quiet again for a few beats and then said, "Earlier, you told me that you have experience with people expecting magic to solve everything. What did you mean?"

Shane set down his fork and considered how much to tell her. He didn't usually talk about this stuff with anyone except maybe Brianna, and even then, only when she cornered him.

"My gift makes cooking easy," he said after a long pause. "I can taste something once and know exactly what's in it. I can look at ingredients and know how they'll work together. I could probably run a successful restaurant on magic alone, no formal training required."

"But you went to culinary school anyway," Rosa said.

He nodded. "Because I wanted people to take me seriously. I needed to prove I could do this without the magic, that I had the technical skills and the knowledge to back up my gift." He picked up his fork again but didn't eat, just moved pasta around his plate. It was delicious, but he didn't feel like eating any more right then. "Even now, though, people in my clan assume the restaurant's success is all because of my magic. They don't see the work. They don't see the hundreds of hours I've put in perfecting techniques and studying flavor profiles and learning how to manage a kitchen."

She was quiet for a moment as she seemed to ponder what he'd just said. "That must be frustrating."

"It is." He finally took another bite of pasta, mostly because he didn't want it to get cold. "But it also taught me that magic isn't enough. Talent isn't enough. You need both talent and mastery, and mastery only comes from work."

"That's what my mother says about being *prima,*" Rosa said softly. "She told me once that I can have all the magical power in the world, but if I don't understand our people and our traditions and how to lead with wisdom instead of just authority, I'll have a tough time of it."

He tilted his head as he lifted another bite of carbonara to his lips. "Your mother sounds smart."

"She is." Rosa's smile was sad. "She's also probably worried sick about me right now, even though I texted her to say I'm okay."

A pang of guilt went through him as he listened to those words. He was harboring a runaway *prima*-in-waiting, keeping her from dealing with the very real problem she'd come to Jerome to solve. That probably made him complicit in whatever family drama was unfolding back in Scottsdale.

"You should call her," he said. "Tomorrow, maybe. I know you texted her to let her know you're all right, but hearing someone's voice is better for that kind of stuff."

Her lips pressed together. "I will…but after the review. After I've shown I can do this."

There it was again—that need to prove herself, to demonstrate competence before facing the harder conversations. Shane understood it because he lived it every day.

"You don't have anything to prove to me," he said. "You showed up, you worked hard, and you didn't quit, even though I know you wanted to about six times today."

Rosa laughed, the sound surprisingly genuine, if somewhat rueful. "More like twelve times. There was a solid hour this afternoon where I was seriously considering just walking out the back door and never coming back."

What would he have done if she really had walked out? Would he have gone after her…or would he have only shrugged and told himself it was to be expected?

"But you didn't."

"No." For a second, her eyes met his. "I didn't."

They finished eating, and Shane collected their

plates and took them to the sink. Rosa followed him, already reaching for the dish soap before he could tell her to leave it.

"I can get this," he said.

"I know you can. But we're supposed to be a team, right? In your kitchen, we work together." She turned on the water and started washing. "Besides, you cooked. The least I can do is clean up."

Shane picked up a towel and started drying, and somehow it felt like they'd been doing this for years instead of just one day. When the last dish was put away and the kitchen was clean, he turned off the lights and led Rosa out the back door.

The night air was cool and clear, the sky overhead scattered with more stars than Rosa had probably ever seen in Scottsdale. She tilted her head back and stared upward, and Shane found himself watching her instead of the sky.

She looked different than she had this morning—softer and more approachable, with those loose strands of hair falling free of the tight braid and her features much more relaxed. When she smiled, the expression transformed her features into something extraordinary.

Shane forced himself to look away.

Don't, he told himself firmly. *She's temporary.*

She's here for a week, and then she's gone. Don't make this complicated.

But as they drove back to his house, Shane couldn't quite convince himself that anything about this was still simple.

Rosa Sandoval was supposed to be a problem he was solving—helping her hide in exchange for kitchen assistance. It was a temporary arrangement that benefited them both, and nothing more.

Except she didn't feel temporary. She felt like she'd always been there, filling a space in his life he hadn't even known was empty.

And that terrified him more than he wanted to admit.

5

Rosa was halfway through dicing her third onion of the morning when she realized she'd spent almost two full days in Jerome and still hadn't talked to Levi McAllister.

The realization hit her with enough force that she paused mid-cut, staring down at the cutting board in Shane's kitchen. She'd come to Jerome specifically to talk to Levi. That had been the entire point. And yet here she was on Tuesday morning, Shane's day off, and she still hadn't walked the few blocks to the big yellow house with green shutters so she could get the clarity she supposedly wanted.

"Is there a problem?" Shane asked. He was standing at the stove, scrambling eggs with the same focused attention he seemed to bring to everything.

"No," Rosa said quickly as she returned to her onion. It wasn't for anything they'd be eating today; she was bagging the onions as she cut them, since he'd said he planned to use them tomorrow morning for brie and caramelized onion omelets. "Just thinking."

She knew she should go today. Right after breakfast, she could tell Shane she needed to run an errand, walk over to Levi's house, and finally have the necessary conversation about consort bonds and failed connections, and what exactly she was supposed to do about all of it.

Except the thought of actually making herself do that very thing made her stomach twist with anxiety.

It was easier here in Shane's kitchen, learning to dice onions and watching him cook. It was easier to focus on knife skills and prep work than to face the reality of her situation. Working at the Asylum gave her something concrete to accomplish, something where she could see herself improving day by day.

Talking to Levi meant confronting all the ways she'd failed.

"So," Shane said as he plated the eggs alongside some toast, "fair warning. We're going to my parents' house for dinner tonight."

Rosa looked up from her onion and sent him a sharp look. "Tonight?"

Ugh. Had that come out as a squeak?

If it had, he affected not to notice. "It's a family thing. We get together on Tuesday nights when I'm off. My mom likes to make sure everyone's still alive and functional." He set a plate in front of her. "You don't have to come if you don't want to, but you're welcome."

Rosa's heart did an odd little flip, but she tried her best to look casual. "And your father will be there?"

"Yes." Shane settled onto the stool across from her, now looking distinctly amused. "The guy you came here to talk to in the first place, remember?"

Right.

So she could spend the day working up the courage to knock on Levi's door as a stranger asking for help, or she could go to a family dinner where she'd meet him in a much more natural, less pressured context.

"Okay," Rosa heard herself say. "I'll come."

Shane nodded, his expression giving nothing away as he picked up his fork. "We'll leave around five-thirty."

They spent the rest of Tuesday morning in Shane's kitchen, where he had her working on more advanced knife skills—julienning vegetables, learning how to properly mince herbs so they released their oils without bruising. Without the pressure of restaurant service looming, the pace was much more relaxed, and Shane took some extra time to demonstrate techniques and correct her form.

"Your grip is better," he said as he watched her julienne a carrot. "You're not strangling the knife anymore."

"I'm trying to let the knife do the work," Rosa said, echoing his words from Monday.

"Good. That's exactly right."

His praise sent a happy flutter through her, and Rosa found herself smiling as she reached for the next carrot.

She was getting better at this. Not expert-level or anywhere close to Shane's effortless mastery, but at least she was starting to be halfway competent.

It felt like an accomplishment in a way that very little had felt like an accomplishment lately.

After lunch—caprese sandwiches that were beyond heavenly—Rosa retreated to the guest room to mull over what she should wear to dinner. She'd brought limited clothing, so her options were restricted, but she settled on clean jeans and a coral-pink sleeveless top that she'd bought last summer.

But should she leave her hair down? It wasn't

as if she was going to be working in a kitchen, after all.

She pulled it loose from its braid, liking the effect of the subtle waves the braiding had left behind, and added a touch of lip gloss.

Hmm. Did it look like she was trying too hard?

This was just dinner with Shane's family, after all, a casual, low-stakes kind of evening.

Except it didn't feel low-stakes, because she'd be meeting Levi, and once she talked to Levi, she'd have to face all the uncomfortable truths she'd been avoiding ever since she arrived in Jerome.

She decided to leave the lip gloss on, just because she usually wore it—well, except when she was working in Shane's kitchen—and she thought it might seem strange that she hadn't taken even that minimal effort when she was going to be a guest in someone else's house.

Shane was waiting by the front door when she came downstairs, and his gaze flickered over her in a quick assessment that made her breath catch.

Was that a hint of admiration in his eyes?

She wasn't sure if she wanted to answer that question.

"Ready?" he asked.

"As I'll ever be."

Since Shane's parents' house was just down the

street, of course they walked. The sun had just begun to go down behind Mingus Mountain, and the early evening air was warm and heavy with the scent of all the flowers that bloomed in people's front yards. Off in the distance, the red rocks of Sedona glowed red in the reflected light of sunset.

"Fair warning," Shane said as they approached the big yellow house, the one whose door Rosa had knocked on only a few days earlier. "Sometimes my family can be a lot. If anything makes you uncomfortable, just let me know, and we'll leave." He paused there for a beat or two before adding, "But with Bree off with Bill on her honeymoon, it'll probably be a little quieter."

"I'm sure it'll be fine," Rosa said, although she couldn't quite ignore the nervous tightening of her stomach. Shane seemed to think things would be more relaxed with his sister gone, but Rosa wasn't sure whether that was a positive or not. If it was just the two of them as guests, that meant his parents wouldn't have anyone else to focus on.

He only shrugged, though, which could have meant almost anything, and then opened the front door without knocking.

The interior of the house was warm and welcoming, with honey-colored wood floors and comfortable, overstuffed furniture and interesting antiques. Voices drifted toward them from somewhere deeper in the house, along with laughter and the clatter of dishes.

"In the kitchen," a woman's voice called out. "Shane, is that you?"

"Yeah, Mom." Shane glanced down at Rosa and gestured for her to follow him down the hallway.

The kitchen was large and clearly the heart of the house, with a big wooden table surrounded by mismatched chairs and counters covered with food in various stages of preparation. A slim, blonde woman stood at the stove, stirring something that smelled incredible, while a man who could only be Levi had positioned himself at a nearby counter, chopping vegetables with the same economical precision Shane used.

Rosa's first thought was that Levi looked surprisingly normal for an entity who had been conjured into existence by a desperate spell. He was tall and lean, with blond hair a few shades lighter than Shane's and kind blue eyes that didn't seem to miss a single detail. When he smiled at her and Shane, its brilliance made him look like a former Hollywood heartthrob who'd decided to retire to a simpler life in northern Arizona.

"There you are," Shane's mother, Hayley, said, turning from the stove so she could pull Shane into a quick hug. She was pretty and didn't seem old enough to have children in their mid-twenties, and was just as blonde and blue-eyed as her husband and son. "I was starting to think you'd forgotten about us."

"I texted you two hours ago to say we were coming," Shane replied, but his tone sounded affectionate rather than irritated.

Hayley's attention shifted to Rosa, and her smile widened. "You must be the young woman Shane mentioned."

"This is Rosa," Shane said. "She's helping out at the restaurant for a while. Rosa, this is my mother, Hayley, and my father, Levi."

"It's nice to meet you both," Rosa replied. An embarrassed flush touched her cheeks as they both looked at her, but she hoped her olive skin would hide most of it.

"Rosa Sandoval," Levi said as he set down his knife. His voice was calm and measured and deep, with an intonation that seemed just slightly more formal than that of most people she met. "Zoe's daughter."

"You know my mother?" she blurted, and then realized that was a stupid question, considering that Zoe was the one who'd brought Levi into existence all those years ago.

"I know both your parents," Levi said. Maybe the slightest twitch at the corner of his mouth belied his inner amusement, but he sounded serious enough as he added, "We've met a few times over the years."

Rosa wasn't sure what to say to that, so she just smiled and hoped she didn't look like a complete idiot.

"Well, sit down, both of you," Hayley said, gesturing past the kitchen table and into the space beyond, clearly the dining room. The curtains had been drawn, letting in a spectacular view eastward toward the Verde Valley and Sedona. "Dinner won't be ready for another ten minutes or so, but I have appetizers. Shane, go ahead and pour Rosa some wine."

The next few minutes passed in a flurry of activity as Shane retrieved wine glasses and Hayley produced a platter of bruschetta topped with tomatoes and fresh basil. Soon enough, Rosa found herself seated at the table next to Shane, trying to absorb the easy warmth of his family's dynamic.

It reminded her of home, actually. Her own family dinners in Scottsdale had the same comfortable chaos—her mother moving between stove and table, her father cracking jokes while he helped with prep, her siblings arguing good-naturedly about whatever topic had captured their attention that week.

Or at least, it had been that way until Zach moved out. Now it was just her and Lira, and half the time, Lira wasn't even home for dinner, instead going over to friends' or cousins' houses, moving through life easily.

Of course it was easy for her. She wasn't the *prima*-in-waiting.

No, Rosa wasn't going to let herself think about that. She needed to focus on the here and now, and not what was happening down in Scottsdale.

For some reason, she'd expected Shane's family to feel different—possibly because of Levi's other-worldly origins—maybe more formal or reserved, but they weren't. They were just…family. In fact, they seemed warm and welcoming, and not particularly inclined to question why she was here in Jerome.

She had to be grateful for that.

"So, Rosa," Hayley said as she set a bowl of salad on the table, "Shane tells me you're studying art?"

"Studio art at Scottsdale Community College," Rosa replied. "Mostly painting, although I work in other media sometimes."

Hayley smiled. "That's wonderful. We have a very active art community here in Jerome. Have you had a chance to explore any of the galleries?"

"Not yet," she said. "I've been pretty focused on learning my way around the restaurant."

"Shane's a demanding teacher," Levi

commented, and Rosa caught the glint of amusement in his eyes. "He always has been. Even when he was young, he expected everyone around him to stick to his standards."

"I don't expect anything of people that I'm not willing to do myself," Shane replied, but there was no real heat in the words.

"True enough." Levi took a sip of wine. "How are you finding the work, Rosa? Kitchen life isn't for everyone."

"It's hard," Rosa admitted. "Harder than I expected. But I like it. There's something satisfying about doing work where you can see immediate results. You prep the vegetables, you plate the dish, you send it out, and people enjoy it. It's very...real."

"Unlike painting?" Hayley asked.

"Unlike a lot of things." Rosa hesitated, then added, "Unlike most of what I'm supposed to be doing with my life, actually."

She felt Shane stiffen beside her, but he didn't say anything.

"And what are you supposed to be doing?" Levi asked. His tone was gentle, not prying, but Rosa sensed he already knew the answer.

It wasn't a secret that one day she would be the *prima* of the de la Paz clan, and that meant she had a destiny ahead of her that very few people shared.

"I'm still trying to figure that out," she said with a smile.

~

Shane was elbow-deep in soapy water, scrubbing the lasagna pan that his mother had somehow managed to burn cheese onto despite having made that same meal dozens of times before, when she materialized at his side with a dish towel.

"I'll dry," she told him.

"You don't have to," Shane told her, already slightly irritated. He knew exactly why his mother had come into the kitchen, and he hoped he could head her off at the pass. "I've got this."

Without replying directly, she plucked a clean plate from the drying rack and started working on it with unnecessary vigor. Yes, the house had a good dishwasher, but they still tended to do dishes the old-fashioned way. A very small hesitation, and then she added, "Rosa seems nice."

So much for avoiding the subject. Shane's hands paused in the soapy water for half a second before he forced himself to keep scrubbing. "She is."

"Pretty, too."

Obvious much? "I hadn't noticed," he said briefly.

His mother laughed then, the sound bright

and disbelieving. "Sure, you haven't. That's why you've been watching her all evening like you're afraid she's going to disappear if you blink."

His jaw set, but he made himself say coolly, "I have not."

She set down the plate and turned to face him. "I don't think I've ever seen you look at someone the way you look at her."

Shane kept his attention fixed on the pan, scrubbing at a particularly stubborn spot of burned cheese. Maybe it was time for a new lasagna pan. "I think you're seeing things that aren't there."

"Am I?" His mother picked up another plate and began to work on it with the dishcloth. "Because from where I'm standing, it looks like you're actually interested in someone for the first time in I don't even know how long. It's been months since you and Sarah broke up."

The mention of his ex-girlfriend made Shane's jaw tighten. "Rosa's not staying. She's here for a week, maybe less. Just until I can find a real sous chef."

His mother's brows lifted, and he could tell she didn't think that was much of an excuse. "She might stay longer if you asked her to."

"No, she can't." Shane rinsed the pan, satisfied that he'd finally gotten rid of that annoying piece of burned cheese, and set it in the drying rack.

"She has a life in Scottsdale and a destiny she's supposed to fulfill."

"A destiny," his mother repeated, but she didn't sound convinced.

"Yeah, that whole pesky consort thing, remember?" He grabbed another pot from the counter and plunged it into the water. "She's the *prima*-in-waiting of the de la Paz clan. She needs to find her consort and settle down. She sure as hell doesn't need some chef in Jerome complicating her life."

"Or maybe," his mother said, speaking slowly as she seemed to ponder the situation, "she needs exactly that. Maybe she needs someone who will see her as more than just her role."

Shane paused again, his hands submerged in the soapy water. He could feel her gaze on him, sharp and assessing.

"I don't have time for a relationship right now," he said at length, since he knew he couldn't just freeze his mother out. "Especially not with someone who's literally hiding from her family and her responsibilities. She's temporary, Mom. She'll go back to her real life, and I'll go back to mine."

This argument didn't seem to prove as effective as he would have liked, because his mother set down the plate she'd been drying and leaned against the counter, arms crossed, and her gaze fixed on him. "Will she?"

Oh, for the Goddess's sake.... "She's good help," he said shortly. "That's all."

For a moment, his mother didn't reply. Then she said, her tone almost chiding, "You're doing that thing you always do, Shane, that thing where you convince yourself that the restaurant matters more than your own happiness."

"The restaurant *does* matter," Shane returned. Anger was flaring, but he knew he didn't want to lose his temper, not with Rosa and his father in the other room. "The *Arizona Republic* is sending a critic this week. If I screw this up—"

"If you screw it up, then you'll fix it," his mother said calmly. "That's what you do. You're probably the most talented chef I've ever seen, and I'm not just saying that because you're my son. But you're so busy trying to prove yourself that you forget to actually enjoy what you've built."

Shane scrubbed at the pot he held, even though it was already clean and he should have put it in the dish drain instead. "I enjoy my work."

"Do you?" Before he could reply, she went on, her voice softening somewhat, "When's the last time you cooked something just because you wanted to? Not for the restaurant or to impress a critic, but just because it made you happy?"

The answer came to him immediately — last night, making carbonara for Rosa in the empty kitchen at the Asylum. He'd enjoyed watching her face light up as she tasted the food, and he'd also enjoyed their easy conversation, the comfortable silence, the way it had felt like they'd been sharing meals like that forever instead of just once.

Of course, he couldn't say any of that out loud.

"The review matters," he said instead. "I need to focus on that. Not on complications."

His mother crossed her arms, the dish towel still hanging from one hand. "So…Rosa's a complication?"

He released an irritated breath. "She's a *prima*-in-waiting who's supposed to find her consort and eventually lead her clan, so yes, I'd call that a complication."

For a long moment, his mother was quiet. Only the sound of running water and the distant murmur of conversation from the dining room filled the space between them.

"You know what I think?" she said at last.

He shrugged. "I'm sure you're going to tell me whether I want to hear it or not."

His mother only sent him a very serious look. "I think you've met someone who makes you feel things you haven't let yourself feel in years, and it's scaring you. So you're already planning her exit instead of seeing where this could go."

Shane rinsed the pot and set it down, then pulled the plug to let the water drain. "There's nowhere for it to go. She's leaving on Sunday. That's reality."

"Reality is what you make it," his mother told him. "I know that better than anyone else. And right now, I think you're making it much lonelier than it needs to be." She set down the dish towel and moved toward the doorway, then paused and looked back at him. "For what it's worth," she said softly, "I like her. I think she might be good for you."

"Mom—"

He didn't get any farther than that, though, because she broke in, "Just think about it." Now her smile seemed almost sad. "You deserve to be happy, Shane. Even if you don't believe that yourself."

Then she was gone, leaving Shane alone in the kitchen.

He dried his hands on the towel his mother had abandoned and leaned against the counter, staring out the window at the darkening sky beyond. Jerome's lights were starting to come on, little pinpricks of gold against the purple bulk of the dusky mountainside.

His mother was wrong. She *had* to be wrong.

Rosa was temporary. That was the deal they'd made. She'd help him through the review, and then she'd go back to her real life.

That he didn't want her to go was irrelevant.

He couldn't afford to care about Rosa Sandoval. Not when she was leaving, and definitely not when she had an entire foreordained life waiting for her back in Scottsdale.

And absolutely not when the *Arizona Republic* critic could walk through the Asylum's doors any day now and judge whether everything Shane had worked for was worth a damn.

Frowning, he pushed himself away from the counter and headed back toward the dining room, where he could hear Rosa laughing at something his father had said. He knew he needed to collect her and head home. Tomorrow was Wednesday — his second day off — but he had prep work to do, inventory to manage, a review to prepare for.

He needed to focus on what mattered.

Even if his traitorous heart kept insisting that Rosa mattered more than all of it.

Rosa was standing in the hallway, pausing to study a collection of family photos on the wall as she made her way back to the dining room from the bathroom—Shane had been a towheaded little kid with a whimsical smile, a smile she had yet to really experience for herself—when she heard Hayley's voice drift out from the kitchen.

"…never seen you look at anyone the way you look at her."

Her breath caught. She knew she should move away, should go back to the dining room where Levi was lingering over the last of the wine. But her feet had apparently forgotten how to work.

"You're imagining things." That was Shane, his tone flat and dismissive.

"Am I?"

Rosa pressed herself closer to the wall, heart hammering. This was wrong. She shouldn't be listening to this. But she couldn't seem to make herself move.

Shane's response was too quiet for her to catch all of it, but she heard fragments: "…not staying…" and "…just until I can find a real sous chef."

He might as well have punched her in the gut.

Of course. That was what she was. Temporary help. A stopgap solution to a staffing problem.

"She could stay longer if you asked her to," Hayley said.

"She can't. She has a life in Scottsdale…a destiny she's supposed to fulfill."

Rosa closed her eyes, Shane's words echoing in her head. *A destiny she's supposed to fulfill.*

He was right, of course. She did have a destiny. She was supposed to find her consort and become the *prima* her mother was training her to be. The sort of training Zoe herself hadn't received, because the previous *prima,* Luz Trujillo, had been struck down by dark magic when she was still in her prime.

Rosa knew she wasn't supposed to be hiding in Jerome, learning to dice onions and falling for a chef who saw her as nothing more than temporary.

Falling for.

No. She wasn't falling for Shane. She couldn't be.

She needed to find her consort. That was the whole point of this mess. Thirty-four failed attempts, and she still had months left before her twenty-first birthday ended and her window of opportunity closed forever. She couldn't afford to get distracted by a gorgeous chef with talented hands and a rare smile that made her breath catch every time she looked at him.

And she especially couldn't afford to get distracted when that chef had just made it clear she was temporary. That she'd be going back to her "real life" soon.

More voices from the kitchen, too low to make out clearly. Rosa forced herself to move, to walk quietly back toward the dining room before anyone caught her eavesdropping.

But Shane's words kept circling through her mind: *She's temporary.*

And underneath that was her own truth, the one she'd been trying not to think about.

She was a virgin, and she had to stay that way until she found her consort. It was tradition — the *prima*-in-waiting remained untouched until the consort bond was confirmed and sealed.

More than tradition, though, it felt like the one thing she hadn't compromised yet, the one choice she hadn't made out of desperation.

She'd failed thirty-four times to find her consort. She'd run away from home instead of facing another round of introductions and awkward kisses and crushing disappointment, and she'd hidden in a stranger's house and taken a job she had no qualifications for just to avoid dealing with her problems.

But she hadn't given up that one thing, that one piece of herself she was saving for the person she was supposed to spend her life with.

Even if part of her was starting to wish that person could be Shane.

Rosa shook her head sharply, trying to dislodge the thought. She couldn't think like that. Shane had made it clear she was temporary. Getting attached to him—getting attached to Jerome, to this strange little life she'd stumbled into—would only make it harder when she had to leave.

And she *had* to leave. On Sunday, or maybe even sooner if Shane found a real sous chef before then.

She returned to the dining room and slipped back into her seat.

"There you are," Levi said, his kind blue eyes studying her with an intensity that made Rosa wonder exactly how much he could see. "I was hoping we might have a chance to talk a little more before you leave tonight."

Rosa's stomach twisted. This was it, the conversation she'd supposedly come to Jerome to have.

The one she'd been avoiding for four days.

"I—" she began, but Shane appeared in the doorway right then, and whatever excuse she'd been about to make died on her lips.

He looked tired. And there was something in his expression—something careful and closed-off—that made her wish she could put her arms around him and give him a reassuring hug.

"We should probably head out," he said, his gaze pausing on her for just a second before it slid away again. "We have an early morning tomorrow."

That was a total lie. Tomorrow was Wednesday, his other day off. But Rosa was glad of any excuse to get away.

"Right," she said as she got up from her chair. "Thank you so much for dinner, Hayley. Everything was delicious."

"Oh, you're very welcome." Hayley flashed her a quick smile, one that showed her previous words hadn't been empty ones, but Rosa couldn't help recalling what she'd said to her son.

She'd be good for you. Was Hayley ignoring the hopelessness of the situation because she herself knew that sometimes the universe had intentions for you that had nothing to do with what you'd planned?

"Come back anytime," she added, and Rosa managed to smile.

"I'd still like that conversation," Levi said quietly as she moved toward the door. "When you're ready."

She met his eyes and saw understanding there — and maybe a hint of amusement, as if he knew exactly why she kept avoiding him.

"Soon," she heard herself say. "I promise."

It was another lie, and they both knew it.

But Levi just nodded and smiled, and Rosa followed Shane outside. The night air was cooler than she'd expected, considering how warm it had been during the day, but she supposed things cooled down faster at this elevation.

They walked in silence for a few moments, the air between them somehow fraught. Jerome's streets were quiet at this time of night, with only the distant sound of music from one of the bars on Main Street and the rustle of wind through the trees along Paradise Lane to break the stillness.

"Your family's really nice," Rosa said at length, mostly because the silence was starting to feel unbearable.

"They liked you," Shane said. His tone was neutral.

She supposed that was something.

About all she could manage was a nod, even as she searched for something else to say, some way to bridge the sudden distance that seemed to have opened between the two of them. But everything felt wrong, weighted with the conversation she'd overheard and truths she was trying very hard not to acknowledge.

She's temporary.

The words echoed in her head with every step.

By the time they reached Shane's house, Rosa felt like she'd been slogging through mud, even though intellectually she understood that today had been far less taxing than her first day at the restaurant. Shane touched his hand to the lock and then held the door open for her, and she slipped past him into the hallway.

"I'm going to turn in," she said, not quite

meeting his eyes. "Thanks for bringing me tonight."

"Sure," Shane said. "Goodnight, Rosa."

"Goodnight."

She went down the hall to the guest room and closed the door behind her, then sat on the edge of the bed and stared down at her hands, at the new scratches on her fingers and the nail she'd broken yesterday. She'd filed it down, but it still bugged her. The Rosa she'd been had always had perfect nails because she'd never had to do any real work with her hands.

Frowning, she lay back on the bed and stared at the ceiling, listening to the sound of Shane moving around in the living room, followed by the shower turning on in the bathroom down the hall.

She thought about Levi's offer to talk, the conversation she kept avoiding, and about her mother down in Scottsdale, worried sick despite Rosa's reassuring texts. Even though she wished she could avoid the topic, she couldn't keep her thoughts from straying to the consort she still needed to find and the destiny she was supposed to fulfill.

Shane's face flashed into her mind, and she remembered how he looked when he plated a dish, his rare smile and the warmth in his eyes when he told her she'd done good work.

She's temporary.

Rosa rolled onto her side and pulled the blanket up to her chin.

She had three more days in Jerome, three more days before she had to go back to her real life and face everything she'd been running from.

And she needed to make those days count. She needed to stay focused on why she'd come here in the first place, on finding answers about the consort bond and figuring out what she was doing wrong.

She absolutely, definitely, could not afford to fall any harder for Shane McAllister.

Even if it was already too late.

6

Rosa was already awake when Shane climbed out of bed the next morning. He found her in his kitchen, standing at the window in an oversized T-shirt and leggings, her dark hair loose and sleep-mussed. She held a mug of coffee—his coffee, made in his French press—and stared out at the mountains like she was memorizing the view because she might paint it later.

Most of the time, he would have been annoyed to find that someone had messed with his coffee and his French press. Today, though, he could only think about how adorable she looked.

"Morning," he said, and she turned, smiling.

Yes, *way* too damn adorable.

"I made coffee," she said at once, as if she hoped that by getting the words out quickly, she might forestall any complaints about making herself free of his kitchen. “I hope that’s okay.”

“It’s fine,” he replied, and knew that he meant it. “How’d you sleep?”

“Great.” She took a sip and gave a faint nod. “I’m not sure if it’s quite as good as yours, but I hope it passes muster.”

Well, that was easy enough to find out. He poured a cup for himself, adding nothing, since he liked his coffee the way he liked his cooking—pure, unadorned, exactly what it was supposed to be and nothing more. And it tasted fine. Of course, some might claim that it was hard to screw up coffee made from beans he’d ground just the day before and made with water that came through the reverse-osmosis filter system he’d put in almost as soon as escrow closed, but still, it was nice to see that Rosa hadn’t botched the process.

“So,” she said after studying his expression for a moment, as if to assure herself that she hadn’t screwed up that morning’s coffee, “what’s on the agenda? You have today off again, right?”

Yes, he did, but a lot of the time, that didn’t make much of a difference. “Well, usually I’d still go to the restaurant and prep and check inventory, maybe take care of any small stuff I don’t have time for when I’m on shift.”

Her full mouth pursed, and he tried not to stare. “So you basically work.”

He shrugged. "Basically."

After he delivered that brief reply, he took a long sip of coffee, watching her carefully over the rim of his mug. Right then, he sort of wished he were a painter, too, just so he could capture the way the morning light awakened deep mahogany and even copper glints in her dark hair and made her skin look positively luminous.

Damn, she was gorgeous.

He cleared his throat and went on, "I was thinking we could stay home today. I could teach you some more stuff in a real kitchen, not a professional one. If you want, of course," he tacked on at the end, just in case she'd decided to use her day off to wander Jerome and sketch or go shopping or whatever.

The way her face lit up at his suggestion shouldn't have affected him as much as it did.

"I'd love that," she said.

After they'd eaten breakfast—his famous brie and caramelized onion omelets, accompanied by potatoes sauteed with more onions and red peppers—and after they'd showered and gotten dressed, they returned to the kitchen so they could start with knife skills. Real ones this time, not the basic cuts he'd shown her for prep work. He set up his cutting board on the kitchen island, the worn butcher block he'd brought from his old apartment, and which Brianna had once quipped he would probably have buried with him. The surface was scarred from years of use, but the wood itself was smooth, since he oiled it faithfully every week.

"Knife skills are like meditation," he said as he laid out three chef's knives of varying sizes. "Most people rush because they think faster is better. But speed comes from being accurate, not forcing things."

Rosa picked up the middle knife. It was eight inches long, German steel, perfectly weighted. Expression thoughtful, she turned it over in her hand. "Show me."

So he did. He stood beside her at the counter and demonstrated the proper grip, the rock-chop motion that let the knife do the work. This was something he always loved, the way his hands moved through the familiar patterns with muscle memory guiding each cut.

"It's like drawing," Rosa said after a minute or so. "The way you move. There's sort of a rhythm to it, isn't there?"

Shane paused mid-chop, a little startled. He didn't think anyone had ever made that comparison before. "You know, I guess it is."

The corners of her mouth turned up ever so

slightly. "Show me again, but a little slower this time so I can really see what you're doing."

He did as she'd requested, even more aware of her attention this time and the way she watched his hands like she was sketching them in her mind. When he finished, she stepped up to the board and tried to mirror his movements.

Her first attempts were clumsy and somehow tense at the same time, showing that she was thinking too much, trying to force exactness instead of letting it come naturally. He moved behind her without thinking, his chest against her back, his hands settling over hers.

"Like this," he said. "Let the knife find its own path. You need to guide it, not fight it."

She relaxed into him. He could feel the moment when it happened, the softness of her shoulders against his chest. His hands moved with hers, the rock-chop rhythm steadying until they were moving together. The onion fell away in perfect dice, each piece uniform.

"There," he murmured, his lips closer to her ear than they should have been. "Did you feel that?"

"Yes," she replied, her voice also low and soft, as if she worried she might break the spell if she spoke any louder.

They stayed like that for a moment longer than was strictly necessary, long enough that

Shane became acutely aware of how she smelled. A scent of vanilla and something floral seemed caught in her hair, mixed with coffee and overlaid by the sharp bite of onion.

Had her pulse just sped up…or was he merely wishing that it had?

He took a step back, knowing he needed to put some distance between them.

"Practice that for a while," he said, and resisted the urge to clear his throat, since his voice sounded way too hoarse. "I'll start on the stock."

Making stock was magic all its own. He'd learned that young, long before culinary school, long before he'd started working at the Asylum. His mother had taught him, realizing early on that her son's curiosity about the kitchen and its working went far beyond a child's simple interest in how the food on their dinner table had been transformed from raw ingredients from the refrigerator and the pantry into something all its own.

He filled his largest pot with water and added chicken bones he'd been saving in the freezer, along with rough-chopped carrots and celery and onion, followed by bay leaves, peppercorns, and thyme. The aromatics would work their magic slowly, over hours, building depth that couldn't be rushed.

"What's your earliest food memory?" Rosa asked from where she still stood at the island.

She'd finished her pile of onions—they still weren't perfect, but they were a lot better—and was watching him with those wide hazel eyes that made him want to loosen his lips and tell her things he'd never told another living soul.

"I was maybe five," he replied as he adjusted the heat on the stovetop. "My mom made bread from scratch—it was just basic white bread, nothing fancy. But I remember watching the dough rise, seeing how it changed shape. And I remember how the whole house smelled while it baked." He paused there, smiling a little at the memory. "Back then, I thought it was magic. And maybe it was, although I know that cooking wasn't my mother's gift."

No, Hayley McAllister had an amazing talent, one that allowed her to expand the magical abilities of anyone around her. What she did in the kitchen, though, was all her.

"So...when did your gift really surface?"

"The way it does for most of us, when I was almost eleven. But I always loved food." He glanced over at Rosa, noting the way she seemed utterly focused on his expression, as though she wished she could pick up a pencil and draw him. "What about you? What's your first memory of art?"

"I was almost five," she said. "My mother was pregnant with my little sister. She was having a hard day—morning sickness—and I wanted to help. So I drew her a picture. It was just crayon on paper, nothing special. But she put it on the refrigerator and said it made her feel better." Rosa paused there, then added, "I suppose I've been trying to make people feel happy through art ever since."

He wished he could see something she'd created. So far, she hadn't seemed too inclined to share that part of herself, although he supposed there hadn't been much opportunity, either. It wasn't as if she could have hidden an easel and a bunch of oil paints in that one tote bag she'd brought with her. "Is that why you paint? To make people happy?"

Her shoulders lifted. "Maybe. I just like creating beauty." For a second or two, her eyes met his before she glanced away. Now focused on the pile of diced onions in front of her, she added softly, "Same as you."

Next, Shane taught her how to make a roux, how to tell when butter was properly browned and the importance of tasting as you go. She asked questions—good ones, thoughtful ones—and he found himself explaining things he'd never articulated before, like how his magic worked, how he experienced food as something more than taste. Somehow, his magic created layers of sensation he didn't have words for and translated them into flavor.

"It's like you're speaking another language," Rosa said as she watched him adjust the seasoning in a sauce by instinct.

"I guess I am. Some people say food is its own language." And he knew he would love to share that language with her. Trying to distract himself, he got out a clean spoon and offered her a sample. "What do you taste?"

She closed her eyes after she put the spoon in her mouth, obviously trying to analyze the flavor. "Butter…thyme…and something sharp…maybe lemon? underneath, though I don't know for sure how to describe it. Warmth, I guess?"

"The warmth is the magic," he told her. "It's not a flavor exactly. It's…." He let the words trail off there as he tried to articulate something he'd only known before as instinct. "It's intent, I suppose, the part of cooking that isn't just technique."

Her eyes opened then, and the flash of understanding in them made his breath catch. "Like how a painting can technically be perfect but still feel empty."

He couldn't help smiling. "Exactly like that."

The hours passed as they tested recipes,

adjusted flavors, and tasted everything twice. Shane found himself cooking differently than he did at the Asylum, with much less focus on precision and a whole lot more on play. Rosa brought out something in him that wasn't about perfection or proving himself. No, this was just the simple pleasure of creating something together.

Around five, they sat at his small kitchen table with tea and the madeleines they'd just pulled from the oven. The cookies were imperfect—they were Rosa's first attempt at French baking, so they were a little lopsided—but they tasted buttery and lemony all the same.

"These are good," he said, knowing he really meant it and wasn't just trying to make her feel better. "Really good."

Rosa broke hers in half, and steam rose from the interior. "Shane, I burned the first batch."

He couldn't help chuckling. "Everyone burns their first batch. That's how you learn." He watched her eat, the glint of happiness in her eyes as she tasted her own work. "You're a natural at this."

"I don't know about that," she said at once. "You're just a good teacher."

"You listen," he told her. "Some people hear, but they don't listen. There's a big difference."

Rosa met his gaze, and something shifted in her expression. "You notice things, too—like the way I work, or how you can tell what I need before I ask for it."

Without thinking, he said, "I notice everything about you."

Subtle, Shane. Real subtle.

But Rosa only gazed back at him steadily. "I noticed."

His heart began to beat a little faster in his chest, even as he told himself that this was dangerous. Rosa wasn't anything close to a permanent fixture in his life. She had a consort to find and her own destiny waiting for her down in Scottsdale. He couldn't—

"We should probably order dinner since we've been cooking all day," he said abruptly as he got up from the sofa and made a show of pulling his phone out of his jeans pocket. "Bobby D's delivers. Do you like barbecue?"

If she was disappointed by the subject change, she didn't show it. Instead, she nodded and replied, "I love it."

The moment had passed…and Shane wasn't sure whether to be relieved or disappointed.

After the food came, they sat in the dining room and ate their fill of smoked brisket and pulled pork, French fries, and cowboy beans. Since he rarely made food like this, it was a welcome change of pace, something he could eat uncritically without feeling as if he had to analyze every mouthful.

The momentary awkwardness from earlier gone, they sat there and talked, alternating sips of Syrah from Chateau Tumbleweed with bites of brisket and beans. Rosa told him about growing up as the *prima*-in-waiting, the weight of expectation that came with knowing your whole life's path before you could begin to choose it for yourself. Shane told her about culinary school, about the brutal hours and the pressure to prove his talent was more than just magic.

"Do you ever resent it?" she asked, and spooned more cowboy beans onto her plate. "You know, how your gift makes everything easier?"

Shane took a sip of wine as he considered her question. "Sometimes. People assume it's automatic, but the magic just gives me potential. I still have to work at it. I'm not some magic genie who can snap his fingers and make a meal appear out of thin air." He set down his glass, then tilted his head at her. "What about you?"

"My invisibility?" Her mouth pursed wryly, and she shook her head. "Pretty much every day. It's the perfect metaphor, isn't it? The girl who's supposed to be the center of everything, blessed with the power to disappear."

He hadn't thought about it that way. Although he was the oldest son and had never shied away from being the center of attention—well, as much as any warlock could be the center of attention, considering how they tried to keep their talents on the down-low—he had no idea what it would be like to be the heir-designate of a witch clan. The pressure must have been enormous.

"Trust me, Rosa," he said. "I don't care what your gift is. You're not the type of person who can disappear."

Now she smiled. "I'll try to keep that in mind."

Outside, the world was growing darker, but that was okay, since he'd lit the candles that sat at the center of the dining room table just before they'd settled down to dinner. The golden light seemed to caress the waves of her hair, to flow over her warm-toned skin.

She reached for the spoon in the container of pulled pork at the same moment he did, and their fingers brushed against one another. That whisper of a touch seemed to send a bolt of lightning up Shane's arm, making every nerve ending suddenly, painfully alive.

Neither of them moved, even though he knew he should have pulled his hand back right away.

Rosa was already looking at him, her lips parted, her pupils dark in the dimly lit room. He knew he could close that distance in a second, could find out if she tasted like dark cherry syrah or tangy barbecue sauce or something else, something that was uniquely her.

The need inside him was almost a physical force, making him tighten with desire. His hand moved without permission, reaching for her face—

And then he stopped.

Because…well, because he knew all of this was utterly insane, even if every cell in his body was screaming at him to close the distance and seal the deal.

So he pulled back, his hand moving toward his glass of wine as if that was always what he'd intended to do. "Um…it's late, and we have an early start tomorrow. We should clean up."

Disappointment flared in her eyes, but she only nodded. "Oh, sure. You're right, of course."

And she got up from her chair and stacked her used silverware on top of her plate, then began reaching for the half-empty takeout containers.

The taut set of her mouth told him everything he needed to know, but Shane didn't try to say anything. All he could do now was let it go and hope that they'd soon forget that fraught moment.

He also picked up his plate, and then went into the kitchen so he could set it on the counter and tell Rosa to go ahead and put the takeout leftovers in the fridge. Her mouth parted, as if she wanted to say something, but she only nodded and set the containers on the top shelf before closing the refrigerator door.

"I'm going to bed," she said at last, her eyes not meeting his. A pause, and then she asked, "Do you think the critic is going to come by the restaurant tomorrow?"

Oh, right. The restaurant critic, the person he'd been stressing about for the past few weeks, ever since he heard of their impending arrival. Now the review in the *Arizona Republic* seemed like the least important thing in the world. "Maybe," he replied. "It's always hard to say."

She managed a limp smile. "Then I guess we'll still need to be at the top of our game. Good-night, Shane."

He nodded and watched her turn to leave the kitchen. For some reason, though, he couldn't just leave it there. "Rosa?"

She paused at the cased opening that framed the living room beyond. "What?"

"Today was good," he said. "I just wanted you to know that."

A small smile flickered at the corner of her mouth. "It was. Sleep well, Shane."

She disappeared through the living room and down the hallway, and Shane stood alone in his kitchen—the space that had felt alive just hours ago—and felt its emptiness acutely.

He was in so much goddamn trouble.

The restaurant was fully booked that Thursday night—they always were on Thursdays, especially now that Jerome was full of summer vacationers —but tonight felt especially significant. The news had come to him through an anonymous email that the critic from the *Arizona Republic* actually was somewhere in the dining room, anonymous among fifty other diners, ready to make or break the restaurant's reputation with a single review.

Intellectually, Shane knew he was ready. He'd been preparing for weeks and had even designed a new tasting menu specifically for this possibility, had trained his staff on every possible contingency. Tonight, he checked and rechecked every station until Mike had to literally tell him to stop hovering.

But hovering was just what he did.

"Heard on the eight-top, table twelve," Mike called from the pass. "Two lobster, three duck, one lamb, two vegetarian tasting."

"Heard," Shane repeated, his hands already moving. The kitchen was carefully controlled chaos—six line cooks, two prep stations, and one dedicated to plating. Everyone knew exactly what they needed to do…or at least, he sure as hell hoped they did.

Rosa worked the plating station with increasing confidence. A few days ago, she couldn't even chop an onion properly, but now she was handling microgreens with tweezers, placing edible flowers with an artist's careful, delicate touch. Somewhat to his surprise, her eye for visual composition had managed to transform his food into even something more than he'd expected.

"Two minutes on the lobster," he called. "Mike, how's the duck?"

"Resting. Ready to plate in ninety seconds."

Everything was going smoothly…maybe too smoothly, and anxiety raised its ugly head.

This kind of perfection never lasted.

Seven-thirty hit, and the kitchen got slammed by ten tables ordering simultaneously. Every station was firing at once, and Shane was at the pass, coordinating, adjusting, tasting everything that came through. The salmon was underseasoned. The risotto needed thirty more seconds. The plating on table six was slightly off-center—

"Chef, we have a problem," Mike said. He sounded calm enough, but tension still underlaid his tone.

Shane's head snapped up at once. "What?"

"The signature dish. Table eighteen." Mike gestured to the spot where one of the line cooks stood frozen, staring at a plated entrée like it had personally offended him. "Kyle plated it backwards."

Shane hurried over to get a closer look. The dish—seared scallops with cauliflower purée, crispy prosciutto, and microgreens arranged to look like breaking waves—was completely wrong. The composition was off, the height was wrong, the visual story was backwards. It looked like an amateur had plated it.

And table eighteen had ordered three of them.

"How long ago did you fire these?" Shane demanded.

Kyle's face looked pale under his early-summer tan. "Six minutes. They're the perfect temp, but I just—I got the arrangement wrong."

Six minutes meant the scallops were already starting to cool. They had maybe two minutes before they'd need to re-fire everything, which meant table eighteen's food would be late, which meant if that table was the critic—

"I can fix it," Rosa said quietly, appearing as if by magic at his elbow.

Shane turned. She was looking at the plates, brows drawn together, as if she was already seeing the solution and mapping it in her head.

Although he knew they needed all the help

they could get, he couldn't help saying, "Rosa, these need to go now—"

"I know. Give me ninety seconds." Even as she spoke, her hands were moving, quick and confident. She didn't replate because there wasn't time. Instead, she rebuilt, moving the scallops with delicate care, redistributing the purée with a clean spoon, rearranging the microgreens and crispy prosciutto into something that made the plating better rather than simply fixing Kyle's mistake.

Now the arrangement was more dynamic, the height more dramatic. It was still Shane's dish, his vision, but it had been elevated by Rosa's artistic eye into something almost transcendent.

Even more amazing, she finished all three plates in eighty seconds.

"Wow," Mike breathed.

Shane could only stare down at her work. She'd saved the service...and saved his reputation. And she'd done it like it was nothing.

"Run them," he said briskly.

Everything after that seemed to pass by in a blur. He was aware of Rosa at the plating station, slender fingers moving nimbly, gaze focused and intent, and how there were multiple times when she caught small issues before they became problems, her instincts for composition making every plate better.

And through it all, he couldn't stop thinking about how much he wanted her.

By midnight, the kitchen was empty except for the two of them. His staff had finished cleanup and departed, leaving Shane and Rosa alone with stacks of dishes and the comfortable silence of exhaustion…and a job well done.

"That was intense," Rosa said. She was scrubbing sauce off a sauté pan, just as focused as ever, but something about the way she stood told him how tired she really was.

"No, that was perfect." He came over so he could stand beside her at the sink. "You seriously saved my ass tonight. Kyle's been with me for eight months, and he's never screwed up a plate that badly. If you hadn't fixed it—"

Her shoulders lifted. "You would have figured something out."

"Maybe." Shane took the clean pan from her and set it in the drying rack. "But you made it better. I'm not talking about just fixing it—it was better. You see things that I miss."

Rosa turned to face him, her back against the sink. A few strands of shining dark hair had escaped their braid and fell against her cheeks like a caress. "You make it sound like I did something special."

"You *did* do something special." The words kept coming and were way too honest, but he was too tired to stop them. "You make everything better, Rosa. The food. The kitchen. My—"

Life, he almost said. *You make my life better.*

But that was far too much. He wouldn't have said those words to a woman he'd been dating for six months, let alone a woman he'd known for six days.

Even if he knew they were the truth.

"Let me teach you something else," he said instead, casting about for some way to dispel the tension in the room. "Something I should have shown you when we first got started."

While she watched him with curious eyes, he retrieved his favorite chef's knife from its case—ten inches of Japanese steel that had cost him two months' pay when he was fresh out of culinary school. The edge was dull from heavy use, and he knew it was time to fix that.

He set up his whetstone on the prep counter and filled a small bowl with water. "Knife maintenance is sacred. You take care of your tools, they take care of you."

"That sounds like something a chef would say to avoid therapy," Rosa said, but she was almost grinning now, clearly ready to focus on something else as well.

"Maybe," he allowed. "But come here."

She took a few steps and paused beside him, close enough that their shoulders almost brushed.

While she watched, he demonstrated the angle and pressure and steady strokes that would restore the blade's edge.

"Your turn," he told her once he was done.

Rosa took the knife carefully, obviously trying to mimic his grip. But her angle was wrong, her pressure too light. He moved behind her without thinking, his chest against her back, his hands covering hers.

"Like this," he murmured. "Fifteen-degree angle. Steady pressure. Let the stone do the work."

He guided her through the motion, once…twice…three times. The rhythmic scrape of steel on stone was a kind of meditation and definitely the most intimate thing Shane had done in months, despite being completely non-sexual.

Or maybe it was exactly because of that. Maybe intimacy was this—teaching someone you cared about a skill that mattered to you.

Rosa's breath hitched slightly. Shane realized his lips were close to her ear, his nose nearly in her hair. That warm scent again—vanilla and something floral—winning out against the scents of cooking oil and dish soap that filled the kitchen.

His hands went quiet on hers, and neither of them moved.

The kitchen was silent except for their breathing and the distant hum of the walk-in cooler. He could feel her pulse where his fingers touched her wrist—rapid, fluttering, matching his own racing heart.

He knew he should step back, should force himself to think of all the reasons why this was a bad idea.

But God, he wanted to know what she tasted like.

She turned her head slightly, and suddenly their faces were inches apart. Her eyes were dark and wondering, her lips just slightly parted.

Shane began to close the distance—

A loud bang from the back door made them both jump.

"Delivery!" someone shouted. "Anyone here?"

Shane stepped back so fast that he nearly tripped, and Rosa set down the knife she'd been holding with shaking hands. They stared at each other, the moment shattered, but the need was still there, almost impossible to ignore.

"I should—that's the linen service," he said, knowing how hoarse he sounded. "I don't know why the hell they're here at this hour. They're supposed to come tomorrow."

"Right," she said. "Um…I'll just—" She gestured vaguely toward the dining room. "Clean the tables."

And she fled.

Shane stood alone in the kitchen, his hands gripping the edge of the prep counter hard enough to hurt, and tried to remember how to breathe.

This was bad. This was worse than bad. Because he knew he wasn't just attracted to Rosa anymore. This was a hell of a lot more than just being fond of her, or impressed by her, more than enjoying her company.

He was falling for her.

Damn it.

He dealt with the linen delivery guy on autopilot, signed forms without reading them, and sent the driver away with a tip he probably didn't deserve, considering how he'd shown up here after the restaurant was officially closed. Then he stood in his restaurant's back entrance, staring up at the stars wheeling overhead, trying to find some kind of balance.

He couldn't do this. Rosa needed him to be her refuge, her safe space while she figured out her life. The last thing she needed was another complication.

By the time Shane reentered the kitchen, she'd finished cleaning and was pulling on her jacket. She didn't meet his eyes.

"Ready to go?" he asked, aiming for casual and knowing he sounded anything but.

She nodded. "Yes. It's been kind of a long day."

They drove back down to Paradise Lane in

silence. Rosa stared out the window at the darkness, her hands folded in her lap. Shane kept his eyes on the road and tried not to think about how close they'd come to crossing a line that couldn't be uncrossed.

"Thank you," she said as they pulled up to his house. "For teaching me about the knife thing, I mean."

"Anytime."

They went inside, and Rosa headed straight for the guest room, although she paused at the entrance to the hallway.

"Shane?"

He forced himself to look at her. The vulnerability in her expression made him ache inside. "Yes?"

A smile that was as brilliant as sunlight despite the weariness in her face. "I'm glad I'm here. Even if it's temporary."

Somehow he managed to say, "Me, too."

She disappeared into the guest room, and Shane stood there for a long moment, his thoughts warring with themselves until they finally gave up and told him to acknowledge the truth he'd been so desperately trying to avoid.

He was in love with Rosa Sandoval.

And there wasn't a damn thing he could do about it.

7

The next few days were a blur, and Shane could only be glad of that. Being busy meant he didn't have to pause to examine what had passed between him and Rosa on Thursday night. If he kept his head down, then he could pretend it had never happened.

Well, except for the part where his traitorous mind wanted to dwell on that sweet moment over and over again.

But he was glad to see that Rosa had become part of the kitchen's rhythm. She still worked with the careful deliberation of someone who knew she wasn't yet fluent in this language, but she no longer looked completely lost. Also, Kelli had stopped shooting her suspicious glances, and Mike had started asking her opinion on plating compositions. Even Carlos, who rarely spoke to anyone outside of dessert-related emergencies, had complimented her knife work yesterday.

The tension between them remained, however, unspoken but far too tangible nonetheless. It hummed beneath every interaction, every time their hands brushed against one another as they reached for the same ingredient…every moment Shane stood behind her to correct her grip on a knife or her angle on a cut. He could feel it when she laughed at something Mike said, when she tucked a stray piece of hair behind her ear, when she concentrated so hard on a task that she bit her lower lip.

Shane had been trying very hard not to think about that lip.

And Sunday came and went, and neither of them said a single word about it. Shane knew she had said she wouldn't stay past that first week, and yet as Monday rolled around, she continued to remain silent. Was she waiting for a signal from him that it was time to go, that she needed to pack her things and head back to Scottsdale to face the responsibilities she'd left behind?

Possibly. But he was too much of a coward to tell her to leave, and since it seemed that she'd kept her mother at bay with reassuring texts here and there where needed, and she'd somehow managed to avoid her grandparents, he decided it was none of his business anyway…especially since he hadn't even begun to find a suitable replacement for his sous chef and he needed every extra pair of hands in the kitchen that he could get.

His next day off was Tuesday again, which usually meant he'd spend it at the restaurant anyway, testing new recipes or doing inventory or finding other minor details that needed his attention but he couldn't deal with while he was working. Being at the Asylum felt far safer than having too much time to think.

But on Tuesday morning, as Shane stood in his kitchen drinking coffee and deciding whether he could justify going in early to reorganize the walk-in, Rosa appeared in the doorway. She was wearing jeans and an embroidered turquoise sleeveless top that made her hazel eyes look almost green. Pink-polished toes peeked out from under those jeans, and he wondered when she could have found the time to paint them.

"So…what are you doing today?" she asked.

He shrugged. "Probably heading to the restaurant. There's always something that needs attention."

Her brows drew together. "It's your day off, though."

He said, "I usually work anyway," before he raised his cup of coffee to his lips.

In response, she leaned against the doorframe,

her expression now thoughtful. "What if we didn't?"

He tilted his head at her. "What if we didn't what?"

"Didn't work," she replied with a smile. "What if we actually explored Jerome today? Like, *really* saw the town, not just your house and the restaurant?"

The suggestion made him blink in surprise. Shane had lived in Jerome his entire life, but he couldn't remember the last time he'd done anything remotely touristy there. The galleries, the shops, the overlooks that brought visitors from all over Arizona—they were just background noise to the constant hum of work that filled his life.

"I don't know," he said slowly. "Aren't you supposed to be lying low?"

Her smile faded a little. "My mother knows I'm here—and so do your parents. And I'm assuming if your parents know, then so do the elders and Connor and Angela. For all I know, my mom told my grandparents as well. So I'm not sure I'm really doing that much lying low. And it would be nice to get out. I checked the weather today, and it's supposed to be cooler, only in the mid-eighties. It's not going to get any better than that."

Well, she had him there. "Okay," he said after

a long pause during which he tried to think of a good excuse to shoot down her idea and couldn't find anything that wouldn't sound obviously obstructive. "We'll head out after breakfast."

~

As she'd said, the day was perfect. The early June sunshine warmed them without being scorching, and a light breeze ruffled their hair and somehow brought with it the scent of ponderosa pines from the mountain above. Shane found himself looking around as if he was a tourist himself, seeing the familiar surroundings with fresh eyes.

Rosa stopped at every gallery window, pressing her nose to the glass like a kid at a candy store. As they walked, she pointed out architectural details Shane had never noticed—the way the old brick buildings caught and held the light, the color combinations in the painted storefronts, how the steep angle of the hill created unexpected perspectives and compositions.

"See that building?" She gestured to a turquoise-painted shop across the street, one that currently housed a boutique that sold clothing and jewelry from local artisans. "The way the shadows fall across the balcony creates an interesting geometric pattern. And the color is almost the exact shade of oxidized copper. I bet the person who painted it knew it would create a kind of callback to the town's mining history."

He gazed at the building—which he'd probably walked past a hundred times—and shook his head. "I never would have noticed that."

"You notice flavors and textures," she said. "I notice color and composition. They might be different languages, but they're kind of the same idea."

They wandered through every gallery they could find, some that showcased local artists, while others featured work from across the Southwest. In one space, Rosa stopped in front of a large abstract landscape, all bold oranges and deep purples with slashes of turquoise that suggested sky or maybe water. She stood there for so long that Shane came over to join her, trying to figure out what held her attention so intensely.

"What do you see?" he asked.

Rosa tilted her head, her gaze tracking across the canvas. "The artist started with the darkest colors in the lower left—see how your eye wants to start there? Then they built up layers, creating depth and movement. The composition pulls you diagonally across the canvas, from that dark corner to the lighter area in the upper right. It's a journey. From earth to sky, from weight to lightness, from sorrow to hope…maybe." She paused, still studying the painting. "They're saying something about transformation, I think." Another hesitation, and then she added, "Or maybe I just sound like a pretentious jerk."

"I don't think you're pretentious," he replied. "I like hearing how you talk about art. It's something I never paid all that much attention to. Now I'm starting to realize how much I missed."

They stood there in the gallery, surrounded by tourists who spoke in murmurs and paused to study a painting just as they had, and he experienced an odd shift deep inside. It wasn't just attraction, although the Goddess only knew that was there, too. For the first time, he was with someone who seemed to truly understand the drive to create, to communicate through art. It wasn't a quality everyone possessed, and finding a woman who did felt like stumbling onto a treasure he hadn't even known existed.

"Come on," he said as a sudden idea occurred to him. "I want to take you somewhere."

Her hazel eyes glinted with amusement. "I bet you say that to all the girls."

But she didn't argue as he led her out of the gallery and then back up the hill to the house so they could climb into the van where it was parked in the driveway. Although he'd bought it for its utility and not its ability to pick up chicks, he found himself wishing he had something fun to drive, maybe a convertible so he could pop the top and let the warm wind flow over them as they drove to their destination.

However, since he couldn't snap his fingers and make a Maserati appear—although that would have been a fun talent to have—he went ahead and backed out of the driveway, then drove up Highway 89A as it twisted its way toward the peak of Mingus Mountain. The town disappeared behind them as they ascended, and he pulled off onto a rutted track that finally ended at a small turnout. From there, a short walk led to a rocky outcropping that overlooked the entire Verde Valley.

"This is my spot," Shane told Rosa as they picked their way across the uneven ground. He realized he probably should have told her to swap out her sandals for some tennis shoes before they'd even gotten in the van, but that couldn't be helped now. However, she didn't seem too worried about her footwear, and followed him gamely and without complaint. "I come here when I need to get away from everything."

They reached the outcropping, and she drew in a sharp breath. The valley spread below them, a sea of golden grass with the dark ribbon of the Verde River and its surrounding cottonwoods cutting through the landscape. In the distance, the red rocks of Sedona glowed in the late afternoon light. The sky above them was that particular shade of deep, almost sapphire blue that seemed almost too saturated to be real, a sky he believed you couldn't see anywhere else in the world.

"It's beautiful," she said softly.

"It's late afternoon," he replied. "Wait a few minutes, and it'll get even better."

They sat on the warm rock, their shoulders touching, and for a long moment, neither of them spoke. He couldn't help being acutely aware of her bare shoulder against his and the way her breathing seemed to match his own. The resiny scent of juniper seemed to hang in the air around them.

"Can I ask you something?" Rosa said at last.

"Sure," he replied, and hoped he wasn't making a mistake by responding that way.

She was quiet for another moment, as if weighing her words. "Do you ever feel like you're performing? Like the person everyone expects you to be isn't quite the same as the person you actually are?"

He hadn't been expecting that question, and it hit a lot closer to home than he would have liked. For a few seconds, he was silent as he thought about how much work went into maintaining his image of the casually confident chef who turned out perfect dishes night after night, and how carefully he had to balance his natural gift with acquired skill so no one in the clan could say his success was only due to his magical talents and nothing else.

"Yes," he said. "All the time."

That response got a thoughtful nod, as if she'd somehow anticipated what he was going to say before the words had even left his mouth. "I've been performing my whole life," she said. "I have to be the *prima*-in-waiting, the dutiful daughter who'll help her clan by finding the right consort and having the right magic and doing everything the way she's supposed to." She made a frustrated gesture with one hand, as if trying to wave all that away. "I don't even know if I really want to paint portraits, or if I just do it because it's the safe choice. Maybe I want to paint abstracts, or landscapes, or—I don't know." A pause, and she released an exasperated breath. "I've never let myself find out."

Shane understood that feeling, the weight of expectations and the fear that if you deviated from the script, everyone would see you were a fraud. "Everyone thinks the magic makes cooking easy for me," he said, his gaze fixed on the golden landscape far below them. "But the magic only makes it possible. The rest is all just work and lots of practice. Sometimes I wonder if I'm working this hard because I love it or because I'm afraid of what might happen if I stop. Like if I slow down, everyone will see I'm not actually that good without the magic doing the heavy lifting."

"You're brilliant without the magic," Rosa said without a second of hesitation. "I've watched you work, Shane. The magic is just one ingredient… and one ingredient isn't enough."

The certainty in her voice seemed to loosen something tight and worried inside him. "You're brilliant, too," he told her, recalling how a few days earlier, she'd let him peek inside the sketchbook she'd brought with her to Jerome. "Those portraits I saw in your sketchbook are incredible. You're able to capture something essential about a person with just a few pencil strokes."

She shifted on the rock so she could look at him, her hazel eyes searching his face. "But what if that's not what I want to do?" she asked. "What if I want to paint something else entirely?"

"Then paint something else," he replied.

Although she didn't quite roll her eyes, he could tell she wasn't too happy with his answer. "It's not that simple."

Maybe it wasn't, but he thought the only way she'd get through these walls she'd placed around herself was to challenge the reason why she'd put them there in the first place. "Why not?"

She opened her mouth, then closed it again, as

though she wasn't sure whether what she'd planned to say was the argument she truly wanted to present. Shane waited, knowing he needed to give her space to work through whatever internal argument she was having with herself.

"Because I'm supposed to be the *prima* someday," she said at length. "And the *prima* has responsibilities and traditions and a role to uphold. Part of that role means being the kind of person people in my clan expect. A lot of the de la Pazes are super traditional. I suppose that makes sense, since our family has been here for so many hundreds of years. Even my mom stopped being a rebel and made herself all girly when it was time for her to do the consort search. And that just makes me think my art can't be weird or experimental or—" She stopped there and made a frustrated gesture with one hand.

"Not yourself?" he prompted.

A bitter chuckle. "Apparently not."

"That's bullshit," he told her, and she blinked at him in surprise. Although he usually didn't care what he said in the heat of the moment when things got crazy at work, he'd tried to rein it in ever since Rosa had started helping out in the kitchen. The casual profanity had clearly surprised her. "Sorry," he went on, "but it is. You're allowed to be yourself *and* be the *prima*. Those things don't have to be mutually exclusive. Your mother found a way to be both, didn't she?"

"My mother tried to create her perfect consort with forbidden magic," Rosa pointed out with a curl of her lip. "I wouldn't exactly call that a conventional path."

"That's what I mean," he said without missing a beat. "She made her own rules when the traditional ones weren't working for her. Maybe you get to do the same thing."

Rosa stared at him without responding, and Shane could practically see the way she struggled with what she'd been told versus what she wanted to be. He wanted to tell her to choose herself, to choose what made her happy. But he remained silent, worried that saying those words would cross some line from concerned friend to something more...to something he desperately hoped for and yet knew could never happen.

The sun had begun to set behind the mountain, sending a wash of rose and gold and deep purple over the valley's shadowed areas. Rosa's skin glowed warm in the golden hour light, and Shane had to curl his hands into fists to keep himself from reaching out to touch her cheek, to see if she felt as warm as she looked.

"Favorite food," Rosa said out of nowhere, breaking the unspoken tension between them. "Go."

Shane blinked at the subject change, then couldn't help smiling at the way she'd tried to steer the conversation into calmer waters. "You mean, besides everything I make?"

She nodded. "Besides everything you make."

He didn't even have to think about his answer. "My mom's pot roast. She made it every other Sunday when I was a kid, and it was always perfect—the meat falling apart, the vegetables caramelized, the gravy thick enough to coat a spoon. No magic, just time and care and love."

"Well, I could already tell your mom was a great cook after having her lasagna last week."

That was true. Hayley McAllister possessed a very great magical gift, but she'd always seemed content being what she laughingly referred to as "a domestic goddess." "She is," he replied, "and I learned a lot from her. Of course, it would be nice if she would stop asking when I'm going to find a nice girl and give her some grandchildren."

What in the world had made him say that? Usually, he guarded his words, but when he was with Rosa, those cautions seemed to fly out the window. His ears heated with embarrassment, and he made himself stare forward, as if the sunset landscape beneath them was the most important thing in the world.

But Rosa only laughed, the sound bright and genuine. "My mother does the same thing. Well, sort of. With her, it's all about finding my consort and fulfilling my destiny, so I guess it's not quite as warm and fuzzy."

"What about you?" Shane asked then, figuring he should guide the conversation back to safer ground. "Favorite food?"

"My grandmother's mole," Rosa said without hesitation. "She makes it for special occasions, and it takes her two days to prepare. There are something like twenty-five ingredients, and each one has to be prepared exactly right—the chiles toasted, the smallest pinch of Mexican cocoa, all the spices ground fresh. I know she doesn't have your magical cooking gift, but it still tastes like magic to me."

"I'd love to try that someday," Shane said. He'd made mole himself a couple of times, wanting to get familiar with the process even though it wasn't something they'd serve at the Asylum, but he thought it would be great to understand the flavors that had shaped her childhood.

"Okay, what about your worst kitchen disaster?" Rosa asked with a grin. "And you can't cheat and tell me you've never had one."

He couldn't help grinning back. "Define 'disaster.'"

"Something that required a fire extinguisher, an evacuation, or a *really* expensive repair bill."

He chuckled. "That's easy. My second year of culinary school. I was trying to make a complicated French dessert—a *croquembouche*, which is basically a tower of cream puffs held together with caramel. The caramel got too hot, I tried to save it, and I ended up with third-degree burns on my hand and molten sugar all over the kitchen floor. They had to close the school kitchen for a day to clean up the mess."

Rosa winced. "Yikes. Did you finish the dessert?"

Oh, you sweet summer child. "Hell, no," he said. "I was in the emergency room getting my hand wrapped in gauze and getting a very stern lecture from my instructor about respecting hot sugar." And although he understood why the school had whisked him away to the emergency room, he wished he could have gone to one of the de la Paz healers to get fixed up, since he'd been in Phoenix at the time. He held up his left hand, showing her the faint scars across his palm. The McAllister healer, Roslyn Campbell, had done her best to lessen the damage, but since he'd gone to her after the burns had already started to heal, she couldn't completely get rid of the scarring. "These are my reminder to always respect the ingredients."

A solemn nod. "Now I really respect all those people who do pulled sugar on *Halloween Wars* and shows like that," Rosa said. "That stuff is dangerous." She stopped there and gave a self-deprecating chuckle. "My story isn't nearly as exciting, but I did once set a microwave on fire making popcorn."

Now, that required some skill. "How in the world did you manage that?"

She shrugged. "I was fifteen and wasn't paying attention. I hit ten minutes instead of one-zero-zero seconds, and by the time I realized what was going on, there was smoke pouring out of the microwave and the fire alarm was going off. My mother came running, my sister thought we were being attacked by dark magic, and my father just opened the microwave and let loose with a fire extinguisher. He wasn't super-thrilled with me, since it was one of those built-in ones that are a lot more expensive to replace."

Shane just had to laugh, even though he guessed at the time, Rosa had been mortified. Actually, they were both laughing now, their earlier tension dissolving into shared amusement. In fact, she was laughing so hard that she tipped her head back in a way that exposed the long line of her throat.

Somehow, he managed to tear his gaze away. Did she have to be so distractingly enchanting?

"Okay, embarrassing childhood story," he said next. He needed to keep the conversation moving before he did something stupid like stare at her mouth for too long. "Your turn."

"What, you don't get to go first?"

"I'm still trying to think of one," he replied. "I have a lot to choose from."

She chuckled again. "Same here. But…okay, here's the first one that popped into my mind. When I was seven, I decided I was going to paint a mural on my bedroom wall. Without asking permission, of course. I got about halfway through painting what was supposed to be a magical forest scene before my mother found me and had a meltdown. But even though she was angry, the mural stayed up for three years because she couldn't bring herself to paint over it." Rosa stopped there, looking thoughtful. "She really should have, though. It was kind of terrible."

"That's not embarrassing," Shane said. "That's adorable."

She lifted an incredulous eyebrow. "The forest had purple trees, and the deer had six legs. It was a nightmare. In fact, I think it gave *me* nightmares."

"It was creative," he told her. "Your mom kept it because she saw your potential, even if the execution wasn't perfect yet."

Rosa looked at him with an expression he couldn't quite read, something that was soft and wondering and maybe a little sad. "How do you do that?"

He wasn't sure what she was talking about. "Do what?"

"See the best version of everything," she replied.

Oh, he didn't know about that. In fact, a couple of his ex-girlfriends would probably say that he did the exact opposite.

"I could ask you the same thing," he said, doing his best to keep his tone casual. "You did it earlier today in that gallery, with that crazy abstract painting I couldn't make heads or tails of. You found the beauty in the chaos."

For a moment, she didn't reply. The sun had fully set now, and the valley below them was purple with dusk. The temperature had begun to drop, and Shane could feel Rosa shivering slightly beside him in her sleeveless blouse. He knew he should suggest that they head back, should put some necessary distance between them before this moment turned into something neither of them could take back.

But instead, he reached out and tucked a strand of hair behind her ear, his fingers lingering on her cheek. Her skin was soft and warm, and when she leaned into his touch, her eyes fluttered closed. His resolve crumbled like over-beaten meringue.

"I know this is a bad idea," he said.

Rosa opened her eyes, and their usual cloudy

hazel was dark in the fading light. "Terrible idea," she agreed, and her voice was almost breathless.

"Probably the worst."

She nodded. "Absolutely the worst."

They leaned in toward one another anyway.

The embrace was tentative at first, almost questioning—her lips soft against his, her breath catching, his hand still cupped against her cheek. Then something seemed to change between them, and the kiss deepened, became searching and sweet and edged with desperation. Rosa's hands came up to grip his shoulders, and Shane wrapped his other arm around her waist, pulling her closer.

He could taste her—something like honey and mint. She made a small sound in the back of her throat that sent heat racing through him, and Shane forgot why this was supposed to be a bad idea, forgot everything except the feeling of her mouth on his and the way she fit against him like she'd been made for exactly this moment.

Maybe deep down, he'd been hoping that their kiss would spark the consort bond, would show that they truly were intended for each other, and that their flirtation over the past week had only been a necessary step to bring them to this moment.

That hadn't happened, though. Oh, it was probably the best kiss he'd ever shared, and yet he'd heard that the consort kiss was supposed to be transcendent, was supposed to basically set your nerve endings on fire and bind you to that woman for all eternity.

No, this had been simply a kiss.

And he had no idea what the hell he was supposed to do about it.

8

HOW COULD SHE BE DOING THIS? HOW COULD she be ignoring everything she'd ever been taught? She was only supposed to kiss someone she thought could be a possible consort, and she knew Shane couldn't be that. He was too old—all the consort candidates had been between twenty-one and twenty-five, and she knew he'd turned twenty-eight back in April—and he hadn't been carefully vetted to ensure that he would be a good fit.

She was sure the de la Paz elders would think he wasn't a good fit at all, not when his life was so firmly centered in Jerome.

That didn't matter, though. This wasn't a consort kiss. No, this was just aching, terrible need, the horrible realization that she loved Shane

McAllister and at the same time knew he wasn't her consort.

What the hell was she supposed to do now?

They finally pulled apart, both breathing hard. Sure, she'd been kissed before—dozens of times, in fact, during those awful consort trials. Clinical kisses, hopeful kisses, desperate kisses that all ended the same way…with absolutely nothing. No spark, no magic, no recognition from the *prima* power sleeping inside her.

This was nothing like those kisses.

This kiss had sent electricity racing through her veins, had made her toes curl and her fingers tingle and the base of her spine light up with want. This kiss had tasted like Shane—like coffee and woodsmoke and something uniquely him that she couldn't name but would recognize anywhere. This kiss had felt like coming home and jumping off a cliff at the same time.

But it hadn't awakened the *prima* power within her, that intangible quality which was supposed to know right away when she'd shared an embrace with the right man.

So…what was she supposed to do now?

She realized that her fingers were still tangled in his shirt, her forehead pressed against his shoulder as she tried to catch her breath and make sense of what had just happened. She could feel his heartbeat hammering against her cheek, almost as fast and frantic as her own.

Logically, she knew she should tell him that even though this had been great, she couldn't let things go any further. A horrible fate had decreed that she had to give herself body and soul to the man who'd awakened the consort bond, and it didn't seem as if Shane was that man. Yes, she needed to make her de la Paz forebears proud and tell him that she wasn't in a position for casual amusements, that she had to focus on finding the man who would be her companion for the rest of her life.

But those terrible words wouldn't come. They stuck in her throat, heavy and sharp-edged, because saying them out loud would break this perfect moment and would turn it from something beautiful and spontaneous into something weighed down by duty and tradition.

"We should probably talk about this," Shane said. The words buzzed against her hair, and a shiver went through her body.

However, she sounded normal enough as she replied, "Probably."

"But not today?"

Relief flooded through her so intensely that it practically made her dizzy. "Not today…if that's all right."

"It's fine."

She lifted her head to look at him, and even in the gathering darkness, she could read the uncertainty in his eyes. He was scared, too, frightened of what this might mean, of where it could lead. She understood that fear intimately, because she'd lived with it her entire life in different forms.

But underneath the fear was something else, something hopeful and impossibly fragile at the same time. That hope made her want to be brave enough to see where this could go, even while knowing it might end badly.

Actually, that it *had* to end badly, since he wasn't her consort.

They sat there for another minute, neither of them quite willing to let go and face the world of what happened after they shared that kiss. At last, the cold drove them back to the van, but Shane reached for Rosa's hand as they walked, and she laced her fingers through his without hesitation.

His palm was warm and slightly rough from the scars he'd shown her earlier, his fingers strong and careful as they intertwined with hers. Somehow, holding hands felt even more intimate than the kiss they'd just shared. The kiss could have been a moment of weakness and nothing more. But this—walking hand in hand through the twilight, choosing to maintain that connection even after the heat of the moment had passed—this felt like a promise, even if neither of them was ready to say what that promise meant.

Her thoughts kept tumbling over themselves as Shane drove back down to Jerome, but she didn't say anything. She knew she should be feeling guilty. After all, she'd come here to hide from her consort problems, not create new ones.

But she couldn't make herself regret this. Not yet, anyway. Maybe tomorrow morning, when she was sure reality would come crashing back in, or maybe even when the day came that Shane found a new sous chef and she'd run out of excuses for staying in Jerome. Right now, though, with Shane's hand warm in hers and the memory of his kiss still tingling on her lips, Rosa felt more like herself than she had in months.

Maybe more than she ever had.

Shane had looked at her today and had seen Rosa—not the *prima*-in-waiting, not the dutiful daughter, not the girl who couldn't find her consort after eight months of trying. Just Rosa. The woman who loved art and saw the world in colors and compositions…the woman who wanted things she hadn't let herself want before.

It was dangerous…and more than a little terrifying.

When they pulled up to his house, Shane killed the engine but didn't immediately get out. "Rosa—"

"I know," she said, cutting him off before he could go any further. "I know we need to talk about this and about all the reasons this is complicated. But can we just have tonight? Just tonight, where we don't think about tomorrow?"

His mouth tightened. Right then, she wished she had the ability to read minds, to see what he was thinking. Was he chastising himself for making a horrible mistake? Warlocks were supposed to know better, right? They were supposed to know that a *prima*-in-waiting was off-limits to anyone who wasn't involved in the consort search.

That wasn't fair, though. They'd both leaned into that kiss, had moved at almost exactly the same time. It wasn't as if he'd tried to seduce her or anything close to that.

Why would they have such insane chemistry if he wasn't the one?

She didn't know. As far as she could remember, she'd never heard of a situation like this before. Then again, if it turned out that it wasn't so uncommon for a *prima*-in-waiting to have a connection with a man who wasn't her consort, she kind of doubted anyone would want to advertise that fact.

"Okay," Shane said after a long pause. "We have tonight."

They went inside, and Rosa started to head for

the guest room, which she knew was the safe choice, the choice that would let them both pretend nothing had changed, but Shane caught her hand before she could disappear down the hallway. She turned back to him, her eyebrows raised in question, her heart suddenly pounding.

"Stay with me?" he asked, and there was a vulnerable note in his voice that made her ache to hold him again. "No pressure, just—let's hang out for a while."

She managed a shaky smile. "Sounds good."

They ended up on the couch, with her curled against Shane's side, his arm around her shoulders, and a soft blanket thrown over them both. Maybe they didn't strictly need the blanket, but it felt good after that chilly wind up on Mingus, and she liked the illusion of coziness it provided, almost as if she could imagine being here months hence, in the wintertime with snow falling outside the windows. She'd never seen snow before, and she loved the idea of experiencing it for the first time with Shane at her side.

The position they shared should have felt awkward—they'd only kissed for the first time an hour ago, after all—but instead it felt natural, like her body had been designed to fit exactly here, in this space against his ribs, with her head tucked under his chin and her hand resting over his heart.

She could feel his heartbeat beneath her palm,

steady and strong and real. Maybe too real. And the way he held her—carefully, like she was something precious he was afraid of breaking—well, that was real, too.

They talked about meaningless things at first, as though they knew it was best to keep things light. He told her his favorite movie was *Chef*, while hers was *Chocolat*. Then they went on to their worst haircuts—his involved a disastrous attempt to dye his hair blue in high school, while hers was the time she'd cut some bangs at age twelve and looked like she'd been attacked by hedge trimmers right before school pictures were supposed to be taken. Things got spirited when they talked about whether pineapple belonged on pizza—he said absolutely not, while she argued that the sweet-savory combination was exactly what made it work, and in the end, they agreed to disagree on that one.

But gradually, the conversation turned toward more important topics, as if they'd both decided it was okay to go a little deeper. Shane told her about the day he started work at the Asylum, about the terror and exhilaration of knowing he was the youngest person to have ever held that position in the forty-odd years that the restaurant had been open, and about how he'd stood in the empty dining room the night before he began and wondered if he'd made the biggest mistake of his life.

"But you didn't make a mistake," Rosa told him. "You've built something amazing there."

"I'm not so sure about that," Shane replied. "The Asylum is a Verde Valley institution. About all I had to do was continue the tradition without screwing things up."

Amazing how someone so talented could still be so insecure about the thing that was the most important to him. "There's no way you could have screwed it up," she said. "You're an amazing chef, and you work harder than anyone I've ever met. You care about every single detail and every person who walks through your door. There's no way someone like that could have messed up the restaurant."

His arm tightened around her shoulders, pulling her closer. When he spoke, his voice was quiet, almost contemplative. "I think you see me differently than most people do."

"I see you clearly," she corrected him. "Most people just aren't paying attention. Their loss."

Shane pressed a kiss on the top of her head, and her eyes drifted closed as she savored the simple affection of the caress. This comfortable closeness, this feeling of being exactly where she belonged—this was what she'd been looking for in all those awful consort kisses. Not magic or destiny or some cosmic recognition from her *prima* power.

Only connection, choosing someone…and being chosen in return.

Rosa told him about the first painting she ever sold, right after she turned nineteen. It was a small landscape of the desert at sunset that she'd done almost on impulse, more for herself than for anyone else. She'd been shocked when someone at a local art fair had offered her three hundred dollars for it, had experienced a strange mix of pride and vulnerability at the idea of releasing her art into the world.

"It felt like I was giving away a piece of myself," she admitted. "Like that person was going to take that painting home, and I'd never know if they really saw what I was trying to say with it, if they understood the moment I was trying to capture. Or whether they got tired of it after a week and stuck it in the garage or the spare room or something."

His fingers played with the ends of her hair. "I doubt that would ever happen," he said. "But anyway, that's what makes it art. If it was just pretty colors on canvas, it wouldn't matter. But you put something of yourself in that painting, and that's what made those people want to own it."

Rosa tilted her head back to look at him. "Is

that how you think about food? That you're putting truth in it?"

He was silent for a moment, clearly pondering her question. "I think about food as communication. I suppose you could say that every dish is a conversation—I'm saying something with the flavors and textures, and the person eating it is responding. If I've done my job right, then they'll feel something, or they'll be transported somewhere. It's been proven many times that food can fix memory just as much as sound or sight. And that's what I'm trying to create—something that's more than a meal and is a real experience, a moment of connection."

Who knew that the soul of a poet hid inside that no-nonsense exterior?

"That's beautiful," she said.

He chuckled. "You make me sound way more poetic than I am."

"I make you sound like what you are," she said firmly. "And that's an artist."

For a moment, he didn't respond, only sat there in silence. She could feel the tension in his body, as if he was wrestling with something he wanted to say but wasn't sure he should.

"What is it?" she prompted, but gently. She didn't want to disturb this quiet, contemplative mood by asking for more than he was ready to give.

"I don't usually talk like this," he said. "About the 'why' behind what I do. Most people just want to eat good food and don't care about the philosophy of it all. And my staff—sure, they care about technique and execution, but not really about the deeper meaning. It's just work to them, you know? A job they're good at. And they are good at it. But for me, it's…."

He didn't finish the sentence. Maybe he couldn't find the right words.

"It's who you are," she finished for him.

At once, he nodded. "Exactly. Most people don't get that. They think I'm obsessed or a workaholic or just too intense about food."

Rosa shifted on the sofa so she could look at him properly. "I get it. Because painting is who I am, too. Not the *prima* thing—that's what I'm supposed to be, I guess. But art… *that's* me. That's the truest thing about me."

They gazed at each other in the dim light of the living room, and it was as if she could feel something changing between them, growing into something new. This was a deeper recognition, a seeing that went beyond physical attraction or even emotional connection. No, this was about souls recognizing each other, as sappy as that sounded when she tried to articulate it to herself.

"I should probably tell you something," Rosa

said, then stopped herself. All those words about her consort deadline, about not getting involved with anyone and the knowledge that this idyll in Jerome couldn't last forever—they all felt too heavy for this moment, too sharp-edged and reality-soaked for the soft cocoon they'd built here on Shane's couch.

"What?" he asked.

With him looking at her like that, she knew she had to think of something. "Just…thank you, I guess. For today, and for the overlook and the conversation and the—" She gestured vaguely between them. "For this."

"You don't have to thank me for that," he said, his tone quiet but intense. "This has been the best day I've had in years."

She snuggled closer, leaning against him. Her eyelids grew heavy, and she felt the pull of sleep trying to drag her under. She knew she should get up from the couch and go into the guest room, should maintain some kind of boundary, even though they'd already blown past so many others today.

But Shane's heartbeat was steady beneath her ear, his arm warm and secure around her shoulders, and he made her feel like she was in the safest place in the world. Her fingers tightened on his shirt, holding on as though he was an anchor that kept her from drifting away.

"Stay," he murmured, as if he sensed that she was thinking about leaving. "Just stay."

So she stayed. She let herself have this—one night of feeling wholly herself, of being with the man who'd shown her there could be so much more than the life that had been planned for her. One night of believing that maybe, impossibly, this could work.

Even though she knew better. She knew that tomorrow would bring complications and consequences and the hard conversations they'd avoided today.

But tonight, Rosa let herself hope. She let herself imagine a world where she didn't have to choose between duty and desire, where being herself and being the *prima* weren't mutually exclusive...where kissing Shane McAllister could be the beginning of something rather than a beautiful mistake she'd have to pay for later.

Tomorrow, she would be realistic and would face all the impossibilities, would remember all the reasons why falling for Shane was the worst thing she could possibly do right now.

But tonight, wrapped in his arms and lulled by the steady rhythm of his breathing, Rosa let herself believe in fairy tales.

Even if she understood that they didn't come true for girls like her.

9

THE NEXT FEW DAYS SETTLED INTO AN EASY pattern that Rosa thought was both dangerous and inevitable, like watching storm clouds gather on the horizon and knowing you should seek shelter but standing still anyway, mesmerized by their beauty.

She worked in the kitchen four nights a week now, growing more confident in her developing skills with each shift. Now she no longer needed Shane to stand behind her to guide her knife work, although sometimes she caught herself wishing he would anyway, just to feel the solid warmth of him at her back, the careful pressure of his hands over hers.

And she'd started sketching him, too, but she was careful not to let him see those drawings. They were only quick studies of his hands as he worked, or maybe the concentration in his profile when he tasted something or when he was figuring out the details of a new recipe. Each of those sketches felt like a secret she was keeping, a way of holding onto moments she knew couldn't last.

Because that was the thing neither of them talked about—the expiration date stamped on whatever this was between them. She got a call from her mother every couple of days, her voice carefully neutral, asking how her daughter was doing and whether she'd made any progress on "figuring things out."

Rosa knew exactly what that meant.

Are you ready to come home and resume the search?

The answer was still no. With each passing day, Rosa became more certain that the reason she couldn't find her consort was living in his pink house in Jerome, making her laugh over breakfast and teaching her the proper way to deglaze a pan.

She knew her mother wouldn't be this patient forever. Honestly, she'd been pretty much a saint so far, and Rosa could only imagine the blowback she must be getting from the people in their clan. Proper *primas*-in-waiting didn't act this way, and everyone knew it. The only reason Zoe had put up with her daughter's nonsense for this long was that she understood what it was like to think you'd never find your perfect match.

And maybe she was also hoping that Rosa would find her match among the McAllisters, just as she had.

They'd spent that particular Wednesday the way they'd fallen into spending his days off, by working side by side in his home kitchen. Tonight, Shane was testing a new dessert for the Asylum's menu, something with dark chocolate and chili that made Rosa's mouth water just from the aroma that wafted through the kitchen. She was supposed to be helping by preparing the garnishes, but mostly she just watched him work, fascinated by the way he moved through the familiar space with such confidence and grace.

"You're staring again," he said without looking up from the ganache he was whisking.

Heat rose to her cheeks. "I'm observing," she remarked airily. "There's a difference."

"Is there?" He glanced up at her, and the corner of his mouth quirked in a way that made her heart beat a little faster.

"Artists observe things," she said, trying to sound dignified. "It's part of the process."

"Uh-huh." He set down the whisk and moved

closer to her, and suddenly the kitchen felt about three sizes too small. "And what have you observed?"

That I'm falling in love with you, Rosa thought, but luckily, what came out of her mouth was, "You taste everything at least three times before you're satisfied with it."

"Quality control," he said, now sounding amused.

"And you have this little crease between your eyebrows when you're concentrating really hard on getting something exactly right," she went on.

He reached up and touched the spot she'd mentioned, as if he was trying to feel the crease there. "I do?"

"Yes." Rosa found herself moving closer, drawn by some gravitational force she couldn't seem to resist, and she pointed up at his face. "Right there."

His hand dropped, but his eyes stayed locked on hers, coolly blue and intent in the warm kitchen light. "Rosa," he said, and her name sounded different in his mouth, raw and real, like he was tasting it the way he tasted his food. "We should probably—"

Whatever he was about to say was lost as Rosa closed the distance between them and went on her toes so she could kiss him. It was exactly the kind of thing the old Rosa—the careful, dutiful Rosa—

would never have done. But that Rosa felt like a stranger now, someone who'd existed in a different lifetime, long before she'd tasted what it felt like to want someone this much.

Shane made a surprised sound against her mouth, and for a terrible half-second, she thought she'd made a catastrophic mistake, that maybe he was going to push her away and say that they couldn't do this. But then his hands came up to cup her face, and he was kissing her back with an intensity that stole the breath from her lungs.

This kiss was different from the one they'd shared at the overlook. That one had been tentative, questioning, almost sweet in its hesitation. This one was hungry, eight days of accumulated need compressed into this single moment. She grasped Shane's shirt, pulling him closer, and he made a low sound in the back of his throat that sent heat spiraling through her entire body.

They stumbled backward together until her back hit the counter and his body pressed against hers, solid and warm and absolutely perfect. His hands slid from her face down to her waist, his fingers spread wide against her sides, and even through the fabric of her shirt, his touch seemed to burn.

She arched into him, seeking more contact, more heat, more…everything. One of Shane's hands moved up her ribs, his thumb brushing the underside of her breast through her shirt and her bra, and a wave of pleasure shot through her so intense that it was almost painful. She gasped against his mouth, her head falling back, and Shane took advantage of the exposed line of her throat, pressing hot, open-mouthed kisses there that made her knees go weak.

"God, Rosa," he breathed against her skin, and his voice was ragged, barely recognizable. "You're—"

His hand slid higher, cupping her breast properly now, and Rosa tensed. It was involuntary, a full-body reaction she couldn't control, and she hated herself for it even as it happened. At once, Shane froze, his hand going still, and then he was pulling back, putting some space between them.

"Hey," he said, and his voice was gentler now, almost worried. His hands moved to her shoulders, steadying and respectful. "What's wrong? We don't have to—"

"I know," she said quickly, but her voice sounded trembling and weak. Damn it. She could feel tears prickling at the corners of her eyes, which was ridiculous. "I'm sorry. I didn't mean to—"

"You have nothing to apologize for," he said. He ducked his head, trying to catch her gaze. "Rosa, look at me."

She forced her eyes upward and saw only

concern, none of the judgment or frustration she'd been expecting. That made something seem to break inside, as if the careful wall she'd been building around the truth she needed to tell him had suddenly shattered.

"I want this," she said, and the words escaped her lips with far more desperation than she'd intended. "I want you. But I—there's something I need to tell you. Something you deserve to know."

Shane's hands tightened on her shoulders briefly, then relaxed. "Okay," he said simply. "Let's sit down and talk about it."

They moved to the living room, to the couch where they'd fallen asleep together after their kiss at the overlook. Rosa tucked herself into the corner, pulling her knees up to her chest in a defensive posture she recognized but couldn't seem to prevent herself from assuming. Shane sat at the other end, clearly giving her space, his expression patient and attentive.

For a long moment, she couldn't find the words. How could she explain something that was tangled up in tradition and magic and her own complicated feelings about her body and her choices? How could she make him understand without sounding like she was from a different century?

"I'm a virgin," she finally said, the words flat and abrupt in the quiet room. "And I have to stay that way until I find my consort. It's tradition—it's more than tradition. It's tied to the *prima* magic, to proving the bond is real before…before it's consummated. It's not like the *prima* has to wait until she's married, but the connection has to be there first."

Shane's expression didn't change, didn't show surprise or disappointment or any of the reactions Rosa had been bracing herself for. He only nodded slowly.

"Rosa," he said after a moment, "I already knew that."

She stared at him in genuine surprise. "You did?"

Now he almost grinned, a reaction she definitely hadn't been expecting. "I might not have been involved in your consort search, but it's not like I've been hiding under a rock. Angela's daughter went through her own consort search five years ago. I get it."

For a second, Rosa could only stare at him. All this angst about her virgin status, and it turned out to be no big deal, something that Shane had known all along? "So…you get it," she said.

Now he frowned. "What else did you think I was going to say?"

"I don't know." She hugged her knees tighter and made herself go on, even though some part of her was trying to tell her it would be better to let this go. "That it's archaic or ridiculous or that you're disappointed or—"

His voice, quiet but firm, stopped her from going any further. "It's not ridiculous. It's part of your tradition, part of who you are. I guess I'm just sorry that you thought it would bother me." He paused there, and his mouth quirked in a self-deprecating half-smile. "Honestly? It makes me like you more, not less."

"Really?" The word came out almost like a squeak, and she wished she'd kept her mouth shut.

"Really." He reached out, his hand pausing in the space between them, as if he wasn't quite sure whether she would appreciate the gesture.

But she did. She wrapped her fingers around his, glad of their strength, their warmth.

He went on, "You're honoring yourself and your values, and I think that takes a lot of conviction. Why would I be disappointed by that?"

Tears stung her eyes again, but this time they felt different, instead reflecting relief and gratitude. "It's the one thing I haven't compromised," she told him, her voice not much more than a murmur. "It's the one choice I haven't made out of desperation. And I know it's maybe stupid in this day and age, but it matters to me. It feels like… like the last piece of myself that's still just mine, you know?"

"It's not stupid," he said, and gave her hand a

reassuring squeeze. "It's not archaic or old-fashioned or any other judgment you're putting on yourself. It's okay. Really."

The tears spilled over then, and Shane made a soft, concerned sound before moving closer so he could pull her into his arms. She went willingly, pressing her face against his shoulder and letting herself cry.

Maybe she should have been embarrassed by falling apart like this, but right then, it just felt good to finally let go of all the tension she'd been holding inside.

"Hey," he murmured into her hair. "It's okay. We're okay."

"But we're not," Rosa returned, the words muffled by his shirt. She shifted slightly before continuing. "Because I want you, Shane, and I want this. But I can't have it. Not really, anyway. Not the way I want to."

His arms tightened around her. "We'll figure it out," he told her, although his voice contained a note of uncertainty he probably hadn't meant to let slip. "We don't have to have all the answers right now."

Since she didn't know what to say, she only nodded.

They sat like that for a while, with her curled against his chest and his hand moving in slow, soothing circles on her back. Eventually, her breathing evened out, and she felt steady enough to pull back and look at him.

"Thank you," she said. "For understanding...and for not making me feel weird about all this."

"You're not weird," he replied. He reached up and brushed away the lingering tears on her cheeks, the gesture almost a caress. "You're perfect. And we'll figure out what this is between us without pressuring you to compromise something that matters to you. I promise."

She really wanted to believe him. Oh, yes... she wanted to believe they could navigate this impossible situation, that they could be together in all the ways that mattered without crossing the line she'd drawn. But even as she nodded and tried to smile, she could feel the weight of reality pressing down on her.

Because the truth was, she'd already compromised. She'd fallen for a man who wasn't her consort, who couldn't *be* her consort, and every day she stayed in Jerome was another day she wasn't fulfilling her destiny, wasn't doing what generations of de la Paz women before her had done.

But when Shane pulled her close again and pressed a kiss to the top of her head, Rosa let herself pretend that love could be enough and that choosing each other could somehow be enough, even when her magic and her duty and her entire future said otherwise.

"Can I tell you something?" Shane asked after a while, his voice almost diffident now, as if he wasn't sure how his words would be received.

She sat up a little straighter. "Of course."

"My last relationship ended because I didn't know how to be present." He paused, and she could feel the tension in his body, the inner struggle it had taken to share this. "She said I was there, but *not* there. That I was so focused on the restaurant, on my career, that I forgot to actually show up for her."

Rosa lifted her head to look at him. "Shane—"

"She was right," he continued, his gaze somehow distant, as if he was looking back into a past he didn't like very much. "Work was safer than intimacy. And you know, I've always dated civilian women. It just seemed easier that way, because there was always this part of me that I had to keep secret from them." He met her eyes, and she saw a raw honesty in his expression that made her ache to reach out and pull him to her. "But with you, it's different. You make me want to show up."

"You *do* show up," Rosa said softly. "Every single day. You showed up when you let me stay that first night, and you showed up when you gave me a job. You did so much more than you had to, and I'll never forget that."

His hand came up to cup her cheek. "Then we're both learning how to show up, I guess."

She leaned into his touch. It felt so good to have him do something as simple as caress her face, and her body ached for so much more.

"I'm scared," she said at last. "I'm scared of what happens when this ends."

"Then let's not think about endings tonight," he replied. "Let's just be here together, for as long as we can."

And because Rosa didn't have a better answer, because she wanted to hold onto this perfect, impossible thing for as long as the universe would let her, she nodded and settled back against him. Eventually, she fell asleep there, safe in the circle of Shane's arms, and if she dreamed of a future where choosing him didn't mean losing everything else, well, no one had to know but her.

He lay awake long after Rosa's breathing had evened out into sleep, staring at the ceiling and trying not to think about how thoroughly he'd fucked up his carefully constructed life.

He'd had rules…good rules, sensible rules. Don't get involved with anyone who couldn't be part of his long-term plan. Don't let emotions compromise the restaurant. Don't fall for someone whose life was fundamentally incompatible with his own.

He'd broken every single one of those rules, and he'd done it with open eyes, knowing exactly what he was doing and doing it anyway.

Rosa shifted against him, her hand resting against the front of his shirt, and his heart seemed to skip a beat. This woman—this brilliant, complicated, beautiful woman—had walked into his life uninvited and had proceeded to rearrange everything he thought he knew about himself.

He should probably be panicking. This was the time when he normally would be planning his exit strategy, figuring out how to extricate himself before this got any messier. Instead, all he wanted to do was pull her closer and promise her things he had no business promising.

Carefully, so as not to wake her, Shane extricated himself from the couch. Rosa shifted in sleep but seemed content to settle against the pillows, so he judged it safe to go on into the kitchen. The dessert he'd been working on earlier sat abandoned on the counter, the ganache probably ruined by now. He should clean it up, should salvage what he could and start fresh tomorrow.

Instead, he only stood there, his hands braced

on the counter, trying to make sense of the tangle of emotions inside him.

Rosa was a virgin. He'd already known that, even though he would never have asked if she hadn't volunteered the information. But hearing her make that admission with such vulnerability and conviction had shifted something in the way he understood what was going on here.

She wasn't just spending time with him because she was hiding from her responsibilities. This wasn't some casual attraction, a flirtation she was indulging in to pass the time. Every moment they spent together was filled with meaning for her, tangled up in tradition and magic and her own sense of self-worth.

And Shane had no idea what the hell he was supposed to do with any of that.

He couldn't be her consort—they'd established that unfortunate fact definitively at the overlook. Their kiss, as earth-shattering as it had been, hadn't awakened any prima *magic* or forged any mystical bond. Which meant that whatever this was between them, it was temporary, and they were on borrowed time.

The smart thing to do would be to end it now. To sit Rosa down tomorrow and explain, gently but firmly, that they couldn't keep doing this. That she needed to go home and resume her search, and he needed to focus on the restaurant and forget any of this had ever happened.

But even as that thought took shape in his mind, Shane knew he wouldn't do it. Not because he was weak or selfish—although he thought he was definitely both of those things when it came to Rosa Sandoval—but because she needed space to breathe, to be someone other than the *prima*-in-waiting for a while. And somehow, impossibly, she'd chosen him as her safe harbor.

How could he take that away from her?

He pushed himself away from the counter and went to the window so he could look out at the yard, which was dimly lit by the solar lighting he'd installed when he first moved in. Tomorrow he'd have to go back to the restaurant and be the head chef again, the man with the laser focus and the exacting standards.

A man who needed to pretend his life wasn't slowly unraveling.

But tonight, he could just be Shane, the guy who'd somehow gotten lucky enough to have Rosa Sandoval fall asleep on his couch, trusting him with secrets that weighed heavily and were precious in equal measure.

A soft sound from behind him made him turn. Rosa stood in the doorway, her hair tousled from sleep, her eyes soft and unfocused.

"You left," she said, and there was a note of confusion in her voice that made him ache inside.

"I just needed some water," he lied, because the truth—*I was spiraling and didn't want to wake you*—felt like far too much honesty for this fragile moment.

She padded across the kitchen, her bare feet silent on the tile. When she stopped in front of him, it was close enough that he could see the sleep-warmth still lingering in her cheeks, the way her eyes were starting to focus and sharpen as she woke up fully.

"You're thinking too much," she told him. "I can tell. You get this look."

"What look?" he asked, trying to sound casual.

"Like you're trying to solve an impossible equation in your head." She reached up and smoothed the crease between his eyebrows—the one she'd mentioned earlier—with her thumb. "It's not attractive. Well, actually, it's extremely attractive, but it also worries me."

Despite everything, a smile tugged at his mouth. "Sorry. I didn't mean to worry you."

"What were you thinking about?"

How I'm falling in love with you and it's the worst possible timing in the history of bad timing, he thought. What he said was, "I'm just thinking about everything you told me."

He could almost see the way her slender form stiffened. "Having second thoughts?"

"No." The word came out more forcefully than he'd intended, but he needed her to understand this. "No second thoughts. I just want to make sure I'm doing this right. That I'm not… shit, I don't know. Taking advantage of or pressuring you or—"

"Shane." Her hands came up to frame his face, holding him still so he had to look at her. "You're not taking advantage of me. You're not pressuring me. If anything, I'm the one who keeps throwing myself at you."

"You are not—"

"I kissed you tonight," she reminded him. "I kissed you at the overlook, and I'm the one who asked to stay that first night, remember? Every step of this has been mine just as much as yours." Her fingers brushed across his cheekbones, and her expression was fierce and tender at the same time. "So stop trying to protect me from myself, okay? I'm a grown woman making grown-up choices."

He covered her hands with his, holding them against his face. "I just don't want to be another compromise you have to make."

"You're not a compromise," Rosa said, and her voice seemed to break a little on those words.

"You're the opposite of a compromise. You're the first choice I've made in months that feels like it's actually mine."

That comment shouldn't have made him fill with warmth and something dangerously close to hope. But it did, and he was too tired and too far gone to fight it anymore.

"Come here," he said, and pulled her into his arms.

She held on to him tightly, her head pressed against his chest. They stood there in the dark kitchen, holding each other, and Shane let himself have this. Let himself believe, just for tonight, that love could be enough.

Even though he knew better.

"Stay?" Rosa murmured against his chest. "Like before?"

"Always," Shane replied, and if the word carried more weight than it should have, more promise than he had any right to make, neither of them acknowledged it.

By some unspoken agreement, they went to his bedroom this time instead of the couch. Maybe that was a mistake, but he wanted to hold on to her while comfortable in his bed, not cramped on a sofa. He gave Rosa one of his T-shirts to sleep in, and she disappeared into the bathroom to change while he pulled on sleep pants and tried not to imagine what she looked like in his clothes.

When she emerged, drowning in a gray cotton tee that fell to mid-thigh, Shane had to look away before he did something stupid, like tell her she was the most beautiful thing he'd ever seen.

Even though it was only the truth.

They climbed into bed, and Rosa immediately nestled into his side, her head on his chest, her arm draped across his waist. Shane wrapped his arms around her and tried to commit this feeling to memory—the weight of her against him, the trust implicit in every line of her body.

"Shane?" Her voice was sleepy, already starting to fade.

"Yes?"

"Thank you."

He pressed a kiss against the top of her head. "There's nothing to thank me for."

"There is, though." She yawned, the words barely audible. "You make me feel safe. That's not nothing."

As she drifted off to sleep, Shane stared at the ceiling and tried not to think about the conversation he'd have to have with her eventually. Sooner or later, he'd have to admit that he was falling for her…but falling for her changed nothing about her situation, or about what she needed to do.

He guessed that he should probably feel guilty.

But as he lay there in the dark with Rosa safe in his arms, he couldn't quite manage it. For the first time in years, he didn't feel like he was just going through the motions of his life.

And if that was selfish, if he was being a terrible person for not sending her home immediately, well, he'd add it to the list of things he'd have to answer for later.

The next morning came too soon, reality intruding in the form of his alarm shrilling into the watery light of dawn. He had prep work to do before the lunch shift began, inventory to check, and a meeting with his produce supplier that he'd already rescheduled twice.

Rosa stirred beside him, making a soft, protesting sound. "Do you have to go?" she asked sleepily.

"Unfortunately." He leaned over and kissed her forehead, allowing himself one more moment of softness before he had to be the head chef again. "But you can sleep in. I'll leave coffee for you."

"Mmm. You're too good to me." And she was already drifting off again, barely awake.

He slipped out of bed and got ready as quietly as he could, trying not to think about how natural all this felt. It seemed as if they'd been doing this for years instead of only a little more than a week. By the time he was dressed and had drunk his morning coffee, Rosa was deeply asleep again, curled up in his bed like she belonged there.

Shane paused in the doorway, just looking at her so he could memorize every line and curve of her lovely face. Sooner or later—probably sooner—this would be just a memory, a beautiful mistake he'd made one summer in Jerome.

But not yet. Not today.

At the restaurant, he threw himself into work with his usual intensity, trying to burn off the restless energy that had been building within him since last night. He prepped vegetables with unnecessary care, adjusted recipes that didn't need adjusting, and generally drove his staff slightly nuts with his nitpicking.

"You okay, boss?" Kelli asked around midmorning after she watched him rearrange the walk-in cooler for the third time. "You seem kinda tense."

"I'm fine," he replied at once, which was possibly the least convincing lie he'd ever told.

She raised an eyebrow but didn't push it. "Well, if you need to talk or whatever, I'm here.

And Rosa's coming in at four, right? That might help."

The mention of Rosa's name made a sharp surge of anxiety go through him. Seeing Rosa at work meant maintaining professional distance and pretending they were just chef and trainee instead of...whatever they actually were.

"Yeah," he managed. "Four o'clock."

The day passed in its usual blur of prep and service and small crises that only felt like emergencies in the moment and were soon forgotten. But Shane found his attention drifting more than usual, his mind always circling back to Rosa and last night's conversation, to the impossible tangle they'd created.

When four o'clock rolled around and she walked through the back door, his heart wanted to skip a beat. She was wearing her usual work uniform—jeans and sneakers, a black T-shirt, her hair pulled back into a French braid—but he could still see the woman who'd fallen asleep in his bed this morning, could still feel the ghost of her weight against him.

"Hey," she said, and her smile was soft and private, obviously meant just for him. "How's your day been?"

"Busy," he replied, which was true enough, even if it left unsaid a whole hell of a lot of things. "You ready to work?"

"Always." She moved past him to wash her hands, and he had to force himself not to stare, not to look at the curve of her slender waist or the way those jeans hugged her hips and her long, slim legs.

He had to be a professional, no matter what.

The evening service went smoothly enough. The whole time, though, Shane remained completely aware of Rosa in a way that had nothing to do with training and everything to do with the fact that he now knew how she felt when she pressed her body against his...how her beautiful mouth tasted.

It was distracting, dangerously so.

As the night wound down and they were doing the final cleanup, he found her at the sink, scrubbing a stubborn pan. He moved up beside her, ostensibly to help dry dishes, but really just so he could be close.

"You did well tonight," he said in an undertone that he knew no one else could hear.

She glanced at him, the warmth in her gaze unmistakable. "I'm learning from the best."

They finished cleanup side by side, working in comfortable silence. The rest of the staff filtered out gradually—Kelli first, then Mike, then Carlos after a final check of his station. At last, it was just Shane and Rosa, alone in the quiet kitchen.

Not that they would be alone for very long. Connor Wilcox had texted him earlier that day, saying he wanted to swing by that evening after service was done so he could talk to Rosa. There wasn't much Shane could do except agree, and when he'd given her the news, she'd only nodded briefly, as if she also knew that protesting such an incursion wouldn't stop it from happening.

"So," she said as she set down the dish towel, "Connor's supposed to be coming by soon, right?"

Shane looked down at his watch. Most people checked the time on their phones, but obviously, that didn't work so well when your job required your hands to be free at all times. "Any minute, probably."

As if summoned by the mention of his name, a knock came at the back door. Shane went to answer it, and sure enough, Connor Wilcox stood there, looking relaxed and casual in jeans and a dark gray T-shirt. He was in his late fifties, but his dark hair was hardly touched by gray, and he looked at least a decade younger than his actual age.

"Hi, Shane," Connor said. "Thanks for hanging around. I know it's late."

"No problem." Shane stepped aside to let him in. "Rosa's waiting to talk to you."

She stepped away from the sink, and Shane saw the way she squared her shoulders, putting on what he recognized as her public face—the one she wore when she needed to be the *prima's* daughter instead of just Rosa.

"Mr. Wilcox," she said as she extended her hand. "It's nice to finally meet you."

"Connor, please." He shook her hand warmly. "And the pleasure's mine."

They moved to one of the dining room tables, and Shane excused himself to give them privacy. But as he busied himself with unnecessary tasks in the kitchen, he couldn't help but notice the earnest way Rosa was talking, the animated gestures of her hands, the vulnerability in her expression.

She was asking Connor about balancing art and duty, Shane realized after a second or two. About how to be a *prima*—or in Connor's case, both a *primus* and the consort of a *prima*—while still maintaining your own identity and dreams.

The conversation went on for more than half an hour before Connor finally got up. Shane walked him to the door while Rosa tidied up their table.

"She's something special," Connor said quietly. "She reminds me of little of Angela, actually. She has that same fire in her belly."

"Yes," Shane agreed. For some reason, he

needed to clear his throat before he added, "She is special."

Connor gave him a long, assessing look. "You're in love with her."

It wasn't a question, but Shane found himself replying anyway. "I don't know if it's that simple."

"It never is," Connor said with a small smile. "But that doesn't make it any less true."

After Connor left, Shane found Rosa standing in the dining room, staring at nothing in particular. He paused next to her and waited for her to speak.

"Connor told me something interesting," she remarked. "He said that the right partner makes you stronger, not smaller, but you have to be honest about who you are."

"That sounds like good advice."

"Is it, though?" She looked up at him, and he saw something raw and aching in her expression. "Because I've been honest with you, Shane. I've told you about the whole consort mess, about the virginity thing, about all of it. And you've been honest with me. But none of that honesty changes the fundamental problem, does it? We can't actually be together, not in the way that matters."

He wanted to argue, wanted to tell her they'd

find some loophole or solution that would make all this work. But he knew such words would be pointless.

"I don't know what to tell you," Shane said at length. "I don't have answers. I just know that being with you—even in this temporary, impossible way—feels more real than anything else."

Her eyes seemed unnaturally bright, but whatever tears had formed there didn't fall. "I know," she whispered. "That's the whole problem, isn't it? This feels real. But my magic apparently says otherwise."

They stood there for a moment, the impossible weight of their predicament pressing down on them. Shane realized that this was the conversation he'd been dreading, the one where they had to acknowledge that no amount of feeling or wanting or choosing could change the fundamental incompatibility of their situations.

But before either of them could say the words that would break this fragile thing between them, Rosa held out her hand.

"Take me home?" she asked. "I don't want to think about tomorrow yet. I just want tonight."

Shane took her hand and pulled her close. "We'll figure it out," he said, even though he had no idea how.

It was a promise he had no business making.

But as he stood there with her in his arms, Shane found himself believing it anyway.

Because the alternative—letting her go, watching her walk away to find the consort her magic demanded—was unthinkable.

Even if it was inevitable.

10

THE RESTAURANT WAS QUIET IN THE afternoon lull between lunch service and evening prep, the kind of peaceful stillness Shane usually savored. Most of his staff had left to have a late lunch of their own, and he'd sent Rosa home earlier to rest after a particularly brutal dinner rush the night before. But then she'd texted him around two, asking if she could come in early, and he'd said yes without hesitation, even though he knew he should probably be maintaining better boundaries and should have found an excuse to keep her away until everyone had come in for dinner prep.

Oh, who was he kidding? All his boundaries had pretty much gone out the window the moment he'd kissed her at the overlook.

Now she stood at the prep station, methodically *brunoise*-ing carrots, brow furrowed in the sort of focused concentration that always awakened a certain warmth within him. She'd come so far in just two weeks—her knife work was clean and efficient now, her movements more confident. It was kind of crazy how much she belonged in his kitchen when he thought about how foreign this work had been for her only a short time ago.

"You're getting good at that," he said as he walked over so he could get a better look at her technique.

She glanced up, a pleased smile touching her lips. "That's high praise from Chef McAllister."

He shrugged. "I don't give praise that isn't earned." He watched her work for another moment, then decided to go for it. The kitchen was empty, and he might as well give this a try. "Put those down. I want to teach you something."

Her eyebrows lifted as she looked at him, expression questioning. "What kind of something?"

"How to make risotto from scratch," he replied.

"Risotto?" Rosa set down her knife and turned to face him. "Isn't that supposed to be really hard?"

"It's technique-intensive," he told her. "But it's not really about difficulty. It's more about patience and attention…and trusting the process."

He went over to the pantry and got out the container of arborio rice, and then headed into the walk-in cooler to fetch white wine, chicken stock, butter, and parmesan. After he'd assembled everything on the counter next to one of the big industrial stoves, he said, "I think you're ready for it."

She followed him over there, and he could practically feel the curiosity radiating off her in waves. "What makes risotto so special?"

"The texture," he replied as he set a heavy-bottomed pan on the burner. "When it's done right, it's creamy without being heavy, each grain of rice distinct but bound together by the starch. It shouldn't be soupy, but it shouldn't be stiff, either. It needs to move on the plate—what the Italians call *all'onda.* Like a wave."

Again, her eyebrows lifted. "That sounds pretty poetic for plain old rice."

He could only smile. "Just wait until you taste it."

They began the process with her heating olive oil in the pan while he diced shallots. Once the oil began to shimmer, he guided her through sweating the shallots until they turned translucent, the kitchen filling with their sweet, pungent aroma.

"Now the rice," Shane said as he measured out the arborio. "Add it to the pan and stir it around in the oil. We're toasting it, waking up the starches."

Obediently, Rosa poured in the rice and began stirring it with a wooden spoon. He moved behind her—closer than was strictly necessary, close enough that he could smell the warm, floral scent of her shampoo mixed with the sharp bite of shallots—and placed his hands over hers.

"Like this," he murmured near her ear. "Keep it moving. You want every grain coated."

He felt rather than saw Rosa's breath catch, felt the way she leaned back into him ever so slightly. The rice made a gentle rattling sound against the pan, and Shane found himself noting every point of contact between them—her back against his chest, his hands covering hers, the way her hips fit perfectly against him. A wave of need went through his body, and he wrestled his attention back to the stove.

"How do I know when it's ready?" she asked, and now her voice sounded slightly breathless.

"You'll see the grains start to look translucent at the edges. There—see?" He guided her hand, tilting the pan slightly so she could get a better look at the rice inside. "Now we deglaze with wine."

He reached around her for the bottle of white wine, his arm brushing against her side. She made a small sound—not quite a gasp, but close—and he had to remind himself that they were cooking and that he needed to maintain some semblance of professionalism.

"Pour it in," he told her. The words sounded too brisk, and he knew he was compensating for the way his body wanted to respond to her nearness. "All at once. It'll hiss and steam."

Rosa poured, and the pinot grigio hit the hot pan with a violent sizzle, steam rising in a fragrant cloud. The acrid smell of alcohol burned off quickly, leaving behind the wine's fruity, acidic notes.

"Now we stir until the wine is absorbed," he said, still standing behind her, still guiding her hands with his. "This is where patience comes in. Risotto can't be rushed. You have to respect the process."

"What if I mess it up?" she asked. She was stirring steadily now, the rice drinking in the wine as she worked. "What if I add too much liquid too fast?"

"Then it won't come together right," Shane replied. He could feel the warmth radiating off her body, could sense the slight tremor in her hands. "You'll end up with rice soup instead of risotto. The magic is in the slow addition of liquid—it allows the starch to release gradually, creating that creamy texture."

A nod, although she didn't look up from the pan. "So…patience is part of the recipe."

"Patience is everything," he responded, and he wasn't entirely sure they were still talking about risotto.

The wine had been absorbed now, the rice looking thirsty and dry. Shane reached for the ladle and the pot of warm stock he'd prepared earlier.

"One ladle at a time," he instructed her, his hand over Rosa's as she scooped up the golden liquid. "Add it, stir until it's absorbed, and then add more. You're building layers."

"This is going to take forever," she remarked, but there was no complaint in her tone. It was an observation, nothing more.

"About twenty minutes," he said. "Which is why most restaurants don't make risotto to order. It's a labor of love."

They fell into a rhythm—ladle, stir, absorb, repeat. He knew he should have stepped away and allowed her to work on her own now that she understood the technique. But he couldn't seem to make himself move, couldn't give up the feeling of her body against his, or the intimate collaboration of their hands moving together.

"Tell me what you're feeling," Shane said after a few minutes. "Through the spoon," he added, realizing there were several different ways she could have interpreted that statement.

Rosa tilted her head slightly as she considered his request. "The resistance feels like it's changing. At first, the rice was hard, almost crunchy against the spoon. Now it's starting to give a little. And the liquid is getting thicker and creamier."

"Exactly," he said, pleased she was able to sense the changes taking place in the pan. "You're feeling the starch release. Just keep going."

The risotto transformed as ladle after ladle of stock was added to the mixture. He'd shifted slightly so he could watch Rosa's face as she worked, and he thought he saw the exact moment when she started to understand what was truly happening in the pan. Her movements became more confident, and he could tell that she was learning to read the rice and trust her senses.

"I keep wanting to turn up the heat and make it go faster," she admitted, a wry smile touching her lips.

"I know." Throughout, Shane had kept one hand on hers, ready to step in if necessary. "But if you do, the outside of the rice will cook too fast, and the inside will stay hard. You'll get the texture all wrong. Sometimes the only way to get what you want is to slow down and let things develop at their own pace."

She turned her head just slightly, and now

their faces were just inches apart. "Are we still talking about risotto?" she asked.

He couldn't help smiling a little. "I don't know. Are we?"

They held each other's gaze for a long moment, the risotto bubbling gently between them. Then Rosa turned back to the pan, but Shane could see the flush touching her cheeks, could feel the way her pulse had started racing beneath his fingertips where they rested on her wrist.

"More stock," she murmured.

Shane added another ladle, and they continued the ritual. The afternoon light slanted through the kitchen windows, turning everything to shades of gold and amber. The restaurant felt like its own private world, removed from reality and all its complications.

"Now we should test it," he said once the rice had absorbed most of the latest addition of stock. He brought the wooden spoon to his lips and tasted, the rice tender but with just the faintest bite of resistance at the center. "Almost there. One more ladle, and then we'll finish it."

She added the final measure of stock, stirring it in with movements that seemed much more assured than they'd been when they started. Once it was absorbed, Shane reached around her for the butter and parmesan.

"Now the *mantecatura,*" he said. "This is where we bring it all together. Take it off the heat."

Rosa moved the pan to a cool burner, and he added a generous knob of cold butter and a handful of freshly grated Parmesan. "Stir it in. Vigorously. This is where that creamy, flowing texture comes from."

He kept his hands over hers as they beat the butter and cheese into the risotto, watching it transform from something that looked fairly ordinary into something luscious and silky. The rice began to move in waves, each grain distinct but bound to its neighbors by the glossy, creamy sauce.

"There," he breathed against Rosa's ear. "Do you see it? The way it flows?"

"It's beautiful," Rosa replied, wonder clear in her voice. "I can't believe I actually made this."

"You did." Finally…reluctantly…he stepped back, although his hands lingered on her waist for just a little longer than they needed to. "No magic, just you."

She turned to face him then, and her eyes were bright with the thrill of accomplishment. "Thank you for trusting me with this."

"You earned it." He grabbed two small plates from the shelf and reached for a fresh spoon. "But we need to taste it while it's perfect. Risotto waits for no one."

Once the dishes were waiting on the countertop, he plated the risotto with care, creating a small mound in the center of each plate and using the back of the spoon to spread it outward in a gentle wave. A drizzle of good olive oil, a few shavings of parmesan, and a grind of black pepper. Simple and elegant, just the way he liked it.

They sat side by side at the prep station. It might not have been quite professional and definitely wasn't appropriate, but Shane was past caring about appearances. Rosa took her first bite, and her eyes fluttered closed in a way that made his breath catch.

"Oh, my God," she murmured. "This is incredible."

"That's all you," he replied. "Your work, your effort."

"And your teaching." She took another bite, savoring it, eyes half shutting again as she appeared to concentrate on all the flavors rolling across her tongue. "I can taste the layers. The toasted rice, the wine, the stock, the butter and cheese—they're all distinct but working together. Like…like an orchestra or something."

"Exactly like that." He finally ate a forkful of his own portion, pleased with how well it had turned out. "Each element needs to be perfect on its own, but the real magic is in how they come together."

They ate in friendly silence for a few minutes, and Shane found himself watching Rosa more than eating. He loved seeing the way she closed her eyes to better focus on the flavors, and the small, satisfied sound she made when something was particularly delicious.

"Can I tell you something?" Rosa asked as she set down her fork.

"Always," he replied. He doubted he would ever tire of hearing about her, about her life before she came to Jerome.

"The first time I really understood what you meant about creating without relying on magic, I was maybe nine or ten." She shifted on her stool so they were face-to-face. "I wanted to paint this sunset I'd seen, and I was so excited about it. But when I showed my mother, she said something that stuck with me."

Shane waited, attentive.

"She said, 'You know, Rosa, your art is the one thing that's completely yours. No magic, no destiny, no expectations. Just you and what you see.' And I realized— " Rosa paused there, her expression appearing to soften as she replayed the memory in her mind. "I realized that painting was my escape. It was the one place where being a witch or a *prima*-in-waiting didn't matter. When I painted, I didn't have to be anything except myself."

"That must have felt like freedom," he said.

"It did. I mean, it does." Her smile turned rueful. "Although that first sunset painting was terrible. The proportions were all wrong, the colors were muddy, and the whole thing was a total disaster."

Shane thought of his first experiments in the kitchen, the utter messes he'd made before his magic truly began to kick in and guided him toward excellence. Now he couldn't help wondering what he would have done if his magical gift had been something else entirely, and he would have had to rely on human grit and nothing more. Lately, of course, he'd prided himself on knowing that he didn't need his magic to be a good chef. When he was a kid, though, he'd enjoyed having that extra boost.

"But you kept doing it," he said.

"But I kept doing it," she echoed. "Because as bad as that first painting was, it was mine. Really, truly mine in a way nothing else in my life was. And that mattered more than being perfect."

He reached over and took her hand, felt her fingers warm and stronger than they looked as they twined with his. "I think that's what makes great artists—knowing when to let go of perfection and just create something honest."

"Is that how you feel about cooking?" Rosa asked then. "Like your magic is a tool, but not the whole story?"

"Exactly." Was there anything more perfect than sitting here in one of his favorite spaces, holding the hand of one of his favorite people? It felt better than he ever could have imagined to be with someone who seemed to understand him so completely. "My magic helps me taste things more clearly, and it helps me sense when something's off. But the actual work is pretty much all me. I like to think that's the part that matters."

Her gaze met his, golden-green in the warm afternoon light. "I love the way you pour yourself into your work, the way you make everything you touch better, more beautiful."

Those words hung between them, filled with all the things they were both trying not to acknowledge. Shane knew he should pull back, should put some professional distance between them before someone walked in and saw them sitting there holding hands like teenagers.

Instead, he leaned in and kissed her. Her mouth was soft and tasted of butter and parmesan.

She tasted amazing, and he never wanted to stop.

When they broke apart, her expression was

worried and yet somehow hopeful at the same time. "We should probably—" she began.

"I know," Shane broke in. "Everyone will be arriving soon."

But neither of them moved. They sat there in the quiet kitchen, hands clasped as the risotto cooled on their plates, and let themselves have this moment of perfect stillness before reality came crashing back in.

Later that night, after service was over and she was back in Shane's guest room—it now felt almost more like home than her bedroom back in Scottsdale, thanks to some handmade odds and ends she'd bought at local shops—Rosa pulled out her sketchbook.

She knew she'd never be able to truly capture what had happened in the kitchen that afternoon, the way Shane had stood behind her, his hands over hers, patient and sure. And a drawing certainly couldn't convey how his voice had dropped to that low, rough register that made her skin prickle with awareness, or the way he'd looked at her when she'd made something beautiful, like she was the most remarkable thing he'd ever seen.

But damn it, she was going to try.

First, she'd begin with his hands. She'd always loved drawing hands—they told so much about a person, the way they moved, the care they took or didn't take. Shane's hands were chef's hands, capable and scarred, strong but surprisingly gentle. She sketched them in motion, stirring, tasting, adjusting. She captured the way his fingers held a knife, the way they curved around a spoon, the way they'd felt covering hers.

Then she moved on to draw his face. It was harder than she'd thought to capture the concentration that transformed his features when he worked, turning his usually guarded expression into something open and almost vulnerable. But at least she could draw the tiny crease between his eyebrows that she'd noticed that first day, and do her best to also sketch out the way his mouth softened when he tasted something that pleased him.

She drew him in profile, his attention on the stove as he was lost in the ritual of creation. Sketching his shoulders made her appreciate all over again the breadth of them, the way his chef's whites stretched across his back when he reached for something.

And as she drew, she let herself feel everything she'd been trying not to feel. The love that had been growing within her was almost a living thing, demanding space, needing acknowledgment. Beneath that love, though, was the grief of knowing this couldn't last, along with the desperate hope that maybe, impossibly, they'd find a way.

Something Connor Wilcox had said to her last night echoed in her mind.

The right partner makes you stronger, not smaller. But you have to be honest about who you are.

Shane made her stronger. He saw her—not the *prima*-in-waiting, not the dutiful daughter, but Rosa. The woman who wanted to create, who wanted to choose her own path, who wanted love that wasn't dictated by destiny or magic or tradition.

But was that enough? *Could* it be enough?

She didn't have an answer to that question. No, she only had this moment...and this sketchbook filling up with drawings of a man she couldn't have but couldn't find the strength to give up.

Letting out a breath, she turned to a fresh page and started drawing them together—Shane standing behind her at the stove, their hands joined, their bodies close. She couldn't see their faces in this composition, only the lines of their bodies and the way they fit together.

As her pencil moved across the paper, she realized this was what she wanted. Forget about destiny, forget about magic. What was really important was two people choosing each other, showing up for each other, making each other stronger.

Unfortunately, wanting something and being able to have it were two entirely separate things.

She finished the sketch and sat there for a moment, gazing down at what she'd created. It was good—maybe some of her best work. She'd captured something true in these drawings, something that mattered.

But she wasn't sure if that was enough.

A soft knock at the door made her look up. "Come in," she called out.

Shane opened the door and leaned against the frame. Just as he did every night after he got home from work, he'd changed out of his whites into sweatpants and a T-shirt, his hair slightly damp from his ritual shower that washed away the day's labors. He looked tired but content, and her heart did that ridiculous fluttering thing it did every time she saw him.

"I'm making tea," he said. "Want some?"

"Yes, please."

She closed her sketchbook—she wasn't ready to show him what she'd been working on—and followed him to the kitchen. Shane moved around the space with easy familiarity, filling the kettle, pulling down mugs, selecting tea bags from the collection in his cupboard.

"Is chamomile okay?" he asked.

"It's perfect."

She knew better than to drink caffeine this late at night.

They waited for the water to boil, both of them fine with being quiet at the end of a long day. Rosa perched on one of the kitchen stools while Shane leaned against the counter, and the quiet domesticity of the moment made her ache even more for all the things she couldn't have.

"Today was good," he said after a moment. "The risotto lesson. You really understood how the dish is supposed to work."

"I loved it," she replied. "The whole process. It felt kind of like a meditation or something."

He smiled in response to that comment. "That's a good way to describe it. Cooking at its best is a form of meditation. You're completely in the moment, completely focused on what you're doing."

"Is that what you love about it?" she asked.

"Partly." He poured hot water over the tea bags, and steam began to rise from their mugs in delicate curls. "But it's more than that. When I'm cooking—*really* cooking, not just going through the motions—I feel like I'm exactly where I'm supposed to be, doing exactly what I'm supposed to be doing. Does that make sense?"

"It makes perfect sense." She accepted the

mug he handed her, wrapping her hands around its warmth. A cup of tea always felt cozy, even on a warm summer night. "It's kind of that way when I paint. Like everything else falls away, and it's just me and the canvas."

He came over so he stood next to her, close enough that their arms brushed. "You should paint more," he told her. "While you're here, I mean. I know you've been sketching, but you should set up in the spare room or something so you can really create. People come from all over to paint the landscapes around here."

The casual way he said *while you're here* made Rosa's throat tighten, as if her time in Jerome had an expiration date. Which it did, of course. She couldn't hide here forever.

But she wasn't ready to think about that yet.

"Maybe I will," she said softly. "If you're sure you don't mind. Painting can be kind of messy."

"'Mind'?" he repeated, then shook his head. "Rosa, I'd love to see you paint. I'd love to watch you create something from nothing the way you watched me today."

They sipped their tea in silence as they stood close in the warm kitchen. Outside, Jerome was quiet, the town settled in for the night. And here, in this small pink house, Rosa let herself pretend that this was her life. That she could stay here with Shane, making risotto and drinking tea and falling more in love with him every day.

It was a beautiful lie.

But for tonight, she'd let it be enough.

"Thank you," she said suddenly. "For today, I mean."

He set down his mug and turned to face her. "It's something I wanted to do. Just like this."

And then he leaned in and kissed her—soft and sweet and full of unspoken promises they both knew he couldn't keep. She kissed him back, pouring everything she felt into the press of her lips against his, the gentle tangle of their tongues, the sweet ache of wanting more than they could have.

When they broke apart, Shane rested his forehead against hers. "Stay tonight?" he murmured. "With me?"

Rosa knew she should say no. Yes, she'd slept beside him in his bed, and nothing had happened, but she still understood that she should maintain some boundaries, should protect her heart from the inevitable breaking that was coming.

"Yes," she whispered instead. "I'll stay."

Because some moments were worth stealing, even when you knew they couldn't last.

And Shane McAllister was worth every impossible, beautiful, doomed moment she could have with him.

11

ANOTHER TUESDAY ROLLED AROUND. IT WAS the kind of perfect June morning that made Rosa understand why people fell in love with this part of Arizona. The sky was cloudless and brilliantly blue, and even though she knew the temperature would warm up as the day wore on, for now it was a pleasant seventy-five degrees, just right for taking a stroll.

After more than two weeks in Jerome, she'd developed her own rhythm separate from her work at the restaurant. Lately, she'd been waking early and slipping out of the house before Shane even stirred, leaving him a note on the kitchen counter so he wouldn't get worried when he awoke and saw she wasn't home. She'd told him she liked to walk around town in the early hours when everything was quiet, which was true enough. What she hadn't told him was where those walks usually ended.

Today, though, she wanted him to see.

They'd had breakfast together—scrambled eggs and toast, some more of that absolutely sublime French roast—and now Shane was looking at her with curious amusement as she grabbed her bag and headed for the door.

"So where are we going?" he asked as he followed her outside. The morning sun glinted down on his hair, turning it to pure gold. "You've been very mysterious about this."

"You'll see." Even as she spoke, however, a nervous thrill worked its way down her spine. She'd been working on the paintings for over a week now, stealing hours in the early morning before the town woke up, but she'd kept them a secret until now. What if it turned out that they weren't good enough? What if Shane looked at them with polite disappointment, and she'd have to see in his eyes that her art was just a hobby after all, nothing that truly mattered?

But she'd decided last night, as she lay in his arms in the dark, that she wanted to share this with him. He'd given her so much, and she wanted to give him something back. She wanted him to see this part of her that had nothing to do with being a *prima*-in-waiting or even learning how to work in a restaurant.

They walked down the steep hill toward Main Street, passing the familiar homes on Paradise Lane before they descended into the more public part of town, walking by galleries just starting to open for the day and coffee shops with locals gathered outside. She led him to a small building she'd discovered about a week earlier, tucked between a jewelry store and a vintage clothing boutique. The sign above the door read "Copper Hill Studio & Gallery" in faded lettering.

"I've walked past this place a hundred times," Shane said as he stared at the storefront with new interest. "I didn't know they had studio space."

"In the back," she told him. As she spoke, she pushed open the door, and a bell chimed overhead. The front room was a gallery space, its walls covered with paintings and photographs by local artists.

"Morning!" Judith called out from behind the counter. She was in her early sixties, with graying dark hair pulled back into a careless bun and perpetual paint stains on her hands.

"Morning, Judith," Rosa said evenly enough, although her cheeks warmed for some inexplicable reason. Maybe it was just that she and Shane weren't out in public much together unless they were at the restaurant. She gathered herself and went on, "Shane, this is Judith Cooper. She owns the studio. Judith, this is Shane McAllister."

"The chef from the Asylum," Judith said, coming around the counter to shake his hand. "Rosa's told me about you. She says you're teaching her to cook."

"She's a quick study," Shane replied, but his gaze had shifted to Rosa, clearly questioning.

"Go on back," Judith said to Rosa as she gave her an encouraging smile. "Show him what you've been working on."

Now his eyes were even more full of questions, but she didn't say anything as she led him through a doorway covered by a beaded curtain, down a short hall, and into the back studio. It was a large, open space with high ceilings and huge windows that let in floods of natural light. Several easels were set up around the room, some with works in progress, others empty and waiting. The smell of paint and turpentine hung in the air, oddly comforting.

In the far corner, Rosa had claimed a space for herself. Three canvases sat on easels, all of them covered with drop cloths. Several more leaned against the wall and were also covered. Her supplies were arranged neatly on a small table—brushes in jars, tubes of paint lined up by color, palette knives and rags.

Shane stood in the middle of the room and looked around with an expression she couldn't quite read. "You've been coming here every morning?"

"Most mornings," she replied. She twisted her hands together and wondered if this had been such a good idea after all. They were here now, though, so there wasn't much she could do except keep going. "I wanted to paint, like you said. But I wasn't sure if anything I made would be worth showing you, and I didn't want to make a mess in your house. So I thought I'd work on them here first and see if they turned into something."

His eyes were very kind. "Can I see them?"

Well, this was what they'd come here for. Even so, Rosa made herself take a breath before she walked over to the first easel. Then she pulled off the drop cloth in one quick motion before she could lose her nerve.

The painting beneath was of Jerome itself, the town cascading down the mountainside in a tumble of colorful buildings and steep streets. She hadn't tried to paint it realistically, though. Instead, she'd rendered it in warm, glowing colors—golds and oranges and deep crimsons, as if the whole town was lit from within. The buildings seemed to shimmer, and if you looked closely, you could see tiny hints of magic woven through the composition—a suggestion of energy in the brushstrokes, a sense of something alive beneath the surface. Anyone not of witch-kind would probably think that was artistic license and nothing else, but she hoped Shane would be able to see the small suggestion of the magic that wove itself through the place, a quality born of generations of McAllisters living there.

He moved closer, his gaze tracking across the canvas. However, he didn't say anything, and worry roiled in her stomach.

Maybe this really had been a horrible idea.

"It's Jerome, but kind of how I feel it," she said, the words tumbling out into the silence. "Like there's this energy here, this magic that comes from the McAllisters, but also the town itself—you know, the history and the art, the way people seem driven to create things here."

Finally, he spoke. "It's beautiful. I've never seen Jerome like this, but now that you've painted it, I can't unsee it. This is exactly what the town feels like."

Relief flooded through her, and she wanted to hug him. That didn't seem like the best of ideas, though, not with Judith just in the other room, so she only replied, "You think so?"

"I know so." The words were emphatic, and he turned away from the painting to look at her. "What else have you done?"

Much more relaxed now that the initial reveal was over, Rosa uncovered the second easel. This one showed the Verde Valley spread out below

Jerome, painted during sunset. The sky was a riot of purples and pale blue and rose, and the valley floor had been rendered in deep golds and greens that suggested mystery and depth. A hawk soared through the sky, its wings spread wide, and something about the way Rosa had captured it made the bird seem like a spirit or a messenger rather than just an animal.

"The overlook," Shane said. "Where we—"

"Where we first kissed," Rosa cut in, figuring there wasn't much point in dancing around what they'd done in that scenic spot. "I couldn't stop thinking about the view and about the moment we shared."

He reached out and took her hand, his fingers warm and callused against hers. "You captured something I thought I felt right then but couldn't put into words. A kind of sense of being suspended between earth and sky, between what is and what could be...if that makes any sense."

It made perfect sense to her. She'd hoped he would understand, but hearing him articulate the sensation so perfectly made her heart ache.

"One more," she said, then gently let go of his hand so she could move to the third easel. This was the one she was the most nervous about, the one that felt the most revealing. But she knew he'd ask if she didn't show him the final painting, so she pulled off the drop cloth and stepped back.

He'd been wearing an encouraging half-smile, but now he went very still.

The painting showed the kitchen at the Asylum, but not as it appeared in harsh fluorescent light or during the chaos of service. This was the kitchen as Rosa saw it…as she saw Shane in it. The whole space seemed to glow from within, rendered in rich umber and soft gold, every surface catching and reflecting light. You could see the stove where Shane worked, the prep stations, the shelves of ingredients. But more than that, you could feel the love in every brushstroke, the care and attention given to every detail. It was a kitchen, of course, but it was also a temple, a place where creation happened.

And in the center of it all, barely suggested but unmistakable, was Shane himself—a figure of dark and light, his hands moving in the work he loved.

"Rosa," he breathed, then moved even closer to the canvas, his gaze seeming to take in every detail. "Is this how you see it? How you see my kitchen?"

"It's how I see you in it," she replied. The words were a hoarse whisper, and she cleared her throat before continuing. "It's like…everything you touch turns to light, turns to something beautiful."

Shane turned to look at her, and she saw

something raw in his expression, something open and wondering. "No one's ever—" He stopped there, swallowed, and then went on, "I've never had anyone see my work like this."

What could she do except take a step toward him? "That's because most people are just eating dinner," she said softly. "They're not watching you create. But I've been watching, Shane. I've seen the art in what you do."

He reached for her then and pulled her into his arms. It felt so good for him to hold her that she didn't even care whether Judith saw them, or if any of the other people who shared the work space might stumble upon their embrace. For a long moment, they only stood there, holding each other in the paint-scented studio while morning light poured through the windows.

"Thank you," he murmured against her hair. "I'm so glad you showed me this."

"I wanted you to see it," she replied. "I wanted you to understand that the art is who I am. Not the whole *prima* thing."

Shane took a single step back, just far enough so he could gaze down into her face. "I know. From the moment you talked about that abstract painting in the gallery, I could tell this was your real language. I don't ever want you to lose that."

Neither did she. Fate, she feared, had other plans for her, though.

~

Standing in the studio with Rosa's paintings surrounding him, Shane thought he felt something shift in his understanding of who she truly was. Sure, he'd known she was talented. After all, he'd seen some of her sketches and had watched the way she observed the world with an artist's eye. But these paintings were something else entirely. They were mature and sophisticated, full of vision and technical skill and a depth of feeling that took his breath away.

Someone who could paint like that shouldn't be doing anything else.

"Could you show me the others?" he asked, and gestured toward the covered canvases that leaned against the wall.

Maybe she hesitated for a moment. She didn't make any protest, however, and went ahead and uncovered them one by one. There was a series of smaller paintings—studies of light and color, experiments with texture and composition. Some were abstract, pure explorations of how colors interacted. Others were more representational, but still loose and impressionistic.

And there, at the end, was a painting that made his breath catch in his throat.

It was him. Or rather, it was an impression of him, one rendered in bold, confident strokes. You couldn't see his face clearly, couldn't make out precise details. But you could get a sense of him, of his dark gold hair and the way he stood, as though he was about to break into movement at any second. His hands were more defined than the rest of him, captured mid-gesture.

"When did you paint this?" he asked. True, it wasn't as if they spent every waking hour together, but he was still impressed at the body of work she'd managed to put together in such a short amount of time.

"Last week," she replied. "After the risotto lesson. I couldn't stop thinking about your hands and the way you move. I wanted to capture it, but not realistically. I just wanted to paint the feeling of watching you work."

Shane moved closer to the canvas so he could really study it. Once again, she'd used warm colors —golds and ambers and deep burgundies—and the paint was thick in places, thin in others, creating a sense of energy and motion. It was beautiful. It was him, but also more than him— an idealized version, or perhaps simply the version Rosa saw when she looked at him.

"This is incredible," he said. She stood a few feet away, and he turned to look at her, needing her to understand what he was saying. "Rosa, this isn't just good. This is real art, the kind that should be in a gallery."

She shook her head, and doubt was obvious in her expression even from this distance. "I don't know about that. I mean, I love painting, but I've never really thought about it as anything more than just something I do for myself."

"Why not?" he asked. He moved over so he was standing in front of the kitchen painting again. "Look at this. You've captured something essential here. I'm not talking about just technical skill, although it has that as well. But it's also deeply felt. You're really saying something with these paintings."

When she replied, her voice sounded small and uncertain. "But what if I'm not good enough? What if my art doesn't matter beyond just being a hobby?"

He didn't answer right away, because he knew he had to be careful about how he replied. She needed to hear this, needed to understand. "Does my cooking matter beyond just feeding people?" he asked at length.

She blinked at him. "Of course it does. You create experiences and memories. You make people feel things."

"Exactly," he said, glad that she was able to see through to the heart of the matter. "And that's what art does—*all* art, whether it's food or paintings or music. It's not about being 'good enough' by some arbitrary standard. No, it's about taking what you feel and see and experience, and translating it into something others can feel and see and experience, too." He gestured toward the kitchen painting again, although he hoped she realized he was talking about all of her work as a whole. "And this—these paintings—they're true. I can feel it, and I think anyone who looks at them will feel it, too."

Unshed tears glittered in the smoky hazel depths of her eyes. "You really think so?"

"I know so." He stepped toward her so he could take her hands in his. "I spend every day trying to create something that matters, something that goes beyond just putting food on a plate. And these paintings? They matter, Rosa. They matter just as much as anything I've ever made."

She clung to his hands as if they were a lifeline, a rope thrown to someone floundering in deep water. "No one's ever said that to me before. My family supports my art, but they also always make it clear that it's secondary to being the *prima*-in-waiting. Like it's a nice hobby but not the real thing."

"Well, they're wrong," he said, not caring if that sounded harsh. "This is the real thing, and if they can't see it, then that's on them."

She let out a shaky laugh. "How did you get so good at seeing people?"

"I'm not," he told her. "Usually, I'm terrible at it. I'm too focused on work, too caught up in my own head. But with you—" He paused there, trying to find the right words. "With you, it's easy. You're easy to see because you're brave enough to show yourself."

They stood there for a moment, hands clasped, surrounded by those magnificent paintings and the sharp tang of turpentine. Then an idea sprang into his head.

"Can I watch you work?" he asked. "I mean, if you're comfortable with it. I'd love to see your process."

Surprise showed clearly in her lovely, luminous eyes. "You want to watch me paint?"

"I want to understand how you do what you do," he told her. "The way you watched me in the kitchen. I want to learn to see the world through your eyes."

A smile spread across her face, tentative at first, then growing more confident. "Okay," she said. "Yes, I'd like that."

She went to set up a fresh canvas on one of the easels, and Shane found a stool to sit on, positioning himself where he could watch without being in her way. Once she had the canvas set where it caught just the right angle of morning light, she tied her hair back, selected her brushes with care, and began squeezing paint onto a palette. The colors seemed random at first, but Shane suspected she knew exactly what she was doing.

"What are you going to paint?" he asked.

"You," Rosa replied simply. She glanced at him, and there was something mischievous in her expression. "But not realistically. I want to capture the feeling of you. Does that make sense?"

"Perfect sense," Shane said, thinking about the risotto lesson, about how he'd talked about trusting the process. "Show me."

She started with broad strokes, blocking in shapes and colors with a confidence that surprised him. The work went quickly at first as she covered the white canvas with washes of color—warm golds and cool blues, deep burgundies and soft greens. Shane could see her making decisions in real time, adjusting her color choices, changing the angle of her brushstrokes.

"I'm not thinking too much right now," she said as she worked, her voice almost impersonal, focused. "That comes later. Right now, I'm just feeling my way through it, responding to what the painting needs."

"Like tasting as you cook," Shane replied. "Adjusting based on what you're sensing."

"Exactly like that." She stepped back, tilted her head as she considered the canvas for a moment, and then moved in again with a smaller brush. “I’m looking for the essence of you. Not your face or your body, but the quality of your presence. The way you inhabit space.”

He watched, fascinated, as the painting began to take shape. Rosa was using the same impressionistic style as in the other paintings, but this one seemed looser, even more gestural. She was working wet-into-wet, allowing colors to blend and blur on the canvas, creating effects that seemed almost luminous.

“The light around you is different,” she said, more to herself than to him. “It’s focused, intense. Like everything else fades when you’re concentrating on something.”

She added more paint, building up layers, and Shane began to see himself emerging from the chaos of color—or rather, he began to see the impression of himself, the feeling of his presence. It was strange and beautiful and somehow intimate, watching someone translate their perception of him into visual form.

“How will you know when it’s finished?” he asked after she’d been working for over an hour.

She paused there, her brush hovering over the canvas. “I’m not sure I do know, honestly. Sometimes I just run out of things to say. Or I reach a point where adding more would diminish what’s already there.” After making that observation, she stepped back and studied her work with a critical eye. "I think this one needs to breathe for a while. I'll come back to it tomorrow and see if it needs anything else."

Then she set down her brush and turned to look at him, and he could see the worry in her expression—the fear that he might not like what she'd created, that he might not understand what she was trying to do.

He got up from the stool where he'd been sitting and came over so he could stand beside her and look at the painting. The figure on the canvas was barely human, more suggestion than reality, but he recognized himself in it anyway. Rosa had captured his intensity and focus, but he thought she'd also found something softer underneath, a kind of longing or searching that he hadn't even realized he projected.

"Is that really how you see me?" he asked.

"It's how you feel to me," she replied. "When I'm around you, when I watch you work. Like you're always reaching for something just beyond your grasp, always trying to create something perfect."

It was strange to be seen in this way, both uncomfortable and exhilarating. He wasn't used to people recognizing so much of him. "I didn't realize I was so transparent," he remarked, trying to sound casual.

He didn't know if he was entirely successful, though.

"You're not," Rosa said quickly, as if she was worried he might have taken offense. "To most people, you probably seem completely self-assured. But I've been watching you...*really* watching. And I see the questions underneath the confidence." She paused there so she could reach out with her paint-stained hands and wrap her fingers around his. "That's what makes your cooking so beautiful, though. You never settle. You always push yourself to be better."

He couldn't help smiling a little. "Is that a good thing or a bad thing?"

"Both," she said, and he loved her that much more for the way she hadn't flinched away from that question. "It's what makes you brilliant. But I think it's also what makes you lonely. It's hard to let people in when you're always working, always trying to push to the next level."

He pulled her closer and touched his forehead to hers. "You got in, though," he murmured.

"Maybe that's because I'm not trying to take anything from you," she said quietly, almost in an undertone. "I'm not asking you to be anything other than what you are. I just want to be here with you, creating beside you."

They stood like that for a long moment, surrounded by paintings and morning light, and

Shane couldn't help thinking this was exactly where he needed to be.

"Will you teach me more?" he asked next. "About painting the way you see?"

She stared up at him, her expression one of hope…and maybe a little confusion. "You want to learn?"

"I want to understand your language," he replied. "Just like you've learned mine. It's only fair."

A smile spread across her face then, and it was so full of joy and wonder that his breath caught.

"Yes," she said. "Of course I'll teach you. We can start today if you want."

"That sounds perfect."

So they spent the rest of the morning in the sun-filled studio, their roles now reversed. Rosa showed him how to hold a brush, how to mix colors, how to see negative space and value and composition.

Admittedly, he was awful at almost all of that, his painting clumsy and uncertain compared to her confident work. But he didn't care. What mattered was the way she lit up when she talked about her art, the way her hands moved with grace and sureness when she demonstrated a particular technique.

They took a break around noon, sitting on the floor with their backs against the wall, sharing a bottle of water Rosa had brought in her bag. At some point, they'd probably go out for lunch, but for the moment, they were content to be just where they were.

Shane's hands were covered in paint—blues and greens and yellows smeared across his palms—and he found himself staring at them with new appreciation for how Rosa must feel about his hands when they were dusted with flour or smelling of garlic and herbs.

"Thank you for bringing me here," he told her.

She leaned her head against his shoulder. "Thank you for understanding what all this means to me."

As they sat there, he found himself thinking about futures and possibilities. What would it be like if Rosa could stay in Jerome, if she could set up a studio and paint every day while he cooked at the Asylum? That would be incredible, wouldn't it?

But he didn't mention any of that to her, mostly because he didn't want to break this perfect moment with talk of the impossible.

Instead, he pressed a kiss to the top of her head and let himself pretend, just for a little while longer, that this could last.

12

FOUR WEEKS. ROSA HAD BEEN IN JEROME FOR an entire month, and Shane knew his life had been transformed in ways he couldn't have imagined that first night when he'd found her invisible, huddled form lying on his couch.

She worked four shifts a week at the Asylum now. When he'd tried to discuss some kind of payment for all the work she was doing, she'd looked at him as if he'd lost his mind and told him she was still learning, and everyone knew interns generally weren't paid.

Maybe so. Rather than arguing the point, though, he'd quietly put the money aside the whole time, figuring he could give it to her whenever she left.

If she left. That day seemed farther and farther in the future, and even though he knew they kept moving toward her October birthday and the deadline for her to find her consort, it was only early July now, and that meant there was still plenty of time remaining before she had to go back to Scottsdale and fulfill her duty to her clan.

Rationalizations, of course, but his life seemed to be full of them now.

At least it seemed as if the staff at the restaurant had fully accepted her as part of the team. Kelli had stopped giving him knowing looks every time Rosa walked in, and Mike had started asking her opinion on presentations. Even Carlos, who tended to keep to himself unless there was a creme brulée disaster or some other catastrophe, had complimented her palate several times.

But Shane knew it was more than that. She'd had woven herself into the fabric of his existence in ways that went far beyond the professional. Where before he would have used his days off to take care of any niggling chores at the restaurant that he didn't have time to attend to when he was actually creating dishes for the patrons at the Asylum, now they were spent with her. They explored Jerome, painted together in the studio behind Judith's gallery, and cooked together in his home kitchen as they either experimented with new dishes or tried new twists on old favorites. His nights ended with her curled against him in his bed, both of them carefully maintaining the boundaries she'd set…but both of them growing increasingly desperate for more.

At least, he assumed Rosa felt the same way. Although he'd gotten good over the years at sublimating his physical impulses when necessary, he knew his body ached for her, that every moment he spent with her, he yearned for the connection they would have if she could find a way to give herself to him body and soul.

She would never do that, though. She had to remain a virgin for her consort.

Despite those barriers…or maybe because of them…Shane realized he'd never been in love like this before. He'd thought he might have been with Sarah, his most recent ex-girlfriend—mostly because he'd been with her longer than any of the other girls he'd dated—but now he knew that had only been comfortable affection, the easy rhythm of a shared and familiar routine. This was different, though. This thing with Rosa…it was waking up every morning wondering how he'd gotten so lucky, and going to bed every night scared shitless that it would all disappear.

Which it would. He forced himself to remember that painful truth every day in the vain hope that it might not hurt so much when the time came for her to finally leave.

But now, as he stood in his kitchen on a Wednesday afternoon with the latest issue of the

Arizona Republic spread out on the counter in front of him, at least he could feel something close to vindication.

The review was stellar, the kind of write-up chefs dreamed about. The reviewer had given the restaurant five stars, a perfect score. He'd praised everything from the innovative menu to the impeccable technique to the warm, welcoming atmosphere.

But it was one particular paragraph that had made Shane's throat tighten as he read it.

> *The plating at the Asylum has reached new heights in recent weeks. Each dish is a carefully composed work of art, with attention to color, texture, and visual balance that elevates the dining experience beyond mere sustenance. McAllister's food has always been technically excellent, but this new aesthetic sensibility suggests an evolution in his vision —a marriage of culinary skill and artistic eye that makes every plate a small masterpiece.*

The critic hadn't known it, but that was all Rosa, with her artist's eye and her understanding of composition and color, and also the way she'd leaped in to fix that one badly plated scallop dish, probably saving the night.

Shane had texted her the news as soon as he'd

finished reading the review, and she'd responded with a string of excited emojis and a promise to come over after her painting session that day, which had extended far into the afternoon. Now it was almost six, and he was putting the finishing touches on a celebration that had been consuming his thoughts ever since he'd read that review.

He was going to cook for her. *Really* cook—this wouldn't be a lesson or a demonstration, but a full tasting menu designed specifically for Rosa. Every course would be a love letter, an expression of everything he felt about her but hadn't quite found the courage to say out loud.

The front door opened and then quietly shut, and Shane's heart did the now-familiar skip it seemed to make every time she came home. He wiped his hands on a towel and went to meet her in the living room. Today, her hair was loose around her shoulders, and she wore a green dress that brought out the hazel in her eyes. He could tell she'd scrubbed her hands hard in the bathroom at the gallery, since they were briskly clean except for a few traces of paint around the edges of her fingernails.

"Congratulations," she said as she gave him an incandescent smile. "I'm so proud of you."

He pulled her close so he could kiss her and taste her smile, feel her joy. "It's your victory, too," he murmured against her lips. "The critic specifically mentioned the plating."

"That's all you," she protested. "I just made a few suggestions."

"No, you did a lot more than that. You made it better." He took her hand and led her toward the dining room. "And I want to celebrate properly."

Rosa's eyes widened as she took in the transformed space. He'd borrowed a proper tablecloth from the restaurant and had set out his good plates and wine glasses, had even found candles that weren't the emergency-preparedness kind.

"Shane," she breathed. "What *is* all this?"

"Dinner," he said simply. "A private tasting menu. Just for you."

Her eyes widened. "You didn't have to—"

"I wanted to." He guided her to the table, then pulled out her chair. "Let me do this. Please."

The protests died on her lips, and she nodded as she sat down and Shane poured her a glass of wine, a crisp Albariño he'd been saving for a special occasion. Then he disappeared into the kitchen to retrieve the first course.

He'd planned this menu with care, thinking about Rosa's preferences, her memories, the things she'd told him about her childhood and her family. The first course was simple—tostadas with fresh ceviche, lime and cilantro bright against the tender fish. It was the kind of thing Rosa had mentioned eating at a relative's house in Phoenix, on summer afternoons when the heat was oppressive and nothing tasted better than something cold and acidic.

Rosa took her first bite, and her eyes closed for a second, lashes thick and black against her cheeks. "Oh, my God," she said. "This tastes like summer."

"That was the idea," Shane said as he took a seat across from her. "You said your cousin Anna made the best ceviche in Arizona."

"She does." Rosa took another bite, and he could see the way she analyzed the flavor, diving into her memories of the dish to compare it to what she tasted now. "How did you get it so right? I didn't even give you a recipe."

"You described it," he replied. "The way the lime cuts through the richness, the cilantro adds that fresh brightness, the texture of the fish. All I did was listen."

She reached across the table and took his hand. "You always listen. That's one of the things I love about you."

The word hung in the air between them—*love*—and his heart thudded in his chest. She'd said it casually enough, but the remark still felt monumental to him.

The second course was butternut squash soup,

but not the way most restaurants made it. No, he'd infused it with warming spices—cinnamon and allspice and a hint of chili—and had garnished it with pepitas and a drizzle of crema. It was inspired by the *calabaza con puerco* that Rosa had mentioned was one of her favorite dishes from yet another de la Paz "cousin's" kitchen. He knew that people in the various witch clans referred to all their relatives as cousins, no matter how distant the relationship, just because it was an easy shorthand rather than trying to say "my great-great-aunt once removed."

"This is incredible," she said after tasting a spoonful of the soup. "It's like the best parts of fall and winter all at once."

"Your cousin's *calabaza*," he replied. "I wanted to capture those flavors, but in a way that felt like my style. I hope that's okay."

"It's more than okay." She shut her eyes again, savoring the symphony of flavors in each bite. "It's absolutely perfect."

The third course was something more experimental—a play on elote, with charred corn, cotija cheese, lime, and chili powder, but deconstructed and refined. Shane had grilled the corn until it was nearly blackened, then cut the kernels off and tossed them with the other ingredients, serving it in a small bowl with a quenelle of lime crema on top.

"This is my childhood," Rosa said, chuckling after she scooped up a bite with the homemade tortilla chips he'd served alongside the elote. "I swear, you could get elote at every street fair in Phoenix. But it's also a lot fancier."

"I wanted to honor where you come from," Shane told her. "The flavors that shaped you."

The fourth course was his favorite—a dish he'd been working on for weeks but didn't think he'd perfected until now. It was a mole negro served over perfectly cooked duck breast, the sauce complex and layered, with chocolate and chiles and more than thirty ingredients that had taken him hours to source and prepare.

Rosa took one bite and went still for a moment before lifting another forkful to her mouth. Then she set down her fork and looked at Shane, tears shimmering bright in her eyes.

"Rosa?" he said at once, worried that he might have messed up something about the dish. "What's wrong?"

"Nothing's wrong," she replied at once, and gave him a watery smile, as though to assure him that her reaction had nothing to do with the quality of the food itself. "This is—Shane, this is exactly how my great-aunt's mole tastes. *Exactly*. How did you…?"

"You told me about it," he said. "About helping her toast the chiles, about the smell of chocolate and cinnamon filling the kitchen. About how she'd make it for special occasions, and everyone would go quiet when they tasted it because it was that good."

Rosa shook her head. "I can't believe that you remembered all that and went to all the trouble of re-creating it."

"I wanted to," he said simply. "I wanted to give you something that felt like home."

They ate in reverent silence then, both of them seeming to understand that this was more than just dinner. No, this was Shane telling Rosa everything he felt through the only language he knew how to speak fluently.

The final course was dessert—a simple tres leches cake he'd soaked in the traditional milk mixture and topped with fresh whipped cream and a dusting of cinnamon. It was the ultimate comfort food, the kind of thing he hoped would make her feel warm and safe and loved.

"Perfect," she said after her last bite. "Everything was perfect."

He cleared the plates and brought out coffee, then headed into the living room so he could sit next to her on the couch instead of across from her at the table. She immediately nestled into his side, her head on his shoulder, and he wrapped his arm around her.

"Thank you," she murmured. "That was the most incredible meal I've ever had."

"I'm glad," he said, and he was. All the hours he'd put into preparing the food had been worth it to see the delight on her face as she sampled each course. He kissed the top of her head and breathed in the scent of her hair, soft florals and vanilla. "I like to cook for you."

Neither of them spoke for a while as the candles burned low and dusk fell outside, the busyness of a summer afternoon drifting down to a quiet evening as most of the tourists departed Jerome to return to their ordinary lives. Contentment seemed to radiate through his entire body, and he knew it had very little to do with the five-star review the restaurant had received. No, this was all about Rosa in his arms, both of them full and satisfied, the night stretching out before them.

After a while, though, she stirred, saying, "I have something for you." She sat up and reached for her bag, which she'd put down on the floor near the sofa, and pulled out a small wrapped package.

Shane took it and sent her an amused glance. "You didn't have to get me anything. Tonight was about celebrating."

"I know," she replied. "But I wanted to give you something, too. Open it."

He pulled away the brown paper wrapped

around the package, and his breath caught. Inside was a small painting—maybe eight by ten inches —rendered in Rosa's impressionistic style. It showed his kitchen at the Asylum, but focused on a single moment…his hands working at the stove, light streaming through the windows, everything glowing with warmth and life.

"It's one of my studies," she told him. "From when I was working on the bigger painting. I wanted you to have it, to remember—" She paused there, and her voice wasn't much more than a murmur. "To remember this time we had together."

He wasn't sure he liked the sound of that, didn't like how final it felt. Before he replied, though, he carefully set the painting on the coffee table and turned to face her so he could look straight into her eyes. "Why are you talking like all this has an expiration date?"

She glanced away, expression downcast. "Because it does. We both know that."

"Do we?" he asked.

Maybe it was crazy to push this, but he knew it would be even crazier for him to simply stand by and let fate bear down on them with the inevitability of an approaching freight train.

He took her hands in his, seeing the faint smudges of paint in her nailbeds, the light calluses she'd developed from holding her paintbrushes for hours at a time. It still wasn't too late to remain quiet, to give in.

But he'd never given in before, and he was damned if he was going to start now.

~

Shane stared at her, blue eyes so intense that they might as well have been lasers trying to bore a hole straight into her soul.

"What if we don't know that?" he asked. "What if we're wrong?"

Her heart began to pound. Rosa knew they'd been avoiding this conversation for weeks, had been pretending that they could just exist in this perfect bubble forever without facing reality. But Shane was looking at her with such intensity, such hope, that she knew she couldn't run from it anymore.

"Shane—"

"Stay," he said, cutting off whatever feeble protest she'd been planning to make. "Don't go back to Scottsdale. Stay here with me."

"I can't hide forever," she said. Each word was agony, but she had to lay it out on the line now, couldn't hide anymore. "My mother's been a freaking saint about all this, but that doesn't mean there isn't still a deadline. I turn twenty-two on October seventh, and if I haven't found my consort by then—"

Utter catastrophe, according to her mother and all the elders in the de la Paz clan. A *prima* without a consort would never come into the full strength of her powers, would be unable to protect her clan during a time of crisis. Maybe once that had been an archaic belief and nothing more, but after hearing about the havoc the Escobar warlocks had wreaked upon the Arizona witch clans, Rosa knew none of them could afford to have a *prima* who was anything less than her utterly best self.

And that meant finding a consort, no matter how much she hated the idea.

"But what if you're not hiding?" Shane asked. Clearly, he had no intention of backing down. His hands tightened on hers as he added, "What if you're actually choosing—choosing this life, this town…me?"

Oh, she'd already chosen him, even though she knew that wasn't how any of this worked. "It's not that simple."

"Why not?" His voice was urgent now, almost desperate. "Rosa, I know the consort situation is complicated, and it's not like you can just snap your fingers and choose your own consort. But what if—" He paused there so he could take a breath. "What if there's a way to make this work after all?"

She wanted to believe him. God, she wanted to believe that love could be enough, that choosing each other could somehow override centuries of magical tradition and the requirements of the *prima* power buried deep within her.

His expression had turned very serious. "Tell me what you're thinking," he said.

"I'm thinking—" To her dismay, her voice broke, and she had to stop and gather herself before she could continue. "I'm thinking that I've never been happier than I've been here with you. For the first time in my life, I feel like just Rosa, a woman in love with a man who really sees her."

For a moment, he was utterly still, staring at her as if he didn't quite believe what he'd just heard. "Say that again," he murmured at last.

She could only stare back at him. "What?"

"The part about being in love," Shane said, his tone now almost rough, as if some part of him wasn't sure it would allow him to believe such a thing.

Tears rose in her eyes, hot and stinging. "I'm in love with you," she told him. "I have been for weeks. I'm so in love with you that it scares me."

"I love you, too," he said, the words coming

out in a rush, as though he'd been holding them back for far too long. "I love you, Rosa. I love your art and your laugh and the way you see the world. I love how brave you are, and I love watching you work in my kitchen and paint in your studio. I love everything about you."

The tears were flowing now, although she couldn't begin to say whether they were happy tears…or simply a sign of the heartbreak to come. "But loving each other doesn't change anything," she protested. "I still need to find my consort. The magic still demands it."

He shook his head. "What if I could be your consort?"

The words hung in the air between them, impossible, terrifying…and full of desperate hope.

"We kissed," she said softly. She'd thought this over a thousand times, and no matter how she looked at the situation, she couldn't make it fit into what reality demanded. "Remember that first time at the overlook? If you were really my consort, we would have felt it."

"But we were both scared then," he argued, clearly unwilling to let it go. "We were fighting what we felt. What if we tried again? What if we kissed each other now, knowing how we feel, and saw what happened?"

She wanted to believe such a thing was possible, that love could be enough to wake the consort bond.

That simply choosing Shane could somehow make him the right one.

But she'd kissed thirty-four other men before him, thirty-four carefully vetted candidates. And none of them had worked.

"I don't want to set you up for disappointment," she said. Disappointment already lived within her, so she was much more worried about Shane's reaction if they should try such an experiment and fail. "I don't want to see your face when nothing happens, and you realize I've been lying to myself about this."

"You're not lying to yourself," he replied, his tone firm. He cupped her face in his hands, making it impossible for her to look away. "And even if the consort bond doesn't manifest, that doesn't change how I feel. It doesn't change that I want to be with you, that I want to build a life with you."

"But my responsibilities—" The protest sounded weak to her, but she knew she had to make it anyway.

"Then we'll figure it out," he said. "Maybe you can split time between Jerome and Scottsdale. Maybe there's a way to fulfill your duties without giving up your art…without giving up *us.* We'll find a way, Rosa. I promise."

Rosa searched his face, looking for doubt or uncertainty, but all she saw was fierce determination and a love so clear, so obvious, that it made her ache inside.

"What are you saying?" she whispered. "What exactly are you proposing?"

"I'm saying I want you to stay with me," Shane replied. "Not forever if you can't, but for now. Keep painting, keep working in the kitchen, keep being exactly who you are. Let's see if we can make this work. We need to find out if there's a way for you to be the *prima*-in-waiting and an artist and my—" He paused there before finishing, "My partner."

"Your partner," she repeated, testing the word. It wasn't the same as being a consort, as being a husband.

But it was something.

"My person," he amended. "Whatever that looks like, and however we need to define it. I just know that I don't want to let you go."

Rosa closed her eyes, and she could see it—the life Shane was describing. Mornings painting in the studio, afternoons in his kitchen or up at the restaurant, evenings after they got back from work curled up together on this couch. She'd have to figure out a way to split time between Jerome and Scottsdale, have to learn how to balance duty and desire.

It was impossible...and it went against everything she'd been taught about how her life was supposed to unfold.

And she wanted it more than she'd ever wanted anything in the world.

"Okay," she said at last as she opened her eyes so she could see his reaction.

Shane's own eyes widened, as if he wasn't quite able to believe that she'd agreed to this crazy scheme. "'Okay'?" he repeated.

"Okay, I'll stay." She made herself look at him, knowing she needed to commit fully to the idea. "I'll stay, and we'll try. I don't know how we'll make it work, and I'm scared to death that it will all fall apart, but I want this. I want *you*. So...okay."

He leaned in to kiss her then, and something about that embrace was different from every other kiss they'd shared. This one was promise and hope and fierce joy all tangled together. She kissed him back with everything she had, pouring four weeks of longing and fear and love into the press of her lips against his.

When they finally broke apart, both of them were breathing hard. He rested his forehead against hers as he said, "We're really doing this."

"We're really doing this," she repeated, half-laughing, half-crying. "I'll call my mother tomorrow and tell her I'm staying in Jerome for a while longer."

At once, concern flitted across his handsome features. "What will you tell her?"

"The truth," Rosa said without hesitating. That was the one thing she knew had to happen. She couldn't dance around this, had to be utterly honest. "I'll tell her that I've found something here I don't want to give up and that I need more time to figure out who I am separate from all the expectations. That I'm—" She paused there, knowing she had to say the words out loud. "That I'm in love and I need to see where it goes."

His hands tightened on her arms. "Is she going to want to meet me…or kill me?" he asked, the smile he wore not fooling her for a second.

"Probably a little of both," she responded with a raspy chuckle. "Think you can handle that?"

"I'd face down an arena of tigers for you," he said. "One pissed-off *prima* should be easy."

They kissed again, the embrace softer this time, lingering. The candles had burned down to nothing, and full dark had fallen outside, but here in Shane's small pink house, everything felt bright and warm and full of possibility.

"Stay tonight," Shane murmured against her lips.

"I always do," she replied with a smile.

However, his expression remained serious. "I mean *really* stay. Be here. Be mine."

"I am yours," she whispered. "However that's allowed to look, I'm yours."

They moved to Shane's bedroom, both of them aware of the line they still couldn't cross but desperate for any closeness they could claim. They undressed down to their underwear and climbed into bed, tangling themselves together in the sheets.

The physical tension between them had been building for weeks, a constant undercurrent beneath every touch, every kiss. Now, pressed against each other with so little between them, it was almost overwhelming.

His hands moved over her skin, and she kissed his neck and his jaw, feeling the thunder of his pulse beneath her lips. They both shook with want, with the effort of holding back.

"I wish—" he began, then stopped, as if he realized anything he said might put more pressure on her.

"I know," she said.

"We'll figure it out," he said again, a promise he was making to both of them. "Somehow, we'll find a way."

Rosa wanted to believe him. Lying there in his arms, his heart beating steady beneath her ear, she let herself believe that maybe love really could be enough, that maybe choosing each other was its own kind of magic, one that didn't need the *prima* power's approval.

And if a small voice in the back of her mind whispered that this couldn't last, that magic and duty would eventually tear them apart, Rosa chose not to listen.

Not tonight, anyway.

13

Sunlight streamed through Shane's bedroom window. For a perfect, suspended moment, Rosa let herself simply exist in the warmth of his bed, the steady rhythm of his breathing against the back of her neck, the way their bodies fit together like they'd been designed for exactly this purpose.

Then she saw her phone on the nightstand. She vaguely remembered dropping it there the night before, but at least she thought she'd had the presence of mind to put it on vibrate. Not that she got too many calls these days; she talked to her mother here and there just to reassure her that everything was fine, although it seemed as if the word had gone out to the rest of the de la Paz clan not to bother her while she was on her Jerome sabbatical.

The screen was dark, but something about it seemed ominous, like a bomb waiting to go off. She shifted with care, trying not to disturb Shane, who seemed dead to the world.

Her stomach knotted when she saw the notification count.

Seventeen missed calls.

All from Scottsdale...and all from her mother.

What had happened? Had someone passed away during the night? Rosa couldn't think of any other reason why her mother would have tried to call so many times.

"Shit," she whispered, and Shane stirred behind her.

"What's the matter?"

She looked over at him. Even now, with panic clawing at her throat, he was beautiful. Sleep-rumpled hair, a shadow of dark gold stubble on his jaw, blue eyes still hazy with dreams. She wanted to memorize this moment, this last perfect breath before everything came crashing down on her head.

"My mother called," she said, and held up the phone. "Seventeen times."

He was fully awake now, pushing himself up to a sitting position. Voice sharp with worry, he asked, "When?"

Rosa checked the call log and told herself she needed to remain calm. "It looks like she started around ten last night. The last call was at two in the morning."

"Did she leave any messages?"

"A couple," she replied. Not with every call, but spaced out, as if at certain intervals she'd gotten annoyed enough to leave a voicemail rather than simply hang up and try again. Rosa pulled in a steadying breath and then put the phone on speaker and played the first voicemail. Her mother's voice filled the small bedroom, clipped and tight in a way that meant Zoe Sandoval was working very hard not to lose her temper.

"Rosa, we need to talk. Please call me back."

The second message, from a little before midnight, was even shorter. "Rosa, call me. Now."

The final voicemail came in just before two. "I'm driving up there in the morning. We're having this conversation whether you want to or not."

Rosa ended the playback and dropped the phone onto the bed. It was just an ordinary iPhone, but it felt like a lump of burning coal in her fingers. "She's coming today."

Shane ran a worried hand through his hair. The sheets pooled around his waist, and Rosa had to look away from the bare expanse of his chest, the way the early morning light painted shadows across the muscles of his shoulders. He was so very real. What they had was real.

And her mother was coming to take it all away. Maybe she hadn't said so in so many words, but Rosa couldn't think of a single other reason why her mother would drop everything and drive all the way up here.

So much for reassuring her that everything was fine and she could take as much time as she needed.

"What time?" Shane's voice sounded steady enough, but Rosa still could hear the tension beneath it.

"She said 'in the morning' in the message, so —" A glance at the clock told her it was a little after eight. "Probably not before ten. As pissed off as she is, I don't think she'd want to arrive on your doorstep any earlier than that. But probably a little later, since I doubt she'd want to get stuck in rush hour traffic. No later than noon, though. Or at least, I don't think any later than that."

The silence that followed her little speech was almost oppressive. All the joy from last night—the confessions of love, the promises, the hope—seemed to have drained out of the room as effectively as water through a sieve.

"Okay," Shane said at last. "So we have a few hours."

"To do what?" The question was harsher than Rosa had intended, but fear had sharpened her words. "To figure out how to explain to the *prima* of the de la Paz clan that her daughter has fallen in love with a man who—" She broke off there, not sure how she was supposed to finish the sentence.

His jaw was tight. "Who what?" he demanded. "Who isn't good enough for her?"

At once, she reached out and took his hand. "That's not what I meant. All I was trying to say is that I've fallen in love with a man who isn't my consort."

His expression softened immediately, even as his fingers tightened on hers. "I know. I'm sorry. I just—" He let out a rough breath. "I don't want to lose you. Not now. Not when we just—"

Not when we just told each other that we loved one another.

Rosa's phone vibrated on the bed, and a text from her mother showed on the home screen.

> I'll be there by 1. We're having this conversation, Rosa. Today.

She showed Shane the message, and she watched his expression shift from determination to something that looked almost like resignation. That change frightened her more than her mother's seventeen missed calls.

"We should get up," she said, even though she wanted nothing more than to stay exactly where they were, to hide from the world in this bed until reality gave up and left them alone. "We should—

I don't know. Talk about this and figure out what we're going to say."

But neither of them moved.

Finally, Shane spoke, his voice still tight with tension. "What happens when she gets here? What happens to us?"

"I don't know." The admission felt like a failure, but it was the truth. She was supposed to be the *prima*-in-waiting, supposed to be responsible and prepared and always have a plan. Nothing in the world could have prepared her for this situation, though. "I guess I should have thought this through, but I just—I couldn't—"

"Hey." He squeezed her hand, his skin warm and reassuring against hers. "This isn't on you. We made these choices together."

"But I'm the one who ran away." The words were bitter in her mouth, but she said them anyway. "I'm the one who dragged you into this mess."

An emphatic shake of his head. "You didn't drag me anywhere." His free hand came up to cup her face, his fingers brushing her cheekbone. "I chose this. I chose *you*. Don't you dare tell yourself anything otherwise."

Tears burned behind her eyes, hot and insistent. "Shane—"

"We need to talk about the consort bond," he said.

There it was. The thing they'd been dancing around all night, the elephant that had been sitting on their chests since that first kiss at the overlook.

Her mouth twisted. "I know."

"Should we try?" he asked, watching her carefully, like she was something fragile that might shatter at the wrong word. "Before your mother gets here, I mean. Shouldn't we at least know for sure, one way or another?"

Rosa wanted to say yes. Oh, God, she wanted to be brave enough to kiss him with intention, to search for the magical connection that was supposed to ignite when a *prima*-in-waiting found her consort.

But she was so very tired of failing.

"I've tried the consort kiss with thirty-four men," she said. The words came slowly, each one dragged up from some deep, wounded place inside her. "Do you know what that's like? It's like taking a test over and over and failing every single time. It's humiliating. Every single kiss is a rejection—not from them, but from the power that's supposed to be *mine*, that's supposed to recognize my perfect match."

His fingers were still moving gently against her cheek, a steady, soothing rhythm, but he didn't interrupt, as if he understood that she needed to work through this on her own.

"And what if—" Her voice cracked on that final syllable, and she had to stop, had to breathe through the fear that was trying to strangle her. "What if we try and it doesn't work? What if you're not—"

"What if I'm not your consort?" He asked the question gently, without accusation, just stating the terrible thing she couldn't bring herself to voice.

Rosa nodded, unable to speak around the lump in her throat.

For a long moment, he was quiet, caressing her cheek, looking at her with those impossibly blue eyes that saw too much.

"We had our first kiss," he said at length. "And nothing happened then."

"I know," she whispered. Even now, disappointment lay curled and aching in her gut, the realization that as good as the kiss had been, it still hadn't been the one to awaken the *prima* spark.

"But we were both scared," he said. "We were fighting what we felt, because we knew we shouldn't be kissing each other at all." His tone became more urgent as he continued. "What if that's why it didn't work? What if we were too closed off and too guarded for the magic to really wake up?"

Oh, she wanted to believe him. She wanted to believe that love could be enough, that intention and passion could somehow override thirty-four terrible failures.

"Or," she returned, forcing herself to be honest, "what if it just doesn't work because you're not my consort? What if the magic knows something we don't?"

"Then at least we'll know," he said simply. "At least we won't spend the rest of our lives wondering 'what if?'"

He was right, of course. She knew he was right. They couldn't move forward without knowing, couldn't face her mother without understanding what they were fighting for…or maybe what they were fighting against.

But knowing all that didn't make her any less terrified.

"Okay," she whispered. "But not here. Not in bed. That feels—"

"Wrong," he agreed immediately. "This isn't about sex. It's about—"

"Magic," she broke in. "It's about the bond."

They climbed out of the bed and, by silent agreement, got ready as if this was just another normal day rather than the one that could possibly change everything. They took turns in the shower and got dressed, both of them moving slower than usual, as if they could delay the inevitable by simply taking their time. Rosa put on a sundress and sandals, thinking that maybe looking presentable might help to lessen some of her mother's ire. Shane, on the other hand, dressed in his usual work attire of dark jeans, a plain T-shirt, and the leather cuff he always wore on his left wrist.

After they were ready, they moved to the living room, to the couch where they'd spent so many evenings curled together, talking and kissing and pretending the outside world didn't exist. The painting she'd given him last night still sat on the coffee table, the colors rich and warm in the morning light.

Jerome at sunset. The place where I found you. The place where I fell in love.

But would Jerome's magic be enough to save them?

"So," Shane said. He sat next to her but maintained a careful distance, as if he wasn't sure whether he should touch her yet. "How does the consort kiss work?"

Her hands were shaking. She clasped them together in her lap, doing her best to still the tremors even though the problem wasn't just her hands. Her whole body wanted to tremble. "It's supposed to just...happen. I mean, both people have to be open to the bond, have to want it. If the connection is right, then the *prima*-in-waiting's power will just sort of naturally rise to the surface. I'm honestly not sure what the potential consort has to do. Meet it somehow, I guess. Respond to it."

Shane's expression was thoughtful, focused. "What does it feel like when it works?"

She'd asked her mother the same question once, years ago, back when the consort search had seemed like an adventure rather than a prison sentence. Zoe had gotten this faraway look in her eyes, and had worn a soft, dreamy smile that was very different from her usual wide, friendly grins.

"My mom said it was like recognition," Rosa said slowly, trying to remember everything her mother had said. "Like your soul had been searching for something your whole life and suddenly found it. She said the magic feels like a warm, fierce, golden light suddenly exploding within you. From the outside, it doesn't seem as if anything has changed, and yet you know everything is different now. It's not like gaining something new. Instead, it feels like becoming whole, like you were always meant to be half of something larger."

Shane was quiet for a moment, absorbing her words. "That sounds amazing."

"I always thought it sounded kind of terrifying," Rosa replied. True, she saw the evidence of her parents' love for one another every day, but still, sharing the consort bond sounded like losing a little piece of yourself to a greater whole.

"Needing someone that much, I mean, having your power, your destiny, your *self* tied to another person so completely."

"Is that what you're afraid of?" he asked, his tone now very gentle. "Being tied to me?"

Oh, she had to disabuse him of that notion right away. "No," she said without hesitation. "I'm afraid of trying and failing. I'm afraid of watching your face when nothing happens and you realize that I'm just—broken somehow. That thirty-four men have tried to be my consort and failed, and you'll be number thirty-five."

"Hey." He reached for her hand, and this time she let him take it. "You're not broken. The system is broken. These arranged consort trials with distant cousins you've never met, being paraded in front of you like you're supposed to fall in love on command—that's what's broken. Not you."

She wanted to believe him. Unfortunately, eight months of failure had carved deep grooves into her sense of self, had convinced her that the problem wasn't the system—it was her.

"We should try," she said then, before she could lose her nerve. "You're right. We need to know."

But there was a seed of doubt in both of them now. She could see it in the way Shane's jaw was tight, in the shadows behind his eyes. He was scared, too.

They couldn't allow that to stop them, though.

"Okay," he said, then shifted slightly so they were face-to-face. "Tell me what to do."

Rosa took a deep breath, trying to center herself, trying to reach for the *prima* power that lived somewhere deep inside her. Most of the time, she did her best to pretend it didn't exist, since to her it had always felt like the one thing preventing her from living the life she wanted.

Now, though, she had to let it rise.

"Just—be open," she said, knowing she was flying blind here. It wasn't as if there was a manual on how to do something that was supposed to be pure instinct. "Don't protect yourself, and don't hold back. Kiss me like you mean it, like you're choosing me despite everything."

"I *do* mean it," he said, the words direct, almost hard. "I *am* choosing you."

She nodded, mostly because her throat was so tight, she wasn't sure if she could have said anything anyway.

He leaned in slowly, giving her time to pull back if she needed to. No way in the world would she do that, though. No, she let him come closer, let him cup her face in his hands the way he had that first time at the overlook, let him tilt her chin up so their eyes met.

"I love you," he said. "Whatever happens right now, that doesn't change."

"I love you, too," she whispered.

Then he kissed her.

The touch of his lips on hers was soft at first, almost tentative, as if they were both feeling their way through unfamiliar territory. But then Rosa tried to let the sleeping, frustrated magic inside her awake and reach out, searching for its match.

The kiss deepened. Shane's hands slid into her hair, and she pressed closer, pouring everything she had into this moment. This was their only chance, and she knew it as well as he did. She opened herself completely, let down every wall and defense she'd spent eight months building, and searched—desperately, frantically—for the spark that would tell her he was the one.

The kiss was good. It was beautiful, actually. His mouth on hers felt right in a way that no one else's ever had. The touch of his tongue against hers sent heat spiraling through her body, made her want to push him down on the couch so she could finally rid herself of the burden of her virginity.

But there was no surge of magic, no explosion of golden light within, making her feel as if she was somehow melting into him.

It was just a kiss.

A really, really good kiss between two people who loved each other, true.

But not the consort bond.

They pulled apart slowly, and Rosa already knew what she'd see in his eyes before she forced herself to look into his face. Mirrored there was the same disappointment and fear that was currently trying to drag her under.

Neither of them wanted to say it first, because that would make it real.

But the silence between them was worse than words could ever be.

"Nothing," she finally whispered.

Shane's hands were still tangled in her hair, but they'd gone quiet, frozen in place. "Maybe we did it wrong? Maybe we need to—"

"Shane." She wanted to shake her head but thought that wouldn't be such a good idea, not with his fingers caught in her hair. "There was *nothing.* No magic…and no bond."

He dropped his hands, and she hated that he wasn't touching her anymore, that already it felt as if a terrible chasm had begun to open up between them. "But we love each other," he protested. "That has to count for something. That has to *mean* something."

"It does," she said, and she realized she was crying now, tears streaming down her face even though she hadn't even felt them begin to form. "Of course it means something. It means *everything.* But it doesn't change the fact that you're not my consort. The magic knows. It always knows."

She watched him process her words, watched the hope drain from his expression, replaced by something that looked like grief. He was grieving what they could have been, what they'd hoped they were.

What they'd never get to have.

And she was grieving, too. God, she was grieving so hard that she could barely breathe.

He raised his head. His expression had gone utterly flat, and he looked at her with the eyes of a man who'd just been told he only had a few months to live. "So…what do we do now?"

"I don't know!" She burst out. "I don't—I *can't*—"

She could almost feel herself breaking into a thousand pieces, all the carefully maintained composure she'd built over eight months of disappointment finally crumbling under the weight of this one devastating failure.

Because this wasn't just another consort trial. This was Shane, the man she loved. This was the person who'd seen all her quirks and her odd angles and had chosen her anyway.

And he wasn't her consort.

The unfairness of it made her want to scream her denial at the world.

He reached for her again, but she pulled back

instinctively, wrapping her arms around herself. If he touched her now, she'd shatter completely. She needed to hold herself together, needed to give herself space to think.

"Rosa—"

"I need a minute." The words were far too brusque, but she couldn't take them back now. "I just—I need to think."

Hurt flashed across his face, quickly hidden. But she couldn't deal with his pain right now, not when she was drowning in her own.

She got up from the sofa and went over to the window so she could gaze out at the little pink house's small front yard, at the orderly Victorian homes marching down the street and the mountains rising in the distance. Jerome in the daylight. It was a place where she'd been happy, a place where she'd fallen in love.

And now it would be a witness to her misery.

Behind her, she heard Shane rise as well, the couch springs creaking slightly. His footsteps were soft on the hardwood floor, but they stopped before he reached her. He was keeping his distance, just as she'd asked.

"I don't regret it," he said, his tone very quiet.

"I know." Her voice was also barely audible.

"And I don't want to give up on this. On us."

She closed her eyes, willing the pain away, hating herself for what she had to say next.

"Shane, I'll be *prima* someday. I have to protect my clan. And to do that, I need my full powers, which means I need a consort. That's not negotiable. That's not something I can decide doesn't matter because I fell in love with the wrong person."

The silence behind her was deafening.

"'The wrong person,'" he repeated, and his voice caught on the last word.

Rosa turned around. He was standing in the middle of the living room, hands shoved in his pockets, shoulders hunched like he was trying to make himself smaller. The morning light painted him in gold, and he was so beautiful that he made her heart ache all over again.

But if she went to him now, put her arms around him the way so she desperately wanted to, then she knew she'd never be able to walk away. Voice breaking, she said, "That's not what I—God, Shane, you know what I meant. You're not wrong. You're *perfect.* You're everything I want. But the magic doesn't care about what I want. It doesn't care about love or choice or any of it. It only cares about the bond, and we don't have it."

"So that's it?" he asked, and gave a hitch of his shoulders, as if he'd intended to move toward her and then realized that was a terrible idea. "We just give up?"

She made an anguished, impatient gesture

with one hand. "What choice do we have?" He didn't respond right away, so she went on, "Tell me, Shane. Tell me how we make this work when the basic requirement of my destiny is something you can't give me."

"I can give you everything else," he replied fiercely. "I can give you love and partnership and a life where you're seen and valued and free to be yourself. I can support your art. I can stand beside you as you become *prima*. I can—"

"But you can't complete the consort bond," she broke in, knowing she needed to stop him before he made any more promises she knew he couldn't possibly keep, not with the situation the way it was. "And without that, I'll never have my full powers. I'll be a weak *prima*. I'll be vulnerable, and the past few years have taught us all that we just can't afford for me to put my clan in that position. Everyone in my family knows this. They've been patient with me so far, but there's a deadline none of us can ignore. Because if I do—"

She wouldn't allow herself to finish the sentence, didn't want to utter aloud what would happen if she failed to find her consort before her twenty-second birthday, even though Shane knew those consequences as well as she did.

"I should go," she said abruptly. "I should—we should both have some space. You know, some time to think."

But what she really meant was, *I need to start letting you go before it destroys me completely.*

She saw the moment when he understood, watched the way his expression shifted from determination to resignation to something that looked almost like acceptance.

"Okay," he said, still in that quiet, almost patient voice that didn't sound quite like him. "Whatever you need."

Without responding, she turned away and headed into the guest room, where she started stuffing her things into the tote bag she'd brought with her—the clothes she'd been storing in the dresser, her toiletries from the bathroom. The sketchbook that was now filled with drawings of the man who'd stolen her heart.

She doubted she'd ever be able to look at them again.

As she headed for the door, Shane spoke one more time.

"For what it's worth," he said, "you're not a disappointment. You're amazing. And whoever does end up being your consort—he's going to be the luckiest man alive."

She knew the words were meant to be kind, but each one felt like a separate knife stabbing into her gut.

Maybe someone else would have been strong enough to reply, to tell him that she thought he was amazing, too, and deserved all the happiness in the world.

She wasn't that strong, though, so she left without responding, closing the door behind her with a soft *click* as final as the tolling of a graveyard bell.

14

Shane stood alone in his living room, staring at the closed door, and tried to remember how to breathe.

She'd left. She'd actually *left.*

And he'd let her go.

He sank back down onto the couch, feeling like someone had scooped out his insides and left him hollow, a flimsy façade of a man. The painting on the coffee table seemed to mock him now. *The place where I fell in love.* What did that matter when love wasn't enough? When magic and duty and centuries of tradition all said that what he and Rosa felt for each other was irrelevant?

His phone pinged inside his pocket, and he stared down at the screen for a moment. The words were all a jumble, unreadable as a bunch of hieroglyphics.

But then he realized it was a text from Mike, who'd taken over sous chef duty until they could find a real replacement.

You coming in this morning? Got some prep questions.

Right. He had a restaurant to run, and he couldn't let himself fall apart just because the woman he loved was slipping through his fingers.

Be there in an hour.

In a way, that simple text was the lifeline he needed. He could focus on work. Work had always been his refuge, the one thing that made sense when nothing else did. In the kitchen, problems had solutions. Recipes had steps. There was order and logic and clear results.

Unlike love…unlike magic.

Unlike trying to build a life with someone when fate itself seemed determined to tear you apart.

He forced himself to go into the bathroom and splash cold water on his face. No need to worry about shaving, since he didn't do that every day anyway and he doubted anyone would notice his current scruffiness. He kept expecting to hear

Rosa coming through the front door, to turn around and find her standing there with some new idea, some new way they could thwart the impossible destiny she'd been saddled with.

But she didn't come back.

By the time he arrived at the Asylum, it was already past nine, and the kitchen staff was deep in prep for lunch service. Mike looked up from the cutting board where he was breaking down chicken.

"Chef," he said after a brief glance in Shane's direction. "No offense, but you look like hell."

"Thanks," he muttered, then grabbed his knife roll and tied on his apron.

"Where's Rosa?"

The question hurt a lot more than it should have, but his voice sounded surprisingly even as he replied, "She isn't working today."

Mike raised an eyebrow but had the wisdom not to push. "Got it. Well, we're almost done with chicken prep. Carlos is on vegetables. Kelli called in sick, so we're down a server."

Shane nodded, trying to focus on the immediate problems rather than a dark, nebulous future. "I'll cover expo. We'll make it work."

But nothing was working. His hands, usually so sure and steady, fumbled with simple tasks. He overcooked a test batch of bacon for the lunch special, and he underseasoned the soup, forcing him to taste it three times before he finally got it right. His mind kept drifting, replaying that kiss, that devastating moment of *nothing*.

"Chef." Mike was standing beside him, voice pitched low so no one could overhear them. "You sure you're good?"

"Fine," Shane said tersely, even though he knew he was the opposite of fine.

Somehow, they got through the next couple of hours, even though everything was an utter blur, something he hoped would flush itself out of his short-term memory sooner rather than later. Around two, as lunch service slowed down, he stepped out of the kitchen for some fresh air and leaned against the brick wall next to the rear entrance to the building. He'd smoked once, a nasty habit he'd picked up in culinary school, before his mother had made him promise to quit. Right then, he would have given anything for a cigarette, for something to do with his hands, for any kind of distraction from the dull ache within that didn't seem to want to go away.

A car pulled up in the small parking lot adjacent to the alley. Shane glanced over automatically, then froze.

It was a silver Lexus with a license plate holder advertising a dealer in Scottsdale.

And the woman getting out of the driver's seat was unmistakably Rosa's mother.

He recognized her at once, even though he'd only seen pictures. She was slight and pretty, like her daughter, with the same dark hair and oval face, and she made up for her lack of height with an air of authority that seemed to radiate from her like heat. She was dressed simply—jeans, a white sleeveless blouse, bronze sandals that echoed the gold hoops in her ears—but there was something regal about her, something that marked her as exactly what she was.

The *prima* of the de la Paz clan.

She spotted him immediately. There was no way he could pretend he hadn't seen her, as much as he would have liked to duck back into the kitchen like a coward.

"Shane McAllister?" Her voice was friendlier than he'd expected but still firm, the tone of someone used to being listened to.

"Yes, ma'am." He straightened, suddenly aware of his chef's whites splattered with the Goddess only knew what. "Mrs. Sandoval."

"Zoe, please." She walked toward him, and Shane had the distinct impression of being assessed, catalogued, weighed, and measured in a matter of seconds. "Is my daughter here?"

"No. She left earlier this morning. She's been staying at the Clinkscale." The lie came easily, because he sure as hell wasn't going to tell Rosa's mother that her daughter had been sleeping in his bed.

Even if nothing had happened.

Zoe nodded slowly, almost as if she'd expected this answer. "I see. And do you know where she is right now?"

"No. She didn't—we didn't—" He stopped himself there before he could sound any more like an idiot than he already had.

"You're in love with her."

It wasn't a question.

Shane met Zoe's eyes. They were very much like Rosa's in shape, but instead were dark brown. Most likely, Rosa got her hazel eyes from her McAllister father. "Yes."

"And she's in love with you."

"Yes."

Zoe was quiet for a long moment. "But you're not her consort."

Thanks for the gut punch. His jaw tightened. "No, I guess not."

"You tried the consort kiss." Again, it wasn't a question. Somehow, the *prima* already knew.

"This morning. Nothing happened." The admission tasted like ashes in his mouth, but he wouldn't clear his throat, wouldn't let her see how much all of this hurt.

Zoe's expression softened slightly, and for a

moment, Shane saw genuine sympathy there. "I'm sorry. I know that must have been difficult for both of you."

"'Difficult' doesn't begin to cover it." The words were far harsher than they should have been, considering that he was speaking to the *prima* of another clan, but he couldn't seem to control his tone. "Your daughter is brilliant and brave and deserves every good thing in the world. And I can't give her the one thing she actually needs."

"No," Zoe said quietly. "You can't."

The bluntness of those words stole his breath.

"But you love her," Zoe continued. "And she loves you. That's not nothing, Shane."

"It's not enough, either." He shoved his hands in his pockets to keep them from shaking. "She needs a consort. She needs her powers to fulfill her destiny. And I'm just—I'm just a chef from Jerome who fell for the wrong woman."

"Or maybe," Zoe said gently, "she's a *prima*-in-waiting who fell for the wrong man at the wrong time. Believe me, I understand what she's going through. I fell in love with Evan even though finding a consort among the McAllisters was the last thing on my mind."

Except everything had worked out just fine for Zoe and Evan, hadn't it?

Somehow, Shane doubted he and Rosa would get the same happy ending.

He looked away from Zoe, his gaze moving past her to the crowded parking lot beyond the spot where they stood. "So…what happens now? Are you going to take her back to Scottsdale and make her go through more consort trials?"

To his surprise, Zoe smiled. "She's twenty-one years old and is an adult with her own rights, so I can't really 'make' her do anything. But yes, I'll strongly encourage her to come home and continue the search. She only has a little more than three months left, and that's not a lot of time."

"I know." Goddess, did he know. Every day with Rosa had felt like borrowed time, like they were living on the edge of a precipice, just waiting for the inevitable fall.

"But I wanted to meet you first," Zoe went on. "I wanted to see the man who made my daughter happy enough to hide from her family for more than a month."

Shane forced himself to look at the *prima* again. "And?"

She studied him for another long moment. "I think I can see why she loves you," she said at last. "You're not like anyone else in her life, and I can tell that you see her as more than just a *prima*-in-waiting."

"That's because she *is* more than that," Shane returned. "She's a brilliant artist, and she deserves to make her own choices about her life."

"I agree," Zoe said, and there was steel in her voice now. "But some choices aren't really choices at all. Some things are written into our blood and our magic. And whether any of us likes it or not, Rosa was born to be *prima*. That's not something she can run from forever."

"I'm not asking her to run from it," he protested. "I just want her to have the space to figure out who she is separate from all the expectations."

"And you've given her that," the *prima* replied calmly. "This time in Jerome was probably the freest she's felt in years. But that freedom was always temporary, Shane. And I think both of you knew that, even if you didn't want to admit it."

Zoe was right, of course. He'd known it from the start, from that very first night when he'd found Rosa sleeping on his sofa, looking lost and desperate and so, so young. He'd known she was temporary.

He'd just been stupid enough to fall for her anyway.

"I need to find my daughter," Zoe said as she pulled her phone from her purse. "But Shane—thank you for taking care of her. And for loving her, even knowing it would hurt."

"I'd do it again," he said. "I'd choose her again, even knowing how this ends."

The *prima* smiled, a smile tinged with sadness. "I believe you. But knowing how things end doesn't make the ending hurt any less."

She walked back to her car, and Shane watched her go, feeling like the last thread connecting him to Rosa had just been severed.

A minute or so later, his phone vibrated inside his pocket. He almost didn't want to look at the screen, but he made himself do it anyway.

The text was from Rosa, of course.

My mom's here. I'm at the hotel.
I'm sorry.

He stared at the message for a long time, trying to figure out what he could possibly say in reply. *It's okay?* Well, it wasn't okay. *We'll figure it out?* No, they wouldn't.

I love you? She already knew that, and it changed nothing.

In the end, he only said,

I know. It's okay.

That lie felt like the kindest thing he could offer.

Shane went back inside, back to the controlled

chaos of the kitchen, where everything had rules and order and made sense. Mike took one look at his face and wisely said nothing, and instead handed him a knife and pointed him toward a cutting board full of vegetables that needed prep.

He worked mechanically, forcing his mind to focus on the simple, repetitive motions. Dice. Slice. Chop. Don't think about Rosa. Don't think about the way she'd looked at him this morning, hope and fear warring in her beautiful eyes. Don't think about the feel of her in his arms, the way she fit against him like she'd been made for that exact space.

Don't think about how empty that space felt now.

Around three o'clock, his phone pinged again. It was another text, this time from Brianna.

> I heard Zoe Sandoval is in town.
> You doing okay?

The McAllister family grapevine was apparently alive and well.

If he ignored the text, his sister would just message him again.

> Been better. At work. Will call later.

But he knew he wouldn't call. What was there

to say? That he'd fallen in love with Rosa Sandoval, the *prima*-in-waiting of the de la Paz clan? That they'd tried the consort kiss and failed?

No. Some pain was too private to share, even with family.

By the time evening service rolled around, Shane had perfected the art of not thinking or feeling. No, he was just moving through the familiar rhythms of the kitchen, calling orders, plating dishes, maintaining the careful orchestration that made a restaurant run smoothly.

He'd become what he'd always been good at pretending to be. Just the chef, just the man behind the line, creating something beautiful and ephemeral that would be consumed and forgotten.

At least in the kitchen, he knew his place.

Outside the kitchen, in the real world where magic and destiny determined who you could love —out there, he was lost.

Around nine o'clock, once the dinner rush had finally slowed, Shane stepped out behind the restaurant again. The sky was dark now, stars brilliant against the velvet black. It was the same sky Rosa had painted so many times, capturing the particular quality of light that made Jerome feel like nowhere else on earth.

His phone pinged one more time.

Can we talk?

Rosa, of course.

He stared at the message, his thumb hovering over the keyboard. Part of him wanted to say no. That would be the smartest thing, of course, to protect himself, to start the long, painful process of letting her go. Part of him wanted to say yes to anything she asked, anything at all, just for the chance to see her one more time.

In the end, he wrote,

Tomorrow after work?

Maybe that was wishful thinking. After all, he had no way of knowing where she even was. Quite possibly, she was already back in Scottsdale.

Or maybe her mother was allowing her to stay in Jerome for a day or so more, just to help her ease into her transition to the world she'd left behind.

Her response seemed to indicate that was exactly what was going on.

Okay. Tomorrow.

He shoved his phone back in his pocket and tilted his head back as he stared up at those impossible stars.

"I love you," he whispered to the night, to the mountains, to the ghost of the woman who'd changed his entire world in such a short amount of time. "And I'm so sorry that's not enough."

The stars didn't answer.

They never did.

15

The hotel room was actually very nice—clean and comfortable, with furniture she guessed was newish but looked antique to match the 150-year-old-building—and yet Rosa still couldn't help feeling like an animal in a cage. She'd been staring at the same green-painted wall for the past hour, sitting on the edge of the bed with her phone in her hands, trying to find the words to text to Shane.

What could she even say?

I'm sorry my mother showed up and ruined everything?

I'm sorry I'm not brave enough to stay and fight for us?

I'm sorry the magic says we're wrong for each other even though my heart says otherwise?

In the end, she'd just sent, *Can we talk?* and waited.

When his reply came—*Tomorrow after work?* —she couldn't help being simultaneously relieved and devastated. Of course she was relieved that he still wanted to see her, but she couldn't help also being devastated that apparently they needed a whole day to prepare themselves for whatever conversation was coming.

A knock at the door made her jump.

"Rosa?" Her mother's voice. "Can I come in?"

She set her phone aside and opened the door. Zoe stood in the hallway holding two cups of coffee she'd probably gotten from the hotel lobby, and wearing an expression that was equal parts concern and resolve.

"I thought we could talk," she continued. At least she sounded more worried than anything else, which possibly was a sign that she didn't plan to read her daughter the riot act.

Rosa stepped back to let her in and accepted one of the coffees, even though she didn't particularly want it. Her mother settled into the room's single armchair, while Rosa returned to her perch on the edge of the bed.

Neither of them spoke, both choosing to sip coffee rather than open a conversation they both realized was utterly fraught.

"I'm not angry," Zoe said at last. "Just in case you were wondering."

"You called me seventeen times," Rosa pointed out. She sounded almost mild, which she supposed was a good thing. Right then, she felt oddly detached from herself, as if all of this was happening to someone else. Coping mechanism, she supposed. "You dropped everything so you could drive all the way up here. That doesn't exactly scream 'not angry.'"

"I was worried," her mother said gently. "There's a big difference. I hadn't heard from you for several days, even though you agreed to keep in touch in exchange for staying here in Jerome. So I started imagining all sorts of terrible scenarios. And yes, once I realized you were fine and were just ignoring my calls, I got annoyed. But that doesn't mean I'm angry, Rosa. I'm just concerned."

Rosa looked down at the coffee cup in her hands and watched steam curl up from the small opening in the lid. "All right. But I still know what you're going to say."

Zoe's hands tightened around the coffee cup she held. "Do you?"

"That I need to come home and keep looking for my consort. That I'm running out of time and can't afford to waste it on—" She broke off there, knowing she couldn't finish that sentence. There was no way in the world she would call what she had with Shane a waste, even if that was what everyone else would probably think.

"On a man you love?" Zoe said softly.

Rosa stared at her in shock. "I—"

Her mother cut in, but almost kindly, as if she thought she might make it easier if she went ahead and laid it all on the line. "Rosa, I talked to Shane today. I could see it in his eyes when he spoke of you, and I can see it in yours now." Zoe stopped there and sent her daughter a direct look. "You're in love with him."

There was no point in denying it. "Yes," Rosa said simply.

"And he's in love with you."

She nodded. "Yes."

"But he's not your consort."

Those words might as well have been a punch in the gut, even though her mother had made that statement in the same calm, almost quiet voice. "No," Rosa said. "This morning, we tried to share the consort kiss, both of us open and searching and—" Her voice caught, and she had to pause for a moment to gather herself before she went on. "There was nothing, Mom. Just a really good kiss between two people who love each other. But no magic, no consort bond."

Zoe was quiet for a moment as she studied her

daughter's face. "I'm sorry," she said at last, and the sympathy in her voice made Rosa's eyes burn with unshed tears. "I know how much that must have hurt."

"I don't understand," she said, and now the tears were falling, hot tracks down her cheeks that she didn't bother to wipe away. Her mother could already see how she felt, so what was the point in hiding it? "How can I love him this much and have him not be the one? How can something that feels this right be wrong according to the magic? It doesn't make any sense."

"No, it doesn't," Zoe said. "But love rarely does."

"Did you feel this way with Dad?" Rosa knew she sounded desperate, but she didn't care, not if her desperation might lead her to a solution she hadn't yet thought of. "Before you knew he was your consort, did you love him? Did it hurt like this?"

Her mother's expression shifted, becoming almost distant as she remembered those crazy days almost thirty years earlier, when she'd first encountered Evan McAllister as he came to Phoenix to help her with the monster she'd conjured, the monster that would soon enough turn into Levi McAllister. "Yes and no. I started falling for your father almost from the moment I met him, but I also knew there were so many reasons why he couldn't be my consort...he was too old, he was from a different clan, he was divorced from a civilian woman. And the more time I spent with him, the more I fell in love with him, and in the end, we tried the consort kiss because we couldn't go on anymore the way we were."

"But it all worked out for you," Rosa said, and she couldn't quite keep the bitterness out of her voice, not when she knew that she and Shane had done almost the same thing but with the opposite result. "The bond was there, and you got your happy ending."

"Yes, I did," Zoe said simply. "That doesn't mean I wasn't still scared out of my mind about what would happen if your father and I hadn't bonded." She paused there, and her brow furrowed, as if she was trying to determine the best way to explain what she needed to say next. "The bond requires you to be open to it," she continued. "I know I was open because I couldn't imagine a future without your father in it. But if you're closed off—if you're trying to protect yourself from disappointment—then the bond has a much more difficult time forming."

Rosa stared at her mother, an icy sensation settling somewhere in her stomach. "What are you saying?"

"I'm saying that the *prima* magic responds to

truth," Zoe told her. "If you're not being truthful—with yourself or with him—the magic knows. It can't complete a bond when one or both people are holding back."

Rosa stared at her mother, not sure she wanted to believe any of those words. "So…what? Are you saying it's my fault it didn't work?"

Once again, her mother was silent for a few beats before she spoke. "I'm saying that maybe you went into that kiss already expecting it to fail. Thirty-four failed attempts had taught you to protect yourself, to brace for disappointment. And it's possible that Shane did the same thing, although for different reasons. Maybe you were both so afraid of failing that you couldn't be fully open to what the consort bond really means."

Rosa wanted to protest, to insist that she'd been completely open, that she'd wanted the bond with Shane to work more than anything in the world.

But…had she? Or had some part of her been holding back, already protecting her heart from the inevitable disappointment she knew waited for her?

"I don't know how to not be afraid," she said, the words brittle as spun glass. "I don't know how to try again when every attempt has ended in failure."

Zoe reached over and took her daughter's

hand. "I know. And that's why I think you need to come home for a little while. Not necessarily forever or to give up on Shane. Just to give yourself some space and hopefully gain some perspective."

"You want me to try more consort candidates," Rosa said, rebellion already stirring in her. True, her mother hadn't come right out and said anything close to that, but she somehow doubted that the *prima* of the de la Pazes was going to abandon the whole prospect just because her daughter was dragging her feet.

Far too much was riding on this to give in to individual whims.

"I want you to have options," her mother said, and now her tone had turned almost brisk, as if she thought they'd turned a corner and it was time to start focusing on the future. "Right now, you feel like Shane is the only choice, but maybe that's because you've been in this bubble with him for more than a month. Maybe if you step back a little, you'll be able to see the situation more clearly."

"Or maybe stepping back will only prove that he's exactly what I want and I'm letting the magic dictate my life instead of living it for myself," Rosa retorted.

Sympathy flickered in her mother's dark eyes, but that didn't prevent her from responding,

"Maybe. But Rosa, now you only have three months left. If you don't find your consort by then—"

Rosa cut her off. "I know. Diminished powers, blah, blah, blah. I know all of this, Mom. I've known it since I turned eleven and my powers developed, and everyone decided I was the strongest de la Paz witch of my generation. Don't you think I know what's at stake?"

"Then you understand why I'm asking you to keep trying," Zoe said. "Not because I don't think Shane seems like a good man, and not because I don't want you to be happy. But your responsibility to the clan has to come first. That's what it means to be *prima.*"

Rosa pulled her hand away and wrapped her arms around herself. The air conditioning in her hotel room was set way too high, and she was chilled right through.

Or maybe the ice that seemed to have taken up residence in her body had absolutely nothing to do with the temperature.

The words sounded petulant even before she said them, but she asked the questions anyway. "And what if I don't want to be *prima?* What if I just want to be me?"

"It doesn't work that way, Rosa, and you know it as well as I do," her mother replied, her voice gentle but with a hint of iron underneath nonetheless. "The magic decides who the *prima*-in-waiting is. The only way to be free of it is to die so it will pass on to the next-strongest witch in our clan, and I sincerely hope you aren't planning to do anything like that."

Of course she wasn't. This hurt worse than anything she'd ever gone through before, but as much as she hated the idea of spending a life without Shane, she wasn't anywhere close to ready to leave this existence.

"No," she said, hearing the defeat in her tone even as she spoke. "Of course not."

"Then you'll do what you have to do," Zoe said, her voice brisk again. "You can stay in Jerome for another day or two so you can spend time with Shane and say whatever goodbyes you need to say. And then you'll come home, and you'll keep looking and keep trying. Because that's what being *prima*-in-waiting means."

Shane spent the next day in a fog, going through the motions of running the restaurant while his mind was elsewhere. Mike had given up trying to make conversation and was instead communicating through a series of grunts and pointed looks that somehow managed to keep the kitchen running smoothly.

Around two in the afternoon, the knock at the back door that he'd both been anticipating and dreading pulled him out of the fog. He opened the door to find Zoe Sandoval standing there again, although today something seemed much more formal about her.

"Hello, Shane," she said. "Do you have a few minutes to talk?"

He should probably say no, should tell her that whatever she had to say, he didn't want to hear it. But he found himself nodding and stepping aside to let her into the kitchen.

Mike and Carlos both took one look at the *prima* and made themselves scarce, disappearing into the walk-in cooler as they muttered about tracking down those lamb chops that had gone missing.

Zoe waited until they were alone before speaking. "I wanted to thank you for being honest with me about your feelings for Rosa."

"Did you come all the way over here just to thank me?" he asked, knowing he sounded downright testy. Well, he'd never claimed to be a saint.

"No," she replied, appearing not to take offense. "I came to ask you a question. Do you love my daughter?"

He'd already answered this question yesterday, but apparently she needed to hear it again. "Does it matter if I do?"

"It's the only thing that matters," she said.

Shane chuckled, a dry rasp with absolutely no humor in it. "Then yes, I love Rosa. I love her stubbornness and her art and the way she sees beauty in things other people overlook. I love how brave she is, even when she's terrified. I love everything about her."

"But?" Zoe prompted.

He couldn't keep the bitterness out of his reply. "But love isn't enough, is it? She needs a consort, and she needs her powers to fully manifest so she can protect her clan and fulfill her destiny. I can't give her that. I'm just a chef from Jerome who happened to fall in love with the wrong woman."

"Or maybe you were exactly what she needed for this time she spent here," Zoe replied. "Maybe she needed someone who could see her as Rosa, not as the *prima*-in-waiting. But that doesn't mean you're meant to be with her forever."

That sounded utterly unappealing. Frowning, he replied, "So…you're saying I was temporary. A distraction."

"I'm saying you were important," Zoe said, but her tone was gentler now. "You gave her what she desperately needed—freedom, space, understanding. But that doesn't mean she doesn't have a responsibility to her clan. I need her to come home and continue her search. There are still several potential consorts she hasn't tried yet. Good men from the Castillo clan, a few from the Wilcoxes she missed during the first round. She has almost three months left. There's still time."

The thought of Rosa kissing all those men made him want to scream his anger at the world. "And you seriously think she's going to do that? Just meekly go back to Scottsdale and kiss a bunch of strangers, hoping one of them lights up the magic the way I couldn't?"

Unruffled, Zoe said, "I think she's going to do what she has to do because that's who Rosa is. She's scared and confused right now, but ultimately, she knows where her duty lies."

He wanted to argue, wanted to insist that Rosa would choose him…would choose the life they'd been building together.

But deep down, he knew Zoe was right.

"When?" he managed to ask.

"I'm asking her to come home in two days," the *prima* replied. "I'm giving her time to say goodbye, to make her peace with this. But Shane—I need to know that you'll let her go when the time comes and that you won't make this harder than it already is."

"'Let her go,'" he repeated. The words were English, but his brain still had a hard time wrapping itself around them. "You're asking me to just step aside and watch her leave."

"I'm asking you to love her enough to want what's best for her," Zoe said without hesitation. "Even if that's not you." She paused, then added in a much softer tone, "I'm sorry, Shane."

Without waiting for a response, she turned and headed out the door.

After she left, he stood alone in the quiet kitchen and tried to remember how to breathe.

Two days.

He had two days left with Rosa.

And then she'd be gone.

That evening, Rosa came to work at the Asylum, just like she had every other night for the past month. But everything felt different now.

Shane could already sense the distance between them, a new awkwardness that hadn't existed before. They moved around each other in the kitchen like strangers, careful not to touch, careful not to meet each other's eyes for too long.

The easy intimacy was gone, and their friendly silences had turned sharp and painful.

Rosa worked her station with the same skill and accuracy she'd always shown, but now her movements were joyless. Shane caught himself watching her when he thought she wasn't looking, trying to memorize the way she moved, the way she bit her lower lip when she was concentrating, the way those few strands of hair always managed to escape the French braid she wore while she was at work.

Two days. That's all he had left to memorize her.

"Chef?" Mike was standing beside him, looking concerned. "You okay?"

"I'm fine," Shane said, even though he knew he was the opposite of fine. "Let's get through service."

But it was all torture. Every ticket that came in felt like another minute ticking off the clock, another moment closer to losing her. Shane threw himself into the work with an intensity that bordered on obsessive, micromanaging every plate, redoing perfectly good dishes because they weren't exactly perfect, snapping at his staff for minor infractions.

"Chef, that scallop was cooked perfectly," Mike protested after Shane sent back his third dish of the night.

"It's overcooked by thirty seconds," Shane shot back. "Do it again."

The kitchen staff exchanged worried looks, but they didn't argue. They all knew better than to push him when he was in this kind of mood.

Around eight o'clock, Shane saw her—his ex-girlfriend, Sarah, walking into the dining room with a group of friends. She hadn't been to the restaurant in months, not since their breakup last year, and seeing her now felt like some kind of cosmic joke.

Sarah looked good. She always did. Her warm blonde hair fell loose on her shoulders, and she wore a black sleeveless blouse and black sandals with her jeans. Not much makeup, because she didn't need any. The tasting room where she worked probably got extra business because of all the men who came in to talk to her and flirt with her and spend as much time as possible in her company.

Some men might have been jealous of the attention she attracted, but he hadn't minded. Sarah wasn't the kind of person who would cheat. If she'd tired of Shane before he'd tired of her, she simply would have broken it off and said it had been fun, but it was time to move on.

She was exactly the kind of woman Shane used to think he wanted.

From her position at the *garde manger* station, Rosa had a clear view into the dining room. Shane saw the moment she spotted Sarah, saw her expression shutter closed, as if she'd immediately recognized something special about her.

"Old friend?" Rosa asked, her tone carefully neutral.

"Ex-girlfriend," Shane said, because there was

no point in lying. "Sarah Knowles. We broke up about a year ago."

"She's beautiful."

He shrugged. "Yeah."

They went back to work, but Shane could feel Rosa's gaze flicking toward the dining room every few minutes, could sense her watching as Sarah and her friends laughed and talked and enjoyed their evening.

After the dinner rush slowed, Sarah stopped by the kitchen on her way out. She'd done this during their relationship, too, always making a point to compliment the food and to thank the staff personally. Managing a wine tasting room wasn't quite the same as working in a restaurant, but it was still a forward-facing job where you needed to keep people happy, so she'd always been sympathetic toward those working in food service.

She greeted him with a warm smile. "Shane! Everything was amazing as always. I told my friends they had to try the duck."

"Thanks," he said as he wiped his hands on his apron. "I'm glad you enjoyed it."

"How have you been?" She leaned against the doorframe, completely at ease, as if they hadn't been broken up for more than a year. "I feel like I haven't seen you in forever."

His shoulders lifted again. "I've been busy. You know how it is."

"I do." She laughed, and it was such an easy, uncomplicated sound, completely devoid of subtext. "I've been meaning to stop by more often, but work has been nuts. Maybe we could grab coffee sometime and catch up properly?"

Shane felt Rosa go very still beside him.

"Maybe," he said, his tone noncommittal.

Sarah's smile only widened. "I'll text you. It was good to see you, Shane."

After she left, the temperature in the kitchen felt like it had dropped about ten degrees.

"She seems nice," Rosa said, her voice far too calm, too measured.

"She is nice," Shane replied, because it was true. Sarah was nice. She was also safe and simple and absolutely not the person he wanted.

But Rosa didn't know that.

All she could see was a beautiful, confident woman who knew what she wanted and didn't have to worry about consort bonds or magical destinies or stupid birthday deadlines.

"Did you smile at her?" Rosa asked out of nowhere.

Shane blinked. "What?"

"When she was talking to you. Did you smile?" Rosa's voice was tight now, almost accusatory. "Because I haven't seen you smile in two days. Not since we tried the bond kiss and failed. But you smiled at her."

"Rosa—"

"Do you still have feelings for her?" she demanded.

"No," Shane said firmly. "That ended a long time ago."

"But she wants to get coffee with you. She wants to 'catch up.'" Rosa was unwrapping her apron now, yanking it over her head with sharp, angry movements. "And you didn't say no."

"I said maybe," Shane retorted, his own temper flaring. "Which is basically a polite way of saying no. And why do you care? In a day, you're going back to Scottsdale to kiss more potential consorts. Why should it matter to you if my ex-girlfriend wants to have coffee with me?"

"Because you're giving up!" Rosa's voice rose, and the remaining kitchen staff suddenly found reasons to be elsewhere, scattering outside for a smoke break or disappearing into the linen closet. "You're just letting me go. You're not fighting for us at all."

His fists knotted in frustrated fury. "What exactly do you want me to fight, Rosa? Your destiny, or centuries of magical tradition? Or maybe the plain fact that I can't give you what you need?"

"I want you to fight for *me!*" she practically shouted. "I want you to tell me that I matter more than your fear of getting hurt! I want you to tell me that what we have is worth fighting for!"

"And I want you to choose me without needing magic to tell you it's okay!" Shane shot back. It was safe to say those words, since everyone else had already scattered. "I want you to be brave enough to say that what we have matters more than some mystical bond that may or may not exist! But we don't always get what we want, do we?"

They stood there, staring at each other across the kitchen, both breathing hard, both of them realizing this fury had nothing to do with one another and everything with what the universe seemed to be demanding of them.

And both of them were too stubborn to admit it.

"Maybe you were right," Rosa said at last, her voice now cold, distant. "Maybe this was just temporary. A nice distraction before I went back to my real life."

A kick to his gut wouldn't have hurt as much. "Sure," Shane heard himself say, even though it was a lie, even though every fiber of his being wanted to take the words back. "Maybe it was."

Rosa's expression crumpled for just a moment before she locked it down, assuming what he thought of as her *prima*-in-waiting mask, still and perfect, betraying nothing. "I should go."

"Yeah," he said again. "You should."

She walked out of the kitchen without looking back, and Shane stood there alone, surrounded by the wreckage of everything they'd built together, wondering how two people who loved each other so much could hurt each other this badly.

16

Rosa couldn't sleep that night. She lay in her hotel bed, staring at the ceiling and listening to the unfamiliar sounds of the old building settling around her, while her mind replayed the fight with Shane on an endless loop.

Maybe this was just temporary.

She'd said that. She'd actually said those words to him, and the look on his face when she had—

Letting out a groan, she rolled onto her side and pulled the pillow over her head, as if that might somehow block out the memory of her uttering those awful words.

It didn't work. Nothing worked. Every time she closed her eyes, she saw Shane's expression shutting down, saw the way he'd withdrawn from her even though he hadn't moved an inch.

At around three in the morning, her phone pinged.

Her mother? No, she probably would have called, although Rosa couldn't think of a reason why Zoe would be calling her in the middle of the night. They'd already agreed that she would have two days here, and at the end of the time, her mother would return to pick her up and take her back to Scottsdale.

No, she thought she knew exactly who it was, a suspicion confirmed when she reached over and picked up the phone with shaking hands.

Can't sleep.

Me neither.

Come over?

She knew she should say no. She knew she should maintain the distance they'd created tonight and protect what was left of her heart before the inevitable goodbye shattered it completely. But her fingers were already moving, typing out a reply.

Yes.

She dressed quickly in the dark, pulling on jeans and the same top she'd worn earlier, not bothering with makeup or even properly brushing her hair, although she did grab a sweater, knowing that even though the days were warm, the nights were still cold here. If this was their last night together—and it was, even if she didn't want to admit it to herself—she wasn't going to waste any of it.

The walk from the hotel to Paradise Lane took less than ten minutes, but it felt like an eternity. Jerome was silent at this hour, its historic buildings looming dark against the star-filled sky. Her footsteps echoed on the empty sidewalk, and the cool air bit through her thin sweater.

Shane was waiting on his porch when she arrived, still wearing the jeans and T-shirt he'd had on under his chef's jacket. He looked as worn out as she felt, with shadows under his eyes and disheveled hair.

They stared at each other for a long moment.

"I'm sorry," Rosa said, the words tumbling out before she could stop them. "I didn't mean what I said. About this being temporary. I didn't—"

"I know." His voice sounded hoarse, as if he'd been yelling at the kitchen staff all evening. But although his temper had been short, he hadn't raised his voice very much. "I didn't mean it, either. What I said about maybe it was just a distraction. That was—" The words lurched to a halt there, and he shook his head. "That was me upset and lashing out because I didn't know what else to do."

She climbed the porch steps, and when she reached him, Shane pulled her into his arms. They stood like that for what felt like hours, holding each other in the darkness, neither one speaking because words felt too dangerous right now.

Finally, he pulled back just enough to look at her. "Come inside. We need to talk."

The house felt different at three in the morning, quieter and cozy, like the world had shrunk down to everything within its walls. Shane led her to the living room, and they settled on the couch, sitting close but not quite touching, as if they both knew that too much contact would break whatever fragile truce they were trying to build.

"I'm going back to Scottsdale," Rosa said, mostly because one of them had to say something, and it might as well be her. "Tomorrow. Well, today, I guess."

His jaw tightened, but he nodded anyway. "I know. Your mom's right—you need to find your consort. You're running out of time."

"I have almost three months." The words sounded defensive even to her, although she realized he wasn't trying to attack her.

His gaze moved to the window, but the blinds were shut and you couldn't see what was going on outside. Or maybe he was looking much farther away, down to Scottsdale and the life waiting for her there. "That isn't very long when your entire future is on the line."

She pulled her knees up to her chest and wrapped her arms around them in a protective gesture she'd thought she'd outgrown years ago. "I don't want to go."

"I don't want you to go," he replied, voice as intense as it was quiet. "But I don't know how to ask you to stay when I can't give you what you need."

She stared at him, hoping he could see the pleading in her eyes, her need for him to understand this, if nothing else. "Shane, listen to me. What we have—what we've had these past few weeks—it's not nothing. It's not temporary, and it's not a consolation prize. I love you. I'm *in* love with you. And that's real, whether the magic agrees or not."

"Then why are you leaving?"

He'd asked the question simply, as if he truly didn't understand.

"Because—" Rosa paused so she could find the right words. "Because every single day that passes, I feel my birthday bearing down on me like a runaway train. Because my clan is counting on me, and my mother is counting on me, and I'm so tired of disappointing everyone." Her voice cracked on the last word. "Including myself."

Shane reached for her hand and wrapped his fingers around hers. His palm was warm, callused from years of knife work, and somehow that small point of contact felt more intimate than any kiss they'd shared.

"You haven't disappointed me," he said, still in that quiet, intense tone. "Not once."

"Maybe I haven't yet. But I will." Her throat burned with unshed tears, and she had to clear it before she went on. "That's what scares me the most, Shane. What happens in three months when I still haven't found my consort? What happens when you realize you fell in love with someone who's broken?"

Shane's grip on her hand tightened. "You are *not* broken."

"Then why didn't it work?" The tears finally came, hot and fast, spilling down her cheeks. "Why did the kiss fail if I'm not broken? We love each other. We were both open to it. We tried, Shane. We really tried. And there was nothing. Just a really good kiss between two people who aren't meant to be together."

He pulled her into his arms again, and this time, she went willingly, burying her face against his chest while sobs shook her body. He held her through it, one hand stroking her hair, the other wrapped around her waist, anchoring her to him.

"I wish I had answers," he murmured against

the top of her head. "I wish I could tell you why it didn't work, or that everything's going to be okay. But I can't. All I can tell you is that I love you."

She leaned into him, and they stayed like that until Rosa's tears slowed and her breathing evened out, until the only sound in the room was the old house sighing gently around them.

"I need to ask you something," he said at length. "And I need you to be completely honest with me."

Rosa pulled back to look at him, wiping at her face with the back of her hand. "Okay."

"If you could choose—if there was no consort bond, no magical requirement, no *prima* duties—would you choose me? Would you want to be with me?"

The question hung in the air between them, and Rosa realized this was the moment where she had to be brave…or lose him forever.

"Yes," she said, the word fierce and certain. "God, yes. Shane, if I could choose, I would choose you every single time. I would choose this" —she gestured between them—"what we have, what we've built together. I would choose your cranky morning moods and the way you hum when you're cooking and how you see me in a way no one else ever has. I would choose you over everything."

Something in Shane's expression shifted,

although she couldn't quite tell what might be passing through his mind. "Then why does it feel like you're choosing everything else?"

There it was. The real question, the one that cut to the heart of everything.

"Because I'm scared," she admitted. "What if I choose you and it's the wrong choice? What if I give up everything—my responsibility to my clan, my chance at the consort bond, my mother's trust—and in five years, you realize you can't be with someone who failed at the one thing she was supposed to do? What if you resent me for not being enough?"

His eyes narrowed. "I would never—"

"You don't know that," she cut in, her voice urgent now. "You *can't* know that. Neither of us can. And I can't—" She stopped herself there, angry at how hard it was to find the right words. "I can't be someone's consolation prize. I can't be the person you settled for when you could have had better."

Shane's expression hardened. "That's not fair."

"None of this is fair!" she returned. "It's not fair that I have to choose between love and duty. It's not fair that the magic gets to decide who I'm supposed to be with, and it's definitely not fair that we love each other, and it's still not enough!"

His voice rose to match hers. "So what do you want from me? Do you want me to say that love is enough, that we can make this work despite the odds? I can't do that, Rosa. I won't be someone's second choice. I won't be the guy you settled for because you ran out of time and options."

She shuddered at hearing those words, hard and unyielding. "Is that what you think this is?"

"Isn't it?" He untangled his hand from hers and got up so he could stalk toward the window, as if he desperately needed to put some space between them. "You said it yourself—you need to find your consort. You need that bond to be the *prima* you're supposed to be, and I can't give you that. So yeah, if you stay with me, you'd be settling. You'd be choosing the easy thing over the right thing."

"Easy?" Rosa pushed herself up from the sofa, a sort of welcome fury overriding the hurt. "You think leaving you is the easy choice? You think going back to Scottsdale to kiss strangers and hope one of them magically turns out to be my soulmate is easy? There's nothing easy about any of this!"

They stood on opposite sides of the room, both breathing hard…and both realizing they were saying things they couldn't take back.

Shane ran a hand through his hair, leaving it a tousled mess. When he spoke again, his voice was quieter but no less intense. "I don't want to be the reason you fail, Rosa. I don't want to be the distraction that keeps you from your destiny. And I definitely don't want to be the mistake you regret five years from now when you realize you gave up everything for a guy who couldn't give you what you really needed."

"So that's it?" she asked. She sounded defeated, because she knew she was. "You're just going to let me go? You're not going to fight for us at all?"

"What exactly do you want me to fight?" His voice was raw now, stripped of all pretense. "Your clan? Centuries of tradition? I can't compete with that, Rosa. I don't even know how to."

"I want you to fight for me!" The words burst out of her, angry and desperate…and true. "I want you to tell me that what we have matters more than the magic. I want you to tell me that you'd rather have me without the consort bond than not have me at all!"

"And I want you to choose me without needing the magic's permission!" he retorted. "I want you to be brave enough to say that love matters more than duty. But we don't always get what we want, do we?"

The silence that followed seemed to thunder in her ears.

And God, how she ached inside, as if some essential part of her that had been holding on to hope despite everything had finally withered and died. "You're right," she said in a murmur. "We don't."

His expression tightened, and she could see the way he fought for control, putting on a mask of utter blankness. "Rosa—"

"No, you're right." She was moving now, backing toward the door, needing to get out before she fell apart completely. "I should go. This was a mistake."

"Don't." Shane came over to her, catching her hand before she could reach the door. "Don't leave like this. Not when we're both angry."

Rosa looked down at their joined hands, at the way his fingers threaded through hers like they belonged there. "Then how should I leave?"

He didn't say anything.

They stood there in the doorway for a moment, neither of them letting go…and neither of them knowing what to say.

At last, he spoke, his voice barely audible. "Stay. Just for tonight. We can leave the rest of this for tomorrow, but right now—" He broke off there and swallowed hard. "I just need you to stay."

Rosa knew it was a terrible idea. Staying would only make leaving that much harder. But when she looked at his face and saw the naked plea in his eyes, she couldn't make herself walk away.

"Okay," she whispered. "I'll stay."

They went to his bedroom like they had that first night she'd slept there, before everything got complicated. But this time was different. This time, they both knew it was an ending rather than a beginning.

Shane pulled back the covers, and they climbed into bed fully clothed, neither of them bothering to change or even take off their shoes. Rosa curled into his side and put her head on his chest. His arms went around her, and for a few precious moments, they just breathed together in the darkness.

"I don't regret any of it," he said at last, his voice a rumble against her ear. "Just so you know. These past few weeks with you have been the best of my life. Even knowing how it ends, I wouldn't change a single thing."

Fresh tears burned in her eyes. "Me, neither. That's what makes it hurt so much."

His arms tightened around her. "Tell me about them."

"About who?"

His voice was soft in the darkness. "The alternate futures we won't get to have. The what-ifs. I want to know what we're losing."

It was a terrible, beautiful idea—torture disguised as comfort. But Rosa found herself speaking anyway, painting pictures of futures that would never exist.

"We'd have a house," she said, also speaking in a murmur, as if she knew that saying any of this too loud would only make it that much more unreal. "Not in Scottsdale, though. Probably somewhere between here and Phoenix, so it would still be in de la Paz territory, but not so far that you couldn't run your restaurant. It would have a big kitchen for you and a studio for me. We'd paint the walls weird colors that made our guests raise their eyebrows."

He chucked softly. "What color?"

"The kitchen would be that warm gold I painted in the gallery piece. The color of how I see you when you're cooking. And my studio would be all windows, full of light."

Shane's hand stroked her hair, a soothing rhythm that made her want to cry. "What else?"

"You'd win awards for the Asylum. Critics would come from all over to try your food. And I'd paint you constantly—dozens of canvases capturing the way you move through your kitchen like a dancer. Some of them would even sell."

Another chuckle. "Some? Try all of them."

A small laugh escaped her, watery but real. "And on your days off, we'd hike up into the mountains. You'd pack these elaborate picnic lunches that would put normal sandwiches to shame. We'd find a spot with a view and eat and talk and—" Her voice caught. "And we'd be happy. Really, genuinely happy."

"We'd get a dog," he added, picking up the thread of their imaginary future. "One of those scruffy rescue mutts that would need one of those doggy DNA tests for us to tell what it really is. You'd spoil it rotten, and I'd pretend to complain about dog hair in my kitchen."

Oh, that sounded perfect. "What would we name it?"

"Something ridiculous," he replied. "Probably food-related, knowing us. Risotto. Or Saffron."

Rosa smiled against his chest despite the tears that wouldn't stop sliding down her cheeks. "I like Saffron."

"Me, too."

They went quiet for a while, just holding each other while the future they'd never have hung in the air, lovely and ephemeral as a sunbeam.

"Shane?" she asked in a very small voice.

"Yes?"

"Do you believe in soulmates?"

He was quiet for a long moment, and Rosa could feel him thinking, choosing his words carefully. "I don't know. Maybe. But I think—" He paused, his hand going quiet on her hair. "I think if soulmates exist, they're not just handed to you by the universe. I think you have to choose them.

You have to choose to show up and choose to be honest. You have to choose to love them even when it's hard."

"Then why doesn't that matter?" Her voice cracked on the last syllable, and she made herself gulp in a breath before she continued. "Why does the magic get to override our choice?"

"I don't know, love." The endearment slipped out easily, and Rosa wanted to cry all over again at how natural it sounded. "I don't have any answers. I just have—" He stopped again, and she felt him shift ever so slightly. "I just have this. You, right now. And I'm trying really hard to be present for it instead of wallowing in everything we're losing."

She shifted, angling her head so she could look up at him. In the darkness, she could barely make out his features beyond the outline of his jaw, the shadowed hollows of his eyes.

"I love you," she said. Not because it changed anything, but because it was true, and she needed him to hear it one more time.

"I love you, too. That's the one thing I'm absolutely sure of."

They kissed then, slow and achingly tender, both of them trying to memorize the feeling. It wasn't about passion or heat. No, this was about goodbye, about honoring what they'd had together even as they prepared to let it go.

When they finally pulled apart, Rosa settled

back against Shane's chest, listening to the steady rhythm of his heartbeat beneath her ear.

"Stay with me until morning?" he asked, his voice already heavy with approaching sleep.

"I'm not going anywhere," she told him, even though they both knew it was a lie.

Because morning would come, the way it always did. And when it did, they'd have to face the reality they'd been avoiding all night.

But for now, in the darkness of Shane's bedroom, they could pretend. They could hold each other and talk about imaginary futures and dogs named Saffron.

They could pretend that love was enough to overcome everything else.

She closed her eyes and tried to memorize the moment—the weight of Shane's arm around her, the warmth of his body against hers, the sound of his breathing gradually evening out as he drifted toward sleep. She tried to capture it all, to hold it like a photograph in her mind so she could take it with her when she left.

Because she knew, with a certainty that made her ache deep inside, that this was it. This was the last time they'd lie together like this, the last time she'd fall asleep in his arms. It was the last time she'd feel this particular brand of peace that came from being with someone who saw every part of you and loved you anyway.

Tomorrow, she'd have to be the *prima*-in-waiting again. She'd have to put on her armor and go back to Scottsdale and keep searching for a consort who might not even exist.

But tonight, she was just Rosa. Just a woman in love with a man who loved her back.

And for these few stolen hours, that was enough.

Pale morning light peeked past Shane's bedroom curtains, and she hated it. She hated that the sun was shining on the morning when her heart would break forever.

For a moment, she lay perfectly still, letting herself pretend that nothing had changed. This should be just another morning. Soon enough, Shane would wake up, and they'd have coffee together, and she'd go to the restaurant with him, and everything would be okay.

But the weight of reality settled over her like a heavy, smothering blanket, and Rosa knew she couldn't hide anymore.

She realized that Shane was already awake. His breathing had changed, and although his eyes were still closed, she could tell from the tension in his body that he was conscious.

"Morning," she said softly, since she didn't know what else to say.

He opened his eyes, and the expression in them was so bleak that she wanted to cry all over again. But she wouldn't. Crying hadn't solved a damn thing.

"Morning," he replied.

They didn't move, both reluctant to break the spell and let the outside world intrude on this last fragile peace.

Finally, Shane spoke. "When is your mother coming to pick you up?"

"One o'clock." Her voice was almost steady, which felt like a small miracle. "She's picking me up at the hotel."

He glanced at the clock on his nightstand. It was eight-thirty, so that meant they had four and a half hours.

"I'll wait there with you," he said.

Would that make things better or worse? She wasn't sure, but she figured she should make some kind of token protest at least. "Shane, you don't have to—"

"I want to," he said. He sounded calm enough…but he also sounded as if he didn't want her to argue with him on this point. "Let me do this one thing."

She nodded, not trusting herself to speak.

They got up slowly, moving around each other

with a careful politeness that felt wrong in so many ways, she wasn't sure she wanted to examine all of them. She went back to her hotel to shower and pack, while Shane did the same at his house. They agreed to meet at eleven, giving them time for one last meal together.

When Rosa returned to the house a few hours later, she found him in the kitchen, cooking. Of course he was cooking. It was what he did when he needed to think.

When he needed to feel in control.

"I made brunch," he told her without looking up from the pan where he was sautéing mushrooms. "Nothing fancy. Just—" He paused there and finally met her eyes. "Just things you like."

Her throat tightened. She set her overnight bag down by the door and moved into the kitchen, watching him work.

The meal he'd prepared was simple but perfect—fluffy scrambled eggs with herbs, sautéed mushrooms, thick-cut toast with butter and jam, fresh fruit. And coffee, of course. Strong and black, the way they both liked it.

They ate at the dining room table. The conversation felt stilted and awkward, the sort of discussion two near-strangers would make. Both of them were far too aware that the clock was ticking down.

"Will you tell your parents?" Rosa asked at

one point. Intellectually, she knew the food was amazing, but it tasted like sawdust in her mouth.

Shane considered the question, then said, "Eventually. But they'd figure it out soon enough, anyway, even if I didn't say anything. They're annoyingly perceptive."

"Will they be mad that I took off and left you in the lurch?"

"No," he replied immediately. "They'll be sad for me…for both of us. But they'll understand."

Rosa pushed eggs around on her plate. They should have already been getting cold, but some lingering trace of Shane's magic seemed to keep them at the perfect temperature. "What about the restaurant? You'll be shorthanded again."

Because somehow it felt easier to ask about how he'd fare at work with her gone, rather than attempting to see what he would do when he wasn't at work.

"I'll manage. I always do," he replied.

There was something hollow in his voice, though, and they both knew it would be different now. How couldn't it be?

After they finished eating, Shane insisted on doing the dishes himself. Rosa watched him work, memorizing the way his hands moved through the familiar motions, the way he placed each clean plate in the drying rack with careful, precise movements.

This was the last time she'd see him like this, the last time she'd stand in his kitchen and watch him move through his space.

The clock crept toward one o'clock, and at last, Shane dried his hands on a dish towel and turned to face her.

"We should go," he said quietly.

Rosa nodded, knowing her voice would betray her if she tried to speak.

He picked up her tote. She almost protested and said she would carry it, since all she had to carry otherwise was the little shoulder sling for her phone, but she could tell he wanted to do this for her.

Just as it had been when she first arrived in Jerome, Paradise Lane felt oddly empty. Were people at work, or were they simply avoiding her while she made her long, slow walk toward a fate she'd never asked for?

In a way, she supposed this was better. At least with no one around, she wouldn't have to launch into any explanations. No, this way she could just quietly slip out of town.

Just before they reached the Clinkscale, though, Shane paused in the small alley between the hotel and the boutique next door.

"Rosa," he told her, "I need to say something."

She turned to look at him and pressed her lips together. Probably, it wasn't anything she wanted to hear, but she needed to give him whatever grace she could.

"Find your consort," he said, his voice hoarse but determined. "Go back to Scottsdale and find someone who can give you everything. Find someone worthy of you."

The words might as well have been a series of daggers in her heart, even though Rosa knew he meant them kindly.

"Shane—"

"And when you do," he continued, not allowing her to interrupt any more than that, "when you find him and feel that bond click into place—be happy. Let yourself be happy. Don't hold back because of what we had. Don't settle for less than you deserve because you feel guilty about this. Promise me."

Rosa couldn't speak around the lump in her throat. She nodded instead, more of those unwanted and useless tears spilling down her cheeks.

He reached over and brushed them away with his thumb, his touch achingly gentle. "And Rosa? Thank you for these past few weeks. For—" His voice caught, but he forced himself to continue. "For choosing me, even if it was just for a little while."

"It wasn't 'just a little while,'" she managed to say. "It was everything."

Just as she finished speaking, her mother's silver Lexus pulled up in front of the hotel, and Shane handed Rosa her tote bag. He wore an expression that would haunt her for the rest of her life—love and loss and resignation all mixed together.

"Goodbye, Rosa," he said softly.

She wanted to say so many things, wanted to tell him she'd changed her mind, that she was staying, that love was more important than duty or destiny or magical bonds.

But she couldn't. Because none of that changed the fundamental problem—she needed a consort, and Shane couldn't be that for her. No matter how much they loved each other, that fact remained.

So instead, she stood on her toes and kissed him one last time. It was brief, just a soft press of her lips against his, but she hoped it would convey everything she couldn't find the strength to say.

"Goodbye, Shane," she whispered against his mouth.

Then she tightened her grip on her bag, turned away, and climbed into the passenger seat of her mother's Lexus.

Wisely, Zoe didn't say anything as Rosa fastened the seatbelt.

The car pulled away from the curb, merging with the light midweek traffic. The whole time,

Rosa kept her eyes forward and her hands clenched in her lap.

She'd done it. She'd left. She'd chosen duty over love, responsibility over happiness.

Everyone would tell her she'd made the right choice.

So why did it feel like she'd just made the biggest mistake of her life?

Shane stood on the sidewalk and watched the silver car carrying Rosa away from him disappear down the highway.

He stood there long after she'd left, long after any reasonable person would have turned around and headed for home.

Something essential had just been ripped out of his life, leaving a wound that wouldn't heal. He could feel Rosa's absence like a missing limb, a phantom pain that would never quite go away.

He'd known it would hurt and had braced himself for it, prepared for the inevitable pain of letting her go.

But knowing it was coming hadn't made it any easier.

Eventually, he forced himself to move. He turned and began trudging up the hill toward Paradise Lane. As he went, he passed kids pointing and laughing as they looked in shop windows, passed families chattering about what to see next...passed couples strolling along Main Street, enjoying one another's company.

But he ignored them all. He needed to go back to his empty house, back to his restaurant and his kitchen and his perfectly ordered life that suddenly felt horribly incomplete.

Moving mechanically, he walked up the porch steps, let himself inside, and then moved to the couch and sat there for a long moment, staring down at his hands.

The hands that Rosa had loved to paint.

Then he did something he hadn't done since he was a child.

He put his head in those hands and wept.

17

Rosa had been back in Scottsdale for a week, and each day felt like wading through concrete that was slowly hardening around her ankles.

The house where she'd grown up looked exactly the same as when she'd left—the same adobe walls, same desert landscaping, same sprawling hacienda-style building arranged around its central courtyard. Everything was familiar and comfortable...and utterly suffocating.

She stood in her bedroom on a Thursday afternoon, staring at her reflection in the mirror while her sister Lira sat cross-legged on the bed behind her, scrolling through her phone with the enviable ease of someone who didn't have the weight of an entire clan's future resting on her shoulders.

"So, this is the guy?" Lira asked, holding up her phone to show Rosa a photo of a handsome man in his early twenties, with dark hair and an easy smile. "Marco Velasquez? Mom says he's from the Tucson branch of the family, and he's supposedly really nice."

Rosa adjusted the neckline of her dress, a simple, sleeveless navy sheath that her mother had suggested would be "appropriate but not overly formal" for yet another consort meeting and tried not to roll her eyes. "That's what she says about all of them."

"To be fair, most of them have been pretty nice." Lira set her phone down and gave her older sister a sympathetic look. "It's not their fault the bond isn't there."

"I know." Rosa turned away from the mirror. Were there any other twenty-one-year-olds out there who had to use so much concealer to cover up the shadows under their eyes? "It's not anyone's fault. It's just the way it is."

Except that it hadn't felt that way with Shane. With Shane, everything had felt exactly right… until the magic had decided otherwise.

Don't think about him, Rosa told herself. *You're never going to move forward if you keep looking back.*

"You look pretty," Lira said next, clearly trying to be encouraging. "Marco's going to love that dress."

Rosa managed a wan smile. "Thanks, Leelee."

Her sister smiled at the childhood nickname. "Do you want me to come with you for moral support?"

"No, I'll be fine." Rosa retrieved her purse from the dresser. "It's just coffee. An hour, maybe less if things go badly."

"And if they go well?"

Rosa paused at the door, one hand on the frame. "Then I guess we'll try the consort kiss and see what happens."

She could hear the defeat in her own voice, and from Lira's worried expression, her sister could hear it, too.

The meeting with Marco Velasquez was scheduled for three o'clock at a coffee shop in Old Town Scottsdale, neutral territory where Rosa could slip away easily if needed. This was a compromise she'd reached with her mother; she would go through the necessary ordeal of meeting the consort candidates, but she wanted to do it on her own terms, away from the house, and not in the living room with her parents waiting somewhere nearby, the way these meetings were usually handled. No kiss until she thought she had at least a modicum of chemistry with the person involved.

Again, that was breaking with tradition, and yet she wanted to assert her independence wherever she could.

And because Zoe was eager for the process to move forward, she'd agreed…even if she might have harbored a few private fears about her daughter bolting when no one was looking.

Marco was already there when she arrived, sitting at one of the café's outdoor tables with two iced coffees sitting in front of him. Temperatures that day had shot well past a hundred degrees, but the misters on the patio made things mostly tolerable.

He stood as soon as he saw her approaching, and Rosa had to admit that Lira was right—he was handsome, with warm brown eyes and an open, friendly manner that put her at ease immediately.

"Rosa?" He held out his hand. "I'm Marco. It's nice to finally meet you."

"You, too." She shook his hand, noting the firm grip, the slight calluses that suggested he did something other than an office job. "Thank you for the coffee."

"Of course." He pulled out her chair like a gentleman, and they settled across from each other. "Your mother told my mother about your favorite drink. I hope I got it right—iced vanilla latte with an extra shot?"

"That's right." She liked her morning coffee black, but anything iced needed some sweetness to it. After essaying a smile she wasn't sure was at all effective, Rosa took a sip, trying to feel something beyond the blank numbness that had settled over her since she'd left Jerome. The coffee was good, but it might as well have been ashes in her mouth.

They made small talk for a while. Marco had gotten his degree in geology two years ago and now worked for a company that drilled wells for people building off the grid, and he seemed smart and funny—and genuinely interested in her artwork when she mentioned her painting. By any objective measures, he was exactly the kind of man Rosa should have been thrilled to meet.

But there was nothing. No spark, no pull, no sense of recognition. Just two pleasant people having coffee on a Thursday afternoon.

After about a half hour of chitchat, though, Marco set down his cup and sent her a rueful smile. "I can tell you're not feeling it."

Rosa blinked, surprised by his directness. "I'm sorry, I—"

"Don't apologize." He leaned back in his chair, and she thought she saw understanding in his eyes. "Believe me, I get it. This whole consort search thing is awkward for everyone involved. I mean, I knew I might be called to meet you, just because I'm in the right age range and we're distantly related enough that it would be safe for us to be together, but since it's getting kind of close to your birthday, I just figured I hadn't made the cut."

She tried not to wince. "It's been kind of a process," she admitted. "You're number thirty-seven for me.

His dark eyes—so unlike Shane's—widened. "Ouch. That's rough."

"It is." Although she hadn't detected even a single hint of a spark between them, she found herself appreciating his honesty, the lack of pretense. Maybe she should just go for it and see what happened. "Do you want to try anyway?" she asked. "The kiss, I mean. Just in case?"

He considered for a moment, then shrugged. "Sure. Why not?"

Because of the heat, no one else was out on the patio. Still, they both got up from their seats and moved to a more private corner, one where they were sheltered by a couple of big palms in oversized concrete planters. Marco twined his fingers with hers. "Ready?"

She nodded, closing her eyes as he leaned in. Might as well get this over with.

The kiss was perfectly nice. Marco knew what he was doing, and he was respectful and gentle. But there was no flare of magic, no sudden rush of connection.

It was just a kiss.

After they pulled apart, Marco gave her a sympathetic smile. "Nothing?"

"Nothing," she echoed, fighting against the burning sensation in her throat. "I'm sorry."

"Hey, it's not your fault." He gave her shoulder a friendly squeeze. "For what it's worth, I hope you find him soon. You seem like you could use a break."

Wasn't that the truth.

After Marco left, Rosa sat in her car in the parking lot and stared at the steering wheel, trying to breathe through the tightness that had settled in her gut.

Thirty-seven. Thirty-seven failed attempts, and now she had only a little more than two months left.

What if her mother was right? What if she'd ruined her chances with Shane, closed herself off somehow, and now the bond wouldn't form with anyone else, either?

Right then, her phone pinged. Her mother, of course, wanting to know what had happened.

How did it go?

Same as always. Nothing.

I'm sorry, sweetheart. Come home when you're ready.

Rosa set the phone down and pressed the heels of her hands against her eyes, refusing to cry in a coffee shop parking lot like some kind of melodramatic teenager.

But God, she was so freaking tired. Tired of trying, tired of failing, tired of pretending that each new disappointment didn't chip away another piece of her hope.

And most of all, tired of missing Shane so badly that her need for him felt like a physical wound.

By the end of the week, she'd met with two more potential consorts. One was a sweet grad student from Arizona State University who spent the entire coffee date nervously quoting poetry. The other was a gorgeous but cocky Wilcox warlock who'd clearly expected Rosa to be dazzled by his looks and his family's wealth, and was visibly annoyed when the kiss produced nothing.

Three failures in one week. To be honest, her lack of success was almost impressive in its consistency.

Friday evening found her in her studio—a converted casita at the back of the property that her mother had given her when she turned eighteen. She stood in front of a blank canvas, brush in hand, trying to will something—*anything*—to come.

But the colors on her palette looked muddy and uninspiring, and the canvas mocked her with its pristine whiteness. Every time she tried to visualize what she wanted to paint, all she could see was Shane's kitchen bathed in golden light, Shane's hands moving through prep work with artistic precision…Shane's rare smile when she'd said something that surprised him.

She set the brush down and turned away from the easel, fighting the urge to throw something.

Her phone sat on the workbench where she'd left it, and Rosa found herself picking it up, then scrolling to Shane's contact info. She'd saved his number but hadn't called or texted since leaving Jerome. What would she even say?

I miss you…I made a mistake…I can't stop thinking about you.

Every man I kiss feels like a betrayal because he's not you.

She stared at his name for a long moment before she forced herself to set the phone down. She wouldn't do that to him.

A knock at the studio door made her jump.

"Rosa?" Her mother's voice. "Can I come in?"

"Sure."

Zoe entered, then took in the blank canvas and Rosa's defeated posture with a single glance.

She didn't say anything, only went over to the small sofa set against one wall and sat down, then patted the cushion beside her in invitation.

Rosa sank onto the couch next to her mother, suddenly exhausted in a way that had nothing to do with lack of sleep.

"Talk to me," Zoe said. Her tone was gentle enough, but Rosa could also tell that her mother wouldn't be put off with vague comments and even vaguer reassurances. "And I don't mean about the consort search. I mean about what's really going on."

She shrugged. "I don't know what you want me to say. I'm doing exactly what I'm supposed to be doing. Meeting candidates, trying the kiss, moving on when it doesn't work. What else is there?"

"There's living, sweetie." Zoe reached over and took her daughter's hand. "You're going through the motions, but that's all. You've become a ghost in your own life."

Rosa wanted to deny everything, but the words stuck in her throat because they were true.

"I can't stop thinking about him," she said at last. Somehow, confessing everything felt better than the alternative, and the words poured out of her. "Every man I meet, all I can think about is how he's not Shane. How his laugh isn't the same, how his hands don't move the same way, how looking at him doesn't make my heart race. And I know that's not fair to them, but I can't help it."

Zoe didn't respond right away. Then she said, "Do you want to know what I think?"

"Will it help?"

A small smile touched her mother's lips. "Probably not, but I'm going to tell you anyway. I think you're punishing yourself."

Rosa frowned. "What?"

Zoe gave her hand a reassuring squeeze. "You're so convinced that loving Shane was wrong—that it was a mistake or a distraction or a failure—that you won't let yourself grieve the loss properly. You're just marching forward, trying to prove you can do your duty, but you're not actually dealing with the heartbreak."

"There's no time to deal with heartbreak." Rosa pulled her hand away and wrapped her arms around herself. "I have less than three months, Mom. I don't have the luxury of sitting around and feeling sorry for myself."

"And how's that working out?" Zoe's voice was gentle but pointed. "You've tried the kiss with three more men this week. What if pushing yourself this hard is making everything worse?"

Rosa didn't have an answer to that question.

They sat in silence for a while, the studio quiet except for the faint sounds of evening settling over the compound—distant traffic out on Scottsdale

Boulevard, the splash of water from the fountain in the courtyard, the rustle of a gentle wind through the palm trees.

"I miss painting," Rosa said at length. "I used to love it so much. But now every time I try, nothing comes. It's like that part of me just…died when I left Jerome."

"It didn't die," Zoe responded. "It's just sleeping. Grieving, like the rest of you."

That wasn't reassuring at all. "What if it never comes back? The painting, and the ability to feel anything except this"—Rosa gestured vaguely at herself—"this emptiness?"

"It will come back." Zoe sounded very certain, but that could have just been because she didn't want her daughter to continue torturing herself like this. "But maybe not until you stop running from what you're really feeling."

She looked at her mother and saw new worry lines etched in the smooth, warm-toned skin around her eyes. "You think I made a mistake in coming back here."

"No." Zoe shook her head. "I think you made the only choice you could make with the information you had. But I also think…." She stopped there to consider her words before continuing. "I think you might have left Jerome before you were truly ready to leave."

Rosa made an impatient gesture with her free

hand. "Shane and I tried the consort kiss. There was nothing."

"I know. But that doesn't mean—" Once again, Zoe paused, and now she looked frustrated more than anything else. "Magic is complicated, Rosa. It doesn't always work the way we expect it to. Your father and I bonded immediately, but that doesn't necessarily mean it always happens that way."

This was impossible. "Are you saying I gave up too easily?"

"I'm saying I don't know for sure," her mother admitted. "And neither do you. And I think that uncertainty is eating you alive more than the failed attempts with other men."

It was true. Late at night, when Rosa couldn't sleep, she replayed that terrible morning with Shane over and over. Had she been too closed off? Too scared? Had she sabotaged their chance at the bond because some part of her didn't believe she deserved it?

"I don't know how to fix it, though," she whispered. "I don't know how to go back."

"Then maybe you need to go forward differently." Her mother let go of her hand and stood up, smoothing down her shirt as she moved. "I think you should take a break from the consort search for a week or two. Give yourself permission to just breathe. Paint, or don't paint. Cry, or don't cry. But stop pushing yourself so hard when it's clearly not working." A pause, and then she added, "Dinner's at seven," and let herself out.

After her mother left, Rosa sat alone in her studio and finally let herself think about Shane. This time, she wouldn't push the thoughts away, wouldn't try to stay busy enough to avoid them, but would actually sit with them.

She thought about his hands, how they were always moving, always creating. And then there was the way he'd looked at her paintings in the gallery with genuine appreciation, asking questions that showed he really saw what she was trying to express. She remembered falling asleep in his arms, wholly herself for the first time in her life.

And even though it hurt, she made herself think about the invisible walls she'd built around her heart, layer after layer of protection against disappointment.

Her mother was right. She'd been invisible her whole life, not because of her magic, but because she'd never let anyone see the real her…the messy, uncertain, scared parts. The parts that wanted things she wasn't supposed to want.

Shane had seen those parts anyway. He'd even loved them.

And she'd left him standing in front of that

damn hotel because she'd been too afraid to fight for what they had.

Rosa picked up her phone again and opened her messages. This time, instead of going to Shane's contact, she scrolled through their old conversation thread, reading his words from that final night.

Can't sleep.

Come over?

And then, in the morning: *Find your consort. Find someone worthy of you.*

As if he wasn't worthy. As if loving each other wasn't enough.

Rosa set the phone down and finally let herself cry—not the choked-back tears she'd been suppressing all week, but real, ugly, gasping sobs that shook her entire body.

She cried for Shane, for herself, for the future they'd painted in words during their last night together. She cried for the dog named Saffron they'd never get, for the house with the crazy-colored walls, for a life that had felt so real before magic had declared it impossible.

And when she was done, when her tears had run dry, and her throat was raw, she lay on the couch and willed herself to find the strength to go on.

After all, this was what she'd chosen... wasn't it?

~

Shane had been back at work for six days, and everyone at the Asylum could tell something was horribly wrong with their head chef.

"Chef, the scallops are perfect," Mike said carefully as he held up the plate for inspection. "You said five minutes, it's been five minutes. The internal temp is exactly where you wanted it."

Shane stared at the dish, seeing the technical execution but feeling nothing. "Fine. Plate and send."

Mike exchanged a worried glance with Kelli, but neither of them said anything as Shane moved to the next station.

This was how it had been all week. Shane went through the motions, executing dishes with technical precision but no heart. The food was still excellent—his muscle memory and training wouldn't allow it to be anything less—but there was a mechanical quality to everything he produced that hadn't been there before.

He couldn't taste anything. That was the worst part.

Oh, sure, he could identify flavors intellectually. He could tell when something needed more acid or salt or heat. But the joy of tasting, the magical connection to food that had been his gift since childhood—that was gone.

It was like cooking in grayscale when he was used to full color.

"Chef?" Carlos appeared at his elbow, holding a dessert that needed approval. "The panna cotta for table twelve?"

Shane looked at it. Saw that the presentation was textbook perfect, the raspberry coulis artfully drizzled, the mint garnish placed with precision.

"Good," he said without tasting it. "Send it."

Carlos hesitated. "You don't want to try it first?"

"I said it's good." Dimly, Shane realized that his voice was way too sharp, but it wasn't as if he could take back the words. "Is there a problem?"

"No, Chef." Carlos hurried away, and Shane caught the concerned look he shot toward Mike and Kelli.

Shane knew he was being unreasonable, knew that he was micromanaging in some areas and completely checking out in others. His staff was walking on eggshells around him, afraid one wrong move would set him off.

He just couldn't seem to make himself care.

The evening service crawled by with excruciating slowness. Shane snapped at Kelli for underseasoning a sauce, redid half of Mike's prep work even though it was fine, and sent back two desserts that Carlos had executed flawlessly.

By nine o'clock, when the last ticket came through, everyone was visibly relieved to see the end of service approaching.

"All right, people," Shane said as he surveyed the kitchen. "Let's get breakdown started. I want this place spotless before you leave tonight."

The staff scattered to their stations, and Shane retreated to his small office off the kitchen to tackle the paperwork he'd been avoiding all week. But the numbers swam in front of his eyes, and after twenty minutes of accomplishing nothing, he gave up and headed back out to the main kitchen.

That was where he found Brianna waiting for him by the pass.

His sister was dressed casually in jeans and a sleeveless green top, her blonde hair pulled back in a ponytail, and the expression on her face told Shane this wasn't a social visit.

"Bree," he said. "What are you doing here?"

"Checking on you." She crossed her arms, her blue eyes—so like their mother's—studying him with uncomfortable intensity. "Because Mom's worried, Dad's worried, and frankly, I'm worried, too."

"I'm fine," he said, tone flat.

She tilted her head at him, clearly unconvinced. "You're not fine. Shane, look at yourself. When's the last time you actually ate something, or slept for more than a few hours? When's the last time you tasted anything you cooked?"

He stiffened. "I don't know what you're talking about."

"Don't do that." His sister moved closer, lowering her voice so the remaining staff members wouldn't hear. "Don't shut me out. I know you're burying yourself in work because you think if you just stay busy enough, you won't have to feel any of the hurt."

That was his sister, the irresistible force. Well, too bad for her, because he was the immovable object. "Bree—"

"You're miserable," she continued inexorably, cutting off his protest. "She's miserable. You're both idiots."

That comment actually pulled a bitter laugh out of him. "Thanks for the support."

"I'm serious." Brianna reached out and gripped his arm. "Shane, it's so obvious that you're in love with her. And you're just…letting her go? Without a fight?"

"What exactly do you want me to fight?" His voice rose slightly, and he had to consciously lower it again. "Her destiny, or centuries of magical tradition?"

"I want you to fight for her," Brianna said,

undeterred. "I want you to at least try instead of just throwing up your hands and accepting that it's over."

"It *is* over." The words were bitter as gall on his tongue. "The consort kiss didn't work, Bree. The magic said no. What else is there to talk about?"

"Maybe the magic said 'not yet' instead of 'no.'" Her expression softened. "You can't know for sure. It sounds like this is kind of uncharted territory for both of you. And that means there's every chance you gave up way too soon."

Shane wanted to argue, but the words stuck in his throat…mostly because he'd had the same thought a hundred times over the past week.

"Even if all that's true," he said at last, "it doesn't change anything. Rosa's back in Scottsdale looking for her consort. She's doing what she's supposed to do. And I'm here, running my restaurant, doing what I'm supposed to do. That's reality."

"This is your life?" Brianna looked around the kitchen, at the cutting boards and the leftover vegetables that needed to be put back in the cooler, at the big industrial dishwashers that were already humming away. "Just work and more work until you've completely buried everything you actually feel?"

"It's what I have," he told her. "It's what I'm good at. And it's enough."

"Is it?" Bree's eyes searched his face. "Because from where I'm standing, it looks like you're barely functioning."

Before Shane could respond, Mike emerged from the storage area. "Chef, sorry to interrupt, but we need you to check something."

Grateful for the escape, Shane followed Mike to the walk-in cooler, where a delivery had arrived late. As he inspected the produce, checking for quality and freshness, Shane was dimly aware of Brianna talking quietly with Kelli near the pass.

By the time he returned to the main kitchen, his sister was gone. But she'd left a note on his desk in his office:

Call me when you're ready to talk. I love you. - B

Shane crumpled the note and threw it in the trash, then sat down heavily in his chair and stared at the wall.

The next afternoon, Shane was in his home kitchen, prepping for the week ahead, when someone knocked on his front door.

He found his father standing on the porch, wearing an expression Shane knew all too well—

the one that said Levi McAllister was here on official business.

"Bree sent you," Shane said flatly.

"Can I come in?" Levi's voice was mild, but there was steel underneath it nonetheless.

Shane stepped aside, and his father entered the living room, taking in the state of the house with a single sweeping glance. Dishes from last night's "dinner" still sat on the coffee table, unopened mail was stacked on the counter, and the place had the general air of someone who'd stopped giving a shit days ago.

"You look terrible," Levi observed.

"Thanks, Dad. Really helpful."

"I'm not here to coddle you." Levi sat down on the living room couch, and Shane had no choice but to follow. "I'm here because we're all worried. So let's talk about the real reason your sister called me."

"Dad—"

"Let me say this," Levi broke in. "Then you can tell me to mind my own business if you want." He leaned forward, elbows on his knees. "Do you remember what I told you about your mother and me? About how we met?"

Shane nodded reluctantly. Everyone in the family knew the story—how Levi had been summoned by Zoe de la Paz as part of a desperate spell, how he'd taken human form, how he'd eventually found his way to Jerome and met Hayley McAllister.

"What you might not know," Levi went on, "is how close I came to never trying with your mother at all. Even after I met her, even after I felt that immediate attraction—I almost walked away."

This was new. Shane sat up straighter, his full attention on his father now.

"Why?"

"Because I was frightened," Levi replied, his tone matter-of-fact. "I'd only been in human form for a short time. I didn't fully understand what I was feeling—this intense physical attraction, this spiritual pull toward her. And more than that, I was convinced I had no right to pursue her. I wasn't really human. I didn't know if I could age, if I could die, if I could give her any kind of normal future. It felt selfish to ask her to take that risk with me."

"But you didn't walk away."

And thank the Goddess for that, or Shane guessed that he and Brianna would never have been born.

"No. Because your mother was braver than I was." A genuine smile touched Levi's lips. "After our first date, after the demon attack where she saw what I really was, she could have run. Instead, she kissed me and told me it didn't matter where I came from or what I was. That I was Levi, and that was good enough for her."

Shane's chest tightened with an emotion he couldn't quite identify. "And that was it?"

Levi shook his head. "Not quite. I still tried to keep some distance, tried to protect her from the uncertainty of being with someone like me. Your uncle Brandon certainly didn't help—he was convinced I was going to hurt her or leave her or turn out to be some kind of monster." He paused, his expression growing more serious. "But we were facing a crisis. Demons were attacking the town, and the portal they were using to get to this plane needed to be closed. Your mother and I both realized that we didn't want to postpone our happiness because the future was uncertain. We didn't want to let fear make our decisions for us."

Levi leaned back then, watching his son's face carefully before he continued.

"I'm saying maybe you and Rosa are so focused on what the magic says and on what the rules are supposed to be that you're not giving the bond a real chance to form. Maybe you need more time. Maybe you need different circumstances. But walking away without exploring those possibilities—" He shook his head. "That's letting fear make your decisions for you."

Shane wanted to argue, wanted to insist that this situation was different, that Rosa had made her choice and that he'd done the right thing by letting her go.

But the words wouldn't seem to come.

Because deep down, Shane knew his father was right.

"She's in Scottsdale," he said after a long pause. "She's doing what she's supposed to do—finding her consort, fulfilling her duty. What am I supposed to do? Show up and demand she give us another chance?"

"I don't know," Levi replied. "That's between the two of you. But I do know that you're miserable without her. You've stopped tasting your food, which for you is like a painter going blind. You're going through the motions of living without actually being present for any of it."

Shane closed his eyes, feeling the truth of those words settle into his bones. "I did what I was supposed to. I got out of her way."

"And how's that working out?" Levi's voice was very gentle despite what he'd just said. "For either of you?"

Shane had no answer.

They sat in silence for a while, and Shane's carefully constructed defenses started to crumble.

"I don't regret letting her go," he said at last. "I couldn't keep her from her destiny just because I wanted to. That wouldn't have been fair to her or to her clan."

"You're right," his father said. "But there's a difference between letting her go and giving up entirely, between accepting her choice and never telling her how you really feel."

"I told her I loved her," Shane protested. "What else was I supposed to say?"

"Did you tell her you thought the kiss failed because you were both too scared to be fully open to it? Did you tell her you'd be willing to try again, to take whatever time is needed, to work at building the bond instead of expecting it to happen instantly?" His father's tone was still patient, but also unrelenting, a trickle of water wearing away at a stone. "Did you tell her that you think she's worth fighting for, even if that fight looks different from what either of you expected?"

Shane's throat tightened. "No."

"Then maybe that's where you start." Levi got up from the sofa and gave his son another considering glance. "I know you'll do what's right."

After his father left, Shane sat alone in his living room and finally let himself think about Rosa—not pushing the thoughts away, not burying himself in work, but actually sitting with the loss of her.

He thought about her paintings, full of light and color and emotion, and the way she'd looked in his kitchen, learning to use a knife with fierce concentration. The sound of her laugh, her endless curiosity, the way she'd seemed to know exactly who he was in a way no one else ever had.

And he made himself think about the kiss, the one that hadn't worked. Had he been fully open in that moment? Or had some part of him been holding back, knowing he shouldn't want this when Rosa's destiny clearly lay elsewhere?

He didn't have any answers to those questions.

18

Rosa stood in front of her bedroom mirror and barely recognized the woman staring back at her. The dress she wore was beautiful—a deep burgundy silk that she and her mother had bought specifically for tonight, with delicate beading along the neckline that caught the light when she moved. Her hair had been professionally styled into an elegant updo, and her makeup was flawless, applied by a stylist who'd come to the house that afternoon.

She looked like a *prima*-in-waiting, like someone who had her life together and was confidently moving toward her destiny.

But she might as well have been a stranger.

"You look amazing," Lira said from the spot where she sat on Rosa's bed. She was already dressed in her own party outfit, a pretty emerald-green dress that complemented her dark hair and big brown eyes, so like their mother's. "Seriously, Rosa. You're going to blow everyone away."

"Thanks," she managed, but the word was only a set of sounds, nothing with any real meaning.

The party had been her parents' idea. Although Zoe had told her to step back a little and give herself some space, and Rosa had done as she'd said, now they were only a few weeks away from her birthday. August had come and gone, and so had most of September, and there just wasn't any more time for her to get her head together.

Hence, the party, one last push to find Rosa's magical partner before time ran out completely.

"Mom invited at least fifty people," Lira continued as she scrolled through her phone. "And I think there are maybe ten or twelve potential consorts in the mix? She tried to keep the thing manageable, but you know how this stuff goes."

Oh, ten or twelve? Was that all? Ten or twelve more men who would look at her with varying degrees of hope or obligation or indifference…ten or twelve more potential rejections to add to her already impressive collection.

Rosa clutched the edge of her dresser, trying to steady herself. She had to present an image of confidence, of positivity, even if her stomach felt as if it had turned to mush and she wanted nothing more than to sit on the bed next to her sister and cry away all the makeup that had been applied so artfully less than an hour ago.

It had been almost two months since she'd left Jerome. Two months since she'd said goodbye to Shane, climbed into her mother's car, and driven away from the only place where she'd felt as if she could be completely herself.

"Are you okay?" Lira asked, her voice now soft and more than a little worried.

Rosa forced herself to relax her grip on the dresser, to school her expression into something approaching calm. "I'm fine. I guess I'm just nervous about tonight."

"You don't have to kiss anyone if you don't want to," her sister told her. "Mom said you could just meet people, get to know them. No pressure."

But they both knew that was a lie. There was always pressure. Every day that passed without her finding a consort was another day closer to failure. There was just so little time left. Over the past few weeks, she'd tried to remind herself that Angela had gone right down to the wire, that she'd been just minutes away from her twenty-second birthday when she'd bonded with Connor, but that had been different. Connor's evil older brother Damon had kidnapped her, wanting to force the consort connection with a McAllister witch, and had only allowed Connor to perform the kiss when it was clear the spark hadn't been there for himself.

Was that what this required? For her to be taken away by an evil warlock to shock her *prima* bond into action?

Somehow, Rosa doubted it.

She turned away from the mirror, unable to look at her reflection any longer. "We should go down. Mom's probably wondering where we are."

They descended the steps to find the party already in full swing. White bistro lights had been strung overhead in the courtyard, casting a warm glow over the crowd gathered below. Tables draped in ivory linens showcased elaborate floral arrangements—roses and lilies and peonies in warm desert shades of coral and yellow and deep russet—and servers moved through the guests with trays of appetizers and champagne.

It was absolutely beautiful, and she could tell how much effort her parents had put into making sure she'd feel wanted and welcome here.

Unfortunately, Rosa would rather have been just about anywhere else.

She spotted her father on the far side of the courtyard, his dark copper hair a striking contrast to the various blacks and browns of the de la Paz clan. He was talking with her Uncle Zander, and raised a hand in greeting.

Somehow, she managed to smile in response.

"There she is!" Her mother appeared at her elbow, gorgeous in a sleeveless cocktail dress of deep teal that made her dark hair shine. She kissed Rosa's cheek, her smile warm but her eyes assessing. Clearly, she'd been worried about her daughter's late arrival, maybe had even been thinking she might have to go upstairs to bring her down to the party. "You look so beautiful, sweetheart."

"Thanks, Mom." Rosa accepted a glass of champagne from a passing server, more for something to do with her hands than because she really wanted it.

"I want you to meet some people," Zoe continued, already guiding Rosa toward a cluster of young men near the fountain. "Daniel Reyes is from Tucson—he's studying architecture at the University of Arizona. And Alessandro Chavez, whose mother is a de la Paz cousin twice removed, although his father is a civilian. He works in tech and is very successful. And—"

The introductions blurred together. Daniel had a friendly smile, while Alessandro possessed a certain awkward charm. There were three others whose names Rosa forgot almost immediately, all of them perfectly nice, all of them looking at her with varying degrees of interest.

But none of them was Shane.

"It's nice to meet you all," Rosa heard herself say, the words pleasant and empty. "Thank you for coming."

She moved through the party like a ghost, smiling at the right moments, laughing at jokes she didn't find funny, accepting well-wishes from relatives she barely knew. The whole time, she felt like she was watching herself from outside her own body, seeing the *prima*-in-waiting perform her role while the real Rosa—the one who'd learned to dice onions and fallen in love with a cranky, gorgeous chef—screamed somewhere deep inside.

Around nine o'clock, after dinner had been served and a toast to Rosa's health had been made, Daniel Reyes approached her near the edge of the courtyard, where she'd retreated for a moment of relative quiet. Although she would have preferred to escape to her room altogether, she'd thought this was a safe compromise.

Or maybe not so safe. Otherwise, Daniel wouldn't have been able to find her there.

"Rosa?" he asked. He sounded diffident, and she couldn't blame him. She didn't know the guy, but she could guess he didn't have a lot of experience approaching women. "Are you okay? You seem a little…off, I guess."

She should have lied and said she was fine,

just overwhelmed by all the attention. But something in his kind expression made her want to be honest with him.

"I'm sorry," she said, and shrugged. "I know I'm probably not being the best company tonight. It's just...." She gestured vaguely at the party around them. "This is all kind of a lot."

"I get it." He leaned against the courtyard wall next to her. "This whole consort search thing is weird for everyone involved. Trust me, I'm just as nervous as you are."

Rosa managed a wan smile as she said, "You don't look nervous."

"That's because I've had three glasses of champagne." He grinned at her, and she could see why her mother had thought they might be a good match. He was attractive, smart, and apparently kind. "Look, I know your mom wants us to try the consort kiss at some point tonight. But we don't have to if you're not ready. We could just talk and get to know each other. Maybe that will take some of the pressure off."

How had he known exactly the right thing to say? Almost at once, some of the tension in her shoulders eased.

"I'd like that," she said. "Thank you."

They talked for maybe twenty minutes—about his work with sustainable building materials, her art, their shared experience of growing up in a witch clan, with all the expectations and limitations that entailed. She was a little surprised by how easy he was to talk to, and by the time he suggested they try the kiss, Rosa thought she was ready.

Or at least as ready as she'd ever be.

They moved to a more private corner of the garden, away from the main party. Daniel took her hands in his, and he stepped a little closer… although not so close that she felt uncomfortable.

"Ready?" he asked.

She nodded, closing her eyes as he leaned in.

The kiss was…fine. Well, probably more than fine, if she wanted to be objective about it. Daniel clearly knew what he was doing, and as he deepened the kiss, she knew a different Rosa, a Rosa who'd never met Shane McAllister, might have allowed herself to be swept off her feet.

But there was nothing. No spark of magic, no sense that she'd just found her other half.

She supposed she should have been used to that sense of crushing disappointment by now.

When they pulled apart, Daniel's expression was sympathetic, almost worried. "So…nothing?"

"Nothing," she replied, even as she tried to ignore the familiar burning sensation in her throat. She absolutely could not lose it here, no matter how much she wanted to fall apart. "I'm sorry."

"Hey, it's not your fault." He gave her shoulder a kindly squeeze. "For what it's worth, I hope you find him soon."

Somehow, she managed a wan smile as he gave her an encouraging nod before he headed back to the celebration…which felt more like a wake right now.

She also returned to the party, picked another glass of champagne off a passing tray, and tried another potential consort—Alessandro Chavez, who kissed her with considerably less finesse than Daniel and looked relieved when nothing happened—and generally went through the motions until she thought she might scream.

The hour finally crawled past eleven, and Rosa wanted to allow herself the smallest sigh of relief. Less than an hour to go before all these smiling, happy people left, and she could finally retreat to her room and bawl her eyes out.

She was standing near the bar, trying to avoid making eye contact with anyone who might want to talk to her, when she overheard two men around her age talking nearby. She didn't know their names—they were distant cousins from somewhere, probably dragged to the party by their parents in the hope that they might be the one to spark the consort connection.

"So that's thirty-nine failures now, right?" The

first guy's voice was slightly slurred from too much champagne. "Including the two tonight?"

"I think so. Damn." The second guy let out a low whistle. "You think she's defective or something?"

Rosa froze, her champagne glass halfway to her lips.

"Maybe she's cursed," the first guy continued, clearly not realizing Rosa was within earshot. Or maybe he was just drunk enough not to care. "Like, maybe she pissed off some witch from another clan, and now she'll never find her consort. That would explain why she's failing with literally everyone."

"Or maybe she's just broken," the second guy suggested. "Like her magic doesn't work right or something. Imagine being *prima*-in-waiting and not even being able to do the one thing you're supposed to do."

He might as well have come over and kicked her repeatedly in the gut. Rosa set down her glass on a nearby table, her hands shaking, and walked away before they could see the tears threatening to spill over.

Somehow, she made it through the rest of the party. She smiled at more guests, chatted about college—although she wasn't even attending this semester, thanks to all the turmoil in her life—and generally did whatever she could to pretend everything was fine. Her parents shot her concerned looks more than once, but Rosa only shook her head and kept at it. The show must go on, after all.

Because that's all this was. A performance of someone who had it together, someone who wasn't falling apart from the inside out.

By the time the last guest left a little after midnight, Rosa felt like she'd just run two marathons back to back.

"Good night, sweetheart," her mother said, pulling her into a hug at the base of the stairs as her father stood nearby. Lira had long since disappeared, pooping out around eleven. "I know tonight was hard, but you handled it beautifully."

"Thanks, Mom." Rosa returned the hug, drawing what little comfort she could from her mother's familiar embrace, and then looked over at her father. "And thanks, Dad. The party was really nice, but I need to go to bed now."

"Get some rest," Evan said. "We can talk tomorrow about the next steps."

Next steps. Yeah, right. All that meant was more consort candidates, more failures.

More proof that she was broken, defective, possibly cursed, just like those two jerks had said.

She climbed the stairs to her room, closed and locked the door behind her.

Now she could finally give herself permission

to fall apart. She slid down the door, still wearing her beautiful dress, and buried her face in her hands as sobs wracked her body. They were huge, ugly, gasping sobs that had been building for weeks, held back by sheer force of will and the knowledge that breaking down wouldn't change anything.

But now, as she sat there alone in her room with thirty-nine failed consort attempts behind her and no idea of what could come next, she let herself wallow in the fear and the shame and the crushing weight of disappointing everyone who was counting on her.

And underneath it all was the aching, hollow grief of losing Shane.

After what felt like hours, her tears finally slowed. She sat on the floor of her bedroom, her carefully styled hair falling out of its pins, mascara staining her cheeks, and stared at the wall across from her bed.

The wall where she'd hung several of her recent paintings.

Without consciously intending to, she pushed herself to her feet and moved closer, studying each canvas with new eyes.

Half of them were about him.

She hadn't realized it while painting them. No, she'd only told herself she was just capturing interesting subjects, exploring light and color and composition. But now, as she looked at them all together, she couldn't deny the truth.

That painting of a kitchen bathed in golden light? It was Shane's kitchen, the way it looked when he was cooking in it.

The study of hands moving through precise, practiced motions? Those were Shane's hands, the ones she'd sketched a hundred times, the ones that created pure magic out of the simplest of ingredients.

The abstract piece with warm oranges and cool blues swirling together? That was the feeling of falling asleep in Shane's arms, safe and warm and free of all expectations except that she always be herself.

She sank onto the edge of her bed, still staring at the paintings.

"I've been invisible my whole life," she said out loud to the empty room, her voice hoarse from all the crying. "Not because of my magic. But because I've never let anyone see me. The *real* me."

It was true. She'd spent almost twenty-two years playing the role she was supposed to fill—the dutiful daughter who did what was expected of her. She'd hidden the messy parts, the parts that wanted things she wasn't supposed to want.

She'd been invisible not to others, but to herself.

Except with Shane.

Shane had seen her, had looked past the titles and expectations and seen Rosa—just Rosa, with all her flaws and fears and fierce, stubborn hope.

And she'd left him standing in that alley by the Clinkscale Hotel because she was too afraid to fight for what they had.

Or maybe he had made that choice for them by agreeing so readily that she should go.

Her phone sat on her nightstand, and she found herself reaching for it so she could pull up Shane's contact information. For a long moment, her thumb hovered over the call button.

It would be so easy. Just press the button, hear his voice, tell him—

Tell him what?

That she loved him? He already knew that.

That she'd made a mistake? Maybe. But nothing had changed. She still needed a consort, and he still couldn't give her that.

Should she say that she was miserable without him? He was probably miserable, too, but that didn't solve anything.

Rosa set the phone down again.

What would be the point? She couldn't go back to Jerome without a solution, couldn't ask Shane to wait while she kept kissing strangers and hoping one of them would finally trigger the bond.

And she definitely couldn't ask him to be with her if she failed. No way in the world would she ask him to watch her become a *prima* without a consort, struggling with diminished powers while she failed at the one thing she was supposed to do.

Shane deserved better than that. He deserved someone who could give him everything, not someone broken and defective and—

Rosa cut off that thought. No. She couldn't allow herself to start believing what those drunk idiots at the party had said. She wasn't defective or cursed.

She was just scared and tired. And so desperately, achingly lonely that the weight of it threatened to crush her.

After drawing in a breath, Rosa looked at her paintings again, at Shane's kitchen glowing with golden light.

That's what he'd given her, she realized. Light. The ability to see herself clearly for the first time, to understand that being Rosa and being *prima*-in-waiting didn't have to be mutually exclusive.

She just didn't know how to hold onto that light now that he was gone.

~

Shane McAllister had always known exactly who he was. A chef. A McAllister witch with a gift for food that bordered on supernatural—which, he supposed, it literally was. A man who'd built something real and tangible out of talent and sheer bloody-minded determination, a restaurant that people drove hours to reach, a reputation that spoke for itself.

Tonight, as he stood alone in the Asylum's kitchen at half past midnight, he had no idea who he was at all.

Service had ended two hours ago. He'd sent the staff home at their usual time and told Mike he'd handle the final breakdown himself. It wasn't an unusual request—Shane often stayed late, especially on busy nights—but Mike had given him a long look before nodding and heading out, the kind of look that said he knew his boss wasn't staying to clean.

Shane was staying because going home meant walking into an empty house that still smelled faintly of Rosa's shampoo, even after so much time had passed. He'd washed the sheets and opened the windows, had scrubbed every surface she might have touched, and somehow the ghost of her still lingered in every room.

So he cleaned the kitchen instead, even though it was already spotless. He wiped down stations that had been wiped down twice. He reorganized the walk-in cooler, rearranging containers that were perfectly arranged. And after he was finished with that task, he sharpened knives that didn't need sharpening, the rhythmic scrape of steel against stone filling the silence the way conversation used to.

When there was absolutely nothing left to clean or sharpen or reorganize, he stood at his station—the pass, where every dish was inspected before it left the kitchen—and stared at the empty surface.

He hadn't tasted a single thing he'd cooked tonight.

Not the seared duck breast with its cherry gastrique, not the hand-rolled pasta with brown butter and sage, not the panna cotta that Carlos had executed flawlessly despite Shane sending it back twice for no good reason. He'd inspected every plate visually, checking for color and composition and presentation, but he hadn't lifted a single spoon to his lips.

Because there was no point. His magic was gone—not the technique, not the knowledge, but the gift itself, the ability to taste with his whole being, to feel the soul of a dish and know instinctively what it needed. That part of him had packed its bags and left around the same time Rosa had climbed into her mother's Lexus and driven south on 89A without looking back.

He was cooking in grayscale, and his kitchen

knew it, even if no one had the nerve to say so to his face.

His legs gave out slowly, not dramatically. One moment, he was standing at the pass, and the next, he was sliding down the front of the station until he sat on the tile floor, his back against the cold steel, his legs stretched out in front of him. The kitchen was dark except for the emergency lights and the glow of the exit sign, both of which cast a faint reddish wash over everything.

This was his kingdom. His perfect, gleaming, meticulously organized kingdom, where every tool had its place and every process had been refined to surgical precision. He'd built it from the ground up—had convinced the hotel's owner to let a twenty-seven-year-old transform a neglected space into something extraordinary, had poured four years of sixteen-hour days into making the Asylum a destination.

And right now, as he sat on its floor at nearly one in the morning, he would have traded every bit of it for one more evening of teaching Rosa to make risotto.

The thought hit him like a fist, and he pressed his palms against his eyes. God, that risotto lesson. He could still feel the weight of her against his chest as he'd stood behind her, guiding her hands through the motions, could still hear her voice asking if they were still talking about food, and the way his heart had hammered so hard he was sure she must have felt it against her back.

Patience is everything, he'd told her. *Sometimes the only way to get what you want is to slow down and let things develop at their own pace.*

What a hypocrite he'd turned out to be.

Because when it really mattered—when Rosa had stood in front of him, and they'd shared that kiss, the one that was supposed to confirm or deny everything—Shane hadn't been patient at all. He hadn't slowed down. He'd gone into that moment already armored, already certain it wouldn't work and composing his graceful speech about how they'd both be fine and some things just weren't meant to be.

He'd protected himself from disappointment by guaranteeing it.

Shane let his hands drop from his face and stared at the ceiling, at the gleaming hoods of the ventilation system that kept his kitchen cool and clean.

What had his father said? *Maybe the kiss didn't work because one or both of you wasn't ready to see what was right in front of you.*

At the time, Shane had dismissed the comment, filed it under well-meaning parental advice that didn't apply to his situation. But now, as he sat alone on the floor of his restaurant with nothing left to hide behind, he couldn't avoid the truth anymore.

He'd been afraid.

Not of the kiss itself, and not of Rosa. He'd been afraid of what it would mean if he let himself want this—*really* want it, with no reservations, no exit strategy, no carefully maintained emotional distance. Because wanting something that badly meant you could lose it, and Shane McAllister did not lose. He won. He achieved. He built things and maintained them and controlled every variable until the outcome was assured.

You couldn't control magic, and you sure as hell couldn't control a consort bond. You couldn't control whether the woman you loved was destined to be with you or with some stranger she hadn't even met yet.

So he'd done what he always did when faced with something he couldn't control. He'd shut down. He'd kissed her with his walls up and his heart locked away, and then when the bond didn't spark, he'd told himself it was the universe confirming what he'd already decided—that he wasn't enough.

That he was never going to be enough, not without the magic to prove it.

Shane drew his knees up and rested his forearms on them, letting his head hang forward. The kitchen was utterly silent, the kind of silence that only seemed to exist in commercial kitchens after hours, when the fans were off and the burners were cold and the patrons had all gone home.

He thought about Rosa at that party she was probably dreading, wherever it was and whenever they'd thrown it, surrounded by eligible men her parents had handpicked. Men who might be her consort, men whose kiss might do what Shane's hadn't. The image carved something open inside him, raw and jagged.

But underneath the jealousy—and at least he was being honest enough to call it by its real name—lay something worse, the knowledge that he'd had his chance and squandered it. Not because the magic had failed them, but because he had failed her. He'd let Rosa walk away believing she wasn't worth fighting for, that their love wasn't worth the mess and uncertainty and vulnerability of trying again.

He'd stood in an alley outside the Clinkscale and watched the best thing in his life drive away, and he hadn't said a single word to stop her.

Because saying those words would have meant admitting he needed her. And needing someone—truly, desperately needing them—was the one thing Shane had never allowed himself to do.

The realization settled over him, its weight seeming to press him into the cold tile floor. He'd spent his whole adult life building a fortress out of competence and control, and Rosa had walked right through its walls as if they weren't even there. She'd seen him—not the chef, not the guy who had everything figured out—just Shane, stubborn and scared and so hungry for real connection that he'd fallen in love with a woman who'd broken into his house and fallen asleep on his couch.

And then he'd let her go because he was too afraid to be that vulnerable again.

He sat there for a long time, letting the silence work on him the way he'd never let it work on him before. He didn't reach for his phone, didn't get up to find one more thing to clean, didn't retreat into the safety of doing something productive. No, he just sat with the loss and the regret, and for once in his life, he didn't try to fix it or control it or make it go away.

When he finally pushed himself to his feet, his knees ached and his back was stiff from the cold floor. The kitchen clock read a quarter past two.

He had a full house booked for tomorrow. Sunday brunch was always crazy, so he couldn't just leave.

But Monday.

On Monday, he would hand the kitchen over to Mike, get in his van, and drive down to Scottsdale. He didn't have a plan. There was no grand speech prepared, nor any real guarantee that Rosa would even want to see him. All he had was the truth—that he loved her, that he was sorry, and that if she'd give him another chance, he'd go into that kiss with his whole heart wide open this time.

No armor or exit strategy, no protecting himself from the possibility of failure.

Just Shane, choosing Rosa, and trusting that love and patience might be enough after all.

He hit the lights, locked the back door, and stepped outside. The air was cool and thin at Jerome's elevation, sharp with the scent of juniper, and overhead the stars burned with the fierce clarity that only existed this far from the city.

For the first time in six weeks, Shane McAllister felt something that wasn't grief.

It was terrifying.

But it was also, he thought as he climbed into his van and turned toward home, exactly what he deserved to feel.

19

Rosa woke on Sunday morning with swollen eyes and a throbbing headache. That headache was accompanied by a clarity so sharp it almost hurt, so she thought that might be a decent trade-off.

She lay in bed for a long time, staring at the paintings on the wall opposite. In the pale morning light that tried to peek past her bedroom blinds, Shane's kitchen glowed even more vividly than it had last night, the golden warmth of it almost tangible, as if she could step into the canvas and find herself back in that space where she'd learned to dice onions and make risotto… and fall in love.

Last night, she'd talked herself out of calling him. She'd set the phone down and told herself there was no point, that nothing had changed, that she still needed a consort and he still couldn't give her that.

But something had, in fact, changed.

She had.

Rosa sat up slowly, pushing tangled hair out of her face. The burgundy dress lay in a crumpled heap on the floor where she'd finally peeled it off sometime around three in the morning, and her pillow was streaked with mascara. She probably looked like a raccoon who'd lost a bar fight.

But she didn't care.

Because somewhere between the tears and the exhaustion, she'd stopped being afraid of the wrong thing.

For eight months—no, for almost her entire life—she'd been terrified of failure. Of not living up to what was expected of her, of disappointing her family, of being the *prima*-in-waiting who couldn't do the one thing she was supposed to do. And that fear had driven every decision she'd made, from that first awkward consort kiss all the way through to climbing into her mother's car in Jerome and leaving Shane behind.

She'd been so desperate for the magic to confirm her choice that she'd never actually made one.

That was the thing she'd missed. She'd gone into every single one of those thirty-nine kisses waiting for magic to tell her what to do, waiting for the universe to hand her an answer so she wouldn't have to risk being wrong. And with Shane—God, especially with Shane—she'd been so certain the kiss would fail that she'd armored her heart before their lips even touched.

What if that was why the bond hadn't manifested? Not because Shane wasn't her consort, but because she hadn't been brave enough to choose him?

Rosa swung her legs out of bed and stood, trying to ignore the pounding in her head. She went over to the paintings and touched the edge of the canvas that showed Shane's kitchen, feeling the texture of dried paint beneath her fingertips.

She'd painted this from memory. Every detail—the warm light, the gleaming surfaces, the careful arrangement of tools and ingredients—had come from a place so deep inside her that she hadn't even recognized what she was doing until last night.

Her art had known what her heart was too afraid to admit.

She loved him. She chose him. And she was done waiting for permission.

She showered quickly, scrubbing the remnants of last night's makeup from her face, and dressed in jeans and a simple white blouse. She threw some clothes into an overnight bag without much thought—enough for a few days, maybe more.

She didn't know how long she'd be gone. To be honest, she didn't know if Shane would even want to see her.

But she knew she had to try.

Her parents were in the kitchen when she came downstairs, her father reading something on his tablet while her mother sipped coffee and scrolled through her phone. They both looked up when Rosa appeared in the doorway with the overnight bag slung over her shoulder, and she watched their expressions shift from casual greeting to something much more complicated.

"I'm going to Jerome," she said.

No point in easing into it. She was done with careful approaches and strategic conversations, always performing the role everyone expected her to play.

Her mother set down her coffee cup. "Rosa—"

"I know what you're going to say." She dropped the bag by the door and took a few steps so she was now standing at the edge of the table. "It's impulsive, and there are only a few weeks left before my birthday, and I should be here focusing on finding my consort. But Mom, Dad—I think I already have."

Evan lowered his tablet. "Shane McAllister."

Rosa wondered how long her parents had known, how much they'd seen in her face during the weeks since she'd come home, all those times she'd gone through the motions of meeting consort candidates while her heart was two hours north in a little pink house on a street called Paradise Lane.

"Yes," she said. "Shane."

Her mother was quiet for a moment, studying Rosa with those dark, perceptive eyes that always seemed to see more than Rosa wanted to reveal. Then she said, "The consort kiss didn't work with him. You told us that yourself."

"I know. But I think—" Rosa paused, gathering her thoughts, wanting to get this right. "I think it didn't work because we were both too afraid. We went into it expecting it to fail, and the magic—it responds to intention, right? That's what you've always told me. You have to be open to it, or it can't take hold."

Her parents exchanged one of their looks, the wordless kind that came from decades together.

"I've kissed thirty-nine men," Rosa continued, her voice steady despite the way her pulse hammered in her veins. "And with every single one of them, I felt nothing. But with Shane, I felt *everything*—just not the bond. I think that's because the bond needs more than attraction or compatibility or even love. It needs choice. Real, wholehearted choice, even if you don't realize at the time that you're making that choice."

Zoe got up from her chair and came around the table. "Sweetheart, I need you to understand what you're risking. If you go to Jerome and try the kiss again, and it still doesn't work—"

"Then at least I'll know," Rosa cut in. "At least I'll know I gave it everything I had, instead of spending the rest of my life wondering what would have happened if I'd been braver."

"And if it does work?" her father asked quietly.

Rosa felt the sting of tears in her eyes, but these were different from last night's, born from hope rather than despair. "Then I'll have found my consort. He'll be the man I love, and for the first time in eight months, I won't have to choose between my heart and my duty."

Her mother searched her face for a long moment, and Rosa held herself still under that scrutiny, letting Zoe see everything—the fear, the determination, the love she'd been trying so hard to lock away.

Then Zoe smiled, and it was like watching the sun come out.

"Go," her mother said simply.

"Really?" Even after everything, Rosa hadn't quite expected it to be that easy.

"Really." Zoe pulled her into a hug, holding her tight. "You've been carrying this weight alone for far too long, and we should have seen it sooner. Go find your chef, Rosa."

Her father got up as well and wrapped his arms around both of them. "Drive carefully," he said, his tone a little too casual, focusing on the mechanics of the situation rather than the emotions. "And call us when you get there."

"I will." Rosa held onto them both for a moment longer, breathing in the familiar scents of her mother's perfume and the herbal soap her father used, and then she stepped back and picked up her bag.

She was almost to the front door when her mother's voice followed her down the hall. "Rosa?"

She turned. "Yes?"

"Believe in yourself," Zoe said. "You've always been stronger than you think."

Rosa nodded, not trusting herself to speak, and walked out into the bright September morning.

The drive from Scottsdale to Jerome took just under two hours, and Rosa spent every minute of it alternating between conviction and terror.

She was doing the right thing. No, she was making a catastrophic mistake. Shane would be glad to see her. No, Shane would tell her she'd had her chance and blown it. The magic would work this time. No, the magic would fail again, and she'd have to drive back to Scottsdale knowing she'd been wrong about everything.

By the time Highway 89A began its winding climb up to the former mining town, her hands were shaking on the steering wheel, and she'd talked herself into and out of this plan at least a dozen times.

But she kept driving.

Jerome appeared around a bend in the road, clinging to the mountainside the way it always had, stubborn and improbable and beautiful. The sight of it made her ache with a longing so fierce it stole her breath—not just for Shane, but for the version of herself she'd been here, the Rosa who'd learned to hold a chef's knife, who'd painted in the golden afternoon light…the girl who'd fallen asleep on a stranger's couch and woken up to scrambled eggs that tasted like magic.

She wound through town and turned onto Paradise Lane, and there was the house. It was still aggressively, unapologetically pink, the color of Pepto-Bismol, the color of a house that didn't care what anyone thought of it.

Shane's van was in the driveway.

Against all odds, he was home. Had he not gone to work? It was now nearly two, a time when brunch was probably winding down, so maybe he'd just come home to take a break for a few hours.

Only one way to find out, she supposed.

She parked her Prius behind the van and sat there for a full minute, her heart pounding against her ribs. This wasn't a done deal, right? She could still leave. She could back out of the driveway and drive back down the mountain and pretend she'd never come.

Instead, she turned off the engine, got out of the car, and walked up to the front door.

And then she knocked before she could lose her nerve.

For a long, terrible moment, nothing happened. Then she heard footsteps. The door swung open, and Shane was standing there in a rumpled T-shirt and jeans, looking like he hadn't slept much either, his dark blond hair uncombed and his blue eyes wide with shock.

"Rosa?"

He said her name the way he always said it, with that slight catch in his voice that made it sound like something precious, something he was afraid to hold too tightly.

"Hi," she said, and then she added, because she'd driven two hours with her heart in her throat and she couldn't do small talk right now, "Can I come in?"

He stepped back wordlessly, and she walked

into the living room where this had all started—the same couch where she'd fallen asleep that first night, the same Connor McAllister painting on the wall, the same turquoise tile fireplace. Everything was exactly as she remembered, neat and organized and impersonal, a space that belonged to a man who'd never quite committed to making it feel like home.

Except now there was a painting on the kitchen counter, leaning against the backsplash. One of hers—the small study of hands she'd done weeks ago, Shane's hands, moving through the practiced motions of cooking. He must have asked for it before she left, or maybe she'd given it to him. She couldn't remember. But he'd kept it, had placed it where he'd see it every time he walked into his kitchen.

The sight of it nearly undid her.

"Rosa," Shane said again from behind her. "What are you doing here?"

She turned to face him. He looked exhausted—dark circles under his eyes, a tension in his jaw that she recognized as the look he got when he was holding himself together through sheer force of will. He looked the way she'd looked in the mirror last night before the party, all desperation and sheer grit.

"I came to tell you something," she said, and was grateful that her voice held steady. "And I need you to let me get through it before you say anything, because if I stop, I might not be able to start again."

He leaned against the doorframe between the living room and kitchen, arms crossed over his chest, and nodded. She could tell he was guarded now, braced for impact.

Rosa took a breath and began to speak.

"Last night, my parents threw a party. A consort party—fifty people, ten or twelve potential matches, the whole production. I wore a beautiful dress and smiled at everyone and kissed more men who meant nothing to me, and then I went upstairs and cried until I couldn't breathe."

Shane's expression shifted, something raw passing over his features, but he didn't speak.

"And while I was sitting on my floor in my ruined makeup and my fancy dress, I looked at my paintings. The ones I've done since I came home, I mean." She swallowed hard. "Half of them are about you, Shane. Your kitchen. Your hands. The way it felt to fall asleep in your arms. I didn't even realize it while I was painting them, but my art knew what I was too afraid to admit."

His arms loosened slightly, uncrossing just enough that she could see the rise and fall of his chest quicken.

"I've spent eight months looking for my consort," she continued. "Eight months kissing strangers and hoping for a sign, waiting for magic to give me permission to choose. And the whole time, I was so scared of failing that I never once stopped to ask myself what I actually wanted." Her voice broke, and she let it. She needed to be real now, no matter what. "I want you, Shane McAllister. I've wanted you since the morning you made me scrambled eggs, and I told you I was never leaving. I want your terrible early-morning grumpiness and your beautiful food and the way you look at me like I'm the only person in the room. I want all of it."

Shane pushed away from the doorframe and was standing straight now, his eyes bright and intent on her face.

"And I think—I *believe*—that the reason the consort kiss didn't work is because we were both too afraid." She was crying now, tears sliding down her cheeks, but she didn't wipe them away. "We went into it already grieving, already protecting ourselves from the disappointment. And magic responds to intention. You taught me that—not with words, but in your kitchen. Patience. Trust. You have to be fully present for the process, or the risotto turns to soup."

Something happened to Shane's face then—a tremor passed across it, the breaking of a dam that had been holding back a flood.

"Rosa," he said, and his voice sounded like it

wanted to break as well. "I was going to come to you."

She blinked. "What?"

"Tomorrow." He took a step toward her. "I was going to drive to Scottsdale tomorrow. I decided last night, after everyone went home and I was alone in the restaurant, sitting on the floor of my kitchen like an idiot." Another step. "I realized that I'd done the same thing you did—gone into that kiss with my walls up, already convinced it wouldn't work because I was too afraid of not being enough."

"Shane—"

"You came all this way to tell me you choose me." He was close now, close enough to touch. "So let me tell you something, too. I choose you. I should have chosen you weeks ago. I should have fought for you instead of standing in an alley and watching you drive away because I was too scared to admit that I needed you."

His voice broke on that word—*need*—and Rosa understood what it cost him to say it, this man who'd built his entire life around never needing anyone.

"My dad told me that magic responds to intention," Shane went on, "that you can't just half-ass a consort bond and expect it to manifest. And he was right. I went into that kiss already armored, already certain I'd lose you. I never gave the magic a real chance."

Rosa reached up and touched his face, her palm against his jaw, feeling the roughness of stubble beneath her fingers. "Neither did I."

"So maybe we should try again," he said. "For real this time. No armor, no exit strategy, no expecting the worst."

She didn't want to ask the question, but she knew she had to. "And if it still doesn't work?"

"Then we'll figure it out together. Because I'd rather have you without the bond than spend another day without you at all." He covered her hand with his, pressing it against his cheek. "But Rosa—I don't think that's going to be a problem."

"No?"

"No." A faint smile touched his lips. "Because I've never been more sure of anything in my life."

She rose on her toes and took his face in both hands. "Then kiss me, Shane. Kiss me like you mean it."

"I always meant it," he murmured. "I was just too afraid to show you."

And then his mouth found hers, and this kiss was nothing like the one they'd shared in his kitchen all those weeks ago. That kiss had been tentative, fragile, weighted down by dread. This one was fierce and open and raw, full of everything they'd been too afraid to give each other the first time.

Rosa poured herself into it—all her love, all her fear, all her stubborn, desperate hope. She felt Shane do the same, felt the moment he let go of the last of his defenses and gave himself over completely, holding nothing back.

And then the magic came.

It didn't crash over them or explode between them the way she'd always imagined it would. Instead, it rose like dawn—slowly at first, a warmth kindling in her chest, then spreading outward through her veins until her whole body hummed with it. She felt it reach for Shane and find its answer in him, felt the bond weave itself into existence, connecting them at some level deeper than flesh or bone or thought.

It felt like coming home.

Rosa gasped against his mouth, and Shane pulled back just far enough to look at her, his blue eyes wide and wondering.

"Tell me you felt that," he said, his voice barely a whisper.

"I felt it." She was laughing and crying simultaneously, her hands still cradling his face. "Shane, I felt it."

The consort bond settled into place between them, warm and steady and real, as natural and inevitable as if it had always been there, just waiting for them to stop being afraid long enough to let it in.

Shane pressed his forehead against hers, and for a moment, they simply breathed together, letting the magnitude of what had just happened wash over them.

"You came back," he said again, and this time the words held an entirely different weight.

"I came back," she told him. "And I'm not leaving again."

He kissed her once more—gentler this time, a promise rather than a declaration—and then wrapped his arms around her and held on, his face buried in her hair.

They stood like that for a long time in the living room of his ridiculous pink house, two people who'd spent weeks running from the truth and had finally found the courage to stand still.

The bond hummed between them, quiet and strong.

And for the first time in eight months, Rosa Sandoval wasn't afraid of anything at all.

20

THEY SAT ON THE COUCH IN SHANE'S LIVING room—the same couch where Rosa had fallen asleep that first night, exhausted and desperate and running from a destiny she didn't know how to face. It felt like a lifetime ago, and also like yesterday.

Shane's arm was around her, and her head rested on his shoulder, and the consort bond hummed between them like a warm, golden thread woven through every breath they took. She could feel him there, not his thoughts exactly, and not quite his emotions, either, but something deeper than either of those things, an awareness of his presence that settled into her bones as if it had always been there, waiting for them to stop being afraid long enough to let it in.

The afternoon light poured through the west-facing windows, turning the living room to amber and honey. On the wall, Connor's painting of a river at dusk glowed in the warm light. Rosa thought about the first time she'd seen it, how she'd recognized Connor's work immediately and how she'd been too exhausted and overwhelmed to appreciate the beauty of it.

She appreciated it now. She appreciated *everything* now—the warmth of Shane's body against hers, the steady rhythm of his heartbeat beneath her ear, the simple miracle of being here with him and knowing, finally, that she was exactly where she belonged.

They were quiet for a long time, just holding each other and letting the reality of what had happened settle over them. Rosa could have stayed like that forever, wrapped up in Shane and their bond and the golden afternoon light.

But eventually, someone had to say it.

"So what happens now?" Shane asked, his voice a low rumble she felt as much as heard.

Rosa sat up a little, although she kept his hand in both of hers, unwilling to lose contact entirely. "A lot of things, I suppose. But I know we'll figure it out."

"I can move to Scottsdale," he said, and she could tell he was trying to sound casual about it, as if uprooting his entire life was no more complicated than rearranging his walk-in cooler.

"I can find a position there, or open something new."

She was already shaking her head. "Shane, you love Jerome. You love the Asylum. I won't ask you to give that up."

"You're not asking. I'm offering." His fingers tightened around hers. "You're going to be *prima* someday. That means Scottsdale eventually, right?"

"Eventually, yes. But not for decades. My mother is only forty-six, and the women in my family tend to live well into their nineties. She's not going anywhere for a very long time."

She watched the tension ease from his shoulders as he absorbed that information, and she could somehow sense the way that timeline changed the shape of things in his mind, shifting them from urgent sacrifice to something more like a long, slow adventure.

"So we have time," he said.

"We have time." Rosa tucked her knees up beside her on the couch and turned to face him. An idea had been forming since somewhere on the drive up from Scottsdale, crystallizing with each mile, and now it was clear and bright and certain. "What if we found somewhere else? Somewhere that would be ours—not Jerome, and not Scottsdale. It would be something we choose together."

Shane tilted his head. "What do you mean?"

"There are places in my clan's territory that are

small and artsy and quirky, kind of like Jerome. Tubac, maybe, or Bisbee. Places where I could paint and you could cook, where we could build something from scratch that belongs to both of us."

She watched him turn the idea over, could almost see him running through logistics the way he'd work through a prep list—considering angles, weighing options, solving problems before they arose. That was Shane, always planning, always organizing. But now there was something else in his expression, too. Wonder, maybe. Or hope.

"You'd want that?" he asked. "To leave Jerome?"

Rosa reached up and touched his face. "Jerome was my hiding place. I came here to run away from my responsibilities and pretend I could be someone else. But I don't want to hide anymore. I want to find *our* place—somewhere we choose on purpose, not by accident."

"And the Asylum?"

"You can train Mike to take over. You consult, and you visit as needed. But you can build something new, too." She smiled. "*We* can build something new."

"A gallery and restaurant," Shane said slowly, and she could see the moment the idea caught fire in him. "Like we talked about."

"Like we dreamed about. Our art, our food, our life."

"In Bisbee or Tubac?"

"Wherever feels right. We'll explore, and then we'll decide together."

He leaned in and kissed her, slow and sweet and full of promise. When he pulled back, she was smiling at him through tears that she didn't bother to wipe away.

"Together," he said. "I like the sound of that."

They sat with that for a while, working through the practical details the way they always did—when he'd talk to Mike, what to do with the pink house, how to balance the search for a new place with Rosa's trips back to Scottsdale. The consort bond hummed steadily between them the whole time, a warm undercurrent beneath the everyday logistics of building a life together.

But as the conversation wound down and the afternoon light deepened into the rich gold of approaching evening, something seemed to change. Their newly forged bond pulsed, warm and insistent, and Rosa became acutely aware of Shane's proximity—the warmth radiating from his body, the way his fingers tangled with hers, the slight catch in his breathing when she shifted closer.

She looked up and found his eyes already on her, dark and intent.

"Rosa," he said, and the way he said her name made heat bloom low in her belly.

"Yes?"

He lifted their joined hands and pressed his lips to her knuckles, his gaze never leaving hers. "I want you. I've wanted you since the morning I found you asleep on this couch, like some kind of witchy Goldilocks who'd broken into my house and stolen my sofa."

She laughed, even as her pulse quickened. "Technically, I didn't steal anything."

"You stole my peace of mind." A ghost of a smile. "And then my heart. And now that we're consorts, now that I know you're mine and I'm yours—"

The rawness in his voice undid her. Rosa leaned over and kissed him, cutting off whatever careful, noble thing he'd been about to say about waiting or taking their time or making sure she was ready.

She was ready. She'd been ready for longer than she wanted to admit.

"I don't want to wait," she said against his mouth. "I've spent eight months waiting. I've spent my entire life waiting for something I wasn't even sure existed. And now it's here, and I'm done being patient."

Shane pulled back a little so he could look at

her, his expression torn between desire and tenderness. "Are you sure? We don't have to—"

"Shane McAllister." She put a hand on his chest, feeling the rapid hammer of his heart beneath her palm. "Take me to your bedroom."

Something ignited in his eyes at those words. He rose and pulled her to her feet, and she followed him down the hall to the room where she'd spent so many nights sleeping beside him, wrapped in his arms but never crossing the line they'd both drawn.

The bedroom was dim and cool, the curtains filtering the late afternoon light into soft gold. Shane turned to face her, and for a moment they just stood there, looking at each other across the small distance between them.

Then he reached out and tucked a strand of hair behind her ear, his fingers trailing down the side of her neck. She shivered.

"I need you to know," he said quietly, "that this matters to me. *You* matter to me. This isn't just—"

"I know." She caught his hand and pressed it against her cheek. "I know what this is. I know what it means."

She reached for the hem of his T-shirt, and he let her pull it over his head. In the soft light, his body was lean and strong, the body of a man who spent his days in physical work. Then she ran her hands across his chest, feeling him tense under her touch, feeling their bond flare with shared heat.

His fingers found the buttons of her blouse, undoing them one by one with the same deliberate care he brought to everything—every dish, every knife cut, every perfectly composed plate. When the last button slipped free, and the fabric fell open, he drew in a breath that she felt as clearly as she heard it.

"You're beautiful," he murmured, and the reverence in his voice made her eyes sting.

They undressed each other slowly, trading kisses between each discarded piece of clothing. Rosa's nervousness was there—a flutter in her chest, a slight tremor in her fingers—but their connection carried Shane's tenderness to her like a current, steady and reassuring, and she found herself leaning into it the way she'd learned to lean into the rhythm of his kitchen.

Trust the process. Be patient. Let things develop at their own pace.

When they finally lay together on his bed, skin against skin, the sheer intimacy of the moment stole her breath. Shane braced himself above her, one hand cradling her face, and he looked at her with an expression so full of love that she thought she might start crying all over again.

"Tell me if you need me to stop," he said. "Tell me if anything doesn't feel right."

"You feel right," she whispered. "Everything about this feels right."

He kissed her then, deep and slow, and she wrapped her arms around him and let go of everything—all the fear and uncertainty, the months of performing a role she'd never chosen. She let go and fell into Shane, and into the blazing, terrifying freedom of being fully seen and fully loved by another person.

It was tender and careful and imperfect in all the ways first times are—a murmured apology when he moved too quickly, a breathless laugh when they bumped noses, a moment of discomfort that eased when he paused and waited, and kissed her forehead with aching gentleness. Through it all, the consort bond sang between them, amplifying every sensation, turning every touch into something luminous.

And when they found their rhythm together —slow and deep and achingly right—Rosa understood at last what it meant to be truly visible to another person. Not the *prima*-in-waiting, not the dutiful daughter, not the girl who'd kissed thirty-nine strangers hoping for a miracle.

Just Rosa. Seen and known and loved.

Afterward, they lay tangled together in the fading light, Shane's arm around her waist and her head on his chest. His heart beat steady and strong beneath her ear, and she was all languorous contentment and warm honey fire.

"That was—" he began.

"If you say 'better than risotto,'" she broke in, "I'm leaving."

He laughed, a real laugh, the kind she'd heard so rarely when they first met, but that came more easily now. "I was going to say 'worth the wait.' But also yes, significantly better than risotto." A pause, and then he added, "We should probably eat at some point."

She smiled. "Is the chef offering to cook?"

"The chef is always offering to cook." He kissed the top of her head. "But I'm not getting up yet."

"Good," she said, settling against him again, luxuriating in the warmth of skin on skin. "Neither am I."

Outside the window, a cool purple evening settled over Jerome, and somewhere in the distance, she could hear the faint sound of music drifting up from one of the bars on Main Street. Rosa closed her eyes and let herself sink into the moment—the heat of Shane's body, the steady rhythm of his heart, the quiet certainty that this was only the beginning.

They had a future to build and a place to find.

A life to create together.

But all of that could wait until morning.

EPILOGUE

Rosa arrived at Visible an hour before anyone else, her arms full of fresh flowers she'd picked up from the farmer's market that morning. December in Bisbee was cool and crisp, the kind of weather that made her grateful for the vintage leather jacket she'd found in one of the town's thrift shops. The building's keys felt familiar in her hand now after three months of unlocking this door every morning.

She stepped inside and paused, as she always did, to simply look at what they'd created.

The space still took her breath away. On the left, the restaurant side featured exposed brick walls and Edison bulbs hanging from the ceiling, casting warm light over the mismatched vintage tables Shane had spent weeks tracking down. On the right, the gallery walls displayed her paintings alongside work from other local artists, a rotating collection that changed monthly. The two spaces flowed together seamlessly, art and cuisine in constant conversation.

She'd named it Visible. It was both a declaration and a promise.

She set the flowers down on the host stand and began arranging them in the collection of vintage bottles she used as vases. Above her, the floor creaked faintly, and she knew that was Shane getting out of bed, probably smiling as he realized she'd gone on yet another early-morning foray to the farmer's market.

Her phone pinged in her pocket. A text from her mother.

Looking forward to tonight. Your grandmother is very excited to see the space.

Can't wait. See you around six.

She'd found a rhythm over the past three months, splitting her time between Bisbee and Scottsdale. Most of each month she spent here, painting and helping run Visible. But for a few days every month, she drove north to work with her mother on clan business, proving she could be both herself and the *prima*-in-waiting her people needed.

Footsteps on the stairs made her look up. Shane appeared on the bottom step, hair still damp from the shower, wearing jeans and the black button-down shirt he always chose for special occasions. He carried two mugs of coffee, and the smile he gave her made her warm inside despite the December chill.

"Couldn't let you do all the prep work alone," he said as he handed her a mug.

"I was just doing flowers." She went on her tiptoes to kiss him anyway. Even after three months, the simple freedom to kiss him whenever she wanted still felt like magic.

He'd promoted Mike to head chef at the Asylum and consulted there twice a month, timing his visits to coincide with her trips to Scottsdale. The rest of his energy went into Visible's restaurant side—a smaller, more personal menu than what he'd offered in Jerome, experimental and intimate. He was writing a cookbook, too, pages of recipes and stories scattered across their kitchen table most mornings.

He was softer now, she thought, quicker to laugh. The hard edges that had defined him when they'd first met had smoothed into something warmer, more open, and she thought he was now the Shane McAllister he was always meant to be, just as she was now the Rosa she'd been hiding for too many years.

She couldn't wait for tonight.

~

By six o'clock, Visible was full of people laughing and talking and drinking wine from local vineyards in Sonoita and Willcox. The McAllisters had driven down from Jerome—Hayley and Levi, Brianna and her husband Bill, along with various members of the extended family. The de la Paz clan had come from Scottsdale and Phoenix and Tucson—Rosa's mother and father, her grandparents, aunts and uncles and cousins who'd made the trip to see what the two of them had built.

Shane watched from behind the pass as servers delivered his food to the communal tables. He'd planned the menu carefully, choosing dishes that honored both his training and his instincts. Each plate was a small work of art, and watching people's faces as they tasted his creations never got old.

"This is incredible," his mother said, appearing at his elbow with an empty plate. "The mole is perfection."

"Thanks, Mom." He kissed her cheek, then nodded toward the gallery side where Rosa was showing Connor one of her paintings. "Rosa's work is the real star tonight."

"You both are," Hayley replied, her tone firm

enough to close that particular discussion. "And I'm so proud of you. You found your person, and together you've built something beautiful."

From across the room, Rosa caught his eye and smiled, and the connection between them felt so strong that he was a little surprised it wasn't actually visible.

His sister materialized beside him, a glass of wine in hand. "So," Brianna said, with the particular lack of subtlety she'd perfected over a lifetime of being his little sister. "When's the wedding?"

"Spring," he replied, since he knew there wasn't much point in trying to dance around the subject. "Something small, outdoors. Just family."

"Here in Bisbee," Rosa added, appearing at his side and slipping under his arm. "Somewhere in the mountains, but we haven't chosen the spot yet."

"And you're hiring a caterer?" Brianna pressed, sending him a pointed look. "Please tell me you're not trying to cook for your own wedding."

"Absolutely not. I'm going to be too busy marrying this woman."

Rosa laughed and kissed his cheek. "Look at you, learning to let go."

As the evening progressed, he watched their two families mixing—Hayley deep in conversation with Zoe, Evan talking magic with Rosa's grandfather, Levi listening to some elaborate story from Brianna, while Bill stood nearby looking faintly bewildered by the whole affair, as he often did at large mortal gatherings. The two clans were blending beautifully, and Shane let himself breathe.

Three months ago, he and Rosa had stood in his living room on Paradise Lane with their newly manifested consort bond glowing between them, trying to figure out what came next. Now here they were, building exactly the life they'd dreamed about.

It wasn't perfect. There were still challenges—Rosa's future responsibilities as *prima*, the balancing act between Bisbee and Scottsdale, the ordinary difficulties of two strong-willed people learning to share a life. But they were facing it all together, and that made everything possible.

Rosa woke before dawn, the way she always did now. Shane was still asleep beside her, one arm thrown across her waist, his breathing deep and even. She loved seeing him like this—relaxed and content, a stillness in his features that she never saw when he was awake and working.

Carefully, she slipped out from under his arm and padded to the small studio nook they'd set up by the window. The light was perfect at this hour, a pre-dawn glow that made Bisbee's old buildings look like something from a dream.

She'd been working on a new series—portraits of women claiming space, choosing themselves. She called it *Visible*, after the restaurant and everything it represented.

This morning, though, she started something different. A new canvas, fresh and waiting.

She blocked in the composition quickly—the view from their apartment window, the mountains in the distance, the town beginning to wake. But in the foreground, she painted two figures visible through a window, clearly together, clearly home.

Shane's voice came from behind her, warm and sleep-rough. "Couldn't sleep?"

"Didn't want to," Rosa replied without turning from the canvas. "The light was calling."

He appeared beside her with a mug of coffee—she hadn't even heard him make it. But that was Shane, always anticipating what she needed before she knew it herself. He handed her the mug and wrapped an arm around her waist as he studied the new painting.

"Is that us?" he asked.

"It's where we are," she said softly. "Where we chose to be."

They stood together, watching through the window as the sun rose over Bisbee. The sky shifted from deep purple to pink to gold, painting the old mining town in colors that made her fingers itch to capture them. But for now, she just wanted to be here, in this moment, with this man.

"I love this life," Shane said quietly. "I love you."

"I love you, too."

The sun rose higher, washing Bisbee in gold and rose light. Inside the apartment above Visible, the *prima*-in-waiting and her consort were home.

And they were whole.

The Witches of Mingus Mountain series concludes in Healer's Heart.

ALSO BY CHRISTINE POPE

LEGENDARY

(Urban Fantasy/Paranormal Romance)

Silver Linings

Lion's Share

Trial by Fire

Here Be Dragons

VEGAS SLAYERS

(Urban Fantasy/Paranormal Romance)

Speak of the Devil

Devil in the Details

The Devil Went Down to Laughlin

Devil May Care

Devil to Pay

The Devil's Due (August 2026)

The Devil Next Door (December 2026)

THE WITCHES OF MINGUS MOUNTAIN

(Paranormal Romance)

Stolen Time

Borrowed Time

Killing Time

Wind Called

Demon Loved

Christmas Past

Season of Magic

Healer's Heart

PROJECT DEMON HUNTERS*

(Paranormal Romance)

Unquiet Souls

Unbound Spirits

Unholy Ground

Unseen Voices

Unmarked Graves

Unbroken Vows

Unholy Night

THE DJINN WARS*

(Paranormal Romance)

Chosen

Taken

Fallen

Broken

Forsaken

Forbidden

Awoken

Illuminated

Stolen

Forgotten

Driven

Unspoken

Hidden

Written

Given

Mistaken

FAMILIAR SPIRITS*

(Cozy Mystery/Paranormal Romance)

Spells and Spaniels

Cauldrons and Cats

Hexes and Hedgehogs

Charms and Chihuahuas

Runes and Ravens

LATTES AND LEVITATION*

(Cozy Mystery/Paranormal Romance)

Caffeine Before Curses

Muffins After Magic

Pastries and Prophecies

Eclairs and Ectoplasm

Sugar Skulls and Specters

Wedding Cakes and Wishes

HEDGEWITCH FOR HIRE*

(Cozy Mystery/Paranormal Romance)

Grave Mistake

Social Medium

Household Demons

Perpetual Potion

Jingle Spells

Wandering Monsters

Uninvited Ghosts

Prophet Motive

Ballroom Bits

Spell Check

Brew Confessions

Charm School

UNEXPECTED MAGIC*

(Urban Fantasy/Paranormal Romance)

Found Objects

Finders, Keepers

Lost and Found

Finding Destiny

THE WITCHES OF WHEELER PARK*

(Paranormal Romance)

Storm Born

Thunder Road

Winds of Change

Mind Games

A Wheeler Park Christmas

Blood Ties

Healing Hands

Wishful Thinking

Smoke and Mirrors

MISS PRIMM'S ACADEMY FOR WAYWARD WITCHES*

(Fantasy/Academy Romance)

Misspelled

Dispelled

Expelled

THE DEVIL YOU KNOW*

(Paranormal Romance)

Sympathy for the Devil

Charmed, I'm Sure

A Wing and a Prayer

Wish Upon a Star

THE WITCHES OF CANYON ROAD*

(Paranormal Romance)

Hidden Gifts

Darker Paths

Mysterious Ways

A Canyon Road Christmas

Demon Born

An Ill Wind

Higher Ground

Haunted Hearts

THE WITCHES OF CLEOPATRA HILL*

(Paranormal Romance)

Darkangel

Darknight

Darkmoon

Sympathetic Magic

Protector

Spellbound

A Cleopatra Hill Christmas

Impractical Magic

Strange Magic

The Arrangement

Defender

Bad Blood

Deep Magic

Darktide

Star Bright

THE WATCHERS TRILOGY*

(Paranormal Romance)

Falling Dark

Dead of Night

Rising Dawn

THE SEDONA FILES*

(Paranormal/Science Fiction Romance)

Bad Vibrations

Desert Hearts

Angel Fire

Star Crossed

Falling Angels

Enemy Mine

TALES OF THE LATTER KINGDOMS*

(Fantasy Romance)

Dragon Rose

Ashes of Roses

One Thousand Nights

Threads of Gold

The Wolf of Harrow Hall

Moon Dance

The Song of the Thrush

THE GAIAN CONSORTIUM SERIES*

(Science Fiction Romance)

Beast (free prequel novella)

Blood Will Tell

Breath of Life

The Gaia Gambit

The Mandala Maneuver

The Titan Trap

The Zhore Deception

The Refugee Ruse

STANDALONE TITLES

Hearts on Fire (Paranormal Romance)

Taking Dictation (Contemporary Romance)

Golden Heart (Gaslamp Fantasy Romance)

Night Music: A Modern Reimagining of The Phantom of the Opera (Contemporary Romance)

Ghost Dance: A Sequel to Gaston Leroux's The Phantom of the Opera (Historical Mystery/Romance)

Flight Before Christmas (Fantasy Romance)

* Indicates a completed series

ABOUT THE AUTHOR

USA Today bestselling author Christine Pope has been writing stories ever since she commandeered her family's Smith-Corona typewriter back in grade school. Her work includes paranormal romance, cozy paranormal mystery, and urban fantasy, among others. She makes her home in Arizona's beautiful Verde Valley.

Christine Pope on the Web:
www.christinepope.com

facebook.com/ChristinePopeAuthor
youtube.com/@ChristinePopeAuthor
bookbub.com/authors/christine-pope

www.ingramcontent.com/pod-product-compliance
Lightning Source LLC
LaVergne TN
LVHW041054080826
845145LV00007B/1572

* 9 7 8 1 9 4 6 4 3 5 9 2 7 *